MEGAN SHUNMUGAM

THE
MORTAL TRIALS

THE ISLES OF WRATH,
BOOK I

ANGRY ROBOT

ANGRY ROBOT
An imprint of Watkins Media Ltd

Unit 11, Shepperton House
89-93 Shepperton Road
London N1 3DF
UK

angryrobotbooks.com
The heat of his gaze

An Angry Robot paperback original, 2026

Copyright © Megan Shunmugam 2025

Edited by Gemma Creffield
Cover by Sarah O'Flaherty
Set in Meridien

ISBN 978 1 83673 015 6
Ebook ISBN 978 1 83673 016 3

Printed and bound in the United Kingdom by CPI Group (UK) Ltd, Croydon CR0 4YY

The manufacturer's authorised representative in the EU for product safety is eucomply OÜ - Pärnu mnt 139b-14, 11317 Tallinn, Estonia, hello@eucompliancepartner.com; www.eucompliancepartner.com

9 8 7 6 5 4 3 2 1

PRAISE FOR

MEGAN SHUNMUGAM

"Rife with the best sort of physical and emotional sparring and an electrifying romance you can't help but root for, this is a captivating debut and a journey I'll be sure to keep following."
Shalini Abeysekara, #1 Sunday Times Bestselling author of
This Monster of Mine

"A gripping tale of resilience, determination and friendship in the face of despair. Megan has crafted a complex world with ancient curses between elven, fae, gods and mortals that leave you dizzy with anticipation and breathless with every turn of a page."
Hazel McBride, Sunday Times Bestselling author of
A Fate Forged in Fire

"Unputdownable! The Mortal Trials *enchants you with a sharp, insatiable magic that refuses to let go."*
Grace Morrow, author of *We Become Darkness*

"A spellbinding, high-stakes fantasy world with a smoldering, tension-filled romance that will have readers on the edge of their seats."
Taylor Epperson, author of *Second Time's a Charm*

"A fast-paced adventure that will thrill romantasy fans!"
Rachael A. Edwards, author of the Threads of Fate duology

*"*The Mortal Trials *will grip you from the first chapter, and the romantic tension will keep you turning every page. With mysterious histories, a broody leading man, and a feisty heroine, it's everything romantasy readers want."*
Nicole Platania, author of the Curse of Ophelia saga

To the readers and the dreamers.

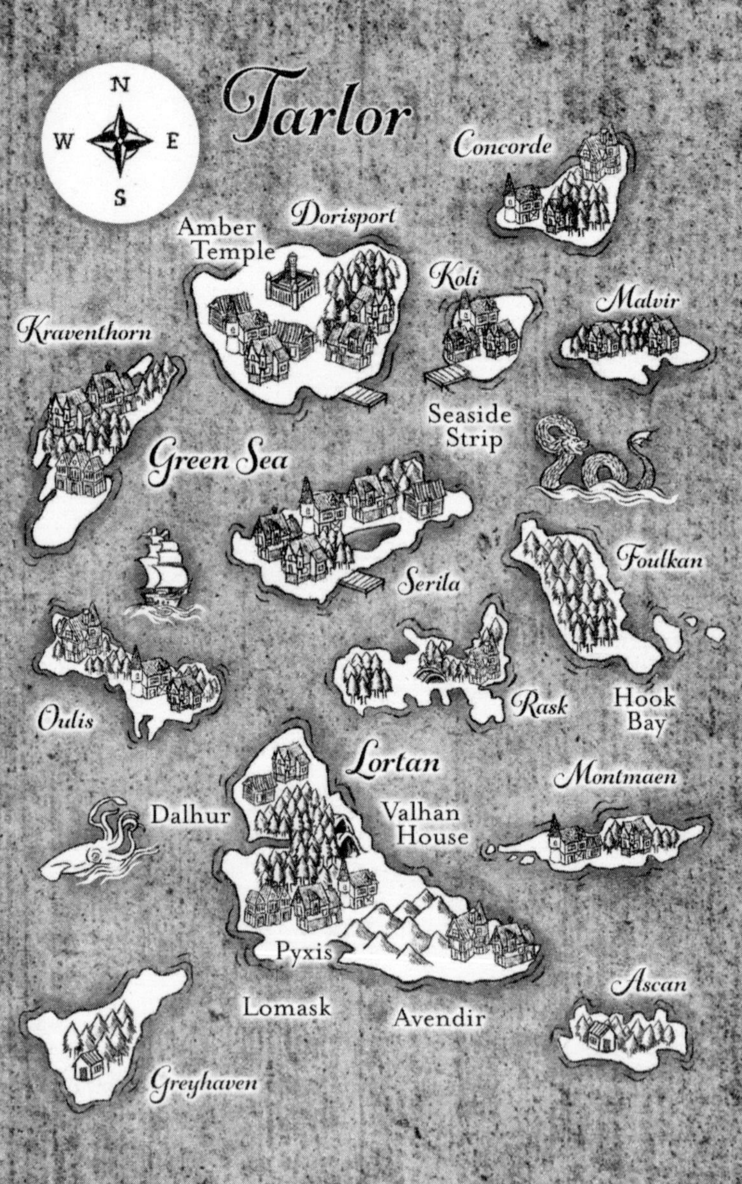

N
W E
S
Tarlor
Concorde
Dorisport
Amber Temple
Koli
Malvir
Kraventhorn
Seaside Strip
Green Sea
Foulkan
Serila
Oulis
Rask
Hook Bay
Lortan
Montmaen
Dalhur
Valhan House
Pyxis
Ascan
Lomask
Avendir
Greyhaven

CHAPTER 1

Eight blades were on the table, their inlaid ruby hilts gleaming in the dying flickers of candlelight.

Umma, the only other person still left in the kitchen at this hour save for me, bustled past, a flour-dusted apron slung around her waist. "Stop dawdling and set those away." She pointed sharply at the knives. "There's still much to do before bed."

I snapped back into gear, reaching for the silverware and a stack of burlap cloth. I grabbed the first knife by its hilt and made quick work of wrapping it before packing it neatly into the cupboard. "How are the morning preparations coming along?"

Umma settled beside me, grabbing a knife and cloth of her own, her fingers nimbly wrapping. "The dough is rising nicely. Although, I suppose we've got to get through tonight first."

I clicked my tongue in dismissal. "You know nothing that's going on out there–" I gestured with the tip of a knife in the general direction of the window, foggy and condensed from the heat of the kitchen "–affects us in here."

Umma gave me a disapproving look. "If it happens in our land, it affects us."

I rolled my shoulders, setting the last of the knives away before turning to her. "We're perfectly safe. The governor's house is the strongest fortress in all of Serila. It hasn't been breached in twenty years."

Umma did not look convinced. "Nevertheless, I'd prefer we take the usual steps to safeguard ourselves. Do you have the salt?"

I nodded, reaching beneath the table to grab the bag of supplies I had packed earlier that day.

Umma pulled her apron over her head, surveyed the floury mess staining its front and placed it in the laundry basket, amidst the other aprons and dish towels. She gave one last cursory look around the kitchen, inspecting the locked windows and the hearth, which only housed cinders. Leaning down so the strands of her graying hair nearly kissed the guttering flames of the sole candle burning on the table, she blew it out. The room was instantly plunged into darkness. I blinked, my eyes adjusting to the moonlit room.

I felt my way along the edge of the table to the doorway, the bag of supplies nestled under one arm like a newborn. Umma reached the door first, shucking it open, and the buttery light of the hallway greeted us.

The stone passages were quiet at this time of night, the only sounds that of old floorboards creaking and groaning as we made our way to the servant's quarters. Umma slid her key into the lock of the door to our shared bedchamber, and we hurried inside, eager to escape the cold draft from the hallway.

I waited as Umma fiddled with the candle set on the small bedside table – the only thing separating our cots from one another. She struck a match and then the room was illuminated. She turned to me expectantly. I set the pack at the foot of my bed, the movement rustling the thin bedsheets, and doled out the supplies.

"Salt for your sorrows, fennel for your fears, a flower for tomorrow and cotton for your tears." I lined up the jar of salt, fennel, a small daisy from the garden, and a strip of rough canvas on my bed.

Umma sat on her own bed, surveying me like a hawk as I crossed to the window above the bedside table, salt in hand. Carefully, I unscrewed the lid and dusted the salt on the sill in a neat line. I repeated the process where the door met the floor. The fennel went beneath our beds, a token of respect to the gods, the flower was wrapped in the canvas and set on the bedside table.

Umma gave me a nod of approval. She moved toward the small washbasin in an alcove beside the door and scrubbed off the day's work from her hands and face. When she was done, I repeated her actions, grateful for the cold water that rinsed away the remnants of dough and flour from beneath my fingernails. We changed into our bedclothes by the dim candlelight and then settled before our beds, on our knees.

The cold floorboards pressed into my skin, and I rested my elbows on the frame of my bed, eyes drifting shut.

Umma spoke the prayer uttered each night before going to sleep: "We give thanks, mighty gods, for the gift of another day. We are most grateful for the sun, the moon, and the stars. For the blessed air we breathe, and the food provided. We are your humble servants and exist only by your grace and mercy. Cloak us in your warmth and safety and allow us to see a new day tomorrow."

I rose to my feet at the end of her prayer, pulled back the bedcovers and crawled into the sheets. Umma reached across to blow out the candle, pausing only briefly to look at me. "I don't thank the gods enough for it, but it's been over twenty years since I found you on the doorstep. I am so grateful for that day."

I blinked back the prickling sensation in my eyes. Umma almost never spoke about the winter she found me, a babe left on the doorstep of the governor's house. I think she feared it would reveal her softer, good-natured side. The side she had taught me was a danger to reveal in a world like ours, where life was so fleeting and fragile, at the constant mercy of the gods. It infuriated and terrified me at the same time.

"Umma, you're going to make me cry," I half-joked.

She waved my words away. "Ugh. It's Augustine. You would think I'd be used to it after five decades, but this day always makes me emotional."

"Why?" I whispered, taking advantage of her rare sharing mood.

Umma blew out the candle, the light leeching from the room in the blink of an eye. Silence rang for a moment, and then she said, "It's easy to carry on ticking like a cog in the well-oiled machine of this house. We forget how fragile our lives are. How miniscule we are in the grander scheme. This day reminds me of that."

I chewed on her words. It was harder for me to process my infinitesimal existence when I had grown up knowing only the walls of the governor's house and its manicured gardens. "Have you ever seen–"

"Do *not* finish that sentence, Lirah," Umma warned shrilly. "Not tonight."

Not on Augustine, when all the things that go bump in the night were out to play.

A shiver skittered across my spine, raising the hairs on my arms, and I pulled my knees to my chest, snuggling closer into the warmth of the duvet. The wind whistled outside and branches battered against the window, but I drowned all sounds out. At some point, I drifted into a deep sleep, exhausted from the furnace that was the kitchen and the constant kneading of dough.

A violent shaking of my arms pried me from sleep and my teeth clattered in my jaw as I was roughly pulled into a sitting position. My eyes snapped open to find Umma's face mere inches from mine, a look of wild terror in her eyes.

"Umma." I blinked. "What's wrong? What time is it?"

The room was still dark. Daylight had not yet crept above the horizon, which meant we weren't due to wake up and put the bread into the oven. My heart stuttered. It was still Augustine.

Umma's head whipped to the door, then back to me. "You need to get dressed. The house has been breached."

"What do you mean?" I asked, even as I shoved the bedcovers away, reaching for my slippers at the foot of the frame.

Umma shook her head at my shoe choice. "Not those. Wear your boots. We have to go out through the window."

I shoved my feet into my boots, haphazardly lacing them as I peered up at her. "How do you know we've been breached?"

"I heard them," she whispered. "The music I've only ever heard once before, when I was a child."

She pressed my cloak into my arms and swiveled to pull her own winter cloak on. "Hurry, Lirah. We only have min–"

The entire room shuddered as the frame around the door splintered. A screech of crackling wood resounded through the room, sharp as a whip, and then the door was pulled clean off its hinges. Umma shrieked as a harsh male outline stepped right across the salt boundary and into the room.

Moonlight cut through the shadows wreathing his body, revealing a handsome face, light hair and golden eyes. But it was the pointed tips of his ears that had me sinking to the ground in horror.

Elven.

He was the stuff of nightmares. Power reeked from him, a palpable scent in the air as he raised his hand toward me, golden rings glinting on nearly every finger. Those bright, menacing eyes flickered over to where Umma stood near the window, then back to me, crouched before my bed, my fingers reaching for the fennel, as if it would ward him off when the salt had clearly done nothing.

It would be laughable, were I not quaking, that we had thought a bit of salt would stop a male like this.

"You can come quietly, or I can throw you across my shoulder and take you. Your choice," he said. I heard it then, the music Umma had mentioned. His voice was melodic, at odds with the hard set of his jaw, a lilt that would have mesmerized me under very different circumstances.

Umma took a tentative step forward, her hands clasping my shoulders as she wrenched me to my feet. "There will be no need for force." Her voice was strong, but the shaking of her fingers betrayed her fear. "We will come."

The blond elven stepped aside, leaving the hole where the door once stood unbarred. A silent command.

Umma's fingers fell from my shoulder, along my arm, until her hand brushed mine. Fingers entwined, she led me past the male and into the hallway. Several other residents from the second floor of the servant's quarters stood outside their bedroom chambers, dressed only in their night things, surveyed by yet another elven. This one had red hair and a gruesome, jagged scar that cut along half of his jawline, as if someone had taken a blade to him but hadn't managed to finish off the job.

His eyes flickered to me, then to the blond elven striding out from behind us. There must have been a silent command received from his counterpart, since the red-haired male shoved at the man closest to him and said, "Move. All of you. To the main hall."

The man scuttled forward, nearly tripping on his feet as he hurried along the passageway, the others around him, all cooks and cleaners, following suit.

Something hard and sharp dug into the spot beneath my shoulder blade and I was propelled forward. I shot a look over my shoulder at the rounded hilt of a dagger that was now being re-sheathed by the blond elven.

"Move," he said. "Or I will make you."

Umma's grip on my hand tightened just as my stomach twisted. We had no control over the situation. We were completely at the mercy of the elven. I felt sick, like I would throw up all over the hardwood floors, but there wasn't time to even gather my thoughts. My emotions roiled as Umma pulled me to join the throng of servants shuffling through the passage and up the set of steps that led into the upper house. Glass crunched beneath my boots as we entered the main hall. I squeezed Umma's hand as I scanned the debris littering the floor and the host of people already within the room, scrunched along the edges of the walls and pressed into corners.

A dark-haired elven held court at the center.

Where his friends were lean, this one was broad, muscular, and so tall his head nearly brushed the chandelier dangling from the ceiling. I could not see him very well from where I stood near the corner, but I could tell he wore armor, as if he were going into battle. The hard lines of the metal cut ridges across his abdomen, angular and unforgiving. There was nothing soft about him.

I had gone from wondering whether elven truly existed to now being in the presence of three. And it was petrifying. The power emanating from them was dizzying and electrifying. It felt like the ground was spinning beneath my feet and there was no way to stop it.

The governor of the house, Unferth Golund, a portly man with a graying moustache and dark eyes, clutched the arched banister at the base of the steps leading to the second floor, his knuckles white. The curtains were thrown wide, revealing the dark silhouette of the gardens beyond, and a chill wind whistled through one of the smashed windows. Salt lay scattered futilely across the floors.

I clutched at my cloak, pulling it tight across my shoulders as the blond elven and his red-haired friend strode past me and straight to the one in the center.

The elven exchanged murmured words and, over one shoulder, silver eyes met mine for a second so brief I wondered if I had imagined it. Then the others stepped away, one on either side of Silver Eyes, as if falling into position.

Silver Eyes stepped forward, and the breath left my lungs when he turned his attention to the governor.

"Where is your daughter?" he asked. But there was no melody in his voice, no musical lilt like the other. This voice was lethal calm, gravel, and death. He strode forward, inching closer to Unferth, a glint of metal at his side catching my eye. "We have searched the house and cannot locate her. I am not a male who likes to repeat himself, governor. You would be wise to tell us where she is."

Unferth released his death grip on the banister, if only to take a step backward, away from the approaching elven.

Why were they searching for the governor's daughter? No one had ever seen the girl; Unferth kept her locked away. It was rumored that she was my age and so sickly that Azrael, the God of Death, would soon collect her.

Unferth cast his wide eyes around, as if hoping a solution would drop from the heavens. For a moment, I thought he might actually confess her location. And then his eyes landed on me.

My heart pounded furiously. I realized what was happening the second after Umma breathed, "No."

"She's over there." Unferth raised one thick arm, a finger pointed directly at me. "I'm so sorry, my elven master, I only sought to keep her safe in the servant's quarters where she would be most unsuspecting. Forgive me."

The commanding elven with the mercurial eyes looked to me again, and the hairs on the back of my arms rose. I tried to swallow, but my mouth was dry, my tongue numb. Umma shifted her grip on my arm, pulling me behind her. "She is not–"

"Silence."

The word did not come from Silver Eyes, but from the scarred one to his left.

Umma opened her mouth, but no sound came out. Flashes of emotion, ranging from confusion to panic to horror, filled her face. She kept straining to speak to no avail. My knees went weak and fear unlike anything I had ever known gripped me. I tugged at her, steering her to face me properly.

"Umma. Umma, what's happening?" I swiveled to Scar Face, a cruel smirk now creeping across his lips. Anger pulsed red hot through me, tinging my vision. "What did you do to her?"

The smirk faded as malevolence touched his eyes. "You dare speak to me? You impertinent mortal."

Lightning flashed outside, near enough to bathe the room in lashes of brilliant white.

Umma clutched my forearm, but still I stepped forward, fury dousing my terror. "What. Did. You. Do?"

Thunder clapped overhead as if it felt my fury. The sheer impossibility of the situation was not lost on me. I was so small and fragile, so utterly *human* against these three elven who could do anything they wanted to me and get away with it. My stomach was a knot of twisted vines.

Scar Face stepped forward, his fingers reaching for the dagger at his side.

"Stop," their commander ordered, a bored look on his face. "You, daughter of the governor, come forward."

There was no use in challenging it. No one around us looked remotely as if they would corroborate my plea of false identity if I voiced it. Only Umma still held on to my arm, her desire to protect me evident in the beseeching look on her face. But defending me would come at too great a cost for her.

I gently extricated my arm from her grip and stepped forward. Dread pulsed through my body, but I swiftly banished it. I would be strong like Umma had taught me to be. Shards of glass crunched beneath my feet as I picked my way past scattered furniture toward the center of the room. The closer I got, the more I felt it. The raw power. Emanating from *him*. The one with the silver eyes. I had sensed power from Blondie too, but it now seemed tame in comparison. Whatever this was mirrored ruthless chaos, like gathering storm clouds before a flood.

I could make out the details of his armor now, the lethal looking blades strapped to his sides, hair the color of midnight, like wings of a raven, against tanned skin. His features were angular. Unyielding. He was beautiful, in the way death might seem to some.

"Your name." It was not a question, but a command from someone used to dispensing them.

"Lirahna." I was proud when my voice did not waver.

His eyes scanned my face, my body, probably musing about how easy it would be to snap me in half.

His gaze returned to my face as he spoke, his words loud and clear for all to hear. "We have come to collect one mortal from Serila, as is customary on Augustine, to compete in the Mortal Trials. This year, we choose Lirahna of the House Golund."

Even though I had anticipated his words, dreaded them, they still hit me with a terrible force. Despair rocked through me – despair and utter hopelessness.

A thumping echoed behind me, and I whirled around. Umma had begun to rush forward, tripping over glass and an upturned table in her haste to reach me.

I turned quickly to see Scar Face flexing his fingers, an amused expression on his face. Bitter bile rose at the back of my throat.

They knew my weakness now. Umma's too. Foolish and contrary to the tough façade she had worked so hard these many years to maintain, desperation shone on her face as she raced forward.

It is vulnerable to feel – to love – Lirah. In a world like ours, we are not afforded that luxury.

"Stop!" I shouted, both to Scar Face and her. "No one needs to get hurt." As if we ever stood a chance of wounding *them*. No, I was doing this for Umma.

I was scared. So terrified my bones threatened to quiver, but they did not need to know that. Umma had shouldered so many burdens for me. Had taken me in when my own mother didn't want me. She had loved me and cared for me. I would be strong for her now. I would protect her now.

"I will come with you." I faced Silver Eyes. "I will not run. Just don't hurt her."

He surveyed me with the same uninterested expression, as if he kidnapped mortal girls all the time and this was a dreadful bore to him. "Say your goodbyes. You have one minute."

I broke his stare before he had even finished his sentence, swinging around to hurtle the remaining distance to Umma. She met me halfway, words choking in her throat, unable to pass her lips. She clutched me in an embrace so tight it hurt, pulling away only to stare at me with glistening eyes.

Love shone clearly through her eyes and the kiss she pressed to my temple. I dropped my forehead to hers as cold misery embraced me.

"I know," I whispered. She did not need to speak to convey her message. "I will come back for you. Once this is all over. I promise."

Umma drew back, shaking her head ferociously.

Run, she mouthed.

I blinked, hot tears trickling down my cheeks. "I will not. I will keep you safe."

Umma's eyes were wide and feral as she pushed something into my palm. I glanced down for just a second, noting the burlap. Umma must have pocketed one of the blades earlier, as a precaution before bed, when I wasn't looking. I shoved it into my cloak before anyone could notice.

Rough, large hands wrenched at my shoulders, pulling me away. Yanking me from the only family I had ever known. I didn't even get a chance to tell Umma I loved her before I was shoved out the door.

Something hard slammed against the side of my head. And then I was falling.

Sinking into nothing.

CHAPTER 2

There was daylight and nightfall.

I woke intermittently either at dusk or dawn, but never the same time in a row. I couldn't comprehend how many days I had been asleep for, since I was never allowed to remain awake for longer than the minutes it took my captors to realize I was conscious. Then they'd force something with a sweet scent beneath my nostrils, and I would drift off into a dreamless sleep until the next day. In the twilight zone between wakefulness and sleep, I thought I saw a glimmer of silver peering down at me. It carried through to my befuddled dreams.

Once, the disorientation faded momentarily for my body to register a soft rocking beneath the hard surface I slept on. An almost imperceptible swaying had my stomach twisting, threatening to upturn whatever meager contents remained. That was before the ever-present guard swiftly sent me back to sleep.

When my eyes eventually fluttered and stayed open for long enough to assess my surroundings, it was early morning. A strip of pale sky was visible through a window near a slatted ceiling, illuminating a large room. Its walls were painted an eggshell white and a solid wooden door was wedged near the left corner. I sat slowly, wincing at the crick in my neck and the ache in my joints from having slept far too long and uncomfortably.

Where was I? Memories slotted through my brain, foggy and condensed. Umma, the elven, the Trials–

"You're up."

The words came from my right. I turned to find a girl who looked to be about my age, seated in a bed similar to the one I occupied. She was pale, paler than most of the people in Serila, so I assumed she was from one of the northern islands, perhaps Concorde. And she was ethereally beautiful, so much so that I had to triple check her ears to make sure she was not elven. Strands of lilac framed her face, but the rest of her hair was the color of cornsilk, her eyes a cool blue. Dark circles shadowed those eyes. She looked as tired as I felt.

She tracked my face too, no doubt also making a mental note of everything she saw there. She gingerly folded back the covers of her duvet, swinging her legs off the side of the mattress and letting out a loud yawn.

"Gods, I feel like I've been asleep for years," she muttered, stretching her long limbs.

It seemed like a good thing to do considering how sore my body felt, so I pulled my arms before me, tentatively rotating the joints. My muscles winced in protest, and I gave up stretching in favor of rubbing the knots out.

"As do I," I said. "Do you know how long we've been asleep for?"

She snorted. "I tried counting for the first week. Gave up fairly swiftly."

A week? We had been asleep for a *week*, maybe even longer? My heart stuttered in my chest at the thought of Umma, voiceless and unable to do anything about it. I wasn't even there to help her.

"I take it you're another one of the candidates, then?" she asked.

"Hm?" I fixed my gaze back on her, though my thoughts still lay with Umma.

"One of the candidates," she repeated. "Chosen for the Mortal Trials."

"Oh. That. Yes."

"Yeah. *That.*" She leaned back against one of her pillows, sighing loudly. "You look like you're from one of the eastern isles. Let me guess – Foulkan?"

"Serila."

"Huh." She levelled those cool blue eyes at me. "You do *not* look like you're from Serila."

Maybe I wasn't. Maybe my mother – my real mother – had been from Foulkan, where the islanders had brown skin and dark hair, obsidian eyes, and sharp tongues. It didn't matter. I was taken from Serila. From the person who did not birth me but was more of a mother than anyone else would ever be.

"What about you?" I changed the subject.

"I'm from the mainland," the girl said. "Dorisport."

My brows raised on their own accord. I had lived a cloistered life in the governor's house, but still, I had heard stories about the mainland from Umma, from the other cooks and cleaners, and even the men who tended the gardens.

"I've never met someone from Dorisport," I hedged, not wanting to offend her with my next question. "Is it really as… religious, as they say?"

"Oh, yeah." The girl's eyes fluttered closed as if she hadn't just slept for days. "There's a monument on practically every corner. You can't walk four feet down the street without one of those zealous Children of the Gods preaching fealty. My family are super religious," she said this last part like it was a secret, shared between old friends.

"And you aren't?" I couldn't help but question, fascinated to have met someone so far from Serila. Citizens of the mainland hardly ever traveled to neighboring islands. There was no reason for them to when the mainland housed the most important temple. The one that was said to have once been the hallowed crossing ground for the gods themselves eons ago, when they had deigned to leave their land and visit our world; a tale so outlandish I had trouble believing it.

The girl blew out a breath, lifting her head to study the ceiling. "To an extent, I am. You can't not be, living in Dorisport. Not with the Amber Temple at your doorstep." She seemed to be choosing her words carefully. "I'm just not as… fervent, as most. I perform the rituals on the holy days, and usually do my nightly prayers, but I don't really know if they're ever listening."

"The gods are always listening," I said. "Whether they *hear* you is another story."

It was the most I could say without my words venturing into treason. To speak ill against the gods was not only careless, but dangerous too. From what Umma had told me, the gods were a petty bunch. Whispered enmity had once wrought floods of devastation and destruction upon Concorde several years ago. They were still rebuilding to this day.

She gave me a curious look. "You're surprisingly candid for someone from Serila."

"Is there talk that we're deceitful?"

"Your governor has a reputation for dishonesty. It has made trading with Serila most risky. My father's a tradesman," she added as an aside.

Being a tradesman could be a noble profession, but there were many who were crooked, and a side effect of the job was exposure to corruption, from secrets to black market deals. It made the occupation trickier to navigate than others. "Is that why you were taken?"

Her eyes flickered to me, then over to the ceiling.

"I'm sorry," I hastened, "if that was too invasive."

She let out a soft chuckle. "There's nothing invasive about it. You were also taken. It's not a secret. To be quite honest, I don't know why I was taken. All I know is that three elven arrived halfway through Augustine and took me."

"And your family–" I paused, not knowing whether I should finish that sentence.

She scoffed. "What were they supposed to do? I have three younger sisters. It was either me or one of them. I'd rather it be me. And it's not like anyone will ever rebel against the Mortal Trials. If they do, the elven will stop blessing the isles, all our crops will die, and then we'll starve to death."

"What do you mean they bless the land?" I asked. This was the first I was hearing of it.

Her brows scrunched. "Have you been living under a rock?"

Close. The governor's house was a fortress, the kitchen my prison. I had only ever heard whispered rumors of the elven. I had even been half-convinced that Augustine was a cautionary tale, a bedtime story told to children so they would behave.

She shook her head at my silence and continued, "Every month, an elven representative visits each isle. They drop a seed of magic in the soil, and it ensures our crops are healthy."

"What happens if they stop?"

She shrugged. "I don't know, and I don't want to find out. There's a reason why we coexist so peacefully with the elven, why no mortal will ever raise an army to challenge them. It's a battle we would not win. I suppose the loss of thirteen lives every decade is far better than the countless who would lose their lives in a war." She sucked in a deep breath. "I am glad they took me and not my sisters. Everyone knows no one makes it out of the Trials, anyway."

Her words made me feel queasy. The truth behind them echoed hollowly in my chest. The thought of me not making it back home, of never seeing Umma again, was too painful to bear. I had to make it back. I made a promise. "Don't say that."

She rolled her eyes. "You don't mean to tell me you actually think you're getting out of this alive? I know you Serilans are an untrustworthy bunch, but I didn't take you for naïve."

I wasn't naïve. Everyone in Tarlor knew what the Mortal Trials were. Umma had explained it to me before I was six.

Every decade, on Augustine, the elven were entitled to take thirteen mortals, one from each of the islands of Tarlor, to compete in an elaborate series of twisted challenges designed to weed out the strongest of the lot, the ones most genetically compatible for the final challenge, the Rite. Participating in the Rite would bestow the ultimate gift upon the winner – immortality – and thus a chance to become elven.

The choice of which mortals were taken was always at the discretion of the elven. Volunteers were never considered. There was no age limit, but generally, most candidates were in their twenties. And the girl seated across from me was right. No one ever made it through the Rite.

It was horrifically dangerous to even compete in the challenges, and the few who passed through and made it to the end swiftly found Azrael, the God of Death, waiting on the other side.

All but one. The only mortal to ever turn elven in the past seven decades.

Augustine Devior.

"But August–"

"Don't start with the *'but Augustine managed to survive, so there's hope'* delusion. There's no hope. There's only gruesome death, painful death, and semi-painful death. You should take your hope and place it on the third."

"You're just a ray of sunshine, aren't you?" I muttered, leaning back against my pillows.

"The irony that that is the meaning of my name is not lost on me."

"What? Sunshine?" I rolled onto my side to look at her properly.

"Solana. But you can call me Lana. My friends do."

"Are we friends now?"

She shrugged, rolling off the bed and standing. "If we're going to die here together, we might as well be."

I mimicked her movements, pushing the duvet off and getting to my feet carefully. They felt wobbly. "I'm Lirahna. Lirah for short."

"Lirah and Lana," she mused. "When they sing the song of our deaths, at least it will be poetic."

I didn't respond. Her words, though pessimistic, were not wrong. But I owed it to Umma to at least try to make it out of here. Hope was a dangerous thing, but deciding you'd failed before even trying to survive meant certain death.

I watched as Lana padded to the wooden door at the corner of the room and thumped twice. Nothing happened. She tried the doorknob, but it didn't give.

"It's locked," she huffed, facing me. I smoothed down the crumpled night clothes I still wore from Augustine and surveyed the rest of the room. Two identical cots, a narrow window, door, ceiling, walls. No other furniture save for a small wooden chest built like a safe and painted the exact eggshell white of the walls, so that it camouflaged into its background. My gaze would have skipped right over it were it not for the small indentation near the side where one might open it.

"Look." I pointed, crouching down to run my fingers over its edges.

"What is it?" Lana asked, coming to stand beside me.

I slid a nail into the crack between the indentation and the edge and the chest popped open. Several objects were stored inside. I pulled them all out and placed them in a line before us.

The first two items were a set of identical clothing. Sturdy black pants that molded perfectly to my body when I tried them on. The top was fashioned into a corset, made of hard leather. Three gold buckles strapped down its center. The boning was slitted on the sides to store… I didn't even know what.

"A corset?" I said, staring down at the garment in distaste.

"A cuirass," Lana clarified. "It's meant to go over your long-sleeve. Protects the torso."

Right. Another reminder that I was now in a situation where my torso would need protection.

"It looks like a corset."

"Compete for your lives but make it fashionable?" She shrugged. "I can't understand the elven."

I pulled the corset – cuirass – on, buckling it into place as Lana reached for the third and final item laid out.

It was a small page, dark lettering in sprawling curlicues stretching from end to end.

"What does it say?" I asked, stepping behind Lana to read over her shoulder as I secured my hair into a bun atop my head.

My eyes flitted across the page once. Then twice. Lana's fingers trembled as she read aloud:

> "'Atop a hill lies a cabin on a cliff,
> Surrounded by jagged peaks frozen stiff.
> For survival to be earned, it must be unlocked
> Or you will find yourself plunging down to the rocks.'"

She looked at me with concern. "What is this?" she breathed. "A riddle?"

I shook my head. "No. It's an instruction."

As if on cue, a tile not three feet away from us began shaking. It quivered with the force of a mini earthquake, vibrating and fissuring, tiny cracks spiraling across its surface. I watched in horror as more pieces began chipping off, a cold draft billowing in through the fractures in its surface.

I wasn't surprised when I peered through the cracks to find snowcapped summits yawning for miles beneath.

"There's a key hidden somewhere in the room," I muttered, my eyes spinning around the sparse space I thought I had thoroughly analyzed. "There has to be, to unlock the door."

"Shit," Lana said as the next tile began to split.

Shit was right. The Mortal Trials had begun. Whether we liked it or not, the only way out now was through.

The entire room stretched and groaned, like a beast waking from slumber.

"We have to move quick." Lana crouched before the wooden chest, her fingers running the lengths of its compartments, up and down, searching for the key.

I tested the floor in front of me gingerly, the toe of my boot tapping once before I hopped onto the next tile, until I made it back to the beds. Around me, other tiles shivered, but I couldn't focus on them. Not when the key could be buried beneath our sheets and the floor might give way at any second. I started at my bed first, wrenching the cream duvet off in a flourish and shaking it. Nothing fell.

The sheet stretched taut over the mattress was plain cotton, and I knew without checking that the key was not underneath. I pulled it off anyway, running my hands across the divots in the mattress. Even if the key was miraculously stored within, I would not have a tool to cut it open anyway.

Lana huffed her abject frustration behind me. She leaped across an open patch of the floor, which revealed more snowy peaks and dark rocks jutting out in menacing, bone-splintering angles.

"We're going to die in here," she muttered, ripping off her own bedcovers.

I didn't waste any precious seconds to respond. I pulled the mattress off the bedframe, not caring where it landed, my eyes scanning the iron frame. Still no key.

I dropped to my hands and feet just as the tile beneath my right hand began to shake. I had seconds. Seconds to stay alive. I stuck my head beneath the frame, my left hand extending to sweep the surface of the floor. And then it gave out.

My right hand fell straight through, the tile dropping with it. I keeled forward face first, my body crashing into the shuddering surface as my entire arm sank into the air. I floundered, terror gripping me with icy tentacles. My heart hammered against my ribcage as I shoved myself up and away from the broken tile with my other hand, yanking myself back.

My sleeve got stuck on a ragged edge of floor that had not yet fallen. I pulled violently, desperately wanting away from the plunging drop below, and the material tore. The jagged tile scraped painfully along my wrist as the sleeve tore off and a cool breeze stole it from view.

"Lirah, your arm." Lana stood poised with her mattress, her gaze on my wrist. Scarlet blood oozed through the gash, dripping onto what remained of the floor.

"Don't worry about it," I said, pushing the pain into a lock box to deal with later. "Keep looking."

Lana tossed her mattress aside, her voice wobbling as she said, "There's nothing here. It's pointless."

"Keep trying." I gritted my teeth, eyes flicking around the room in search. The wooden chest had been camouflaged earlier. Maybe the key was hiding in plain sight? Several tiles had broken free near the wall, and I took a running jump to clear the empty space, stumbling as I landed. I ran my hands across the eggshell surface, ignoring the twinge in my forearm and my ribs as I moved.

Wait – my ribs?

My fingertips faltered on the walls and then they were running the length of my torso, because there was definitely something digging into my ribcage. I had thought it was the impact of falling onto the floor and the boning of the cuirass stabbing into me, but…

My fingers felt for the slits in the boning, the ones I had thought might be good for storage.

"Lirah, watch out!" Lana yelled. Through the daze of my realization and the quivering of the room, I hadn't realized that the floor where I stood had begun fissuring, my weight speeding things along. "MOVE!"

I flung my entire weight to the side, landing awkwardly on my elbow, My arm protested in pain as I pushed myself to a seating position. There was no time to spare to think about my brush with death; I scooted away from the latest patch of tiles to my right that had begun trembling.

Nowhere in the room was safe.

I fumbled along the cuirass once more, my eyes nearly shuttering with relief as my fingers grazed cold, hard metal. I pulled the key out and Lana's eyes widened. She rummaged along her own gear, pulling out the twin to my key.

"It was on us the entire time. Those *fucking* bastards," she breathed.

I would have laughed, had the tiles right before the front door not begun to vibrate.

"We have to go. Now."

Lana did not hesitate. She jumped across the open space, landing with a grace I would never possess. She hurried to the door, dropping to her knees and shoving the key into the lock. She twisted the knob, and I heard the most satisfying click as it swung open.

Lana crossed the threshold and shouted, "It's just a hallway out here! It looks safe." She glanced back at me as I scrambled across the room, dodging tile after broken tile. The patch before the door quivered ferociously, hairline cracks coalescing. My heart plummeted to my feet. I wasn't going to make it before they fell. I was going to die.

Panic clawed at my lungs, but still I raced for the door, watching horror-stricken as the floor before it finally gave way, plunging into nothing.

"You have to jump!" Lana called.

"It's too wide. I won't make it," I managed to get out, my voice high-pitched with fear.

Lana gripped the doorframe, her other hand outstretched toward me. "I'll catch you."

My eyes caught hers. Even though we had just met, intrinsically, I trusted her. Aside from not having an alternative choice, a cold fire gleamed in those blue eyes, steely and determined.

My feet met the edge of emptiness, and I lunged, legs kicking wildly. My fingers grazed hers. Gravity pulled hard, but Lana's hand wrapped around my uninjured wrist. I reached for the doorframe, my nails digging into the grooves. My knees dangled hopelessly beneath me, torso wedged against the threshold.

Lana yanked and my fingers scrabbled, every ounce of my willpower focused on swinging my legs to the side. Lana grunted as she wrenched my arm, and I had to bite my lip to stop myself from screaming at the excruciating pain in my shoulder joint. Instead I concentrated on using the momentum to swing my legs once more. My foot mercifully found purchase on the lip of the threshold.

Lana tugged once more, finally hauling me over the edge. I scrambled forward, just as the entire room gave a final shudder and the rest of the floor fell at once.

Tremors racked my body, my breaths coming out in pants. Lana sank to the floor beside me, quivering hands scrubbing her face.

"Are you okay?" she heaved, breathless from the exertion.

As the adrenaline of the last few minutes subsided, I became acutely aware of the throbbing in my wrist, the cramp in my calves and the ache in my shoulder. But I was alive. "I'm okay. Thank you. For saving me."

"Lirah and Lana," she said shakily. "Our deaths need to be far more poetic than falling through a floor."

I gave her a weak smile. It turned into a flat-out grin, one she returned. "We made it."

A soft cough, sounding a lot like someone clearing their throat, resounded through the passage. I looked away from Lana to survey the hallway we now sat in. Green vines snaked along the walls, illuminated by warm lights, nestled into sconces spaced evenly along it. At the end of which, an elven stood.

"You haven't even *begun* to make it yet," Blondie said.

CHAPTER 3

Lana and I shared a reluctant glance as we followed the elven, too exhausted to even ask where he was taking us. He had been leading us along a series of hallways, all of which were so similar. I lost track of the various twists and turns we took to get to a wider, open space. It looked like a sparring hall, with rubber mats spaced equidistantly on the ground and a rack of vicious looking weapons to one side. The ceiling was covered with moss and fern, spiny tendrils snaking along the walls, and a cool breeze seemed to drift in from absolutely nowhere.

Anxiety speared my gut at the lack of windows and the others who already stood waiting in the room, near the weapons rack. From my count, there were eight mortals and three elven, one of which I recognized as Scar Face.

His eyes met mine and an arrogant smirk crossed his mouth. A soft hiss escaped my lips at the haughty look.

Lana nudged me in the ribs. "What's wrong?"

I shook my head silently at her, but Blondie tutted from where he stood a few steps ahead. "Making enemies already, are we?"

I opened my mouth to bite out that this was none of my doing and all *their* fault, but he was already striding away toward the others in the center. Lana elbowed me forward and we took position beside two other mortals: a boy who looked a few years older than me, and a girl no older than sixteen.

"Hi," Lana said to them, clearly the chattiest of our bunch.

The girl surveyed us shrewdly. She sported a nasty gash above her eyebrow, while her counterpart crossed his muscled forearms.

"This is Lirah," Lana continued, pointing me out. "And I'm Lana."

"It's nice to meet you," I said, in an attempt to be friendly.

"Is it?" the girl drawled.

She clearly did not want to be friends.

The boy clicked his tongue at her. "Ignore her. She's pissy because the arrows nearly caught her."

Arrows?

"*Nearly*?" the girl shrieked, pointing to the cut on her brow. "I beg to differ."

The boy ignored her. "I'm Moric. From the isle of Foulkan."

"Rayna, from Oulis," the girl grumbled. She held a tiny lighter in her hand, which she flicked on, then off.

"They let you keep that?" I asked, noting that the blade Umma had given me was missing. Kidnapped and now defenseless. Just great.

Rayna shrugged. "Seems like it. You look terrible." She said the last part specifically to me. "What happened to you guys?"

"We had to find a key to unlock our door before the floor dropped out," I summarized.

"We had to find a key too," Rayna said, the little flame in her hand striking again. "Our floor didn't fall, but we had about ten dozen arrows shooting at us."

I didn't know which was worse.

"What are we doing here?" Lana asked, peering at the elven gathered in front. "It looks like they're waiting for something."

"Yeah. The last three." Moric's eyes scanned the other mortals. "There should be thirteen."

Rayna scoffed bitterly at the elven. "What even stops us from leaving? I didn't ask to be kidnapped in the middle of the night. If I don't die from these dumb challenges, I'll die during the Rite. So, what'll happen if I refuse to compete?"

"They'll kill you," Moric muttered.

"None of us are getting out of here alive," Rayna said. "Whether I die now or later, it doesn't matter."

"It *does* matter," a deep voice boomed from across the room, and all heads swiveled to survey the elven now entering.

Dark hair, familiar silver eyes.

"I think he heard you," Moric said.

"No shit."

Great. I filed away super hearing in the mental cabinet I was slowly beginning to grow on all things elven.

"And you *will* compete," Silver Eyes continued, striding purposefully across the room. He was so tall and his shoulders so broad that I didn't even notice the two mortals trailing behind him, until he swerved around our group to join the other elven.

The remaining mortals joined us, their faces ashen. Tear tracks marked the face of an older woman. She was the eldest of the group, it seemed.

"Aren't there supposed to be three of them?" Lana whispered.

"Thank you for joining us," Silver Eyes said, his voice filling the room. He was clearly in charge here. If the position in which he stood a few steps ahead of the others, who had shifted into formation behind him – Blondie at his right, Scar Face at his left and two others behind them – did not indicate his dominance, then the power radiating from him did.

Just like the night they had taken me, I sensed his energy like a tangible beast, prowling the radius of our group. It felt like midnight rain and forest fires, ocean salt and unyielding granite. It was a different kind of deadly brutality. One that rippled and undulated with lethal calm. And lurking at the edges of that power was something unspeakably wild.

"We barely did," Rayna snapped.

Moric elbowed her in the ribs, earning him a cold glare.

"What? It's the truth." Rayna's voice rang loud and clear across the room. "If this was the first Trial, I can't imagine what fresh horror you're going to throw at us next."

My gaze flickered to Silver Eyes, waiting for a display of brutality. For Scar Face to step forward and silence Rayna, just because he could. Anger bubbled beneath my skin, hot and vicious.

But Scar Face didn't so much as glance at our group. His focus was on his nails, which he was cleaning with the tip of his dagger, looking infinitely more entertained by the blade than us.

Silver Eyes didn't so much as bat his eyelashes at Rayna's outburst. Instead, his brows knitted together in an expression I could only call pitying.

Blondie beside him grimaced.

"I'm afraid to tell you," he said, "but that was not the first Trial."

Moric shuffled uncomfortably beside me as Lana's lips parted silently. Rayna's eyes widened, but even she seemed to have been rendered speechless.

It was the eldest woman of the group that spoke. "What do you mean that wasn't the first task? A man *died* trying to make it out of that room!" Her voice broke, tears threatening to spill again from her brown eyes.

"That was most unfortunate," the elven said, as if reporting on bad weather. "But a necessary consequence of the Mortal Trials. As you will find out, the Trials are not as linear as you may think and will also consist of several *unofficial* Trials within the actual challenges themselves."

This caused a spattering of murmured grumbling and outrage within our group. Granted, no one had ever made it out of the Mortal Trials alive – with the exception of Augustine – so there wasn't really a lot of knowledge on the challenges themselves within the mortal isles. But the general consensus was that there were three Trials and then the Rite. I was relieved that the news of the unofficial Trials seemed to be a surprise to everyone. Additional challenges seemed brutal on top of what we were already forced into. I shouldn't have expected anything less.

"Let me explain," Silver Eyes said, his voice like liquid night, silencing the murmurs. "I am Kilian Valhan."

Kilian Valhan. Even sequestered in the governor's kitchen my entire life, I knew who he was. Elven, like mortals, had a hierarchy system. Kilian was upper elven, and he ruled over other elven who resided on the isle of Lortan.

That had to mean…

"You've all been brought to Lortan. More specifically, Lomask, where the Mortal Trials will take place."

That explained the sea legs I had felt upon waking earlier, and the several days of unconsciousness. It had definitely taken over a week to sail from Serila to Lortan. The bridges and pathways used to enter Lortan were forbidden to mortal eyes. The elven were allowed to cross over to the mortal isles, but humans could not set foot on Lortan or Greyhaven, the isle of the lower elven – those who did not possess the power of the upper elven, but had lower magic.

"You have all been chosen to compete in three Trials, along with any unofficial challenges we may determine at our discretion. Those who survive will have the privilege of participating in the Rite for the chance to join us here in Lortan, in everlasting glory and life as upper elven," Kilian said.

As if sensing Rayna's next question, Kilian continued, his tone sharp as knives, "It is important to note that there is a very specific reason why mortals are not allowed to cross into Lortan, or even Greyhaven. Once a mortal sets foot on elven soil, they are bound to remain there for all eternity."

A silence rang through the room. My sluggish brain tripped and lurched over its thoughts, turning the sentence over and over in my head, until finally it sank in. I could never leave.

Not as a mortal, that is.

I promised Umma I would return. I promised to go back for her. Fear clenched at my heart unlike anything I had ever known, its grip a steel vise. My eyes met Lana's, the determination I had seen burning in them earlier now guttering into cinders.

She had been right all along. We would either die competing in the challenges or die living as mortals on an elven isle, where everything from the food to drink could be poisonous to our fragile human bodies.

And even though I knew hope was nothing but kindling to my pyre, the only chance I stood of ever making it back home was to try to get to the Rite. And, if by some miracle, I passed the challenges but my body failed at that final hurdle, at least I would have tried my hardest to return to the only person who had ever truly loved me.

Perhaps then, when Azrael collected my soul, it would have found peace.

"The first challenge will take place in one week," Kilian said. "You'll need to use the time to prepare. The sparring room we're in is available for all. Make use of the facilities provided in

Valhan House and Lomask. You are free to wander the city and visit the libraries, but do bear in mind that Lomask's citizens do not take kindly to deserters. They have been warned not to offer you any elven food or drink or harm any of you for the duration of the Mortal Trials, but should you choose not to participate, you will no longer be afforded the protection of the Trials."

Kilian glanced to Blondie at his right and took a small step back. "Septimus will explain the rules."

Septimus cleared his throat. "The first challenge will test your survival skills. For this one, you will be split into three groups of four. Split at your own discretion. It does not matter to us." He gave us an expectant look, accompanied by a shooing motion, the rings on his fingers glinting as they caught the light. "Well, go on."

There was a hustle of activity as people broke off, chatting to those closest to them. Lana and I shared a look. We did not need to say anything further to know we would stick together. We turned to face Rayna and Moric.

Rayna gave us a dubious look, her nose scrunching slightly. "I'd offer to pair with you, but honestly, you don't look like you'd last very long in a survival challenge." Rayna's eyes scanned the torn material of my sleeve, the cut on my wrist and tense set of my shoulder, the joint having nearly subluxated. "Maybe you'd manage," she said to Lana, "But I doubt you'd consider pairing without Lirah?"

Lana shook her head. "It's going to be a hard no."

Tears nearly welled in my eyes at how fiercely loyal Lana was to a girl she had met only an hour ago. But Rayna was right. This was a survival challenge, and only the strongest stood a chance. I had grown up peeling vegetables and cooking stew. I had not traveled Tarlor. I had not even met anyone from any of the neighboring isles. I was inexperienced in survival.

"Lana," I said to her. "It's okay. Rayna's right. You need to do what's best for you."

"I know. And what's best for me is sticking with you," Lana said simply.

Rayna nodded. "Good luck to the both of you." She turned to Moric. "What about you? Are you coming or staying?"

Moric shook his head. His eyes, a striking shade of hazel which contrasted against his dark skin and the jet-black hair cropped close to his head, narrowed. "It's a *survival* challenge. If it comes down to sticking a knife in my back so that you stay alive, I know you wouldn't hesitate."

There was a bite in his words, and I wondered what exactly had happened during their unofficial challenge.

"I'm staying."

Rayna shrugged. "I won't apologize for prioritizing my survival."

With that, she pocketed her lighter, turned on her heel and headed toward another group.

"That means nothing if you lose your soul in the process," Moric muttered at her retreating form.

"Welcome to the Mortal Trials," Lana said sardonically.

I scanned the rest of the room. There was one group that had broken off and formed a quartet. Rayna stood near three men, all twice her size. There was only one other person who stood on her own farther out, a distant look on her face.

I jerked my head toward the older woman. "What about her?"

Lana gave me a look that clearly asked if I was being serious. "She's too old. She'll never be able to keep up with us."

I pressed my lips together, biting down with my teeth. The woman *was* old. Perhaps the same age as Umma. And though she might slow us down during the challenge, she had probably seen five different Trials. Maybe she had heard stories of how others had passed various challenges. Besides, it seemed Rayna had joined the group of men and now stood with them next to the other squad.

"It doesn't look like we have a choice," Moric said, observing the same.

Lana groaned as Moric waved the woman over.

"If she gets us killed, I'm going to be *so* mad at you," she hissed.

The woman crossed over to us, a questioning look on her face.

"We'd like you to join our group," Moric said when she had reached hearing distance.

"Me?" Surprise colored the word. "Are you sure? The others said…"

"We're sure." I gave her a soft smile, one I usually reserved only for Umma. I knew it was stupid and probably just because she was older, but something about her reminded me of my mother, of baked bread and warm fires. Of home. "What's your name?"

"Anama," she said. Like the herb that only grew on the western isle of Kraventhorn.

"We're Lirah, Lana, and Moric." I pointed us out, our names starting to feel like the childhood game Umma used to play with me where we kept adding items to a list, seeing if we could remember each one.

With the groups finalized, Septimus said, "You will find your dorms in the hallway beyond this room. Bathrooms are shared and at the end of the hallway. Tomorrow morning, you will each be assigned an instructor who will guide you through the Trials. Meals will be served in the mess hall one floor above. Any questions?"

"Yeah," Rayna said. "How do we know our food won't be poisoned?"

Septimus rolled his eyes. "It won't be. Everything in Valhan House is safe for mortal consumption."

Valhan House. That had to mean… Kilian owned the building we would be living in for the foreseeable future. It had to be massive to accommodate us all.

"You serve us no good if you die before the Trials begin," Kilian added.

You serve us no good if you die before the Trials begin.

"Why?" I surprised even myself with the question. But my voice was clear and echoed throughout the room. "Why does it matter whether a human turns elven? What do you get out of this?"

It had been nagging at the back of my mind from the time Umma had first told me about the Mortal Trials. I had never voiced it aloud before.

Kilian's silver eyes gleamed as he narrowed them at me. "That is of no concern to you, mortal. Pass the Rite and you will find out."

I rolled my eyes with bravado that could only have been sent from the heavens. "Why bother with the Trials at all, then? Just stick us all in the Rite and let's see what happens. Unless this is all just a game of sport to you? I wonder, do you place bets on our lives?"

Kilian's gaze darkened and the temperature increased several degrees. "The Rite isn't designed for all of you. Only the strongest are able to enter. We cannot determine who is the strongest if we do not test you. But right now, *you* are testing my patience. And if you continue to do so, you might find you won't even make it to the first Trial."

Lana gulped audibly beside me.

"Question time is over," Kilian snapped, jerking his head to the doorway. "You're all dismissed."

My gaze didn't leave the upper elven until he and the others had disappeared from the room, anger sizzling beneath my skin. How dare they kidnap us from our homes, bring us to a land we literally could not leave and tell us that their motive was not our concern? Threaten to eliminate me from a Trial I didn't even *want* to be a part of? I wanted him to return just so I could throw something at his head.

"Are you okay?" Lana nudged me gently.

"No," I blurted. "I don't understand *why* they're doing this. How is everyone on all thirteen godsdamned isles just okay with this happening? How do we know the elven won't just kill us if we pass the Rite? Has anyone ever even seen Augustine?"

Anama shuffled awkwardly beside Moric, then said softly, "I have. He's visited the Great Library of Kraventhorn on occasion. I am – *was* – a scholar at the library. I've worked there for decades."

"Of course," Lana said. "Augustine was the candidate from Kraventhorn during his Trial."

Anama nodded. "He's a scholar himself. He's checked out nearly every book on upper magic. And yes, he's very much elven."

I shook my head in doubt. "It still doesn't make sense to me. It hardly seems like they'd turn us into elven out of the goodness of their hearts."

"Well, they're not. Not really, at least," Moric said. "Nobody else has ever made it through the Rite. So, they're not actually turning anyone."

"Anyway." Lana linked her arm through my uninjured one, tugging me toward the doorway where the other groups had already exited. "I don't have the mental capacity right now to dissect whether there's a nefarious purpose behind the Mortal Trials, when it hardly seems likely I'll even make it to the Rite. As it is, I'm struggling to process the fact that I can't leave this godsforsaken island as a mortal and likely won't see my family again."

"We've all got family we're worried we'll never see again," Moric said, not unkindly. "Little brother," he clarified at my questioning look. "It's just the two of us."

I looked at Anama, hoping she might share too.

Her gaze diverted from us and around the hallway as we exited the sparring room. The hallway branched off into different directions like the veins on a leaf, doors nestled into alcoves which presumably led to bedrooms. The doors were blank and unmarked, yet the others who had left before us seemed to have claimed most of them.

We had almost reached the shared bathroom at the end of the hallway when Anama said, "No family. It's just me."

She stepped toward one of the unclaimed bedrooms. "I think I'll take the afternoon to rest. It's been an eventful day."

"Agreed." Moric stifled a yawn with the back of one hand. "Maybe I'll see you guys at dinner."

It was hard to believe that with everything that had happened, it wasn't even suppertime yet.

"I don't know if I'll be up for dinner tonight," Lana murmured, backing toward the door on Anama's right. "I seem to have lost my appetite."

"Me too," I said. I felt emotionally drained, numb and exhausted. I supposed sailing for over a week, nearly plunging to your death and then being told you had basically zero chance of ever seeing your loved ones again had that effect.

I claimed the room beside Moric and gave the others a slight wave before heading inside. I shut the door and let loose a long breath before turning to survey my surroundings.

I had barely registered a small desk, chair and bed before a tiny black dart whizzed out from the shadows and flew straight at me.

CHAPTER 4

The dart had eyes. They glowed bright and silver as a creature stopped a hairsbreadth away from my face. Dark wings beat the air, stirring a gentle breeze.

Quick as a whip, the creature zoomed around me, flight path zigzagging along the length of my body. It couldn't have been bigger than my index finger and cloaked so entirely in shadow that it looked like it wore a dress. Wings sprouted from its back, paper thin and delicate, but strong enough to carry it across the length of my body and back up to my face.

"Who are you?" Her voice was high-pitched in tenor but contained a hard edge.

"I'm Lirah," I whispered, afraid that if I startled her, she might zoom straight back into the shadows.

I shouldn't have been worried about scaring the creature, though. Those silver eyes narrowed menacingly at me. "I am so *sick* of meeting new mortals."

I blinked. "Who are *you*?"

"Me?" She fluttered her wings, spreading them wide so that I could see the veins in the near translucent folds. "I am Calendula Mirau, the fourth. Descendant of the magnificent Mirau Titan, spear leader of the shadow sprites. And make no mistake, I do *not* answer to you, mortal."

She was a shadow sprite.

Umma had told me bedtime stories about the sprites who mainly resided on elven soil, but I hadn't thought they were

32

real. She looked so dainty and fragile, but the angry glint in her eyes told me that she was not to be trifled with.

"I'm sorry," I hedged. Keeping my tone as polite as possible, I asked, "But why are you here?"

This was the wrong thing to ask. The shadow sprite huffed angrily, wings propelling her higher and higher to the ceiling. Silver embers sparked and drifted to the ground with each movement.

"I told him I didn't want to do it." Each word was punctuated with a sharp flap. "Every decade it's the same story. Every decade they all die. I'm *sick* of it."

"Are you my instructor?" I asked, remembering Septimus saying that we would be introduced to our instructors the next morning.

Calendula pivoted, spiraling back to eye level. "Of course not, silly mortal. I'm your sprite. For however long you survive the Trials, anyway. After that, I'll wait another decade to accompany another stupid mortal to their death." She gave a long, dramatic sigh, floating to sit on the edge of the desk. I realized the shadows were part of her actual body, shifting as she crossed one leg over the other. "You mortals are all the same and this existence has been painfully long. I just want to go home."

"Why can't you?" I asked, still frozen by the door.

She propped a hand beneath her chin. "I can't. I'm stuck here with you until you die. I'm supposed to help you pass the challenges so you can make it to the Rite. But this decade, I've decided not to help. And he can't force me to."

The casual way she spoke about my impending death was… unsettling, to say the least, but I forged on, curiosity outweighing my discomfort. "Who can't force you?"

Calendula rolled her eyes, annoyance pursing her lips. "Your instructor. I told you, I'm only your sprite until you die. Each candidate gets an instructor, and each instructor lends their candidate a sprite for the duration of the Trials. Once you die, I'll get to go home."

My instructor. Who was…?

I didn't need to voice the question though. It was evident in the darkness that clung to Calendula's skin. Her silver eyes that shone as bright as moonlight. And the faint power thrumming with each beat of her wings. "It's Kilian Valhan, isn't it?"

Those silver eyes widened slightly. It was all the confirmation I needed.

"You'll find out tomorrow," was all she said. "In the meantime, perhaps you should take a bath. And clean that wound. There are medical supplies in the cabinet and clothes in the dresser. Once you've claimed a room, it's been spelled to supply items for its resident."

Calendula yawned wide, her mouth gaping open to reveal nothing but darkness. "I had forgotten how tiresome you mortals are."

She stretched her arms above her head before getting to her feet. Spreading tiny hands in front of her, the shadows rippled and undulated, branching out to form a small hammock which floated in midair a few inches above the desk. I watched as she crawled into the hammock, made herself comfortable and promptly fell asleep.

Only when she was softly snoring did I let myself properly survey the chamber. The walls were a pastel gray. The furniture was sparse, but there was indeed a dresser, and another cabinet above a small sink. A few shelves were mounted on the wall, presumably for storing books, but the real highlight was the bed. The mattress was larger than anything I'd ever slept on, including the bed I'd awoken in this morning. I ran my fingers across the duvet, relishing the feel of the soft, luxurious fabric.

I examined the dresser next, pulling open the first drawer to find more cuirasses, long-sleeves and tunics for layering on top. The second had an array of pants, ranging from soft linen sleepwear to sturdy leather. Underwear and socks graced the third drawer, and beneath it, two pairs of flat boots with rubber soles sat on the floor.

I pulled out the medical kit from the cabinet next, finding it well stocked. I chose the gauze, a bottle of liquid whose label read *Antiseptic*, and a roll of tape, setting them neatly on the desk, careful not to disturb Calendula. Although, the shadow sprite seemed fast asleep, her mouth slightly agape as she snored.

Rolling my torn sleeve up, I assessed the damage to my wrist. The cut wasn't as deep as I initially thought, I noted with relief, running my wrist under cool water from the sink to clean the dried blood from around the wound. The water felt so good against my clammy skin that I found myself splashing it onto my neck and face. Succumbing to the overwhelming need to scrub my skin clean, I grabbed a set of pajamas before heading to the bathroom.

Twenty minutes later, I was clean and nestled beneath the duvet. For the first time in my entire life, I had gone to bed without reciting my nightly prayer to the gods. After everything that had happened to me, I no longer felt them deserving of worship. It was treasonous to even think that, but I didn't care. What worse could the gods do to me now? The sound of Calendula's breathing was soft and steady as I replayed the day's events. I twisted over the rules Septimus had laid out, and the fact that I could never leave Lortan as a mortal. Anger festered in me as I recalled the hard set of Kilian's jaw, the glare he had given me when I had asked about the motive behind the Mortal Trials.

He had done nothing to prevent his friend from cursing Umma. He had simply watched, then ripped me away to a land I could never leave.

I tossed and turned throughout the night, considering all the ways I might escape the Mortal Trials, and coming to the same end result each time.

Death.

Even if I managed to make it to the edge of Lortan, I would not be able to leave. I was imprisoned here, and no one was coming to save me.

That was fine, I decided with a huff, flipping onto my back and staring furiously at the ceiling. I would just have to save my own godsdamned self.

I fell asleep, restless and annoyed, and awoke to a shrill ringing in the morning. "What is that godsawful noise?" I groaned, rolling onto my side to pull my pillow over my head.

Calendula seemed chirpier this morning as she flitted to perch on the corner of my bed. "It's the breakfast bell."

Breakfast? It felt like I had just shut my eyes ten minutes ago.

"You'd better get ready if you want to eat before the day's activities. The first week is always the hardest for you mortals."

"You don't know me," I snapped. The anger that had been simmering last night threatened to boil over. "I don't know what you've got against me, but I'm not like the others."

Sure, I may not be experienced on a sparring mat or as worldly as Lana, but I was no stranger to hard work. I had worked every single day of my life, perhaps twice as hard as others, to earn my keep as an abandoned stray in the governor's house.

Calendula's silver eyes widened for a fraction of a second before narrowing with hostility. "Fine, mighty mortal. If you think you know better than I do, I won't burden you with useless information." She shook a tiny fist at me before turning tail and zooming off into the shadows.

I sighed. Grabbing some toiletries and a new set of clothes for the day, I got ready and made my way outside, stopping to knock on Lana's door. When she didn't answer, I traced our steps from yesterday down the hallway to the doorway beside the sparring room. A set of staircases curled up and down.

The mess hall, one floor above our dormitories and the sparring room, was full. Four rectangular wooden tables filled the length of the space, one of which was occupied by mortals, separated into our groups from yesterday. Elven crowded the other tables, keeping a wide berth from the rest.

I approached my group. Lana and Moric were opposite Anama, their plates piled high with scrambled eggs and bacon, slices of toast and fruit. All untouched. Jars of pale, creamy butter and glossy jams were placed in the middle of the table, with sets of shiny cutlery. Perched atop Moric's shoulder sat a curvy sprite, her figure the perfect hourglass shape. She was made of vine and green moss. Brown branches snaked along her legs. Her wings were lime green and looked as delicate as Calendula's.

Lana shot me a look of relief as I slid into the seat beside Anama. "I was worried when you didn't answer your door this morning."

"You came looking for me?" I reached for an empty saucer. As soon as I set the plate in front of me, food appeared, the same items that sat untouched before the others. "I must have been in the bathroom. I tried your door before I came up too. Why's no one eating? You don't all still think it's poisoned?"

Three pairs of sheepish eyes stared back at me. I shook my head at them and reached for a fork. Spearing a piece of pineapple, I put it in my mouth, then chewed and swallowed. Five seconds passed before I said, "It's tangy."

That was all the confirmation Lana needed. She dug into her food with a fervor, ravenously shoveling eggs into her mouth. Moric and Anama were a little more dignified, but both seemed equally starved.

"Didn't anyone come for dinner last night?" I asked, popping a grape into my mouth. Its sweet juice coated my tongue as I bit into it.

Anama shook her head, her mouth full.

"We were a bit preoccupied with our sprites." Moric gestured to the green sprite on his shoulder, who had an annoyed look on her face.

"I told you the food wasn't poisoned," the sprite said in a tinny voice.

"I'm sorry," he mumbled through a mouthful of toast.

"You're going to have to start trusting me if you have any hope of making it through the Trials." The sprite folded her arms across her chest, then stomped the length of Moric's shoulder. She settled at the base of his neck, curled on her side and closed her eyes.

"Is she *asleep*?" Lana eyed the sprite.

"Sprites are notoriously low on energy," Anama said. Her voice was soft, like she hadn't quite gotten used to speaking to us yet. "It's because their bodies are so small, and they expend so much energy flying. They either need to eat a lot or sleep to maintain themselves."

"Did yours tell you that last night?" I asked.

Anama shook her head. "I've worked for many years in the Great Library of Kraventhorn, with little to do but read. My sprite is very… shy. She's hardly spoken to me since arriving."

Much like Anama herself, I couldn't help noting. If our sprites had been chosen for our personalities, I shuddered to think what that said about mine.

"I'm sure she'll come around. What about yours?" I asked Lana.

Lana took a sip of her orange juice and opened her mouth to respond, but a tiny shape whizzed above her head, dropping to land before her plate. He was pure sunlight. Where Calendula was shadow and night, yolky light leaked from the sprite before me. He had a handsome face, his features sharp and pointed, his eyes a familiar gold. He wore a suit, the starched white shirt beneath his coat crisply pressed.

"This is Osmanthius," Lana introduced.

Osmanthius gave a deep bow. "At your service."

I blinked, but there was no animosity in Osmanthius' eyes as he straightened. Was it just my sprite that hated my guts?

"Where's yours?" Lana asked, her eyes tracking Osmanthius' movements as he picked his way around her plate, inspecting the food on the table. He tugged at a piece of leftover toast, breaking off a breadcrumb and popping it into his mouth.

"I think I pissed her off," I grumbled.

Anama winced. "Bad move. Aside from being extremely lethargic, sprites hold grudges for lifetimes."

"Speak for the others, but *I'm* not lethargic," Osmanthius protested, his golden wings ruffling even as he yawned.

"Of course," Anama hastened to assure him. Turning to me, she said, "You should give her a peace offering."

"A peace offering? Like what?"

She shrugged. "Find out her favorite food. You're going to need her for the rest of the Trials."

I opened my mouth to ask her how I was supposed to find out Calendula's favorite food when she had stalked off to the shadows, when the same trilling that had awoken me this morning echoed through the room. The plates, food, cutlery and condiments disappeared in the blink of an eye.

"I was still eating that," Moric griped.

The elven who had been steadfastly ignoring us now stood, filing out of the mess hall in an orderly line. As they exited, a smaller group entered through the double doors to the right, led by Kilian Valhan.

He donned his usual armor, daggers glinting at his sides, jaw set in the same grim expression he seemed to wear each time I saw him. His dark hair was ruffled, soft curls spilling over his forehead like ink across parchment.

"Welcome to your first day in Valhan House," Kilian said as he reached our table, but there was no warmth in his voice.

"Assignments will be called out. Once you've been allocated an instructor, please join them in the center, where you will take the sacred oath." He offered no further explanation before pulling out a roll of parchment.

"Rola Doul," Kilian read from the sheet.

A woman from the first quartet nervously stood.

"You'll be paired with Palisa."

A stunning dark-skinned, silver-haired elven branched off from the elven group to meet Rola in the center of the room. Palisa whispered something inaudible to the mortal woman and they joined hands. And then it was done. I watched as the pair exited the room without a backward glance.

"Is that it?" Lana whispered. "Seems a bit anticlimactic."

The assignments carried on like that for the next few minutes. Moric was called up, disturbing his sprite, much to her annoyance, and paired with an elven male with forest green eyes. Anama's instructor was a willowy elven female with sun kissed skin and silky copper hair that ran down her back. She was easily the most beautiful female I had ever seen in my life.

"Rayna Forlun," Kilian drawled in that bored voice that told me he had done this for far too many decades. "You're with Echon."

My heart shriveled in my chest as Scar Face – Echon – stepped to the center. I didn't particularly like Rayna, but I wouldn't wish that elven on my worst enemy.

Rayna seemed smaller, younger, beside Echon, his signature cruel smirk etched across his lips as they took the oath and he led her out the mess hall. I swallowed the hard lump in my throat and blinked against the hot tears pressing at the corners of my eyes as the memory of what he had done to Umma resurfaced.

I will not cry. Not in front of them.

Lana's name was called next, and it distracted me enough for the fog of sorrow to clear momentarily. It did not come as much of a surprise when Lana was paired with Septimus. His golden eyes, so similar to Osmanthius', skimmed the length of Lana's body as she stood from her seat and made her way to the center. I knew that look on his face, the appreciation that gleamed in his eyes.

He murmured something to her, his lips nearly brushing her ear as he leaned down, and then she nodded. Their hands joined and it was done. Lana turned, giving me a watery smile as she was led out the door.

And then it was just Kilian and I. Alone. My heart gave a nervous contraction, all of yesterday's adrenaline-fueled bravado vanished.

He gave me an uninterested look. "As you may have astutely ascertained, you'll be under my instruction, Golund."

Ignoring the misnomer of my surname, I swung my legs over the bench and stood. "What a shocker."

His brows raised and then his eyes narrowed. "You knew."

"Your shadow sprite has a shitty poker face."

The corner of his lip curled infinitesimally. "Speaking of, you've offended Calendula gravely."

"She offended me first." Each step I took toward him brought me closer to his unmistakable power. It was so heady that I felt lightheaded, but I carried on until I was standing in front of him.

"You should offer her strawberries. Works like a charm."

"Strawberries?" I peered up at him. The top of my head barely skimmed the planes of his broad shoulders. Up close, I could see faint embers of gray in those bright silver eyes.

"They're hard to come by in the Shadow Soil, where she usually lives. Are you ready to take the oath?" His voice still had that hard edge to it, but there was something curious in his gaze as he searched my own.

I nodded, commanding my thumping heart to calm down.

His eyes held me captive, just as they had the night he had taken me from my home. "Do you swear to complete the Mortal Trials to your best ability and accept my guidance for the remainder of your mortal life?"

I paused, my lungs squeezing painfully in my chest. I had gone over this again and again last night while I tossed and turned in bed. There was no escaping the Trials without death. I had no choice but to participate. It was the only slim chance I had of survival.

I nodded once more and took a step forward so that our hands would join.

Callused fingers engulfed my own, his skin rough against mine. A current shot up the side of my palm, tingling along my entire arm like a shockwave.

I yanked my hand from his grip. "Did you feel that too? What just happened?"

"It was the oath." Kilian shoved his hand into his pocket. "We've been linked."

"What does that mean?" I was aware of how high-pitched my voice had become, but I felt *different*. More awake. My surroundings were crisper, the air cleaner, colors brighter. And I was acutely aware of *him*. Stranger still, I felt anger, so stark and raw it made me tremble. I loosened a breath, trying to expel some of it. It didn't work.

"The sacred oath is upper magic," he said, casual indifference in his voice. "It links a candidate to their instructor so they might know when their candidate is in danger, how they're feeling, if they're intending to defect from the Trials. It's a helpful tool to determine whether your candidate has died during a challenge."

How they're feeling? The nonchalance in his tone proved that he either did not understand or simply did not care about how invasive and utterly intrusive that would be. My bet was on the latter. My anger intensified, hot as a poker.

"Why didn't you tell me first?" I snapped.

"Would it have changed your decision to accept?"

He knew it would not have. I had no choice but to accept the oath, to accept my position in the Mortal Trials. *Accept, accept, accept*. I was a lamb brought to Lortan for the slaughter and both he and I knew I had no say in anything that happened here. Fury whistled in my ears, my emotions heightened to their breaking point. I wanted to punch something. I wanted to punch *him*.

I ought to douse the entirety of Valhan House in gasoline to find out whether elven flesh burned the same as mine.

"To link us, the oath transfers a grain of my power to you. Only a grain," Kilian continued, as if he was oblivious to the rage singing in my bones. "It's barely even registrable, but it allows me to keep tabs on you at all times. So, if you were thinking of doing something stupid..." Silver shards of ice hardened in his eyes. "Don't. There is nowhere you can run where I won't find you."

CHAPTER 5

I tried to run anyway.

I spun on my heel and sprinted for the door.

Kilian groaned behind me, but I didn't chance a glance back. My feet skidded on the polished floor, and I clawed at the doorframe before hurtling out of the mess hall and into the corridor.

There were no pounding footsteps behind me – or maybe I couldn't hear them over the blood rushing in my ears.

I tripped at the end of the corridor, arms flinging forward to grasp at a banister. Then I was bolting down the staircase. I didn't have a second to consider where I might be going, only believed that if I reached the bottom, I'd surely end up outside.

My breaths came out short and sharp as I ran, my hand grasping the banister.

I glanced over my shoulder, panicked, but the staircase was empty.

I paused for a second to catch my breath. And then I continued, a bit slower this time, my ears straining for any sound.

When I reached the bottom of the stairwell, I cracked open the door and peered out. A blast of cold air immediately hit me, and I shivered, my teeth chattering. The interior of the house was definitely temperature regulated because it was *freezing* outside.

Stone pillars were the first thing I saw. The ground was a checkered slab of white marble and gray granite, and large columns towered at regular intervals on the outer edges. I peered up at the ceiling where a fresco of a battle scene was depicted in great detail. From what I could see, there was a courtyard beyond. It was empty.

I still didn't know what I would even do if I escaped, but I'd consider it afterward. *If* I managed to make it through the courtyard.

I steeled myself to make a mad dash for it.

I made it to the pillars before a set of arms wrenched me back and, quite literally, off the ground.

"Let me go!" I yelled. My words echoed off the columns and bled out into the vacant courtyard.

"Every decade, one of you tries to run," Kilian muttered. "That one *has*, in fact, become a bet. And I've had my money on you since I first saw you."

I squirmed in his arms, grunting as I tried to free myself from his iron grip.

"What's your plan?" His voice was at my ear.

"Like I'd fucking tell you." I tried jabbing at his ribs but only met solid armor.

He snorted. "You can't because you don't have one."

My fingers closed around the hilt of something strapped at his side. I couldn't see what I was drawing out of its sheath, but it felt light enough to be a dagger. "I have a plan. It starts with killing you."

I thrust blindly, aiming for whatever flesh I could find, and hitting metal instead.

Kilian's hand clamped over mine and he twisted my wrist. It didn't hurt but the angle loosened my grip, and he easily yanked the blade from me.

"With my own weapon, no less?" He tutted. "How original."

"I'm making the most with what I have at my disposal. It's called being resourceful."

"Ah, I see. I imagine this resourcefulness will come in handy when you're out in Lortan, struggling to find shelter and food that won't poison you?"

"That's my problem. Not yours."

"I hate to break it to you, but once you accepted the oath, you became my problem."

"So unlink us then. Problem fucking solved."

"I can't. It's binding. You accepted it."

"That was before I knew how invasive it would be. I had no *choice*."

"Semantics. It's too late to back out now. Bad things happen to those who break oaths."

I gave one more shove at his arms.

He released me.

I stumbled forward, clutching at the nearest pillar to steady myself.

Kilian passed by casually, dagger in hand. A glint of red caught my eye and my jaw dropped. "That's *my* dagger."

"Is it?" he asked mildly.

"*Yes*." The fucking audacity. I was a hairsbreadth away from stomping my foot in rage. "Give it back!"

"I quite like it."

"It's *mine*!"

"How about we make a deal? You go back inside, like a good candidate, and I'll return the dagger?"

My eyes narrowed. "You can't make deals over things that don't belong to you."

He waved a haphazard hand. "My house, my rules."

Anger swelled like a rising tide, swift and brutal. "I'm not going anywhere."

He turned to look at me. He spread his arms wide. "Where else will you go?"

I stepped off the marble and granite. Cold air kissed my cheeks and my gaze flitted around the surroundings.

Snowy summits enclosed us, bleak, white and endless. Valhan House was nestled somewhere in between two slopes and was imposing in both size and structure. It was triple the size of the governor's house in Serila and striking in its architecture, grandiose like something reminiscent of another time.

I swallowed, turning back to find Kilian staring at me.

"I don't know. Maybe I'll be lucky and find someone who'll help me survive. The elven can't all be soulless monsters like you."

His ensuing huff could have been construed as laughter. "None of them will help you. They're all as invested in the outcome of the Trials as I am."

"Why?" I glared at him.

He gave me a bored look. "Because they care about saving the world."

My lip curled. Of course he was going to give me some sarcastic, illogical response.

"We're wasting time out here," he drawled. "Everyone else has already started on the training, so if you're done trying to escape, can we go back inside?"

I pressed my lips together, trying to figure out my next course of action. How I might wrest my dagger from him and drive it into his nearest artery. I was enraged at how absolutely powerless I was over the situation. I had zero control over what happened to me, or when it happened.

Even if I did somehow manage to get away, Kilian was right. Where would I sleep tonight? The air was so frigid I feared I might become hypothermic if I stayed out in the courtyard for another few minutes. What would I eat? Elven food was toxic to the mortal digestive system. I'd be dead in minutes. In fact, I was struggling to come up with a solution that did *not* result in me dying in minutes.

The glaringly obvious one was, of course, returning inside and continuing with the Trials.

"Your lips are turning blue," Kilian remarked.

My teeth clattered against each other, and I just barely resisted rubbing my hands over the thin fabric of my long sleeve.

"You're not going to make me haul you over my shoulder and carry you back inside, are you?"

The fight sizzled out of me. Icy cold seeped into my bones and lodged itself in my marrow. My survival instincts shuffled around, recognizing not freezing to death as an immediate priority.

I crossed to him and reached for my dagger. To my surprise, he didn't resist. I stared at him warily as I sheathed it into my belt loop.

"Come on, then," he said, like I was a sheep he was herding back into its pen.

I'd tried to escape, but I knew a lost cause when I saw one. The cards had never been stacked in my favor.

Sighing, I started back toward the house.

* * *

Kilian Valhan faced me across the rubber mat, his arms folded casually across his wide chest.

We were in the sparring room. The other candidates and their instructors were posed similarly. In the time that I had spent freezing out in the courtyard with Kilian, they had begun their training.

"How much fighting experience do you have?" Kilian asked, his question drawing me back to our mat, the pent-up tension bottled in my shoulders. My fingers flexed, aching to hit him now that I'd thawed out.

"Not much. I am pretty handy with a knife, though. Would you like me to demonstrate how well I can cut?" I said sweetly.

"As enticing as that sounds, I don't think we have time for knife play."

I flushed. That was *not* what I meant, and he knew it.

"You may be surprised to find that having less training might work to your advantage, though," Kilian continued. "It means you won't have to unlearn any bad habits. Start with your feet shoulder-width apart, your left foot slightly back. Further… Yes. And don't keep it so straight, you want to be standing at a nice thirty-degree angle."

Gods, he was bossy.

"Keep your hands near your face. Your fists and legs are your best weapons in close combat. You want to keep your face, ribs and torso protected at all times. And you want to aim for an opponent's face, ribs and torso, because that's where they'll be aiming on you. I'm going to show you a basic block and dodge before we get into attacking."

He stepped closer to me and large hands encircled my wrists. A tingle of warmth fizzled beneath his touch, zinging like the current from the oath. He maneuvered my fists in front of my face, fingers sliding down my arms to direct my elbows. He showed me several positions to block my ribs and sides, all complicated contortions my limbs were completely unused to.

"Stop looking at me like that and pay attention," he snapped.

"Like what?"

He leveled me with a cool stare. "Like you want to hit me."

"I do."

"You'll get a chance once you've proven you can block and dodge." He took a step back, taking up the same stance he had just shown me.

And then he lunged. Quick as a whip, he slammed out with his palm, and I was never going to be ready for it. My movements were clumsy and unpracticed, and he landed a solid jab to my ribs. Not enough to break them, but hard enough to send the message that he clearly could if he wanted to. The force sent me skidding along the rubber mat, and I stumbled backward, clutching at my bruised side.

"Again," he ordered.

I dragged my feet along the mat into position once more, shaping my arms so they blocked my ribs and face. He darted swiftly, muscled arm reaching out to swat the side of my head. My head swiveled from the impact, my ears ringing, and I fell to the ground, landing sprawled on the mat. My ribs ached at the collision. I glared up at him, anger quickly replacing the humiliation.

"You didn't block *or* dodge." He clicked his tongue impatiently.

"You've had years to gain experience. It's my first day."

"That won't matter when you're in the challenges. Blocking and dodging is basic survival."

"Please, tell me more about how I can't even master the basics." Sarcasm dripped from my voice.

He reached out a hand to help me up. "Again."

I tried and pitifully failed my next few attempts to block and dodge, receiving blows to the other side of my body – after which, Kilian smugly reminded me that an attacker would not repeat their moves. I heaved for air as I climbed back to my feet, ignoring the hand he offered.

I hadn't had a chance to catch my breath, let alone survey the others in the room, but I took a moment now to quickly assess them. I was relieved to find that they didn't seem to be much better off than I was. Anama's skin was a mottled red from where her instructor had just dealt her a blow to the face, and Rayna's cut above her brow was bleeding again as Echon prowled around her, like a jaguar hunting prey.

I allowed myself to be distracted by the others for five seconds. That was all it took for Kilian to sweep a leg beneath mine. I keeled forward, my hands slamming out just in time to prevent me from breaking my nose. The impact rocked my bones. I winced as I rolled onto my back, staring up at him.

"Don't ever lose focus during a fight," he intoned.

I huffed, shoved to my feet and stalked toward him. His brows rose as I made it all the way to his chest and jabbed a finger right in the center of his breastplate. "If you're so great at blocking and dodging, then why don't you take all this fancy armor off and show me how it's done? Unless you're afraid you'll get hurt?"

"Hurt?" He scoffed. "By you?"

I didn't know whether to be offended or angry. I settled for both. "I would have successfully stabbed you earlier if it weren't for this." I poked the armor again. "So, yeah. I'd say you have something to worry about."

His fingers reached for the sides of his breastplate, deftly working at the buckles. The metal fell to the ground with a clatter, revealing a plain white shirt, the material loose against him. I watched in horror as his fingers caught the hem of his shirt, pulling the thin fabric over his head to reveal...

I actually couldn't breathe.

I wasn't sure if it was from the impact my fall had on my lungs or just sheer stupidity, but *fuck*. His abdomen rippled as he moved, the muscles firm and taut beneath acres of tan, golden skin, marred only by thin silver flecks and jagged ridges of scar tissue where it looked like a blade had slashed him several times.

"No one asked you to take your shirt off." My tongue was dry. "The armor would have sufficed."

"You implied that I needed protection. I don't feel like leaving that up for debate. So, go on." He motioned for me to come closer.

I *really* didn't want to, but my traitorous, prideful body stepped forward. I braced my feet against the mat, one arm raised to my face, the other angling for his ribs. I channeled my fear of not passing the first challenge, the sizzling hatred I felt toward Echon, toward Kilian, and even Septimus for hauling me to this land to die. I channeled my worry for Umma, voiceless in Serila, and the new, tentative friendships I had made so far. The adoration I felt for Lana, which would cause nothing but misery and heartache if she didn't make it through the Trials.

And then I swung. With every bit of loathing and wrath my aching muscles could muster.

Bone crunched as it met a forearm that may as well have been made of granite. Sharp pain sluiced through my arm, and it took me a second to realize that it wasn't his bone that had fractured, but mine.

"*Motherfucker*," I groaned, cradling my hand to my chest.

His forearm hadn't even bruised. It was as if I hadn't touched him. Fury pulsed through my pain, and I jerked my leg forward, aiming for the one spot I *knew* would bring him to his knees.

But Kilian blocked with ease, one hand gripping under my knee and twisting so that I no longer faced him. The forearm I had uselessly attacked wrapped around my throat. He pressed hard enough to tell me I was well and truly trapped, but not enough to block my airflow. His body was warm stone behind me. His muscles tensed when I dropped my head against his chest, exhausted from the exertion of staying upright.

"Are you going to give up this easily?" he taunted. His breath skirted across my cheek, tickling the hair plastered there. I felt something dark and ravenous replace the wrath in my core. "Like you did the night we took you from your home?"

Cold fury leaked through my veins until my vision tinged red. If he was trying to goad me back into fighting, it was sure as hell working. I stomped down on his foot, *hard*, and it surprised him long enough for me to get out of his hold. Dropping to the mat, I swiveled, sweeping my ankle against his. But it was like trying to kick at stone. In one motion, he had me pinned on my stomach, face pressed into the rubber. His hand gripped my arms above my head and his knee dug into my lower back.

"If you ever have the element of surprise, you'll need to be stronger than that. That was a pitiful attempt. Do better, Golund."

That was it. The final straw. If he was going to pummel me to a crisp, he should at least have the decency to call me by my real name.

"My name isn't Golund," I ground out against the rubber mat. "It's Aldhur."

The pressure on my back disappeared, and I nearly moaned in relief. I didn't have time to relish the feeling, however. Kilian rapidly rolled me around to face him.

"What do you mean your name isn't Golund?" His voice rumbled as he towered above me, all gilded skin and storm cloud eyes. "You're the governor's daughter."

I was keenly aware of the scene he was making, his voice loud and harsh in the now silent sparring room, the others all turned to observe us.

"Am I?" I rose into a sitting position, too enthralled with the rage curling his lip to even feel the pain that engulfed my entire body.

His jaw clenched so hard I was surprised his teeth didn't break. "We searched the entire house. You are the same age. The governor confirmed it."

"Yet I am not her." I didn't know why he needed the governor's daughter, but it was clear she had been the intended candidate of choice. Not me. Satisfaction coursed through me as his eyes flashed thunderously. "Had your lackey not silenced my mother before she could tell you, you would have known that I am *not* the governor's daughter. I am Lirahna Aldhur, scullery cook, and now your prized candidate in the Mortal Trials."

His face contorted with pure rage. Lightning – brilliant, purple strands of pure energy – sizzled along his skin. The air crackled, and the walls of the large hall seemed to shrink. Thunderclouds boomed so loud they might have been inside, and with such a ferocity that my teeth chattered.

The room plunged into darkness as every single sconce of light shattered, shards of glass raining down on the floor. The only illumination in the room was the purple energy vibrating from Kilian, and the golden orbs of Septimus' eyes as he crossed the room.

He placed one hand tentatively on Kilian's shoulder, the lightning skittering along Kilian's skin not seeming to bother him. Septimus murmured something inaudible to the elven staring down at me with pure, undiluted wrath. Kilian ground his teeth together, nodding once in Septimus' general direction. He grabbed his shirt and armor from the ground and strode from the room without another look.

Septimus heaved an exasperated sigh as soon as Kilian left. The room cooled down with his exit, and my skin no longer felt like it was on fire. Septimus waved a hand and soft, golden light filled the space.

"You should have told him sooner," Septimus said, his voice tired and strained. He reached a hand to help me up, but I ignored it as I pushed off the ground. I flinched at the explosion of pain in my ribs, the side of my head, my wrist – yesterday's wound bleeding afresh – and pinky. In fact, there wasn't an inch of my body that *didn't* hurt.

"When was I supposed to do that?" I shot at him, trying to ignore the pounding of blood in my ears. "When your friend cursed my mother? When you drugged me and put me to sleep for a week? Or perhaps I should have said something while I was fighting for my life in the death trap I woke up in." The words clawed out of me, spiteful and bitter, as if they had a life of their own.

Septimus shook his head. "It is regrettably unfortunate how events have unfolded."

"Unfortunate? I have lost *everything*. We all have." I gestured to the others around me. "It is not *unfortunate*. It's a godsdamned tragedy."

Tears prickled at the corners of my eyes, and I turned quickly so the elven wouldn't have the pleasure of witnessing my heart break, just as my fragile bones had. Without waiting for a dismissal, I marched for the door, my steps so hurried I was nearly running.

I exited the sparring room, turning right at the stairwell, unsure where I was even going. We were surrounded by nothing but icy mountains.

"Hey. Wait up!" The voice was female, but not one I was familiar with. It sounded both old and young. Harmonic, like several chords had struck together to create it.

I paused on the steps and turned to see Anama's instructor a few feet behind me. The female elven was staggeringly beautiful. Her copper hair, tucked behind her pointed ears, shone even in the dim lighting of the stairwell.

"You're in a hurry. Going somewhere?" she asked, falling into step beside me.

"It's not like I could go anywhere without one of you finding me and dragging me back here." The words had more bite to them than she was owed, but it was true. I had barely made it fifteen steps without an elven on my tail.

"I understand how awful this situation must be for you. For all of you. It has never been fair for us to take you from your homes and sentence you to death." Her voice was gentle. So at odds with Kilian's harsh disposition.

"Why do it, then? None of us have asked to be elven. Release us and be done with it."

The female gave me a sad smile. "I never introduced myself. My name is Syrina. I've been paired with your friend Anama for the Trials. I see a lot of myself in her. It's why I don't instruct very often. You may think the Trials are hard on you, but each decade we form bonds and attachments to our candidates. And each time, we watch them die. No one hates the Mortal Trials as much as I do. I do not relish a single drop of blood spilt – mortal or otherwise."

"Watching someone die is not the same as dying."

"No. It is far more painful. Take a left here." Syrina gestured to a doorway on the lower landing of the stairwell. "We should get you to the med hall to fix that hand of yours. I don't know what you were thinking, riling Kilian up like that. You might as well have signed your death certificate."

I shouldered the door to find a long stone passage, exposed to the elements on the left side. Aside from the chill, the view was breathtaking – different higher up than on the ground floor. The jagged mountain range on either side was clearer, the frosted peaks rising and falling around us. It reminded me of the tiny snow globes which had decorated one of the governor's living rooms.

A railing coated in a fine dust of snow trailed the length of the passage. To the right stood rooms, their doors labeled with things like *Supply Hall, Staff Dinner Hall,* and right at the end of the passage, *Med Hall.*

"I feel so much anger every time I'm near him," I said as Syrina held the door open for me.

The med hall was a cluster of white beds. All were empty save for one, atop which an elven male was sprawled, fast asleep, his torso wrapped in bandages. Syrina led me to a bed away from him and ordered me to sit.

"Kilian has that effect on people," she responded. "Try not to let him get under your skin. I don't."

I gave her a skeptical look. "He riles you up too?"

"All the time. You think I want to be here, training another candidate to go through the worst experience a mortal should ever have to endure? I'd much rather be in my studio with my paints and pottery, creating things that will actually survive."

"So why are you here, then?" There was no hostility in my question, only curiosity.

"He asked me to be," she said simply. "And you'll soon learn just how difficult it is to say no to him."

"Are you two…?" My question hung in the air. The way she spoke about him, with a casual indifference that only came from knowing someone a very long time, made me wonder whether they were together.

"No. Definitely not." Syrina laughed. It was a tinkling sound that reminded me of windchimes. "He's like my brother. And besides, he's not my type."

I blinked. It was hard to imagine Kilian not being anyone's type.

"Sure," Syrina continued, her eyes light with amusement. "I can admit he's attractive, if you're into the whole tall, brooding, capable of slaying his enemies with half a thought kind of thing, but it's not for me. I prefer my partners to be softer, feminine, but who can still kick some ass, you know?"

Despite wanting to hate her, I couldn't. A smile broke across my face. "An excellent combination."

A door flapped open to the side and a male elven entered. He wore a white coat and sported a tired expression as he crossed over to us. "Syrina," he said by way of greeting. "Are you well?"

"Perfectly so, Midius," Syrina replied. "I've brought my mortal friend, Lirah, for some healing. She fractured her wrist punching Kilian."

Midius gawked at me in disbelief. "Are you able to rotate the joint?"

"No." I didn't even try. My wrist throbbed even when I didn't move it, the skin hot, blood-slicked and swollen.

"May I?" The elven's fingers hovered above my wrist but did not touch me.

I nodded.

Cool fingers pressed gently to my wrist, then to my temple. "You've had a minor dislocation to your fifth metacarpal and a superficial laceration," he murmured. "There's some fracturing to your vertebrosternal ribs and a few muscular contusions. Nothing serious."

Nothing serious? It hurt when I fucking *breathed*.

"I'll leave you in the capable hands of Midius," Syrina said, backing away. "If you ever need to chat or things become too much – more than it already is, I mean – I'm here."

"Thank you," I said, and genuinely meant it.

Midius' fingers softly scraped along my wrist and an icy menthol sensation licked at my bones. It was a foreign feeling but not an uncomfortable one.

"Is this upper magic?" I asked the healer, curious.

"Of course," Midius answered. "Upper magic and a lot of experience. It takes a certain skill to reset bones and repair muscles."

"How long have you been practicing for? I would have thought the magic would make it easier."

"Oh, decades, my dear. Decades. The magic only gives you the ability. It's how you hone it that distinguishes you."

When he was done, I rotated the joint carefully, marveling at the instant relief. If I had dislocated a bone in Serila, it would have taken months to heal.

The icy sensation slowly leeched out of my body, leaving me with no physical pain. Only the blistering ire in my heart that seemed to never wane.

I doubted even Midius would be able to fix that.

CHAPTER 6

Calendula did not reappear that night, nor was she there the next morning when I woke. I made it my mission at breakfast to pocket as many of the fat, red strawberries that appeared on my plate as I could, unsure how many it would take to curry her favor.

Lana, Moric and Anama came to the table just as I was stuffing the last fruit into my already bulging pocket.

"You're up early this morning." Lana's cornsilk hair was tied up today, only the front strands of lilac curling gently against her cheeks. She looked better rested, the dark circles beneath her eyes fading to be near imperceptible. Her skin was less pale too, her cheeks tinted a rosy pink.

"What?" she asked, catching my stare. "Do I have something on my face?"

I shook my head. "No. You look nice this morning."

"Have I looked like shit the other days?"

Moric hid a grin behind a piece of buttered toast and Lana chucked a grape at his head.

"You'd be amazed at what a good night's sleep and solid meals can do for my well-being," she grumbled.

"I didn't think you were getting much sleep with all the fantasizing you've been doing about a certain golden-eyed–"

"Oh, for fuck's sake." Lana shot him a glare that could have cracked ice. "Don't start with me."

Moric swatted a hand at the invisible threat like it was an annoying gnat. "Relax, he's not here."

Anama gave a rare chuckle as Lana upped the stakes of her next threat.

"What are they on about?" I whispered to her as Moric lobbied another retort at Lana that made her cheeks turn beet red.

"He's teasing her about Septimus," Anama whispered back. "He thinks she's got a crush on him."

"I do *not*." Lana scowled at us. "Anyway, enough about me. Let's talk about Lirah and the fiasco that was yesterday's sparring session."

Lana was clearly trying to take the heat off herself, but it worked. Moric took the bait. "What *was* that about, Lirah? We came to get you before dinner last night, but you didn't answer."

"After Midius healed me, I was so exhausted I slept straight through dinner. I didn't even hear you knock."

"That's not what I'm asking about," he pressed.

"I know." I explained the events that had transpired the night I was taken.

When I was done, Lana let out a low whistle. "That explains why Kilian was so pissed. What's so special about this governor's daughter, anyway?"

"I have no idea. Rumor is she's so ill she can barely stand. The governor probably had her moved somewhere safer for Augustine. Anyway, it doesn't even matter. I'm here now. And we won't stand a chance of making it through the survival challenge unless we start figuring out Lomask and its citizens."

"I agree," Anama said. "To survive on an isle, you need to know as much about it as possible. I'd say a trip to the library is needed."

We hurriedly finished our breakfast and agreed to meet outside the stairwell ten minutes later. I had something I needed to do before we left.

I slipped inside my room and rifled in my pocket for the strawberries. Setting all five of them on the table, I stepped back. "I know you're there, Calendula. I'm sorry for offending you the other night. I could really use your knowledge for the rest of the Trials."

A few seconds transpired into minutes, and I was aware that the others would be waiting for me. My shoulders slumped in disappointment, and I turned to leave. At the rustling behind me, I paused. When I looked back, three of the strawberries had disappeared and the shadow sprite sat perched on the edge of the table.

"I see Kilian's taught you how to bribe," Calendula said tartly.

"I wouldn't call it bribing… I'm just trying to make amends," I said. "I know we started off on the wrong foot. I really didn't mean to snap at you. I know it's not an excuse, but these past few days have been very overwhelming."

Her eyes softened, and she rose to the balls of her feet, rolling another strawberry toward her. The fruit was half her size, but she crouched down to take a dainty nibble from its side. After she swallowed, she said, "It was difficult for me… after my last mortal died. It's been ten years, but I still think of her sometimes."

After speaking to Syrina yesterday and now hearing the raw pain in Calendula's voice, I understood. "I guess I'll just have to try my godsdamned best not to die, then."

The joke was halfhearted but there was truth to it. I did not want to die. I wanted to fight. Through each challenge thrown my way, I wanted to claw my way out, tooth and nail. I wanted to see Umma again. I wanted to live.

Calendula gave me a doubtful look but launched into the air, a blur of darkness. She flew straight toward me, landing gracefully on my hand. Her tiny wings stirred the air around my fingers, tickling me as they settled on my palm. She yawned softly. "Where are we going?"

We exited through the stairwell and into a sun-drenched courtyard. Despite the warm rays on my face, the air was still freezing. The snow from the mountains drifted like dandelions through the air, sticking to Moric's hair. He shook his head, dispelling the flakes, and puffed a breath of hot air into his cupped hands.

"It's cold as all fuck," Lana muttered, stepping into the courtyard proper. "Where is this library, again?"

Calendula snored softly from where she had tucked herself into the large pockets of my cloak, no help at all.

Lana's golden-eyed sprite Osmanthius flew a few feet ahead of us, wings flapping erratically to keep him suspended at eye level. "It's not too far. Follow me," he said.

We scurried along the courtyard, dodging elven carting baskets laden with unusual fruit and sweet-scented loaves – all elven food by the look and smell – until we reached a big archway. I looked over my shoulder to find Valhan House stretched out like a magnificent beast against the backdrop of the icy summits. The house was impossibly tall, some turrets even towering over smaller peaks. I could not see the med hall from my position near the archway and knew it would be on the opposite side, facing the summits.

It was too cold to even speak as we followed Osmanthius down the cobblestones leading away from Valhan House. The path followed a winding road, marked with strange signs in what I assumed was the elven alphabet. I could not read it, but Osmanthius seemed to know exactly where he was taking us as he flitted across the road, cutting right along a narrow passage. The alleyway opened onto a large area that reminded me of the courtyard at Valhan House. Towering buildings lined the sides of the space. Most of them looked like residential homes, flattened one on top of the other, but the ground units were almost entirely storefronts.

There was everything from clothing shops boasting the latest designs in cloaks and gloves, spun from premier elven silk, to patisseries, with roasted coffee and delicate, sugar-dusted confections nestled against the windowsill. Elven passed from store to store, clutching mugs of hot cocoa and large shopping bags. The colors were so vibrant, unlike the dull browns and drudgery of Serila. And the scents were so overwhelming, I could not identify where one ended and the other began. I couldn't help but feel this place was not meant for mortal eyes. We did not belong here.

Though they noticed us, the elven did not pause their shopping or give us so much as a cursory glance. There was no hostility in the space they gave us either. It was simply as Kilian had said: we had been bestowed the protection of the Mortal Trials. We passed the front of a boutique which sold small trinkets and tokens, and I stopped when a sparkling silver piece caught my eye.

"See anything you like, dearie?" An elven female was stooped so low arranging the stock beneath the table that I hadn't noticed her at first. As she straightened, I saw she wore long, pastel blue robes with intricate designs that I could spend all day studying and still not have time to appreciate every detail. Silver dripped from her neck, an abundance of pendants littering her chest.

"Your pieces are stunning." I eyed the rack.

Lana and the others had paused a few feet away, eyes wide as the elven female reached over to grab the token I had initially admired. It was solid silver and flecked with onyx dust, the pendant shaped like a diamond. In the center of the diamond, an open eye stared back at me. A delicate, short chain was affixed to its outermost points.

The elven stretched her arm toward me and pressed the bracelet into my hand. Stunned, I looked down at it, a feeling of warmth settling in my bones at the contact.

"Take it," the female said.

I shook my head, even though I desperately wanted it. "I can't. I don't have any coins to pay for it, and it's far too lovely to just give away."

"It was never mine to begin with." The elven returned to stocking her shelves, no longer paying me any attention.

Lana clutched at my hand, pulling me away from the stall before I could protest further.

"When an elven grants you a trinket, you take it," Osmanthius huffed from Lana's shoulder. "It is considered gravely rude to refuse any offering."

"I didn't know," I murmured, turning the piece over to inspect the back. A thin sentence was engraved along the diamond, barely legible, and written in the elven alphabet. Perhaps Calendula would be able to translate it for me when she woke.

I wrapped the bracelet around my wrist, securing the metal clasp as we came to a stop before a tall, face-brick building. I peered up at the elven signage, which was written in gold and then, in smaller print beneath, in Grilish, the mortal tongue –

Pyxis.

"What does it mean?" I whispered to Anama, as if the library could hear me.

"Pyxis? It's the name of the library," she said. "The Great Library of Lortan is further north, in Dalhur. This one is smaller and belongs to the elven of Lomask. Its name is derived from the box once used by the gods as a storage vessel and is meant to represent the information stored within."

Anama really was a walking encyclopedia.

We followed Osmanthius inside, where it was infinitely warmer. The reception was small and cozy. Flyers and leaflets were tacked onto a bulletin board on the wall closest to the front desk.

A petite elven dressed in beige robes sat behind the bureau. She looked young, even by elven standards, barely older than Rayna. She stared at us, noting the flush in our cheeks from the cold, Osmanthius – who looked exhausted from the flight, blinking sleepily – perched on Lana's shoulder, and the fragile mortality coursing beneath our skin. "How can I help you?" she asked.

"Good morning." Anama took the lead. Her entire demeanor had shifted as soon as we had entered Pyxis. She seemed… calmer, more confident and at ease inside the walls of the library. I realized as she spoke to the elven, scholar to scholar, that this place must remind her of home. "We're looking for information on the birthing of Lortan, the history of Lomask and the Mortal Trials. And anything on the topography, wildlife, plants and herbs native to Lomask."

The scholar nodded, sliding out from behind her desk to escort us around the corner into the library proper, and I gasped at the sight. Being sequestered in the governor's kitchen had hardly left time for me to explore Serila and its own library. This was my first time being somewhere filled with so many books. And there were troves and troves of them. Texts lined shelves for miles, stretching and curling along a wide staircase that spanned multiple floors, all the way to the ceiling. The scholar led us along the winding staircase, the musty scent of old books and parchment intoxicating. I struggled to keep my fingers at my side – they itched to run along the spines of shelved hardcover tomes.

I spotted several other scholars in the same beige robes, sorting books, as we passed the first floor.

"You'll find what you're looking for here," the scholar said, leading us to a wall of books on the second level. Several desks sat nestled between the shelves, and a few cozy armchairs were pushed near the window, through which the courtyard below was visible. "No eating or drinking amongst the books is permitted and, unfortunately, mortals are not allowed to check out any of the books. You're free to visit whenever you want, though. If you need help, any of our scholars will be able to assist."

With that, she turned and left, leaving us to examine the rows upon rows of books.

"Where do we start?" Lana asked, a defeated expression already on her face.

Anama rubbed her hands together, a glint in her eyes I had never seen before. She was *excited*. Moric chuckled but didn't say anything as Anama went to work, examining the books on the shelf closest to us. She pulled one out from the third level and handed it to Moric. "Let's start by categorizing the ones we're going to study. Four piles: one for the history of Lortan, one for the Mortal Trials, another for the structure of Lomask and the last for nature indigenous to Lomask. We'll split the work between us and then share our knowledge when we're done."

"Sounds like you do this for a living," Lana teased. "I'm happy to take the section on the history of the Trials."

"I'll do the structure of Lomask," Moric said.

"Lirah?" Anama asked, giving me the choice between the history of Lortan or its nature.

"History," I said, more drawn to events and timelines than herbs and plants.

Anama nodded and shifted her attention to the shelves. We spent the next hour playing pass the book, sorting each one Anama handed to us into makeshift piles. Once she had covered the entire length of the wall, we collapsed into chairs beside a desk, exhausted.

I stared at the books before me. I knew the history of Lortan would not be a quick read, but I did not anticipate there to be twenty-eight books to sift through. Frustration gnawed at me.

Pale early morning light had given way to bright midday. Only a few days remained before the first challenge. Before I had to fight for my life.

Huffing a breath, I pulled the first book forward and began reading.

* * *

I knew the evening had arrived when the light slanting through the window and onto the desk shifted to hit me directly in the face, golden rays arching brilliantly across parchment and the hastily scribbled notes I had made. Moric had sourced a notepad and a few quills from one of the scholars so that we could document our findings. I now had nearly five pages of barely legible script on the pad before me.

Lana shifted in the armchair she was occupying. The piles of books she had been studying stretched the length of her calf at the foot of the chair. Her head rested against the back of the armchair and her eyes were closed.

I rubbed my eyes violently against the glare of the dying sunlight, stifling a yawn with the back of my hand. My brain felt like a soggy towel that had been wrung dry too many times.

"Shall we call it an afternoon, team?" Moric glanced at the rest of us.

Anama closed the cover of a thick tome she had been poring over. "I think so. I doubt any more information is going to stick if we keep going at this rate. Should we compare notes before we leave?"

Lana cracked one eye open. "Can someone else please go first? I need a minute to wake up."

"I'll go." Moric reached for the notepad on his lap. He rifled back to the first page, sticking his tongue out as his eyes scanned its length. "Okay, so as you may know, Lomask is one of Lortan's three cities. Lomask is structured like a bowl, surrounded on one side by the summits and the other by the Forests of Dalhur. The buildings are either made of iron, ore or brick and you'll hardly ever find amber anywhere."

"That's a huge 'fuck you' to the gods," Lana mumbled. And she was right.

Amber was the material gifted to the mortals by the gods centuries ago. It was the material used to construct the Amber Temple in Dorisport and usually adorned each household as a sign of fealty and respect. The lack of the precious gem in Lomask announced clearly how the elven felt toward the gods.

Moric flipped to the next page on his notepad. "The Forests of Dalhur are not a great place to be stranded overnight."

"Then that's most likely where they'll put us for the survival challenge," I said. "Why? What lives in the forest?"

"All manner of creatures, ranging from woodland sprites to a species of gargantuan lacertilia, flesh-eating plants and panthera."

"Wonderful," I muttered.

"On the bright side, there are a bunch of caverns and tunnel systems along the borders of the forest. So, if we *are* dropped in the middle of it, our safest bet is to make it to one of the caves. That's all I've got for you guys today. Tomorrow, I'll start researching the summits." Moric shut his notepad and stretched his long legs out in front of him.

Anama grabbed her notes next. "Notable plants indigenous to Lomask include sloughberry, impid root, willowbark trees, frostlis leaf, and several species of flowers." She pointed out an image of each item in a textbook. "Impid root is fantastic in the treatment of open wounds and encephalitis, a condition affecting the tissues of the brain. And sloughberry, most interestingly, is not poisonous to mortals. We shouldn't eat it in large quantities as it might cause some... distressing bowel movements, but small quantities should be fine."

"Bowel movements?" Lana raised a brow. "What, like diarrhea?"

Anama cringed. "Precisely."

"Gods above. Please continue."

"Willowbark trees are only found on the summits of Lomask. The bark is useful for its antibiotic properties when properly combined with a mixture of fennel and hot water. A species of wild nanuuq is native to Lomask and reside near the snow caves, which should be avoided at all costs."

"I was going to talk about that tomorrow..." Moric muttered, his eyes closed.

Anama placed her notepad and textbook onto the table.

"Thanks. Is it my turn now?" I asked her.

She nodded, and I reached for my own stack of notes. "You can't really speak about the history of Lortan without the history of Tarlor – the two are interwoven so closely."

Anama nodded again, urging me to continue.

I scanned my notes and the open book on my lap, eventually settling on a passage that summarized everything quite nicely. I read from the page, "'Tarlor was once the land of the gods, and they roamed free upon its soil until they grew tired of only each other's company. In a blaze of power, the gods joined to cleave Tarlor into the islands we have today. They set their home beyond Dorisport, in Tuscan. It is said that the only way to enter Tuscan is through the Amber Temple.' But, of course, no one knows exactly how that's done," I added as an aside.

I scanned the next paragraph. "'The fae – distant ancestors of the sprites – were created first, by the goddess of life, Winipyr. But they were wicked and vain, and sought to challenge the gods. This resulted in their extermination by Azrael. Winipyr breathed life into the elven next, carving them in the image of the gods, with beauty, grace and power, hoping they would prove better than her first attempt. But the elven, with their power and magic, were irrepressible. Even though they did not seek to challenge the gods, they could not be controlled. So, the gods sent the upper elven to Lortan and the lower elven, those with less magic, to Greyhaven, thereby creating a class system and a natural hierarchy.'"

"Do you think they have a good relationship, the upper and lower elven?" Moric asked, curiosity in his voice.

"The lower elven are at an obvious power disadvantage, but I understand there are regular meetings held between Kilian and the lower elven representative to address any concerns," Anama volunteered.

"Right. Sorry, Lirah," Moric said. "Continue."

I consulted the passage again. "'Lastly, Winipyr created the mortals in the image of the elven, but with no power or magic. Mortals were designed to be a duller, less potent version that would be more malleable to the wishes of the gods. And to avoid the stain of elven influence on her perfect creation, Winipyr forbade mortals to ever set foot on elven land, or they would remain there forever.'"

"So that's why we can't leave," Lana breathed. "It's not an elven command. It's the gods' will."

I nodded. "'Each of the thirteen gods bestowed their power upon Tarlor, to ensure mortals and elven alike never rose beyond their station.'" I skimmed my notes. "'Pain from

Osiren, deceit from Eros, storms and downpour from Fury, cruelty from Kadax, war from Aerie, and death from Azrael.' We were also granted gifts from the gods, to placate us and keep us praying to them. 'Luck and fortune from Adonitis, art from Solinia, pleasure from Mahleia, the hunt from Roriola and bonds from Toriosys. Only Primus reserved his power, since Winipyr believed that if the God of Curses bestowed his gift upon Tarlor, we would destroy each other wholly.'"

I slid my notepad onto the desk, exhausted and parched.

Lana sat up straighter in her seat, and I thought she was getting ready to regurgitate her own information about the Mortal Trials, but her gaze was fixed on something over my shoulder. I turned, just as a cloyingly sweet smell filled my nostrils. A scent I'd last smelled on the ship that had brought me here.

My vision went hazy, my limbs slackening as the book propped on my lap tumbled to the ground. All I saw before darkness swallowed me was a pair of gleaming silver eyes.

CHAPTER 7

Through half-lidded eyes, I could vaguely make out a metal rack. I blinked, my vision clearing.

Moric lay slumped on the ground. His eyes were shut but his breathing was even and regular; he was fast asleep.

Lana leaned against the wall of the sparring room, her eyes fixed threateningly on the male pacing before her.

"Drugging us was not necessary," she hissed. "We would have come willingly."

"Wrath really brings out the blue in your eyes, sunshine," Septimus cooed.

I propped myself up on one elbow and Lana immediately dropped to a crouch before me, her hand outstretched. I took it, allowing her to help me up. I felt groggy and irritable. I brushed the dust from the floor off my back and scrubbed my face. Pieces of hair had come loose from the braid I had so carefully entwined this morning. I shoved the strands away from my cheeks, annoyance bleeding into anger as I surveyed Moric and Anama still sleeping on the ground. A few feet away, the other survival squads also slept.

"What the actual fuck just happened?" I asked.

Lana ground her teeth, looking just as upset as I was. "Septimus and his cronies thought it would be entertaining to drug and haul us back to Valhan House for another one of their unofficial challenges."

"They're designed to help you face the real challenges. You can thank me later, sunshine," Septimus said. He was the only elven in the room, and looked exceptionally impatient. He strode back and forth while the others began to rise.

"Stop fucking calling me that," Lana seethed.

"What vicious words for such a pretty mouth." Septimus stared at her dead on, unfazed. "I wonder what else it can do."

The blush that tinged Lana's cheeks had nothing to do with the rouge staining her skin. I noted it with curiosity, wondering if there had been some truth to Moric's teasing earlier.

The raised voices, it seemed, had woken Anama and Moric. They both stirred, blinking blearily as they looked up at us.

"What's going on?" Anama asked as I helped her to her feet.

There was no need to explain though; everyone was now awake. Septimus crossed to the center of the room, eyes alight with amusement. "I hope you all had a good rest. The second unofficial challenge begins now. The good news is that it's highly unlikely one of you will die during this challenge. Unless you manage to royally piss off your instructor." He flashed a set of even, white teeth at us. "Your task this challenge is to steal something – anything, really – from your instructor. The bad news is that each of your instructors has been made aware of this challenge, and they'll be on the guard. You have one hour."

Septimus sauntered toward our group, his golden eyes fixed on Lana. "I'm afraid you won't manage to steal anything from me, sunshine, but I'd love to see you try."

The look Lana gave him was positively murderous, but Septimus had already walked off, exiting the sparring room without a backward glance.

"Fucking elven." She scowled.

I vehemently agreed. How was I supposed to steal something from my instructor when I didn't even know where he was? The last time I had seen him, he had nearly hurled a bolt of lightning at me. Frustration sizzled in me. I didn't realize my hands were clenched at my sides, nails biting into my palms, until Anama gently touched my shoulder.

"Are you okay, Lirah?" she asked.

I exhaled a calming breath through my nose, though it did little to soothe my frazzled nerves. "Yeah. No. I don't know. I just feel so… angry. At everything. And all the time."

"Hmm. Have you ever felt like this before?"

"I've been angry, sure. But–" I shook my head, "– never this kind of… fury. It's like a constant ache in my chest that never fully goes away. It feels like I'm a hairsbreadth from snapping all the time." I rolled my shoulders, but they were still tense springs.

"You know," Anama hedged. "When you take the sacred oath, it's not only *your* feelings that are shared. The link is… reciprocal."

I froze.

Was she saying what I thought she was saying? Fuck, *no*.

"Anama, I need you to be perfectly clear with me. Are you telling me that this *rage*, this eternal battle not to scream every single second of every single day, is not even *mine*?"

She winced. "If it's a new feeling, it's most likely stemming from the link."

From Kilian.

I was going to fucking kill him.

"How do I find him?" I asked her, my gaze skipping across the other survival squads who were in conversation, most likely trying to figure out the best plan to win. I didn't care about the challenge. I wanted to make him *bleed*.

"I suppose you could use the link. As if you were tugging on it," Anama said. "Follow the feeling. The angrier you get, the closer you are."

Excellent.

I wasn't just going to make him bleed. I wanted to make him suffer first.

I muttered a thanks and, ignoring Lana and Moric's protests that it was a really bad idea, charged for the stairwell. They couldn't possibly understand how agonizing it had been, going to sleep each night absolutely livid and waking with a desire to incinerate the entire world.

"What's happening?" Calendula, who it seemed had slept her fill and had chosen that ripe moment to wake up, fluttered out from my pocket, easily keeping pace with me as I stalked upstairs.

"I am going to find Kilian," I ground out, passing the mess hall floor and continuing upstairs to a part of the house I had never explored.

"You look mad."

"Do I?"

A look of pure glee crossed the shadow sprite's face and dark embers sparked along her wings. "You found out about the link."

I paused my death march to glare at her. "Thanks for the heads up."

"Oh, it's so much more fun with you finding out this way."

I didn't respond, the anger a palpable storm creeping closer with every step I took toward Kilian. Fury swelled in my chest, and I barely felt the burn in my calves from the flights of stairs. I stomped along the landing of the fifth floor, hurtling past several doors until I stood before the one that made my vision darken with splotches of red.

A keypad was fixed to the side of the door, labeled once more in the elven alphabet.

I looked at Calendula expectantly.

She sighed. "He'll exile me to the other side of the Shadow Soil if he finds out I helped you sneak into his bedroom."

His bedroom.

"Then I won't tell him it was you. Give me the code and disappear. He thinks you're still mad at me."

"I *am* still mad at you." Calendula rolled her silver eyes but floated daintily to the keypad. I watched as she palmed each symbol: seven in total. Darkness enveloped the sprite and she whispered, "I hope he doesn't kill you," before slipping away, leaving me with just my rage for company.

I toed open the door, grateful that the hinges did not squeak, and crossed the threshold. The first thing I noticed was the sheer size of the room. High ceilings met dark gray walls, accented by mahogany furniture, with panels of glass windows stretching from floor to ceiling across the length of an entire wall. A bookshelf lined another, filled with tomes haphazardly stacked and strewn across its shelves. The opposite wall housed a rack with an assortment of weapons, from swords to bows to onyx-hilted daggers. A large bed bedecked in black sheets claimed the right half of the room, close to the windows that overlooked the jagged peaks and icy summits. Snow drifted outside and a chill skittered across my spine.

A desk stood beside the door. Papers littered its surface, held down with metal paperweights that were tiny replicas of the daggers on the wall. I picked one up, gingerly examining it, and weighed it in my hand. I quickly pocketed it for the unofficial challenge and turned to survey the rest of the room. If Kilian wasn't here, why did the anger seem to be reaching its crescendo?

There was nowhere else to go. No one else to expend this energy on. And so I did the only thing I could think of. I placed my palms on the desk, on top of the pages, and in one sweeping motion, shoved. Papers flew into the air, drifting for a millisecond before floating and skidding along the hardwood floor. The paperweights scattered across the ground. I hoped he stepped barefoot on one of them.

Hands on my hips, I viewed the wreckage. It was a cute attempt at destruction, but not my best work.

For all the irreparable damage he had caused to my life, I could do better than that.

Rolling the sleeves of my tunic, I stomped to the bookshelf. I placed both hands against the side of the shelf, bracing my feet against the floor. Tensing my shoulder muscles for strength, I heaved. The godsdamned thing didn't so much as budge. I tried again. I managed to move it an inch forward, but it wasn't enough to tip it over, and the case simply rocked back against the wall.

Frustrated, I let loose a breath as I wedged one boot against the corner of the bookshelf and used my knee as leverage. I grunted at the effort, but with the added purchase of my knee pushing from the back, the bookshelf wobbled. Once. Twice. And then it was falling, tipping to the ground. Books scattered in every direction. But the most pleasing sound was that of the heavy mahogany case clattering with resounding finality.

I did that, I noted proudly.

I moved on to the bed next. I yanked the duvet and sheet off, tossing them toward the window in a plume of black. With every piece of destruction wrought, I felt that anger in my chest ease. This was the happiest I had been in days, trashing the room – the personal belongings – of the elven who had uprooted my life as easily as it was to breathe.

"Fuck. You!" I said to no one as I shoved his mattress to land on the floor. I was crossing over to the weapons rack when the sound of the door snicking open stopped me in my tracks.

"What the *fuck* are you doing?"

The anger was back, blooming in my chest as a bubble of viscous acid.

Kilian stood at the doorway, a towel slung low around his abdomen. A very naked abdomen.

Water slicked the curls in his hair, dripping onto his chest.

And my mouth. Went. Dry.

He crossed the threshold, eyes scanning the disaster that was his room. The scattered pages, upturned bookshelf, and chaotic mess of sheets on the floor. And then they narrowed at me. "What are you doing in my bedroom? What have you done to my bookshelf? Those are fucking *battle briefs* you're standing on!"

His mouth twisted into a thin line of pure wrath as I took my boot and scrunched the page beneath my feet. He moved so fast my mortal eyes barely tracked the movement; he was standing at the door and then right before me, his face mere inches from mine.

"Leave."

"No." I leaned into the anger, letting it wash over me, relishing the blistering heat it left in its wake. "Do you realize what you've done by swearing me to this oath? I have been living with your rage for the past two days. It's been fucking *miserable*! Why are you this angry? Surely you can't get any work done when you feel like snapping people's necks in half all the godsdamned time!"

I mustered enough courage to poke him in the chest, but realized immediately that might have been an even worse idea than trashing his room. Firstly, I really had no business knowing how hard and warm his muscles were beneath his chest. Secondly, the menacing glint in his eyes turned to granite-flecked steel.

He caught at my wrist before I could whip it away.

"If you wanted to touch me, you could have just asked."

I tried to tug my arm away, but he had found the thin bracelet gifted to me that morning and I feared the chain would snap. His fingers curled around the pendant now. Something akin to recognition flickered in his eyes. "Where did you get this?"

"It was a gift, from an elven near Pyxis." I paused. "Why? What is it?"

His brow rose at my question. "You don't know what it symbolizes, yet you wear it?"

Asshole.

"Are you going to tell me what it means, or not?"

"It's a charm. The outer layer signifies continuity. The inner eye means caution. It's upper magic, a protection spell of sorts, to watch over you as you continue your journey. The elven have hope that a new mortal will pass the Rite."

"Why do they want that?" I asked my question again, knowing it would be a waste of time. "Why are the Trials so important?"

"I told you before." Ice coated his words afresh. "Pass the Rite and you'll find out."

I wrenched my grip from his, unsatisfied once again. It served no use hitting him when all he would do was block my blows. I would be the one sent back to Midius, likely in a matchbox. But destroying his possessions... Now, that I could do.

I whipped back to the weapons rack, striding forward. But before I could lay one finger on the rack, he had me pinned against its side.

His forearm pressed into the delicate skin of my throat, his body taut and tense against mine. He ran one finger idly down the hooks of my protective gear and my breath hitched. "Do you know how easy it would be for me to end your life, Lirahna Aldhur, scullery cook in the house of Golund?"

"Don't make idle threats, Kilian Valhan. Either you're going to kill me, or you're not." The words came out more confident than I felt. "And I don't think you are."

He huffed and rolled his eyes, but his grip loosened slightly.

"You were upset I wasn't the governor's daughter," I said, switching focus. "What is so special about that girl? Why did you want her instead of me?"

"I don't want her. Not anymore," he said. "But I wondered... No one had ever seen the girl. The governor kept her protected at all times. I thought there might be something he was trying to hide from the elven."

Ah. He thought the governor's daughter might have possessed the ability to pass the Rite. To turn elven.

"And you don't think that anymore?"

"I'm starting to think there was a reason we found you instead. Septimus was drawn to the governor's house on Augustine. I had assumed it was for his daughter. But now, I'm not so sure."

I shifted slightly, the movement causing his hips to press closer against mine, and I felt it again. The anger, yes, but lurking deep beneath, a starving beast. His soft breath skated across my skin like a cool summit breeze, peppermint and ice. And I wanted… Gods, I could not allow myself to think about what I wanted. Not from the elven standing before me.

But it was there in the cold fury of his eyes, the soft parting of his lips, the lines of his body against mine, his forearm at my throat. My core clenched, my thighs shifting imperceptibly to quell the ache. His eyes snapped to meet mine and I froze. He had felt it, subtle as I was trying to be. He was a fucking elven; all his senses were heightened. Embarrassment tinged my cheeks and I tried to hide it, but that beast was back, prowling and hungry.

And gods be damned, I *wanted*.

I could not sense where his anger ended and mine began. It was one and the same. Combined so completely that to remove one from the other would be impossible.

"What are you doing here, Lirah?" His words were soft. The softest I had ever heard from him.

He had never called me that before. Only addressed me in full. Though I had been called the nickname many times by others, I had never noticed how intimate and vulnerable it felt.

His fingers stilled along the seam of my gear, mere inches from my midriff. Surely, he could hear my heart galloping wildly.

"I'm here to make you bleed. To make you suffer," I managed to get out, my voice hoarse, my tongue parched.

He pressed his hips against mine. My core *throbbed*. Fuck me. I had been worried about the challenges when I should have been worried about Kilian Fucking Valhan. I was not going to make it out of this room alive. When Lana eventually came looking for me, she'd find me melted in a puddle of desire on Kilian's bedroom floor.

"I think you've succeeded in making me suffer," he whispered into my ear.

I was contemplating how to make his hips repeat their movement one inch to the right, when the sound of a bell trilled everywhere.

"Candidates," Septimus' unmistakable voice rang out through the hallways, echoing in Kilian's bedroom. "Your hour is up. Please make your way back to the sparring room."

Kilian let out what I could have sworn was a frustrated sigh, but he gently extricated his hold on me. I instantly mourned the loss of contact.

"You'd better go. Before Septimus comes looking for you." Kilian stepped away so I could pass. "Or before I change my mind and make you get on your hands and knees."

Heat blossomed in my cheeks, my stomach dipping as if I were falling.

"To clean the mess you made, of course." A devilish grin pulled at the corner of his lips, and fuck – if I had thought he was beautiful *glaring*, that smile nearly brought me to my knees.

I needed to get out of there. I had to leave before I did something stupid and reckless and irrevocable. I hurried to the door, stepping over the pages strewn across the floor. My hand was on the doorknob when he said, "You stole a paperweight from the desk. Put it back."

Gods above, how did he even know that? My hands clenched into fists at my side, but I didn't turn around. "Make me," I threw out behind me.

"Be careful what you wish for," he muttered darkly as I slipped out the door.

CHAPTER 8

The first official challenge was only hours away and I hadn't been able to get a wink of sleep all night. I had tossed and turned, until finally crossing the hallway to Lana's bedroom and knocking softly on her door. She'd answered immediately.

Now I sat at the foot of her bed, clutching a pillow to my chest. We'd been fully dressed for hours – in fleece-lined leathers and thick winter coats, because we didn't need the threat of hypothermia to add to our problems – waiting for the challenge to start. Nausea roiled in the pit of my stomach. My queasiness had nothing to do with the pepper steak pie I had eaten at dinner the previous night, and everything to do with the gnawing dread that something terrible was about to happen.

It felt like tiny spiders were crawling across my skin, every small sound in the passageway enough to make me whip my head to the door in fresh panic.

"Stop looking at the door. You're going to make me vomit," Lana groaned, covering her head with a pillow.

A knock sounded and both Lana and I's heads swiveled to stare at the door. Lana's face was tinged a sickly shade of green as she crossed to the peephole and looked out. Her shoulders drooped in relief as she unlatched the door. "It's only Moric and Anama."

The others crossed into the room, both also fully dressed.

"How long have you been waiting?" Moric asked, sliding against Lana's dresser to sit on the floor. Anama remained by the door, a nervous look on her face.

"Since midnight," I said.

"Do you think they'll allow us to take any supplies with us?" Moric asked.

"Doubtful," Lana responded.

We sat in tense silence, the only sound that of our sprites' soft snores blending harmoniously. They were ethereal even in sleep, I noted, staring down at where Calendula rested on my thigh. She had given me a few pointers on the survival challenge, warning me to keep hidden during the night, not draw attention to myself by starting a fire no matter how cold it was, and to always stay alert. The survival challenge did not require brute strength or mental reasoning; it tested a mortal's instinctual senses, she had said.

I tried to divert my thoughts to greener pastures, but no welcome distraction came to mind. I had sealed the entire bedroom encounter with Kilian in a lock box and thrown away the key, refusing to allow myself the opportunity to think about just how close I had come to rising on my toes and kissing him. What was wrong with me? He was an asshole, he was elven *and* he was my instructor. And entirely too mysterious for my own good. Besides, there were virtually zero odds of me passing the Rite. I was mortal. There was no future here.

The only good thing to come from that encounter was that the link had been eerily quiet ever since. Anger no longer bubbled in my throat, threatening to spill out of my mouth into hateful words directed at everyone, and I no longer felt like my skin was on fire.

"Do you hear that?" Lana asked, sitting straighter.

Anama nodded. "Yes. It's faint but it almost sounds like..."

I cocked my head to the right, where a soft melody seemed to waft beneath the door and through the cracks in the floorboards. "It sounds like music."

"Cover your–" Anama began, but it was too late.

The music was enchanting. It filled my head, leaving room for nothing else. It felt like lush gardens and vinery, bare feet on dewy grass. Violin strings sang a melancholy tune of loss and heartbreak, the uplifting lilt at the end of each note a promise for a new beginning. It felt like magical places and forbidden spaces. A stolen kiss at the end of time, or an old god coming home. It was both haunting and exhilarating and I did not notice when my eyes glazed over and the others became blurry shapes of color. I was so lost in the melody, I did not register leaving Lana's bedroom, or trudging down the stairwell. And I definitely did not comprehend that despite all our research and preparation, we had failed to protect ourselves at the very start of the challenge.

I knew I had snapped out of the trance when I heard birds chirping overhead. I had been so ensorcelled by the elven tune that it had blocked out all other noise – even my own thoughts.

I came to, my eyes blinking the haze from my mind. The mental fog cleared to reveal densely packed trees surrounding me so completely that only patches of sky shone through the dark leaves. Anama and Moric stood to my left, Lana to my right. All of them looked as confused as I felt. Lana peered up at the trees while Anama scanned the ground.

"You were right, Lirah. We're in the Forests of Dalhur," Moric said.

"It looks like it's nearly midday. We must have been walking for *hours*. Did I ever mention how much I hate these Trials?" Lana muttered, stretching her legs out.

"Where are our sprites?" Moric asked, searching his pockets. I checked my own cloak, but Calendula was nowhere to be found.

"Maybe they're not allowed to help us during this challenge?" Lana suggested, studying the trees, probably for a flicker of gold.

Anama dropped to her knees, her fingers sifting at the soil a few feet ahead.

"What are you doing?" Moric asked, looking at Anama like she had finally lost it.

"This is freshly tilled soil." She stared at the ground. "Something's buried down here."

"Maybe it should stay buried?" Moric suggested, uncomfortable at the prospect of potentially unearthing a rotting carcass.

"No." I fell beside Anama, sinking my hands into the soil. There had to be a reason why we were brought here. "Something was put here for us to find."

I clawed at the ground until my fingers hit cold metal. Anama found something at the same time. She pulled out a piece of parchment covered in sand. I dug the metal object out, pulling it by a long chain. It was a hexagonal shape and had a clasp where the item opened. The metal was burnished, and its intricate swirls and whorls were rubbed off in certain places.

I knew what it was as soon as I unlatched the clasp.

"A compass," Moric breathed over my shoulder.

"And this is a map," Anama announced. She pointed to a large red *X* marked near the top left corner.

"Thank the gods. We have our challenge," Lana said.

"Where are we?" I asked, squinting at the map.

"It doesn't say."

"I shouldn't have expected anything less," I grumbled, wondering whether it was Septimus or Kilian who set this challenge. Or perhaps it had been Echon, eager for us to wander lost and confused in the Forests of Dalhur, with evening swiftly approaching.

"Anyone any good at map reading?" Lana asked.

Moric shuffled. "I wouldn't say I'm *good* at it, but I used to make them for my younger brother. Sometimes, when he missed our parents or had a bad day at school, I'd hide silly trinkets around the garden and make a map for him to decipher. Once, for his birthday, I made one that spanned our entire village."

I bit back my comment that his brother was lucky to have him; it wasn't a compassionate thing to say when Moric had been wrenched away from his home, not knowing whether he would ever see his sibling again. Instead, I said, "That's more experience than I have."

Anama and Lana nodded their agreement, Anama passing the map to Moric. "Walk us through it."

He dropped to one knee on the soil and placed the map flat on the ground, smoothing out its wrinkles. His nose scrunched as he studied it. He pointed his index finger to an illustrated diagram of mountainous peaks. "Those are the summits." His finger dipped an inch, to a sketch of a house nestled between the jagged formations. "And that must be Valhan House. If we follow the trail from there across this road, that should be Pyxis." The structure Moric pointed to vaguely resembled the library, with its tall, symmetrical shape. "We know the Forests of Dalhur act as a natural border separating Lomask to the south and Dalhur to the north."

Moric's fingers skipped across the map to a line of illustrated trees, nearly bisecting the map in half. Near the bottom of the trees, a river snaked all the way across the land toward the Green Sea. He ran his finger along the line of trees, which had to represent the forest. "This would place us somewhere here. The problem is, I don't exactly know where we are on this line. But look at this–" He indicated a cluster of circles between the top and middle half of the line. "I'd bet you anything those are a network of caves. That's our best bet of surviving the night and the only way to mark where we are on this map. It's not too far from the checkpoint, either."

The *X*, which presumably marked the point we were meant to reach, was marked right at the apex of the line, near the top of the map. To get there we would have to pass the caves, and only then would we know for sure if we were on the right track.

"The issue is…" I started, meeting Moric's hazel eyes.

He nodded, his expression grim.

"We don't know which direction to head in," Lana finished.

The map did not contain a compass key to follow. We had to find a landmark to know whether we were going the right way. And that meant picking a direction and simply walking.

It sounded simple in theory, but… nightfall would come in a few hours, and I knew we were not the only creatures roaming these woods. A chill rose the hairs on my neck.

I looked to Anama, undoubtedly the wisest amongst us. "Which way do you think we should go?"

She gave the question some thought, and then said, "Most infrastructure, both man-made and natural, leans toward the rising sun. The sun rises in the west. That's where the caves should be."

The trees around us were so dense I could barely see the sky, let alone the setting sun.

"So, west." Anama's voice was strong and confident. "We go west."

Something *thunked* against the top of my head and I whipped my gaze heavenward to stare at a low-hanging branch above my head.

"What's wrong?" Lana asked, concern dipping her brows.

"Acorn." I pointed to the cluster of massive nuts hanging from the boughs of an old oak. "Be careful."

Lana took a purposeful step away from the tree.

I stepped away from it too, scanning the compass in my hand. "West it is." I rotated on the spot until the dial faced the right direction. And then we walked.

I tried to keep track of the passing hours whenever a copse of trees gave way to reveal a slice of sky ahead, but I knew the sun was sinking below the horizon when the bright light faded to pale dusk. Tree trunks, whitewashed from the day, pressed in on us. The sight of them made me feel nauseated and claustrophobic, like a rat trapped in a maze, desperately trying to find the way out.

The pangs of hunger began, and I was sure everyone else felt the same, yet no one complained. I did not bother covering my yawn when it ripped from my throat.

Lana gave me a sidelong glance, dark smudges back beneath her eyes and more prominent than ever. "Bet you're regretting camping out in my room all night instead of counting sheep."

I gave a lifeless chuckle. Each step felt like I was walking on knives. "I'd give up my mother's secret stew recipe right now to go back in time and enjoy a good night's sleep."

"Woah. If you're giving up a prized recipe, it should be for more than just sleep," Moric said from where he led our group. I had handed over compass duty earlier, and he seemed grateful for the job. I had to admit, taking point on direction was an excellent distraction from the hunger.

"What would you give it up for, then?" I asked.

Moric didn't hesitate. "Another day with my family."

A pang, worse than the combined hunger and sleep deprivation, strummed at my heart.

Trailing behind Lana and me, Anama said, "I'd give it up to eat a bowl of shellfish soup and hot bread on one of Kraventhorn's sandy beaches. I adore the ocean. I used to spend every single minute I wasn't working at the library exploring the tide pools and sea caves and, occasionally, cliff diving."

Anama? Cliff diving? That was surprising.

She did not miss the look that flickered between us all. "I know. It's a lot more adventurous than reading dusty old books for a living, but I really enjoyed it."

"Anama, you're a closeted adrenaline junkie," Lana whispered like it was a secret.

I laughed, nodding in agreement. "Who would have thought sweet and quiet Anama spent her weekends jumping off cliffs for sport?"

Anama rolled her eyes, the gray streaks in her tawny hair shining gunmetal in the moonlight. I only realized then that dusk had turned to nightfall. Leaves rustled overhead, and an occasional bird squawked. I did not allow myself to ponder what else might be lurking in the branches above.

"What about you, Lana? What would you give my mother's secret stew recipe up for?" I asked in a feeble attempt to distract myself from the gnawing fear.

Lana, gods bless her, played along. "I don't want to say."

Even Moric turned to look at her.

"What?" She blushed crimson. "If I'm being truthful, it's not nearly as dutiful as wanting to see my family, or as wholesome as enjoying a hot meal in my favorite place."

"Come on, Lana Banana," Moric teased. "We all went. It's your turn."

"Gods, these nicknames get progressively worse each day," she muttered. "But fine, since we're all out here and might die at any second if a panthera comes shooting out the trees... I'd give up the recipe for one night of casual, no strings attached sex with Septimus."

I choked on my spit.

Anama's eyes bulged in their sockets.

A slow, cocky grin stretched along Moric's face. "I. *Knew*. It."

Lana gave him the middle finger.

"You know you've just signed yourself up for endless teasing," I told her. "He's *never* going to let this one go."

Lana stuck her tongue out at Moric, who was still smirking gleefully. "Wanting something and actually *having* it are two completely different things. Septimus is elven. We hate them."

I pressed my lips together in a thin line as thoughts of Kilian – naked, save for a towel – flitted across my mind like a butterfly.

He was elven too. We did hate them. We most certainly did not daydream of towels slipping and cuirasses coming undone. And we definitely did not wonder what those full lips tasted like.

"I hear hate-sex does wonders for the skin," Moric chirped, sounding infinitely more alert than he had a few minutes ago. His mind was most likely whirring with an endless stream of taunts.

The look Lana gave him was pure daggers. She opened her mouth to retort, then snapped it shut.

"What?" Moric chortled. "Septimus got your tongue?"

"Shh." Lana pressed a finger to her lips. "Can you hear that?"

"All I hear is the sound of your panties dropping for a certain golden-eyed elven," Moric sang.

"I'm being serious. Shut up and listen."

We all stilled, coming to a stop. I glanced around, then murmured, "Is it me or are the trees thinning?"

"I think we're coming to a clearing." Anama squinted through the darkness. "I can see something up ahead."

"Maybe it's the caves." Relief washed over me. We would have a place to rest for the night, somewhere moderately safe to sit and take our shoes off. My toes were scrunched painfully in my boots.

We walked with renewed vigor, only the moonlight glinting off the trees and the promise of a clearing up ahead guiding us. And as we grew closer to the glade, trees branching off to scatter in distant clumps, I heard what Lana had:

The rhythmic gurgling of water flowing over rock, splashing and bubbling as it wended downstream.

There were no caves. Only a grassy bank that gave way to a wide, curving river.

Anama fell to the ground beside me, her knees hitting the grass with a thud.

We had trekked west, but found the river. We had gone the wrong way. The caves were to the east. My stomach sank to my feet, disappointment stinging my chest.

Lana's hand was half-raised to her mouth, her gaze locked on the river. And Moric, compass hanging limply from his hand, was speechless.

Anama pulled out the map, scanning it in the silvery moonlight. "This can't be. I don't understand. The sun rises in the west."

I crouched down beside her and laid my hand atop hers. Her fingers were icy cold. "It's okay. We'll go back."

A tear dripped from her face and onto the map. "I said we should go west. This is my fault."

"Hey." Lana shook her head. "It's no one's fault. We were stranded in the middle of fucking nowhere. We all knew there was a fifty-fifty chance we were going the wrong way."

"No, it's my fault. My fault," Anama muttered, shaking her head. She wasn't listening to us. She got up and began pacing alongside the river. "What if we go around? There's a trail on the map, leading northeast, around the forest. Maybe we can cut–"

I heard the sound before my brain registered what I could see. A faint whizzing and then a wet thump as a spike flew through the air with deadly precision, and landed in Anama's shoulder.

Lana screamed, a bloodcurdling, high-pitched sound that shocked me into movement. I launched forward, gripping Anama before she could topple over into the river.

The river.

A glowing pair of yellow eyes had emerged from its depths. The lower half of the creature's face was submerged within the water, only a scaly scalp and a long, thin tail covered in emerald spikes high above its head visible. The water stirred and its tail bobbed higher, the spines along it prickling as it reared back.

"Get down!" I screamed, pulling Anama with me as a second barb flew inches above our heads.

Blood was dripping down her arm. So much blood, turned black by the moonlight. I didn't want to take the spike out and risk increasing the blood loss. My hands fluttered across her shoulder. *I didn't know what to do.* "Can you move?"

She gritted her teeth and nodded. "I can try."

Moric and Lana were at our sides, Lana looking frantically toward the river. I kept my gaze fixed firmly on Anama. She looked so pale.

"We need to go," Lana cried.

I reached around Anama's torso, hauling her up so she could lean her weight against me.

"We have to go. That thing is coming!" Moric shouted.

Anama blinked sluggishly. Her injured arm hung limply at her side. I guided her one step forward, then another. I didn't dare look at the river.

Anama's legs trembled and she gasped for breath.

"Help me!" The words ripped out of my throat, a guttural sound I did not recognize.

"I can carry her." Moric reached for Anama.

"No." Anama's voice was so soft, so weak. "I'm losing... too much blood. You need... to leave me. I'm sorry... for bring– bringing us... west."

"Don't say that. Don't fucking say that." I scrubbed a hand across my eyes to get rid of the tears blurring my vision.

"Guys!" Lana shouted, and I looked up in time to see that the creature had risen from the water enough to bare the ridges of its exoskeleton. Its abdomen was shiny and round, and several spindly legs protruded from its sides. Yellow eyes stared straight at us as that lethal tail lifted once more.

"What the *fuck* is that?" Lana wailed.

"Arrow-tailed lancer," Moric breathed.

A single, sharp dart flew, aiming right for Lana, but she dodged expertly, rolling along the bank.

Anama clutched at her arm. "Stop," she moaned. "I'll only... slow you... down."

"Moric!"

"On it." Moric heaved Anama into his arms, hands cradling her lower back and thighs. He took one step forward and then staggered as an arrow nicked his leg. Anama lurched forward in his arms, slipping from his grip. They both rolled to the ground, Anama whimpering as she landed on her injured shoulder.

I cast a panicked look at the river. The water stirred violently as the arrow-tailed lancer surged forward. I grasped at Moric, my gaze skirting over his wound.

"I'm fine." He pushed me toward Anama instead.

Grabbing Anama, I wrenched her up. She winced in pain, and her eyes fluttered open, focusing on me.

"Run," she said firmly, even as her legs wobbled.

"*No.*" I dragged her forward as if my sheer will would be enough to get us all out of here alive. The air screamed as another arrow whizzed through it. It hit Anama's torso dead center, the force propelling her out of my grasp. Her eyes bulged, hands rising to her stomach.

"No!" This couldn't be happening. How could everything be occurring in slow motion and so quickly at the same time?

I took a step forward, but Anama rose a shaky hand toward me. I could see the agony and defeat in her eyes. Blood bubbled, trickling from her mouth as she began stumbling away from me.

"Anama. Get on my back!" Lana screamed, trying to tug her over. But Anama shook her head, pushing her away.

"Run," she coughed. "*Please…*"

The arrow-tailed lancer reared back again, its scales bristling, the spines on its tail quivering. Anama swiveled slowly to face it.

Its tail lashed out, quick as a whip, and tore into Anama. And then it was dragging her forward, right to the edge of the bank. I sprinted forward, not thinking, hand thrown out, fingers clawing for her as the arrow-tailed lancer pulled her into the river. My fingers grasped at air and nothing.

Dark blood drifted to the surface.

A choking sob split from my chest, my hand still outstretched. The creature, distracted by its prey, slipped beneath the surface, submerging until even its yellow eyes and arrow tail had vanished completely.

"Anama!" Her name clawed against my windpipes, a rough grating sound that was swallowed by the gurgling of the river. Lana was at Moric's side, her fingers skating across his thigh, ripping at the fabric of his pants to reveal brown skin, marred by a long, thin gash.

"I'm okay. It's a surface wound," Moric said, but there was terror in his voice.

Lana appeared beside me, her hand on my arm. She pulled me to face her. "Lirah, we need to go before that thing comes back." Her eyes were wild.

My breath tore from me in ragged gasps, and I turned one last frenzied look to the river, then to my friends. Moric was injured. And Anama was gone. Adrenaline coursed through me. Every second we spent on this bank put my friends' lives in more jeopardy.

"Are you sure you're fine?" I asked Moric, quickly.

He nodded.

"Then fucking *run*."

CHAPTER 9

My throat was on fire. My calves burned like a furnace had been lit beneath them. And my chest was a hollow, aching beast that threatened to split open and unleash the seven fires of hell upon the world.

We ran all through the night, stopping only to check the direction we were headed in. Pale dawn sluiced through the trees overhead. We had no map to guide us now. It had been with Anama when she was dragged into the river.

I knew her injuries had been too serious for her to survive, whether the creature had pulled her in or not. There had been so much blood. But that didn't make her loss any less painful.

So I ran, my legs pumping faster and faster, as if I were sprinting away from the trauma, the pain and grief. Away from myself.

Lana slowed to a stop ahead of me. Her hands clutched her kneecaps, her breath wheezing out of her. "I – need – a minute."

Moric nodded, stopping beside her. He pulled out the compass and double checked our position. "We should be nearing the caves soon. We can stop and rest there for a bit."

"No," I said. The word surprised my friends as much as it did me. "We need to finish the challenge. The longer we spend in here, the more we're at risk. I won't let anyone else die today."

I hated the look Lana gave me. Her eyes scanned my face, dipping to my hands, which were covered in dried blood.

Anama's blood. "We need rest, Lirah. We'll be useless if we keep going at this pace. And being useless puts us at even greater risk."

I hated how right she was even more. I wanted to be done with this challenge and out of the forest, away from the horror of it all, but my body was truly exhausted.

"I don't think I can keep going, even to the caves," Lana puffed. "My legs are *vibrating*. And I'm so hungry I think my stomach is trying to digest itself."

"Then we have to take a break," Moric said firmly. He looked at our surroundings, which were exactly the same as they had been hours ago. Just trees upon trees, damp soil and green leaves beneath our feet. Several bushes and shrubbery grew at the base of the trunks, and what looked to be ripe berries spilled from their branches.

"Are those strawberries?" Lana's eyes were wide as saucers as she stared at the shrubs.

I crouched down beside one of the plants and viewed the berries. They did indeed look like strawberries, but a faint blue ring tinged the upper portion where the stem grew. "It's a sloughberry. I recognize it from the photos in the textbook Anama showed us."

Another pang ripped through my chest.

"Sloughberry is safe for mortal consumption," Moric said slowly.

"In small quantities, yes. I'm just not sure *how* small, though."

Lana groaned. "I'm starving, but the only thing that could make this situation worse than it already is would be diarrhea."

I didn't disagree. Maybe one would be fine, but that would not fill us anyway.

"I'll take my chances with hunger." Lana plopped down at the base of an oak tree, resting her head against its thick trunk.

"Me too." Moric shook his head at the sloughberries, taking a seat beside Lana.

I still stood, hands planted on my hips despite the quavering of my thighs. My feet had gone numb in my boots long ago, so at least I didn't have that pain to contend with. "Are we really just going to sit here and wait for something to come pick us off?" Paranoia scratched at my brain.

"It's daytime." Lana yawned. "We'll rest for an hour max, and then we'll carry on to the caves. We've been heading northeast for a good while now. We'll reach the caves before nightfall."

I gnawed on my lower lip.

"Sit, Lirah," Moric commanded. "Nothing is chasing us. I'll take first watch. At any sign of trouble, we'll run."

Nothing that we *knew of* was chasing us.

I gave him a hesitant look before finally yielding. Sitting after nearly twenty-four hours of intermittently walking and running through the forest with zero sleep or food was so blissful I nearly cried out in relief. I sank against the base of a mossy trunk, my head nestling into a crevice of soft soil and bark, not caring which insects crawled beneath, and closed my eyes.

A sharp crackle jerked me awake. My eyes snapped open, and I blinked furiously as I rose to my elbows. I stared around, wildly searching for danger and finding nothing immediately threatening.

Lana lay fast asleep. Moric – who was supposed to have woken me for my shift – snored softly. I glanced up at the sky, swearing beneath my breath. It was night. We had slept the entire day.

I crouched before Lana and Moric, shaking their shoulders gently.

Moric jolted, so startled he smacked his head against the tree trunk. "Ow!"

Lana woke more gracefully. Her eyes were wide and alert as she looked around.

"It's okay," I assured them. "We just overslept."

"Is it nightfall?" Lana's eyes shuttered in despair. "We should have listened to you earlier."

I shook my head. "You were right to rest. I feel slightly better."

It was an exaggeration. My stomach still ached something fierce and my legs felt stiffer than ever, but at least I no longer felt like I would collapse at any second.

"Moric?" I asked, peering at him. "You're awfully quiet. What's wrong?"

Moric's gaze was fixed on his leg. On the thin gash the arrow-tailed lancer had inflicted on his thigh. It had now turned a sickly shade of green.

"Can you move it?" I asked quietly, my tone not betraying the absolute horror clutching my heart.

Moric tested the limb, drawing back his knee and straightening it. "It twinges a bit, but yeah, I can move it. The color is… alarming."

"The arrow must contain some form of slow-acting poison." Because it had definitely not looked like this last night. Just how slow the poison was, I did not know. And I really did not want to sit around waiting to find out.

Lana pushed to her feet and extended a hand to help Moric up. I slid an arm beneath his shoulders, propping him against me as he stood. The brunt of his weight was nearly enough to send me to the ground, but I dug my feet in the soil, my muscles screaming in protest.

He extricated himself from our hold. "I'm okay. I'll be fine. Let's keep moving."

I stared down at the compass. The caves were clustered somewhere in the northeast. The checkpoint for the end of the Trial had appeared to be true east.

"I think we should go straight to the checkpoint," I said.

Lana nodded. "There's no need for us to go to the caves now that we've rested."

"Agreed," Moric said. "I'd very much like to finish this challenge."

"Okay. Checkpoint it is." I adjusted our course, and we set off.

The air between us was solemn and exhausted. I jumped at every single branch that rustled in the breeze and every dry leaf that crunched beneath our boots as we continued east. Once, I thought I saw a pair of yellow eyes peering out at me from the treetops and pulled Moric and Lana into a sprint that nearly had us pitching forward onto our faces.

My knees buckled as we broke through a line of trees, and I caught sight of some large, dark formations jutting from the ground. Lana's hand linked through mine, and she squeezed tight. Moric gripped my other hand.

Caves. Four of them, all set in a semicircle almost equidistant from each other.

"Something's not right," I said. The compass needle pointed directly east. "We should be at the checkpoint, not the caves."

Moric's eyes flickered over my head. "Look."

Lana and I whirled around, our gazes tracking Moric's. There, on the trunk of a thick oak, a page fluttered in the wind. It had been stabbed through with two daggers to hold it in place. We approached as one unit, cautiously, as if one of the branches might whip down and strike us.

There was lettering on the page, in the mortal language of Grilish. The curlicue was familiar. I clicked my tongue as I realized where I had seen it: on the letter we had found inside the chest the morning we had woken up on Lortan. Nothing good had happened since then. My stomach gave a nervous flip, and foreboding tingled beneath my skin.

"'Welcome, candidates,'" Moric read aloud. "'To the first challenge.'"

So we *were* at the checkpoint. I had thought the challenge would end once we made it here. And from the look on Lana's face, so had she.

I blew out a shaky breath as Moric continued reading.

"'Set out before you are four caverns. They each lead down to a network of tunnels, created by a monster that slumbers deep beneath. To succeed in this challenge, each of you must choose a cave to enter and collect the set of keys that has been placed within. Once the challenge has been completed, you must make your way back to Valhan House. Should you not return, you will be considered lost to the forest. Good luck.'"

"Well, fuck," Lana muttered.

"Wait." I stepped closer to the trunk, peering at the page. In small print beneath the larger instruction, and barely legible, another sentence was written. "'Hint: The monster cannot see and relies on its ability to collect scents from the air through its tongue.'"

"Like a snake," Moric murmured.

"If there's a giant fucking snake down there, I think I'll puke." Lana flattened a hand against her hair, which was plastered to her face and smeared with dirt. I was sure I looked the same after having spent the night running through and then sleeping on the floor of the forest. But the monster beneath would not care about that. It would only care how we smelled and tasted.

"There are two daggers," I said, jerking my head toward the tree. "You two should take them."

Lana and Moric shook their heads vehemently.

"You can't go in there weaponless," Lana objected.

"I won't be. Don't worry, I have a plan."

I did not have a plan.

Stupidly, I had left the dagger Umma gifted me beneath my pillow at Valhan House. But I would be damned if I let my friends go into those tunnels without some form of protection. I had already lost one; I would not be able to live with myself if I took a chance of survival from Lana or Moric.

Are you willing to give up your life for it? A distant voice whispered at the back of my head. I shook my head to clear it away, but was reminded of Umma's mantra:

It is vulnerable to feel – to love – Lirah. In a world like ours, we are not afforded that luxury.

I don't care, I thought.

The voice came back. *Worry about yourself. You should take those daggers and run into the tunnel, before one of your* friends *does it first. How soon would they betray you to save themselves? Are their lives worth more than your own?*

Yes, I clawed back. Vulnerable as it may be to feel, my friends' lives were more important. And if I had to sacrifice the chance to see Umma again so that Moric could be with his brother, or Lana with her sisters, I would do it in a heartbeat. I just hoped Umma would understand that while the challenges could break my body, they would not take my humanity.

"Take them." I pulled the blades from the tree and pressed one into Lana's hand and the other into Moric's. "I promise I know what I'm doing."

My friends would have to forgive me for the lie, too.

"What happens if one of us gets lost down there?" Lana's voice was a whisper.

I glanced around the forest floor, searching for something, anything, that might help us. Acorns littered the ground from the giant oak above. I crouched down to retrieve a handful and thrust them at her. "Take these in your pocket. Every few feet, drop one. If any of us don't make it back out here, the others will come looking."

Lana nodded and Moric stooped to grab a handful of his own. I pocketed a few myself, stuffing them into every crevice I could find.

Lana threw her arms around my neck in a surprising show of affection. My eyes widened for a second, before I hugged her back fiercely. My gaze met Moric's over Lana's shoulder, and I reached a hand toward him. He took it, enveloping us both in a tight hug. When we parted, the corners of my eyes were wet.

"I will find you," Lana promised. She turned toward the caves, her gaze flickering between the four of them. After a moment, she chose the third from the left and stood before it.

I took the cave next to her. Moric took the one to my left. None of us mentioned the remaining cave. The one intended for Anama.

"Keep your eyes open. I'll see you soon." I gave them a weak smile and crossed inside.

Darkness swallowed me. I reached out a hand to trail along the dry, grainy cave wall to guide me through it. Each step was careful, and I toed the ground ahead before stepping firmly onto the soil. Inside smelled worse than the trash after beef broth preparation day at the governor's house. It was a nauseating mixture of decomposing meat and soil. Something skuttled across my fingers, and it was an effort not to scream and yank my hand away. It crawled off my hand and I carried on down the tunnel, my footsteps continually soft and measured. Every so often I dropped an acorn behind me.

I knew I was descending deeper into the cavern when the floor sloped beneath my feet. The scent was even worse down here, and light was already a distant memory. If I had to pick a truly awful place to die, this would be it. After the maggots and bugs feasted on your flesh, no one would even recognize you. You would belong to the earth. To the darkness of the cavern.

How was I going to find a key down here when I couldn't even see my hands in front of my face?

You don't need light, the voice in my head whispered, *when you command shadows.*

Something happened then. When I blinked and reopened my eyes, my surroundings cleared, hazing into shades of gray. It was like looking at a black-and-white painting.

How…?

But I already knew. The answer was in that distant voice, urging me to be selfish, to prioritize my life over my friends'. It was how shadow had bent and warped around me, my eyes adjusting to see, because my surroundings were no longer the darkest thing in these caves.

I was.

It was the kernel of power Kilian had gifted me during the sacred oath.

It was Kilian *himself* inside my head.

I gritted my teeth as I stomped down the tunnel, scanning the curvature of the walls for any sign of a key. I was grateful for my newfound ability to see – it certainly sped things along – but it was still intrusive as fuck.

The ground shivered beneath me. I peered over my shoulder with my grayscale vision, but there was nothing to see. Blank tunnel stretched on until the wall curved back, blocking my vision beyond. But I knew something was coming. It could only be one thing.

My feet were glued to the spot. I didn't know whether to run forward or backward. But anywhere would be better than just standing still, waiting for whatever had carved these tunnels to find me.

I chose forward and sprinted, my head dipping to avoid the uneven bumps and ridges. I ran like something was chasing me. Something definitely *was*. The soil shook as my feet slammed against it, my heart the only thing pounding faster. Breath squeezed out of my lungs and I gulped, gasping for more. But I was so deep below ground that fresh air was as elusive as the key I was searching for. Still the monster chased. The ground rippled and soil separated from the walls in chunks.

I ran so fast I did not realize I was falling until my arms flailed before me and I collapsed onto the dirt. The ground gave another massive shudder, the walls crumbling as a gaping, black mouth with razor-sharp teeth emerged from below. It snapped upward, loam falling from it in great plumes. I blinked against the dust, my hands clawing me backward and away until, to my absolute horror, my back met the solid cave wall. A dead end.

A black tongue darted out of the monster's mouth. A pair of prongs attached to the tip of its tongue moved independently, tasting the air. The creature lurched forward, saliva dripping from its mouth as it pulled itself into the tunnel with a scaly hand. As it heaved its massive body up, a flash of silver caught my eye.

Four sets of keys jangled on a loop, tied around the monster's thick neck.

Of course that was where the keys would be placed. There was no way I would manage to grab them without coming into dangerous contact with those prongs and flesh-shredding teeth.

I sucked in a sharp breath as a claw raked at the soil mere inches from me. I needed a plan. Something that would not result in me being killed in this tunnel by the predator before me.

If I could confuse it with my scent, perhaps I stood a chance of slipping behind the creature and grabbing the keys.

Hastily, I yanked my cloak off. Rolling it into a tight ball, I launched it across the monster's rising head, to the other side of the tunnel. The prongs on the creature's tongue twisted, following the direction of the cloak, just as I had hoped.

I used the distraction to get to my feet and sprinted around the monster, still only half-emerged from the ground, the rest of its thick, worm-like body hidden in the soil below. It seemed my distraction had run its course though, as those awful prongs tilted back toward me now. Its tongue lolled as hot, reeking saliva dripped from huge teeth that may as well have been daggers with how long and pointed they were.

Its large hand swatted forward, batting me to the ground as if I were little more than a fly. I hit the floor with a thud. A moment later, searing pain sliced through my leg. I looked over my shoulder in time to see the tip of one claw carving the length of my calf. Agony, blistering and hot, shot along my nerves as the talon shredded my skin, straight down to the bone.

The prongs darted along my calf even as I yanked it back, the pain acute and unbearable. The monster reared its head, teeth bearing down to strike. I lifted my arm at the same time, a pressure building inside of me. Razor blades sank deep into my forearm, and heat sizzled through me, not from the pain of the creature's teeth tearing through my flesh but something entirely different. My blood was boiling, bubbling beneath my skin, and just when I thought I would explode from the intensity of it, lightning erupted from my fingertips. Electric blue, so bright it momentarily blinded me. There and gone in a flash.

I screamed, loud and harsh, as hot blood – the monster's or my own, I wasn't sure – gushed down, splashing onto my face, my neck, in my mouth. The taste was bitter and vile, and I gagged. The creature shuddered violently atop me, teeth grinding further as it spasmed from the force of the brief current. The scent of singed flesh permeated the air. My throat was a ragged mess of vocal cords as sounds I did not recognize ripped free from it.

And then, there was light again.

This time, golden and intense. It illuminated the space so brilliantly my eyes shuttered against the glare. I forced them back open, blinking several times. I may have been hallucinating from the pain, but there was Lana, sunlight pouring from her skin, her hair haloed in a wreath of gold as she approached, looking like an avenging angel.

Her mouth twisted into a grim line when her gaze flickered to me, and then she was running, sprinting up the quivering monster's arm. She leaped from its shoulder blade, her dagger arching in a silver blaze as it tore through the air, sinking deep into the monster's skull.

The ground quaked as the creature rolled to the side. Its teeth wrenched out of my arm with another agonizing stab. It twitched once, and then went still.

A slew of curse words strung incoherently from my lips, and I shivered, clutching my arm to my chest.

"Lirah!" Lana's face hovered above mine. "Take my hand."

She helped me up, pulling off her coat and tunic, ripping the sleeves to form a makeshift tourniquet just above the wounds on my arm and calf. Blood flowed much slower from my injuries now, but I still felt so weak and cold.

Lana crossed to the creature, bending over its head to take the set of keys. Propping one arm beneath me, she said, "Let's get the fuck out of here."

"Moric?" I asked as we hobbled away from the monster, stepping carefully around it to avoid the cracks in the earth.

Lana's throat bobbed. "I can't find him anywhere."

My heart sank. "We can't leave him here."

"Let me get you out of these tunnels first. I don't think you realize how much blood you're losing, Lirah."

One thing to be grateful for, I supposed, was that my acorn trail was mostly intact. I breathed a sigh of relief at the pinprick of light that grew steadily bigger as we left the tunnel network behind us. My knees wobbled as we broke free at last, a cold breeze kissing my clammy cheeks. But the feeling of relief was nothing compared to the euphoria at seeing Moric pacing before the caves.

At the sight of us, he rushed forward, his hand reaching out to steady me. "Thank the gods." His voice shook.

"Don't thank them," Lana muttered. "They had nothing to do with killing that thing down there. That was all Lirah."

"*You're* the one who killed it." I shot her an appreciative look. "That's twice now you've saved my life."

Lana shook her head. "I didn't do it on my own. That current you sent through it was lethal. You wrecked your arm trying to kill that creature."

I glanced down at my arm. Blood leaked from it in a steady stream. My calf was a mangled mess of torn flesh and had long since gone numb.

Moric shoved a knotted brown vine into my hand. "Eat that."

"What is it?"

He shuffled uncomfortably before us, his head lowering. It took me a moment to realize he was embarrassed. "I went into the caves when you guys did, but I only made it a few feet before realizing I couldn't see anything. And my leg was burning from where that arrow-tailed lancer pierced it. I'm a fucking coward for leaving you guys in there, I know. When I came out, I did a bit of exploring behind the caves and found this." He gestured to the vine in my hand. "I recognized it as impid root."

He pulled at the torn fabric of his pants, revealing nothing but unmarred brown skin.

"It's healed!" Lana's eyes were wide. "It worked?"

Moric nodded.

It was all I needed to shove the root into my mouth and chew. It tasted how I imagined tree bark would – tough, dry and crunchy – but I summoned the remaining spit left in my mouth and swallowed, the root scratching along my throat as it went down.

It happened like clockwork. I watched in fascination as soft, wet strands of skin stretched and grew, twisting and morphing across the wound. The gaping flesh on both my arm and calf turned rubbery and pink, dried blood crusting its edges, before the upper layer of pigment knitted together, like a puzzle clicking into place.

"I'm so sorry," Moric said as I removed the tourniquets from my healed limbs. My back muscles protested in agony as I bent to reach my calf. A pity the root wasn't a miracle cure for all injuries. "I should have been there to help you."

"It's okay." I straightened. "You wouldn't have found the impid root if you had been inside. If you hadn't found it, I would have probably bled out."

"Besides, it was pitch black down there. I wouldn't have been able to see anything either, were it not for Septimus' light," Lana said.

"We should get a move on," I said quickly, hoping that if I changed the subject fast enough, I wouldn't have to admit that the link to Kilian had proved more useful than not. That his power unsettled – and equally fascinated – me.

Even worse, that it felt more familiar than foreign.

CHAPTER 10

The sprites were arguing.

I heard their shrill voices before we had even cleared the Forests of Dalhur. Moric's memory of the marked checkpoint relative to Valhan House was remarkable. Lana had only questioned him once during the day-long trek back from the caves.

I was beyond starving. My body past numb. My bones felt like brittle bark, chafing beneath my skin with each step. It was a monumental effort not to curl up on the ground and take a nap.

I patted Moric on the back, giving him a weak smile as I stepped toward Calendula. The sight of her made me want to cry. I didn't know exactly where we were, but we had left the tall cluster of trees behind us and that was all that mattered. I didn't want to see a forest again for a *very* long time.

Calendula's wings were fluttering furiously in midair as she yelled at Osmanthius. "Don't you *dare* tell me what I ought or oughtn't do! This is *my* mortal." Silver sparks drifted around her like a hailstorm.

Osmanthius' eyes flashed dangerously at her. "Are you implying that I do not care for my own mortal?"

Calendula made a *pfft* noise. "Obviously. If you hadn't been such a rule follower–"

"I dare you to finish that sentence, Calendula Mirau. You may be the granddaughter of Mirau Titan, but I am descended from Voldun the Fearless."

"Fearless?" Calendula scoffed. "I've seen mortals more fearless than you, rule follower!"

I approached the warring sprites. Moric's woodland sprite, I noted, had been observing the argument from the sidelines and, as soon as she had spotted Moric, floated daintily over to land on his shoulder.

"What is going on here?" I asked, holding my hands out.

Calendula spun to face me. "I tried warning you not to go west."

My brows rose. "You did?"

Calendula nodded crossly. "I threw an acorn right at your head."

My hand lifted automatically to the spot the acorn had hit. "That was you?"

"Yes. And I would have thrown another had Osmanthius over here not stopped me."

Osmanthius shouldered past Calendula, his wings bristling. "We were under specific instructions *not* to assist. What is the point of a survival challenge if their sprites are there to tell them which direction to go?"

"I don't care about the *instructions*. I am a shadow sprite. I bow to no one."

"You're under Valhan rule." Osmanthius rolled yellow eyes at her.

Bright yellow.

"I saw you," I said to Osmanthius. "In the trees. I saw yellow eyes. I thought it had been an animal chasing us… but it was you. You were there the entire time? Even when Anama…?" A lump had formed in my throat. The same one that appeared each time I thought of her. The spark in her eyes when she spoke about her passions. The warm smile I would never again receive from her. My chest constricted painfully.

The cliffs of Kraventhorn would mourn her loss.

Osmanthius nodded gravely. "We are most sorry for her death. There was nothing we could do."

Not exactly true. They could have told us we were going in the wrong direction. That could have prevented Anama's death. But honestly, it wasn't entirely their fault. Osmanthius was right. They had been under instruction. It was the instructor who was truly at fault.

"Where is Anama's sprite?" I swallowed past the hard lump.

Calendula sighed. "She has gone home, to Avendir, where the river sprites reside. She was most upset at her mortal's passing. I don't think we'll see her again next season."

Next season. The thought made me want to be violently sick. But maybe that was also the lack of food, sleep and heavy blood loss.

"Are you allowed to help us get back to Valhan House?" I aimed this question at Osmanthius.

"Of course. We were only barred from assisting you *within* the forest. And I'll have the record show that I care a great deal for my mortal." He squared his shoulders, looking affronted. "There were numerous times I wanted to intervene, but not all of us lack restraint."

Calendula gave him a withering look.

I didn't feel anger toward her. She had done more than she should have – more than any of the others, in fact – to prevent the outcome. I was too stupid not to have recognized the sign for what it was.

I sighed, turning back to wave Lana and Moric toward us. "Take us back to Valhan House, please."

Osmanthius and Calendula were surprisingly quiet on the walk back. It seemed, having aired out their argument, the effort of flying back was now taking its toll on them. Calendula refused to sit on my shoulder, claiming she deserved better than a shoulder perch, earning her a scathing look from Osmanthius, who was nestled against Lana's neck.

Instead, Calendula made me hold out a hand for her to rest on. It was infinitely more effort than my screaming joints and muscles could muster but I ignored the pain, just like I had ignored it for the past three days. I shoved it in the box of things I was too afraid to ever open again. It was getting surprisingly full.

The sun was setting, limning the snowy crests in glistening gold, by the time we started up the cobblestone pathway to the gate of Valhan House. Kilian stood at the arch, arms folded across his chest. As if he had been waiting.

When he saw me trudging up the steps, something inside me flickered back to life. Anger. Panic. No, not panic. *Terror.* Icy fear unlike anything I had ever felt before. Kilian stomped down the pathway, meeting me halfway before I could even cross over into the courtyard. His hands reached for my face but did not touch my skin.

His expression was a mask of fury and rage, and something indescribable. "You've been gone for three days. Three. Days."

I looked up into his impenetrable silver eyes. "I wasn't aware there was a time limit on this challenge. We were told to simply survive." My voice was a cold creature, a beast of ice and snow.

Lana and Moric paused a few feet ahead, but I could see the other instructors waiting just beyond the archway, so I motioned them forward. "Go on. I'll be there soon."

Kilian shifted back into my field of vision before I could get a response from my friends. "I've been waiting–"

"If you were so concerned, you should have sent a servant into the woods to check on us. That way you wouldn't have had to *wait*."

"I'm not in the business of keeping servants," he snapped. "And you're missing the point. I thought you had died."

"Why would you think that? Doesn't your little link tell you if I'm dead?"

"Yes," he said, through gritted teeth. "I felt your pain. It felt like my own body was being ripped to shreds. And then it went silent."

I made to move past him, but he blocked me. "What am I supposed to say? I'm sorry the link was silent. I was dealing with more pressing issues, like staying alive. Besides, I heard you chirping in my head. You asked me if my friends' lives were more important than my own. You told me to take both daggers and run, leaving them defenseless."

"I told you to save yourself. The Mortal Trials are no game, Lirahna. You can't hope to stay alive *and* save your friends. There are no winners. No friendships. There are only survivors."

"I don't want to survive if I lose those most important to me in the process."

"That's a fool's answer."

"Then I am a fool. Let me pass. I have been traipsing the forest for three days. I need to eat. I need to sleep. I need to see a godsdamned medic."

"Are you hurt?"

"I'm fine. I took impid root, but I've lost a lot of blood. I need water, and I need to rest. I don't have the strength to be standing in the courtyard having it out with you. I'm alive. Can you let me go now?"

He took a step closer, crowding my space, his scent hitting me for the first time in days. "You're angry with me."

Despite the swelling of rage in my chest, I hated how my body drew instinctively toward his. It made me even more enraged. I wanted to reach for the blade at his side and sink it into his neck. I wanted to cut him where it would hurt the most.

"Are you serious? My friend is dead because of the challenge you set. Because you commanded the sprites not to help us. Because you kidnapped us to compete in challenges no one asked to be a part of. I'm not angry, I'm fucking *furious*!" I shoved away from him, pushing my legs to stalk off. I just had to make it to the med hall and then I could collapse.

Kilian had the fucking gall to reach for my arm, gripping it firmly enough to whirl me back around. His voice was soft when he said, "Not everyone is going to survive these challenges, Lirah. They're not meant to."

It was the straw that broke my back.

I hadn't even had time to mourn Anama. To grieve the loss of what had truly happened in the forest. And he was implying... what? That everyone I had come to know and love here would die trying to pass the Trials? The thought of anything happening to Lana or Moric made me see red. Sleep deprivation and hunger clouded my vision, anger blossoming into an unruly, wild monster, woken from a century-long slumber.

I wrenched my arm from his grip. The voice I used was colder than any summit snow. "The problem with you elven is that you think you're so much better than mortals. Our lives may be fragile, and death may be on the precipice each moment we breathe, but it takes strength to be mortal. To love, in spite of the overarching threat of death at any minute. To forge real, genuine friendships with no expectation of receiving anything in return. To share in sorrow and loss. To *feel*."

Kilian's eyes darkened. "You think we do not feel? That we are incapable of love, friendship or grief?"

"I don't think it. I *know* it. We have something you will never understand."

"What's that?" he snarled.

I leaned closer to him as I drove my point home. "Humanity. And I feel so fucking sorry for you."

I turned on my heel before he could respond and stalked toward the med hall, ignoring the rage radiating from him and fizzling in my own veins.

I slept for two days straight.

At least that's what Midius told me when I eventually woke. My body had been so low on nutrients and energy that I had awoken attached to a drip and there was a feeding tube stuck inside my stomach. It was a miracle I had even managed to make it up the steps to the med hall before collapsing on a bed beside Lana and Moric.

My friends had woken up a few hours before me. They sat on the side of my bed, Lana drinking juice from a carton, while Midius removed all the various tubes and needles from my body.

"We were the last group to make it back," Moric said after Midius bustled off. "Two others from the first group didn't make it."

That brought the total mortals remaining to nine.

"Were all the groups in the Forests of Dalhur?" I asked, still groggy.

"Two were sent up to the summits," Moric said. "But Rayna's group were in the forest. They were the first to find their keys."

"Kilian was here when I woke up," Lana volunteered.

"Oh?" I sat up, stretching my stiff limbs. "Doing what?"

"Just watching you. Snapped at Midius a few times. He left when he noticed I was awake."

I frowned. "Weird. He probably wanted to make sure I didn't die before the second challenge."

"Probably," Lana agreed.

I hesitated for a moment, not sure I wanted the answer to the question I was going to ask. "Anama... What's going to happen to her body?"

Moric sucked in a sharp breath. He looked gaunt and exhausted. "I asked Ayden, my instructor, about it. He said he doubted there'd be anything left of her to find."

My eyes closed, stomach churning. Yeah, I shouldn't have asked.

"Her stuff was packed up and incinerated since she had no immediate family in Kraventhorn to send it off to," Moric added.

"Right," I said feebly. I didn't know what to do with the pain in my heart. Maybe there would come a time when I would be brave enough to deal with it all. Now was not it.

I had to prepare for the second challenge, only four days away. Which was how I found myself pinned by Lana in the sparring room the next day, for the third time in a row.

"When did you become so good at this?" I grumbled, rolling the arm Lana had trapped behind my back. My blocking and dodging had improved somewhat, but I was still dreadful at the attacking maneuvers.

She stepped lithely back into position. "Septimus has been training me. We've been practicing our magic too."

I raised a brow at her. "Is that all he's been doing with you?"

The blush that crept along Lana's cheek was sinful.

I smacked my foot against the rubber mat and swatted at her. "Solana, you have been withholding information. Out with it. Now."

"I think I hate my full name even more than the nicknames," Lana groaned. "But okay, fine. If you must know… last night, after dinner… he kissed me. There, happy?"

She made to turn, but I stepped in front of her. "I thought you hated him?"

She rolled her eyes. "I don't have to like him to make out with him, you know? Besides, have you *seen* him?"

"Yes. Septimus is hot. I get it. But Lana…" I knew it wasn't my place, and I didn't want to project my anger toward Kilian onto her, but I felt like shaking her awake. "They're responsible for Anama's death."

Lana's eyes flashed with pain, and she nodded, sitting cross-legged on the mat. I sat down beside her, my hands resting idly on my knees.

"I was there when Anama died too," Lana began. "You don't need to tell me. I know the elven are responsible. They're responsible for this entire sick game we're playing. But at the end of the day, we're here to turn elven. And being here, making friends, we've lost sight of that. Even if you don't like it, you need to get your head around it and start accepting the fact that not all of us are going to make it."

She sounded exactly like Kilian. I gritted my teeth, anger bubbling as I prepared a retort.

"Don't give me that look," Lana said, her entire demeanor way calmer than mine. "I lost a friend as well."

"It doesn't seem like you cared all that much about her."

Lana flinched like I had hit her. "Don't you dare say that. I cared for Anama as much as I care for Moric. For *you*. She was part of our survival squad. And I am so godsdamned heartbroken that she died. But the reality is, I might die too. And you, or Moric. And there is nothing in the entire world we can do to prevent it. Life is so fleeting; we need to make the most of it. So, if I want to kiss the hot elven, I'm going to do it while I still can."

I shook my head slowly. I knew, deep in my bones, that she was right. But it didn't make processing things any easier. "I don't know how to cut my emotions off like that, Lana."

"It's not about cutting anything off. It's about accepting your feelings and knowing when to let go of the things you can't control."

I rose to my feet, restless and still annoyed. "I'm going to grab something to eat. Are you coming?"

Lana shook her head, her eyes far away. I thought maybe I had crossed the line, but I was too irritated to apologize.

She extended her legs in front of her, her gaze not meeting mine. "I'm going to take a minute to stretch. Carry on. I'll catch up with you later."

I left the sparring room and headed upstairs to the mess hall. Moric was already seated in his usual spot, a plate of chicken and potatoes before him. He looked haggard and dark circles rounded his eyes. Rayna sat a few seats down, her lighter in hand. She flicked the wheel, staring sourly at the flame before releasing it. Her cut had healed, finally, but she looked like she had aged ten years since last week.

As I slid into the seat across from Moric, I felt a slight pull at the back of my mind. A gentle tug that seemed to whisper my name. I lifted my gaze to find Kilian seated across the mess hall with the other elven, his eyes locked on me. A steady fire stoked the anger that was always present whenever he was near.

Can we talk? The voice was faint but unmistakably his as it scraped along the walls of my mind. I hated this stupid link. Hated that he could hop into my mind whenever he pleased. But just because he could, didn't mean I had to acknowledge it. I decided to ignore him.

Ripping my gaze from his, I stared down at the food that had appeared on my plate.

"How've you been?" Moric asked, oblivious to my inner turmoil.

I shrugged. "About the same as you, I guess."

"So, shit, then."

"You also having trouble sleeping?" I stabbed at a crispy potato before stuffing it in my mouth.

"I keep seeing that arrow-tailed lancer."

My eyes shuttered, the potato turning to ash in my mouth. "I know what you mean." I sometimes expected my hands to still be covered in Anama's blood. "It will take time to heal from that kind of trauma."

"I just keep thinking about how that could have been any one of us. It could have been me at the bottom of that river, right now. And I don't know what's scarier," he whispered. "Knowing that what's left of Anama is down there, or the relief that it's not me."

I forced my food down my throat, my appetite vanishing. Speaking to Lana had left me frustrated, but speaking with Moric made me feel... disgusted.

I pushed away from the table. "I'm tired," I told him, "I'm going to head back to my room."

He nodded, staring blankly at his food. Just as he had been before I had entered the mess hall.

Rayna looked up at me as I passed. "I heard about what happened during your challenge."

I just stared at her, waiting for her to continue.

"Losing your teammate sucks. But they're saying you killed the monster. Is it true?" There was a flciker of respect in her gray eyes.

"I had help."

"I heard it nearly took out your arm. That took guts, Aldhur. I shouldn't have doubted you."

I blinked. "Thank you?"

Rayna shrugged, turning back to her chicken, a small smile on her lips. "Don't get too cocky. You're officially competition."

I couldn't help the swell of pride in my chest at the recognition. It disappeared, however, as I rounded the corner of the mess hall and collided straight into the solid brick wall that was Kilian Valhan.

I sighed, looking up at him. "Can I help you?"

"Can you help me?" he repeated slowly. "Did you miss the part where I asked to speak to you?"

"No. I got that. I just ignored it. I thought it was quite obvious. Do you need me to spell it out for you?"

His eyes narrowed dangerously. "I would choose your next words *very* carefully, Lirahna."

"Or what?" I scoffed. "You'll kidnap me and stick me in a deadly round of challenges where I'm forced to watch my friends die before bleeding nearly to death in a cave while a mole creature viciously attacks me? Oh, wait, you've already done that."

I sidestepped him neatly and stomped down the corridor. He kept pace with me easily. "Look, I get you're upset with me, but we're linked for the duration of the Trials. You need to get over this and let me train you."

"Get over this? My friend died. *I* nearly died. It's not something you just 'get over'. It's actually fucking pointless explaining any of it to you." I exhaled. "Unless you're here to tell me everything I need to know about the second Trial, there's nothing else for us to talk about."

"You need training. If you hadn't drawn from the link, you really would be dead right now."

"But I did, and I survived. *Without* your training."

"You were lucky in the caves to have channeled my magic the way you did. It was an instinctual response, but it won't always be like that. You can't channel out of fear. Let me teach you."

I halted outside my room, spinning around to face him. "Teach me what? How to abandon my friends and desert my humanity? If I ever want lessons on being a fucking prick, you're the first person I'll come to, don't worry."

He slammed his hands against the door, pinning me between it and him. His forehead dipped until his eyes were parallel with mine. Eyes that burned with silver fire. "I am not your enemy."

"Sure as hell feels like it."

He breathed deeply, as if he were asking the gods for patience. I knew how he felt. His frustration was mine. His wrath and fury matched my own, twin flames to a pyre. He stared deep into my eyes, so deep I thought he might be looking straight into my soul. "You will let me train you."

I shook my head, my lips curling into a harsh smile I hadn't even known I was capable of. Kilian made me feel things, act in a way I never had before. Everything was so heightened around him, I felt like a fucking livewire each time he was nearby. Like I might explode if he so much as touched me. It made me livid.

"I would rather die during the second challenge than spend one minute with you."

Instead of recoiling, as I had expected, Kilian smirked. A mirror to my own cruel smile. "Your words bite. But you forget that this link is reciprocal."

"Then you will know for certain how much I loathe you."

He chuckled, a deep masculine sound that resounded along my bones. I wanted to capture it in a musical box and play it forever. "You know, I don't think you do. In fact," he said, and, to my horror, dipped his face lower so that his nose brushed the side of my cheek, his breath a soft whisper on my flesh. "I think you quite like this."

I swallowed, frozen in place against the door. I realized that I was holding my breath. I didn't want to breathe in his scent. I knew the second I did it would be over for me. "I fucking *hate* you."

His lips pressed gently against the hollow beneath my cheekbone, skating along the skin toward my jaw. "What about now?"

"Now?" I couldn't breathe. I was suffocating. Thoughts no longer existed inside my incoherent mess of a brain. There was only feeling. And gods, did I feel. What he was doing to me was excruciating. I struggled to remember exactly what I had been mad at him about.

"Mm." The rumble in his throat vibrated through me, and my thighs clenched involuntarily.

"I – I don't know."

"You don't know? But you were so *sure*, Lirah."

My shortened name on his lips undid me. I breathed. And instantly regretted it. He was peppermint and leather, the saltwater of the ocean and power so heady it disoriented me. His scent was so utterly Kilian. And it consumed me. I wanted to drink it from a bottle and then find the source, so I could guzzle straight from it.

His lips trailed along my jawbone, skirting the underside and my traitorous neck *lifted*. Only an inch, but it lifted, granting him access to my thin, vulnerable skin, and the heartbeat he could undoubtedly feel hammering away beneath.

"I–"

All thoughts vanished entirely as his teeth grazed the dip beneath my ear, his tongue sweeping instantly across the spot. He sucked at the skin, drawing circles with his tongue and my knees... went... weak.

Lust clouded my vision, my eyes shutting as I gave way to the feeling, allowing it to consume me wholly. I needed more. I needed his body pressed against mine and fistfuls of his shirt in my hand. I needed his hair between my fingers and his face between–

"Your friends are coming," he murmured, dragging his mouth back up to my cheek. He pulled away slowly. His eyes were hooded, a smug smirk on his lips.

"If you won't train with me, I'll send someone else. But you *will* train, Lirah." And then he was walking away, as if he hadn't just assaulted my neck in the most tantalizing way and left me completely breathless. "And I'm still waiting for that paperweight you stole."

"Asshole," I muttered.

His answering chuckle set my blood on fire.

CHAPTER 11

I awoke in a panicked fever, sweat trickling down my nape. I stared around my room, but it was pitch dark. When I closed my eyes again, I saw gleaming yellow eyes and blood on my hands.

I pried my eyes open. My legs were tangled in the sheets. Yanking the covers off, I crossed to where a sphere of artificial light the elven seemed to favor over candles – orblight, I'd learned it was called – sat in a sconce. I ran my hand over the cool globe and soft light filled the space.

No arrow-tailed lancer. No blood. Just white sheets, a nondescript dresser and Calendula, curled up on the side of the desk, fast asleep.

My stomach gave a loud grumble. I couldn't go back to sleep. Not when my mind was so agitated. I needed a walk. A midnight snack or a glass of warm milk with honey, like Umma used to make when I could not sleep.

I glanced down at the pajama set I wore – a soft flannel top with matching bottoms – before deciding that I didn't care if anyone saw me. I doubted anyone would still be up and roaming the corridors in the middle of the night, anyway.

I slipped quietly from the room, careful not to disturb Calendula, and made my way to the mess hall upstairs.

As anticipated, it was deserted. The benches stretched out through the space, orblight floating dimly above them. It was eerie, standing in the empty hall with nothing but my thoughts for company. I shrugged off the feeling as I took a seat at one of the tables and waited.

Usually, the food appeared before me. As if it knew I were there, waiting. But now, nothing happened. I tapped a foot against the stone and envisioned warm milk. My nose scrunched in concentration and my eyes squeezed shut. Still, nothing.

I didn't know exactly how the food situation worked here. I was annoyed at myself for not caring enough to figure it out. Perhaps meals were only delivered at designated mealtimes. In which case, I would have to just suck it up and go back to bed.

"What are you doing?"

I swiveled around to stare at the door.

Kilian leaned against the threshold, one ankle casually crossed over the other. He was not dressed for bed. But he did not look ready for battle like usual either. He wore a deep black shirt that hugged the contours of his frame and dark pants. Heavy boots completed his ensemble.

My cheeks burned as I remembered our earlier encounter. I doused my embarrassment in irritation. "Why are you everywhere I go?"

He raised a brow. "In my own home?"

I rolled my eyes. "I forget, sometimes, that this is your house and not a prison for us mortals."

He scoffed. "Good one."

I watched as he uncrossed his ankle and strode toward me. Unhurried. Unbothered. Unaffected.

I swallowed as he took a seat beside me, facing the opposite direction. He leaned his elbows on the table behind him and stared up at the ceiling. I gazed at the broad column of his throat and wondered what it would taste like.

I tore my eyes from him as quickly as the thought flitted through my mind.

He looked at me like he knew exactly what I had thought. Thanks to the link, he probably did.

"What do you want?" I asked, resignation chafing my words.

"I want to know what you're doing up here this late at night when you should be resting."

I sighed. "If you must know, I had a bad dream."

He nodded, understanding, or something akin to sympathy, in his eyes. It was an expression I was unfamiliar with.

"What happened in it?" he asked.

I dug my nails into my palms, unfurled my fingers slowly, repeated the motion. "The arrow-tailed lancer... I watched it kill Anama, just as it had during the first Trial. And then I watched it devour Moric. And drown Lana." I shut my eyes against the flashing mental images, grainy and hazy now, but in the dream, everything had felt so real.

He placed his warm, callused fingers over one of my hands, enveloping it. His thumb ran along the inside of my wrist. "It was just a dream."

I nodded, hastily scrubbing my free hand across my cheek to swipe at the errant tear that had fallen. I hated how emotional the dream had made me. I hated that I was being this vulnerable around him. That he was comforting me, likely out of pity. I tried willing shields of ice and rock around me, but I was too tired tonight. My heart hurt too much.

So, I let him hold my hand, his thumb stroking gently along my skin.

"I have bad dreams too," Kilian said gently.

I looked at him then. Really looked at him. I saw the dark circles beneath his eyes, the haphazard mess of his hair, the shadow sprouting along his jaw. Tonight, he looked like he had seen several centuries and carried the weight of the world on his shoulders.

"What do you dream about?" I whispered, half-afraid he wouldn't tell me. Half-afraid he would.

He tipped his head back up to the ceiling and released a breath. "Gods and monsters."

"That doesn't sound too bad," I said, a halfhearted attempt to lighten the mood.

"No. I suppose it doesn't." He turned back to me, pressed his lips together like he was debating what he would say next. "You know, I am sorry. About your friend. And for being an asshole about it after the challenge."

I blinked. "Did you just... apologize?"

He shrugged. "I understand it wasn't the appropriate time to discuss the odds of survivability then."

I shook my head. "It wasn't about that, though. The way you treat us... it's like we're pawns in a game of chess. Like our lives matter less than yours. It's how you expect me to perform in these Trials. To forsake my morals, the friendships and loyalties I've formed here. To let others die while I continue to live. I cannot carelessly absolve myself of the guilt as easily as you can."

He gave me a level stare. Quiet rage scraped at the boundary of my mind. "You think my guilt doesn't eat me alive? That I go to sleep at night at peace with what I've had to do? Trust me, my guilt has not been absolved by a long shot. But… I do value the lives of mortals. Far more than you will ever realize."

My lip curled distrustfully. His words sounded sincere, but his actions proved otherwise. And it was giving me a headache, staring at him as if I would be able to see the answers to all my questions if I simply looked hard enough.

"You do realize you can just let us all go, right?" I suggested. "If you feel so bad about the Trials."

"I said I valued mortal life, not that I disagree with the necessity of the Trials. The two are mutually inclusive."

"Have I told you how much I hate it when you speak in riddles?"

He looked like he was thinking. "Hm. You've told me how much you hate *me*, so I gather it's included in that package, but if you want to go into specifics on what it is you hate about me, then please, by all means, continue."

Fine, I could go into specifics.

"I hate your house."

He looked around the mess hall, brows drawn. "Why? What's wrong with it?"

"It's too big. Too minimalistic. There's no personality to it."

"Why does it matter whether there's personality to it? It serves its purpose."

"Yes, but it's not a *home*."

"I never claimed it to be one."

"Why do we all have to live here?"

"As opposed to…? Where else would you have me put thirteen mortals where I can simultaneously monitor their treatment and ensure they're training adequately?"

I rolled my eyes. "I hate how argumentative you are."

"Some might call it banter."

"Banter is supposed to be fun. It's not supposed to feel like banging your head against a wall."

"Speak for yourself. I'm having fun," he said dryly. His face was a blank mask, his body all serious lines and unrelenting edges. He didn't look like he'd know the definition of fun if it smacked him in the face.

"I hate the link."

"That I do know. But it did save your life in the caves, so a little gratitude might be nice."

I clenched my teeth. "After *you* put me there."

"Irrelevant."

"I didn't mean to draw from it."

"But you did. And you enjoyed how the power felt."

I glared at him. "Those are private thoughts and feelings."

"They belong to me now."

Anger hissed inside of me like a whistling teapot. "You can't just *do* that. It's not fair, and, in fact, it's emotionally manipulative. You've already kidnapped me. You can't also follow me around and demand I talk to you, listen in on my thoughts or kiss me in hallways."

He raised his brows, amused now. "That wasn't a kiss. I could provide a demonstration if you'd like to do a comparison?"

My cheeks flushed, interest stirring inside of me at his suggestion. "No, thank you," I said primly. "My point is, I'm in a vulnerable position and you're using the situation to take advantage of me."

"It's not *my* fault you're not using the link to your advantage. I keep telling you, it's reciprocal. Maybe if you let me train you, you might be able to find out some useful information. Maybe then there wouldn't be so much of a *power imbalance.*"

"It won't be that easy and you know it," I insisted.

"You'll never know if you don't try," he said in an infuriatingly self-explanatory way.

"*Or* you could just tell me what I need to know," I said firmly.

"But then you'll never learn how to properly channel the magic."

I considered it. All the extra hours we would have to spend together for any meaningful training to occur. Just him and I, nothing but his scent, his voice, his eyes, his all-consuming energy. I thought of his lips on my jaw, how much I'd enjoyed it despite the multitude of reasons why I shouldn't have, and decided that I vehemently did not trust myself around him in a hallway, let alone in dedicated training sessions. Training with him might save my life, but it would not be without a cost. And my heart was too high a price.

I sighed, officially giving up on this exhausting game of tug of war that had no good ending for me.

He tilted his head toward me. "You hate me now, but I think…" He paused, and it was the first time I had seen him struggle for words. Eventually, he said, "I think if you had met me in a different time, in a different place, far from here, you might have actually liked me."

"Maybe," I said. "If you weren't intent on putting me and my friends in jeopardy for Trials you cannot tell me the purpose of."

He gave a grave nod. "Maybe then."

I slanted my head, mirroring his position. "Since we're talking fictional worlds, what else would happen?"

A soft smile caressed the corners of his lips. "Am I elven in this pretend scenario?"

"Oh, no. You'd be mortal."

He snorted. "Okay, sure. Well, if I were mortal, I'd live every day like it were my last. I'd feel my fleeting mortality. I would relish in every single second of it because there is magic in having your days numbered. There is a gift in knowing that you must spend your time wisely and do the things you truly want to because your days are limited. Immortality strips you of that sense of time. It desensitizes you."

I chewed on my lip. "You're right. In this make-believe world, I might have liked the mortal version of you."

"I knew you would." Kilian released his grip on my hand.

I had been so absorbed in our conversation that I had forgotten he was still holding my hand. The absence of his touch left my skin cold. With it came stark realization.

What was I doing, sitting in the mess hall, entertaining a conversation with him, listening to him talk about how things might be if he were not elven?

He *was* elven. And I was mortal. There was no other version of life. No alternative reality where he was not the villain in my story.

"I should go." I stood, my hunger a distant memory. All I wanted now was to leave this hall, to get away from his piercing gaze that saw too much.

He gave a reluctant nod. "You should get some rest."

I didn't look back when I left. I didn't want to see if his gaze followed me through the hall, or if he had returned to staring up at the ceiling, looking as troubled as I felt.

When I reached my room, I collapsed back in the sheets, my thoughts churning over our conversation. When I finally drifted off to sleep, I dreamed of silver eyes and a soft smile.

CHAPTER 12

I was awake and dressed before the crack of dawn, a fiery determination singing in my bones.

I couldn't believe I had talked for so long with Kilian the night before. I had let him hold my hand and speak about his dreams like a besotted teenager. So what if his little monologue about his envisioned mortal life was moving? It didn't make him less responsible for everything that had happened since Augustine.

Valhan House was dead quiet as I exited through the courtyard, not a soul stirring. I tied my hair into a high knot above my head and stretched. I pulled at my hamstrings, the muscles aching. And then I ran.

The air was cold, the mountain snow drifting like someone had tipped a snow globe upside down. It ripped at my exposed flesh, the cold turning the tips of my fingers pale, but I thought that maybe my body was beginning to adjust somewhat to the chill. I pushed my muscles just as I had in the woods, running faster and faster. I ran for Anama and the pain she had endured. I ran from the shitty things I had said to Lana, things I could never take back. I ran from the confusing, messy emotions I felt toward Kilian, who got under my skin like no one else ever had. And I ran for the girl who had died the moment she was taken from Serila. I ran for me.

My muscles burned as I reached Pyxis. I leaned against the library wall to catch my breath.

"You're still wearing it," a female voice called.

I looked up to find the elven who had gifted me the protection bracelet. The charm dangled from my wrist, silver catching in the light.

"Yes," I replied. "Thank you for it."

"Did it work like it was supposed to?"

"I don't–" I began, but… I was still alive. "Yes. It did."

The elven smiled. "I am glad. The upper magic is potent, it should keep you safe from all sorts of dangers and malevolent spells."

"You mentioned that it did not belong to you. Who did it belong to?"

The female paused in arranging her stock. "Another mortal girl, who dwelled here so long ago only the trees and the old elven of Lomask remember."

A mortal. There was only ever one reason why a mortal would set foot on Lortan.

"She died in the Trials," I whispered.

"Yes." The elven nodded. "A tragic loss of life. You remind me of her. She, too, had fire in her eyes and a restless soul. I hope this bracelet serves you better than it did her."

That the female could glean so much of my soul intrigued me, but there was also sadness for the girl who had not survived.

I pulled my sleeve down, covering the bracelet, and the elven gave me an apologetic smile. "I'm sorry. I didn't mean to make you feel uncomfortable."

"It's fine. Thank you again." I pushed off the brick wall, ignoring the stab in my heart as I recalled that the last time I had been here was with my friends. It felt like everywhere I looked there was a reminder of death.

I sprinted back to Valhan House, not pausing to catch my breath. There would be no time to rest if something was chasing me. My muscles and lungs had to learn.

So, I pushed, and I ran. Chasing nothing and everything.

Sweat was streaming down my brow by the time I returned. At the sight of the archway, I swore. I should have never left Pyxis. A golden-eyed elven, dressed in sparring leathers, was waiting in the courtyard. "You're late."

"You've got to be fucking kidding me," I muttered. "He sent *you* to train me?"

"Expecting someone else?" Septimus drawled. "Trust me, there are places I'd much rather be."

"Like my best friend's bed?"

He gave me a wicked grin the devil himself would be proud of. "How quickly you catch on."

"Fetch Syrina. I'd rather train with her."

"Syrina's mortal is dead. She is visiting friends in Dalhur."

I flinched at the casualness in Septimus' tone. Syrina's *mortal* had been Anama. "Fuck you."

Septimus grinned. "*Aaaand* there she is. Kilian told me you were giving him a hard time, but I said, 'No way. Not sweet little Lirahna.'"

"I'm not sweet."

"No," he agreed, "You're rather prickly. But that's not my business."

"*None* of this is your business. Go back inside and leave me alone. Tell Kilian that if he wants me to train, I will do it by myself."

Septimus lifted two fingers, dropping one on each count. "One: I don't know if you've seen yourself train, but you're kind of shit. And two: I don't take orders from you."

I ignored his jab. "You just take orders from Kilian? Then be a good little golden retriever and run back to your master and tell him I'm not playing this game."

Septimus whistled, long and low. "Someone's in a bad mood this morning. You know, exercise is supposed to release endorphins. Maybe you need to take another lap."

"What I *need* is for you to disappear."

"Are you about done?" Septimus' golden eyes were light with amusement. If I had hoped to rile him up, I had not succeeded. In fact, he looked downright entertained. "Because we can banter all day long. I don't have any plans until tomorrow morning."

The elven needed to attend a seminar on what was considered banter, because they had a warped idea of it.

I groaned. "What do I have to do to get you to stop speaking?"

Septimus jerked his head toward the house. "Come for a walk with me. I can't promise I'll stop talking, but I'll make it worth your while."

I gave him a skeptical look. "A walk?"

"Yes, Lirahna. It's when you put one foot in front of the other and–"

"Gods, you're insufferable. What exactly will make this worth my while?"

Septimus considered me for a moment, finger tapping playfully against his chin. "Hmm. What does Lirahna Aldhur want most desperately? Perhaps, the answers to some of her burning questions?" Septimus held his hand to his heart. "I solemnly swear that if you are obedient and do your best to follow my training instructions this morning, I will truthfully answer any three questions you have."

I rolled my eyes at him. "You're lying."

"Am not."

"Fine. Then tell me, what's the second challenge?"

Septimus tutted. "You didn't listen to my rules. I said I will answer any three questions if you follow my training instructions. Have you followed them yet?"

"No," I grumbled.

"Very good. Now." Septimus rubbed his hands together and golden sparks danced from his fingertips. "Let's go for that walk, shall we?"

I didn't have much of a choice but to trust he would hold up his end of the bargain; I had too many questions spinning around my head to pass up the opportunity. Following Septimus, my thoughts churned. When he did not turn left at the stairwell like I had expected him to, I said, "We're not going to the sparring room?"

Septimus shook his head. "I'm taking you somewhere I've only ever taken a few people. My favorite place in the entire world."

I wondered if he had taken Lana where he was leading me now. "What's the deal with you and Lana?" The question rose as I trudged behind him, past Valhan House and up a steep slope, the mountains a towering beast above us.

"Is that one of your questions?"

"No. Just curious, I guess. She's my best friend." I didn't know when that had happened, but somehow, Lana had wormed her way in and now she was the closest thing I had to family in this foreign land.

"And you want to know if my intentions are nefarious?"

"Not nefarious, just… I don't know. It's not my place. Forget I asked."

Septimus extended a hand to help me over a particularly jagged rock on the slope. "I like Lana. She reminds me of what it feels like to be young again."

Septimus hardly looked a day over twenty-five.

"How old are you, anyway?"

"So many questions from sweet little Lirahna."

I glared at him. "Stop calling me sweet."

"Of course," he mocked. "You're a vicious thing. Darkness scatters when you walk."

I puffed out a breath, my calves aching from my earlier run and the grueling hike up the slope. "Is climbing a cliff part of my training, or is this just for your own amusement?"

"Amusement," he sang. "We're not too far off, though. It's just a little farther up. And, for being such a great sport, I will answer one of your, hopefully very well thought-out, questions."

"What's the second challenge?" I repeated.

"It's one of wit and quick thinking."

Wit and quick thinking? "So, it's a mental challenge? Like a puzzle?"

"Is that your second question?"

I glowered at his back, "No. You're not playing fair. You said you'd answer truthfully."

"And I have," Septimus tossed over his shoulder. "It's not my fault your questions are vague."

I gave a frustrated huff. I should have known he would apply a loophole.

Septimus cleared the trail, stepping onto a small landing at the base of another towering mountain. He held his hand out once more, and I let him pull me up before he released his grip and slowly swiveled me around to take in the view.

I hadn't realized how high up the slope had stretched. Looking down, I could see the top of Valhan House and, beyond that, the city of Lomask. Dawn had barely broken, and pale light gilded the treetops and slated roofs of townhouses in the distance.

Septimus pointed a ringed finger to the left, where a tall building jutted out against the skyline. "That's Pyxis. And over there–" His hand swept right to where a thick forest sprouted.

"Those are the Forests of Dalhur. Beyond those lies Dalhur, the city of magic."

I breathed in deeply, taking it in. "I can see why this is your favorite place. Why did you bring *me* here?"

Septimus shrugged. "I thought you might feel more comfortable practicing lower magic up here than down there. It's less noisy."

That was weirdly considerate of him.

"You've been gifted a kernel of power through the sacred oath. Now, mortals can't practice upper magic – your bodies can't handle the current – but some have been known to perform lower magic, on occasion. I heard you already channeled during the first challenge?"

I nodded.

"So, this should be easy for you, then."

"It was… involuntary. I wasn't trying to cast magic."

"In times of stress, your body is capable of great feats," Septimus said. "I'm going to teach you how to draw on the power, the grain of magic gifted through the link, while your mind is in a quiet state. Often, we find that being emotional can lead to… volatile results. So, I'm going to ask you to close your eyes and focus on your breathing."

I did as he asked, my eyes shutting out the magnificent view in front of me. I breathed in, then out. But my mind was restless and my thoughts wandered, breaking off into smaller segments.

"Pull it back," Septimus guided. "You're not focusing. Try to find something to ground yourself in. Like the sounds of the birds. Or the feel of your lungs expanding and contracting."

I tried again, forcing my mind to quiet. To become as still as the snow on the peaks. It was difficult though, and each time I felt my mind inching toward calm, my thoughts intruded. There was simply too much to worry about. The second challenge was in a few days, I didn't have time to be practicing my breathing.

"Stop tapping your foot." Septimus sighed. "You're not grounding yourself properly. You need a still mind for this to work."

I loosened a breath, rolling my shoulders to expel the tension sitting in my muscles. Calming thoughts. What were calming thoughts? There was… one, I supposed. The memory flickered inside my head like a forgotten song. It was thirteen birthdays ago, when Umma had taught me how to bake a cake. She had handed me a leveler, the ingredients and a recipe card, and told me to follow the instructions. She had left the kitchen then, promising to return in exactly half an hour to see how I was managing.

It was the calmest I had ever felt, slowly measuring out the flour and the sugar, carefully whipping the batter and spooning it into the baking tray. Everything had a precise order, an exact measurement and place to go. And when it was done baking, Umma had proclaimed that it was the tastiest cake she had ever eaten.

A gentle wind brushed the strands of hair which had come undone near the base of my neck, and I relished in its cool kiss on my cheek. My breaths came deep and even. And somewhere, flickering inside my chest, something stirred.

"Follow the thread." Septimus' voice was soft and distant.

I tugged on the link and with each pull, a spool unraveled.

Hello, vicious, a voice cooed at the back of my mind, like silk. I startled, not expecting it. It was different to Kilian's voice, far darker, but not foreign. I was sure I had heard it before. *Have you come to greet me?*

My hand reached toward it, my fingers curling around nothingness.

"Let it come to you," Septimus urged.

The magic whirled and undulated, just beyond my reach. *How do you wish to wield me, wicked one?*

I recoiled, pulling my hand back. It rumbled inside me.

Have I offended you? it called, its voice soft as a slithering snake. *Being wicked is not so bad. Indeed, it is far better than being weak.*

My eyes snapped open. Septimus stood in front of me, his gaze on my upturned palm. Floating a few inches above my fingertips swirled a ball of darkness, no larger than a pomegranate seed.

It was fascinating, and I couldn't help staring at it in disbelief. The tiny orb felt warm above my hand, like an extension of my body. Its edges blurred, warping in different directions, whispering to me.

Use me.

Set me loose.

Let me destroy.

Maybe I was losing my mind, imagining a voice of pure midnight and bloodshed. I shook my hand out, the tether to the power breaking instantly. The shadow vanished.

"You were doing great. What happened?" If I didn't know better, I would say the concern on Septimus' face was genuine.

I shifted uneasily, feeling discomforted. Scared. Maybe my mortal mind was breaking under the weight of pressure and grief. If I told him I was hearing voices... granted, I didn't know everything, but I knew *that* wasn't normal. "I don't think the magic wants to help me. It feels... volatile."

Destructive and all-consuming, it felt like the type of world-ending, corrosive power I wanted nothing to do with. The kind that had no use in helping me survive the Trials.

"It does want to help. You just need to learn how to harness it. How to command it. It will obey you if you instruct and shape it to your will. You need practice."

I gave him a dubious look. "I appreciate you taking the time to bring me up here and teach me how to summon this power, but I really don't see how that – or lightning – is going to help me in a challenge of wit," I said.

"Don't think so short-term. You might find use for it another time, in another challenge. The power flowing through your veins is not merely darkness or lightning. You have a kernel of *Kilian's* power."

I raised a brow. "Is that not darkness and lightning?"

Septimus scoffed. "He'll be so offended if he hears that. Kilian's power is wrath and destruction. His power is rage and fury itself. It is death incarnate. It is not some flimsy lightning shower or shadow control. Those are merely manifestations of the power. Kilian could start wildfires and torrential floods. He could annihilate entire isles if he had his full power."

My gaze sharpened on him. "What do you mean?"

Septimus winced. "I wasn't supposed to say that."

The power that I had felt radiating from Kilian was so overwhelming, so electrifying and dizzying that I did not understand how it could not be his full power. "That's my second question. Explain yourself."

Septimus heaved a great sigh. He walked to the edge of the slope and lowered himself so that his legs dangled off its edge. He jerked his head for me to join him. I begrudgingly complied. When I was seated beside him, legs precariously swinging as I resisted the urge to claw back to safety, Septimus said, "There isn't a simple answer to your question."

"And yet you promised to answer."

He sighed again, a burdensome breath that seemed to take some of the light from his eyes with it. "Kilian, Syrina and I have been friends since inception."

This hadn't been the start I was expecting, but I waited, letting him gather his thoughts before he continued.

"Centuries ago, Kilian did something that pissed off some really high-powered beings. To punish him, there was a curse placed on him. On the three of us, really, when Syrina and I aided him. The curse… stripped us of our powers. Left only the barest traces behind. We searched across the entirety of Tarlor for a solution – for someone able to reverse the curse, but no one possessed the ability. We approached every single elven on Lortan and Greyhaven." A faraway look had glazed over those golden eyes.

My thoughts whirled as he spoke, frantically trying to fit the puzzle pieces into place. "If no one can help you undo the curse, then you'll be stuck forever, unable to access your full powers?"

Septimus nodded slowly. "Unless the person with the ability to undo it has not become elven yet."

Oh.

A ragged breath escaped my parted lips. The Mortal Trials… they weren't about turning mortals into elven. I had always suspected there was more to it than that. The entire purpose of the Trials was to find someone with the ability to undo a curse.

Holy fuck.

CHAPTER 13

My mind was reeling. Spinning at a thousand frames per second.

Septimus stood, shaking his head at the questions I hurled his way.

What had Kilian done?

Who had he angered?

Why?

Did they really feel so fucking entitled to restore their full powers that it was worth thirteen mortal lives every decade?

Why had every single elven simply accepted this barbaric practice just for a curse to be broken?

"I've already said far too much, Lirahna. We should head back to the house."

"You promised to answer three questions. You have not answered my third."

Septimus' eyes glowed. "You have asked plenty of questions this morning, and I have been extremely transparent with you. Consider our deal concluded. Now, you can follow me back down to Valhan House or you can remain here all day until a nanuuq comes to eat you. What do you choose?"

I considered my luck with the nanuuq, but ultimately, it wasn't Septimus I was mad at. I wanted to look Kilian himself in the eyes and ask him exactly what the fuck he had done and to whom.

"Don't even think about it." Septimus rolled his eyes, starting down the slope. "He's not here. He's away on business in Greyhaven. He'll be back the night before the second challenge."

I seethed the entire way back, not even saying goodbye to Septimus as we parted on the third floor of Valhan House. I stormed into my bedroom, slamming the door shut behind me.

Calendula jerked awake from her hammock with a start. "Gods above, you scared me."

I gave her an apologetic look, pausing my frustration momentarily to say, "I didn't know you were sleeping."

"I'm always either sleeping or eating." Calendula yawned. "What's got you so wound up?"

"What do you think?" I flopped onto my bed.

Calendula grimaced. "I thought you two were getting along fine. What happened?"

I assumed she was referring to Kilian and me. "Why would you think we were getting along?"

The shadow sprite's wings fluttered, a nervous tell. "I, uhm… I saw the two of you in the corridor last night. It didn't look like you were… *un*happy."

Oh, for fuck's sake. I threw a pillow over my face and screamed.

Calendula said something, but it was muffled by the pillow. I plucked it off and looked at her. "What did you say?"

Calendula huffed impatiently. "I said, don't be upset with him because of Elena. He's been over her for decades."

"What?"

"Elena," Calendula repeated. "That's why you're upset at him, right?"

At the look I gave her, she dropped her face into her hands and groaned, "He's going to exile me to the other side of the Shadow Soil for sure now."

"Calendula," I said firmly, "who is Elena?"

She peeked out through tiny fingers, silver eyes flicking to the bracelet dangling from my wrist.

And everything clicked into place.

The words spoken by the elven female this morning. The recognition in Kilian's eyes as he held the charm on my wrist. No. Not recognition. Sadness.

"He gave this to her, didn't he?" I whispered. Elena. The mortal girl with fire in her eyes and a restless soul.

I unclipped the bracelet and laid it on the table, unable to bear the sight of it. Unable to process how I felt about it.

Calendula's wings fluttered gently. She laid a small hand atop the bracelet, fondly. "She was one of my favorites."

"What does it mean?" I asked dully, my gaze trained on the engraved wording on the back of the pendant.

Calendula did not need to look at it. She murmured, "*'May the fire within protect you throughout.'*"

I didn't say anything. I *couldn't* say anything.

Every look, every touch ever shared between Kilian and I turned to ash and sawdust. Our conversation last night… Was I just the latest mortal in a century-long string? A means to pass the time in an otherwise dreadfully boring immortal existence? I had known from the start that Kilian could not be interested in me beyond the short term. But I had to give him credit. He had played the part of dedicated instructor well. He had stared at me like he saw me. Had spoken to me like an equal. And touched me like he wanted me. He had manipulated *me* into wanting *him*. It was such a clever scheme, all to ensure that I did not run or refuse to participate in the Trials. So that his candidate tried her very best to pass the challenges, to make it to the Rite, and break his curse.

And then, when he regained his full power, he would have no further use for me. He would leave me discarded and wanting and ruined forever.

But not if I discarded him first.

I schooled my expression into one of abject neutrality. "Calendula. I'm feeling a bit strained from my training with Septimus this morning. Would you mind giving me a few moments of mortal privacy?"

"Of course," the shadow sprite said, "I'll come back again in a few hours, if that's fine?"

"Perfect." I feigned a yawn, stretching my back muscles out.

The sprite blended into shadow, disappearing completely. I didn't know how she did that. It was like she became darkness itself, vanishing wholly.

As soon as she was gone, I stood. I rifled through my drawers, grabbing a new set of clothing before heading to the bathroom. Fifteen minutes later, my hair had been washed, and I no longer smelled like I had run five miles then trekked up a mountain. I changed into a violet, corset-shaped leather cuirass and pants, foregoing my usual tunic, leaving only a fleece-lined long-sleeve beneath so I didn't freeze to death when I stepped outside. Lacing up my boots, I decided to leave my dark hair unbound. The steam from the shower had curled the ends so that they just barely skimmed my waist.

I didn't know where I was going. But I knew I was not going to sit around Valhan House, stewing on the fact that Kilian had played me like a fiddle. Even worse, that I had let him. He was elven. I had no one to blame but myself, for letting my emotions and hormones override logic and common sense.

I grabbed my cloak and pulled open the door, stepping into the hallway at the exact moment Lana stepped out of her room. I hadn't seen her since our argument yesterday in the sparring room.

She scanned me from head to foot. "You look hot. Where are you going?"

"Out. Do you want to come?"

Lana's eyes widened slightly. "Out where?"

"I don't know." I lifted my arms slightly. "Lomask is our oyster."

She smiled. "Okay. Give me a second to change."

Five minutes later, I was seated at the foot of Lana's bed, watching as she swiped rouge over her cheeks.

"Where did you even get that?" I tilted my head toward the pink palette in her hand.

"I packed it before I left home. It was my mom's."

"Three elven arrived to kidnap you for the Mortal Trials and you brought makeup with you?"

Lana rolled her eyes. "It's not *just* makeup, you insensitive ass. It's sentimental. It reminds me of home. Now, close your eyes and let me put some on you."

"Oh, no. It's fine, Lana–" I started to protest, but she wouldn't hear any of it.

"If we're going out, you need blush," was all she said as she patted the creamy formula on the apples of my cheeks and then rubbed some on her ring finger before applying it carefully to my lips. "All done," she pronounced, stepping back to survey her handiwork.

I glanced at her work in the mirror above the small sink and, surprisingly, did not hate it.

"I think I know where we can go," she said, stripping her own tunic off and rifling in her dresser. She pulled out a pastel blue piece that perfectly matched the shade of her eyes. A mischievous look glinted in them, and I couldn't help but smile at her.

"Where?"

An hour later, we were seated in a raucous tavern. There were no windows in the space, only dim lighting and tables coated in glistening, sticky fluid. Elven sat on nearly every wooden bench, playing card games or drinking, or playing card games *while* drinking. Beautiful elven females perched on the laps of males, and all of them were either too drunk or engrossed in their games to pay attention to the two mortals who had just entered.

"How did you find this place?" I hissed at Lana as she sashayed up to the elven behind the bar. He was a stunning male, with sapphire eyes and shaggy brown hair that curled delicately around the pierced, pointed tips of his ears.

"Septimus showed it to me on one of our walks through the city," she replied.

One of their walks? How many walks had there been? I cursed myself for not being a better friend and just asking her.

"And," she added, "he told me I was *never* to come in here by myself." She gave me a roguish wink before turning a dazzling smile on the bartender. "We're mortals, if it wasn't already obvious. We might die at any second during the Trials, so could you spare us a drink? One that, obviously, isn't poisonous. I'd hate to cut my time in Lomask short over a cocktail. You can put them on Septimus Mori's tab."

The bartender surveyed Lana appreciatively. "For a pretty thing like you, I've got as many drinks as you want. Take a seat over there." He pointed to an empty booth I hadn't noticed before, in the corner of the tavern. "I'll bring them over soon."

It was hot inside, and I slung my cloak over the side of the booth before sliding in, careful not to touch the greasy table.

Loud music pumped throughout the room, and it was hard to think over the noise. Which was fine. I didn't want to think about anything.

"What prompted this?" Lana shouted across the table.

I wanted to tell her everything. I really did. But this was not the place to do it. "I just needed to get out of the house. It was suffocating me."

"I know what you mean." Lana leaned forward as our drinks came. They were bright blue, and the shimmery powder swirling within made them glow in the dim light. The side of the glass read *Third's Whiskers*.

I didn't bother asking the bartender what was in the drinks before lifting one up to Lana and clinking the side of my glass against hers.

"To surviving the Mortal Trials," she said.

"To surviving."

I lifted the cup and drank deeply. The cocktail was deliciously cool, and tasted of fruit and summer. It did something wonderful to my insides, turning them warm and fuzzy. The music no longer felt as loud as it had when we had entered the tavern and Lana, beautiful Lana, fractured into a kaleidoscope of colors before me.

Before long, Lana ordered a second round.

"I'm so sorry." I clasped her hand after she had placed our order. "For being such a shitty friend. I was wrong about Septimus. He's a decent elven." I meant it, too. The drink, as much as it had made my insides fuzzy, had given me alarming mental clarity. Septimus had been the only one to actually tell me the true purpose of the Mortal Trials.

Lana beamed at me. "I *knew* you'd like him once you got to know him. And, oh my gods, Lirah, can he kiss! I swear I nearly collapsed the first time."

"The *first* time?" I squealed. I felt so blissfully free, talking to Lana about trivial things. Worries had escaped me, the weight of the Trials, Anama's death and Kilian's secrets a distant memory. It was just me and my friend.

I sipped on the sweet liquid, savoring the taste of the alcohol on my tongue. "What was it like?"

Lana cupped a hand beneath her chin, a dreamy look on her face. "You know when you're asleep and you have that dream where you're falling but then you suddenly wake up?"

"Ye-es," I dragged the word out. "That's a bit of a scary dream, though."

She nodded. "It feels scary. Because I'm not waking up, I'm just falling."

I stared at my friend in astonishment. "You're falling *in love* with him?"

Lana scrubbed her face with her hands and then took another deep drink of her cocktail. "I know it's crazy. He's elven and I'll probably die before the Rite. But gods, it just feels right. It's fucking pathetic, and don't ever let Moric get wind of this, but I want to smush my face against his all day."

I tipped my head back and laughed. For the first time in nearly two weeks. And it was like a burden lifted off my shoulders. I raised my second drink toward her in cheers, because, gods, it took courage to admit what you felt. "To Solana, the bravest person I know."

She blushed, angling her glass toward me. "To Lirahna, the kindest, most loyal friend I've ever had."

The next few hours were a blur of drinks and laughter, tears from Lana as she explained how painful Anama's death had been for her, and tears from me as I apologized profusely for accusing her of not caring. Lana had leaned across the table then to hug me tightly, her cornsilk hair smelling of strawberries and pine. She slid out of the booth afterward, dabbing at the corners of her eyes. She proclaimed that this was all entirely too heavy for a girl's day out, and that as soon as she returned from the bathroom, we were going to try another drink.

I grinned as I watched her retreating figure swaying toward the bathroom. I had barely turned back to my drink when the seat beside me dipped. I looked to my left to find an elven male seated beside me, recognizing his forest green eyes immediately. He was Moric's instructor. He looked me up and down, ran his hand through his dark hair and blew out a low breath. "Kilian's going to be pissed when he finds out you're here."

"I don't give a shit what Kilian thinks," I responded coolly, taking another sip of my drink.

"Is that so?" His gaze tracked the curve of my lips around the straw. "I'm Ayden."

"Lirahna."

"Oh, I know who you are. Your reputation in the first challenge precedes you."

I scoffed. "I nearly died."

"'Nearly' being the key word. You killed the monster."

"I had help."

"Are you always this modest?" He winked. *Winked*. Was he flirting with me?

Three drinks in, and I was too buzzed to care. "Do you make it a habit of flirting with mortal women?"

He blinked, and I could tell the question threw him. Good. "No. In fact, I've never met one as striking as you before. The most exquisite females of Dalhur could not compare."

I rolled my eyes. "Does that line actually work?"

He grinned, flashing perfect white teeth, his lips inching closer to mine. "You tell me."

I was being reckless and stupid, and with how I felt toward Kilian… I was so fucking hurt. I did not think. I pressed my lips against Ayden's.

He did not hesitate before sweeping his hands across my waist, dragging me closer. He nudged my mouth open, his warm lips moving against mine. His tongue traced the seam of my mouth, tentatively brushing against my own.

It felt… weird. Not good. Not bad. But definitely wrong.

Those were not Kilian's hands brushing along my collarbone, and it was not Kilian's lips against mine. But those *were* Kilian's eyes that I saw two seconds before Ayden was ripped away from me and thrown across the room, the loud music coming to an abrupt halt.

"Touch her again and I'll fucking kill you." Anger was too light of a word for the expression on Kilian's face. He looked positively murderous.

Septimus stood behind him, observing the bar with disgust written plainly on his face. Lana chose that exact moment to step out of the bathroom. I could have heard a pin drop in the silence. It only lasted a second, though, before Septimus groaned at her. "I asked you *so* nicely not to come here alone."

"I'm not alone," Lana muttered, and Septimus rolled his eyes.

Ayden clicked his jaw, rising to his feet. "I don't understand what the problem is, Kilian. You said you didn't want her."

If my metaphorical wounds hadn't already been bleeding, that would have cut them right open again.

Septimus winced in Ayden's direction. "I'd go back to the house if I were you, buddy. This is not a fight you want to pick."

"Whatever." Ayden shrugged. He picked up his own cloak and left the tavern without a backward glance.

I chanced a look at Kilian again and instantly regretted it. He was so beautiful it made my heart ache. Even angry as he was, lightning skittering off his forearms, I only wanted him. But I hated him, didn't I? He would use me and hurt me before I died in the Trials, if I let him.

Kilian reached across the table for my drink. He lifted it to his nose, scenting it. "This is tainsberry leaf. Who the fuck put tainsberry leaf in your drink?"

Lana's eyes flickered to the bartender, who had slunk so far behind the counter he was barely visible.

Septimus leaned casually against the bar, the ever-present amusement in his tone unwavering. "Do you like your life, good sir?"

"I – I'm sorry. The girls… they wanted to have a good time," the male stammered.

"That's not what I asked," Septimus drawled. "The mortals in Lomask are under the protection of the Mortal Trials, surely you know this. By giving them tainsberry leaf, you've broken the sacred oath of protection."

"No harm can come from giving them tainsberry leaf," the male protested. "It's completely harmless."

"For elven," Septimus corrected. "It's harmless for elven. For mortals, it can cause hallucinations, the bending and warping of light and color, and extreme lightheadedness."

That explained why Lana had looked like a colorful rainbow.

I wasn't sure if I was imagining it, but a thin, golden rope of light flowed from Septimus' index finger, snaking through the air and wrapping around the bartender's wrists. "Someone will be along to collect you to stand trial."

"It's not his fault," I said. "We're perfectly fine."

"I'd like to see you both walk in a straight line first and then still tell me you're fine," Septimus muttered sternly. "He should know better."

With the bartender taken care of, Kilian's attention returned to me. "What are you–" He crouched down before me, eye level with the table, and I had a sudden, extreme urge to run my fingers through his hair. It looked silky and soft, and I wanted to hear what sounds he would make if I tugged gently at his curls. "*What* are you wearing, Lirah?"

His voice was a teasing murmur, and I knew the question was meant only for my ears. He ran a finger along the seam of my gear, over each clasp, and my breath hitched.

"I have a cloak," I said defensively, unsure why it mattered to him what I wore. "What are you even doing here?" I snapped, keeping my hands firmly at my sides. "You're supposed to be in Greyhaven."

"Yes, I *was* in Greyhaven." His voice returned to that commanding tone. "But Septimus informed me that you and Lana had been missing since the morning. I came back to find you."

I folded my arms across my chest. "You mean, you came to hunt down your candidate to ensure she didn't desert before the second challenge."

Confusion flashed briefly in his eyes before being replaced with stony anger. "You don't know what you're saying. You need to sleep the tainsberry off. Come on, we're leaving."

"No."

"No?"

"No. I'm having a nice time out with my friend. You've found me. You can go back to Greyhaven now. Oh, but before you go, would you let Ayden know he can come back? We have unfinished business."

Rage slammed into my chest with so much force I couldn't breathe. Kilian's eyes shone with pure menace. "Not a chance. You're coming back. Now."

I brought my tainsberry-infused drink toward me and slowly raised it to my lips, draining the remaining liquid in the only act of defiance I could think of. Then I slid along the booth, rising to my feet. "Fine, Lord Kilian. Is there anything else you'd like me to do?"

He rose to his full height, towering above me. He grabbed my cloak from the booth and threw it over my shoulders. "Cover yourself up. I'd rather not hurt anyone else tonight."

I wasn't sure if it was the result of the drinks I'd had or Kilian's presence that was messing with my head, but I was very confused. He shouldered open the door, holding it out for Lana and I to exit. The golden glow of the afternoon greeted us, and I was surprised to find that it was still daytime. With the lack of windows and lighting inside the tavern, time had ceased to exist.

I felt groggy and irritable. The sunlight seemed too bright, the colors a haze of brown and yellow, spinning and coalescing into an ugly shade of khaki. I raised my hand to shield against the glare as I stalked ahead of Lana and Septimus.

"I'm taking you straight to bed," Kilian said, falling into step beside me. "I don't know what this little stunt of yours was about today, but if you wanted my attention, you've got it."

"How delusional it must be living inside your head. Nothing about today concerned you," I lied smoothly.

He raised his brows, dark curls spilling across his eyes. "I'm supposed to believe that you kissing another elven *wasn't* to get my attention?"

"Like I said, it wasn't about you. Ayden's hot. I'll do it again if I want to."

Fury blanketed me and was instantly smothered by a layer of ice. He gripped my wrist, pulling me against him. "Why are you acting like this? I can feel your anger. What did I do?"

His thumb caressed the inside of my arm, drawing slow circles. Gods, I hated how that tiny action pleased me more than the entire kiss with Ayden. His fingers paused their gentle assault, and his gaze flickered to my wrist.

"You took the bracelet off." Cold realization dawned in his eyes. "Who told you? Calendula?"

I yanked myself from his grip, breaking easily from his hold as I continued along the winding route I, astoundingly, remembered Lana showing me earlier. "I don't know what you're talking about."

"Oh, come on, Lirah. It's so obvious."

"Could you leave me alone? I really don't want to talk about it."

"Then when will you want to talk about it? Because Elena... That was a *really* long time ago. And I'm happy to tell you whatever you want to know. You just have to ask."

Gods, her name felt like a cheese grater against my skin. I was so irrationally, uncontrollably jealous of a human girl who had died decades ago.

Valhan House appeared and I nearly sagged in relief. I was stupid for allowing myself to be hurt, to be distracted by Kilian when the second Trial was swiftly approaching. I needed to get my head back in the game. But not today. Today, my limbs felt heavy. The aftereffects of the drink hazing my vision and jumbling my thoughts.

"I'm not interested in hearing about all the mortal women you've fucked," I shot over my shoulder. "And I'm *really* not interested in being added to the list. So, if that's your intention, you might as well give up. It's not going to happen."

"That is not my intention." His deep voice rumbled behind me.

"Oh, right, I forgot. What was it Ayden said?" I whirled around. "You don't want me."

"*Ayden* is not a reliable source." His lip curled in distaste.

"At least Ayden didn't drag me here to be a mouse trapped in a death maze," I retorted.

"Can you *stop* talking about him." He groaned. "It's bad enough I have the image of you two kissing imprinted on my retinas."

"You should be glad you arrived when you did and that's all you have an image of."

I enjoyed watching his gaze darken, the silver in his eyes sharpening at the suggestion in my words. Anger licked at the bounds of the link.

"Has provoking me become your new hobby, Lirah?"

I crossed my arms. "It certainly has an air of entertainment to it."

He shook his head slowly. "People who provoke me do not have a habit of staying alive."

"It's just as well, then, that I'm participating in the Trials. Only a matter of time now. Let me enjoy my remaining days, will you?"

He leaned closer, voice like velvet. "If enjoyment's what you're looking for, I can recommend other activities that will be far more satisfying than kissing dim-witted elven."

I stepped forward, drawn to his magnetism. "Bold of you to assume kissing Ayden was not pleasant for me."

He scoffed, lips tilting into a sinful smirk. "Not all kisses are simply meant to be *pleasant*."

I sucked in a breath, a quick, sharp hit of his scent that stressed out my nervous system.

"Maybe I'm happy with pleasant." It was a weak retort and from the humor crinkling the corners of his eyes, he knew he had won whatever game we were playing.

His gaze skipped down to my lips. "No. I don't think you are."

"The world doesn't need to shatter for a kiss to be good," I insisted, sticking to my point now that I'd made it.

"Spoken like someone who's never had a world-shattering kiss."

I pressed my lips together, a flush rising along my neck.

I pictured it then, what it would be like to kiss Kilian Valhan. To feel those lips that had been on my neck just last night, slanted against mine. I wondered if it would be soft or rough. If his tongue would curl around mine in a single, shared breath. If time would stand still and the world would, indeed, shatter. I already knew it would.

No, no, no. This was *not* happening. He had already forcibly inserted himself in my space, I couldn't let him get in my head too.

"And I suppose I never will. Your fucking Trials will kill me before that ever happens." I spun around and nearly ran the last few steps toward the house. I marched up the staircase to the third floor. Lana and Septimus had long disappeared whilst Kilian and I had been arguing in the courtyard.

Much to my disgruntlement, Kilian followed me, all the way to my bedroom. I shoved the door open. There was no use in telling him to leave me the fuck alone. I wasn't wasting my energy on him anymore.

I crossed to the dresser as he stepped inside. The door shut behind him with a snick and I was acutely aware of how much space he took up in the small room.

"Are you just going to stand there?" I asked, forcing myself not to look at him as I rifled through the drawer.

"I want to make sure you're in bed before I go."

"Suit yourself." I grabbed a pair of cotton shorts and, with liquid courage blazing through my veins, began shimmying out of my pants.

Kilian inhaled sharply. "What are you doing?"

"I'm getting ready for bed," I said, matter-of-factly. "You don't expect me to sleep in sparring leathers, do you?"

I ignored the flush of embarrassment I knew I would feel tomorrow morning when I woke sober and remembered this moment. For now, I didn't care. I just wanted to sleep.

Kilian's eyes were glued to my exposed skin as I pulled my pants off, his eyes traveling up my legs. I drew the shorts up slowly, relishing in the agonized look in his eyes, the tense set of his jaw and shoulders. His body was coiled, like it might spring forward at any second.

He swallowed hard as I bent across the bed to pull the covers.

"I–" His voice was barely leashed, those silver eyes roaming my body.

He stepped forward slightly as I climbed into bed. I pulled the sheets over me and nestled into the pillow. He didn't touch me, though. Instead, he reached for the duvet. Strong hands wrapped the cover around me with surprising gentleness. Kilian's scent overwhelmed me, stronger than the tainsberry. A drug all on its own. He stared down at me for a moment, like he was contemplating something, before drawing back.

He pulled out the chair at my desk and took a seat, stretching his long legs and crossing his ankles.

The haze of the tainsberry washed over me again, and he fractured into splintering color. He wasn't leaving. He was supposed to go after I got into bed. Did I want him to go? Not really. I'd miss him if he left. But I shouldn't. My head ached.

"Why are you staying?" I whispered.

"To make sure you don't choke on your vomit if the tainsberry comes back up," he deadpanned.

"How gallant," I muttered, burrowing deeper into the covers. "I didn't even drink that much. You don't need to babysit. Surely there are villages of mortals out there in need of terrorizing."

He snorted softly. "You think so highly of me."

"Don't conflate your ego." My eyes fluttered closed. "I hardly think of you at all."

"Oh, now that's a lie and you know it."

"Prove it."

"I don't need to. We both know the truth. I'll let you in on a little secret of mine, though, since you're so bad at reverse engineering the link."

I yawned. Kilian's voice was soft and soothing, his presence making the room feel warm and safe.

"For each thought you have of me, I have two of you," he murmured. "I think of your eyes – onyx and unyielding, especially when you're glaring at me. I wonder how your hair would feel between my fingers. I wake up, excited for the first time in decades, for the fresh hell you're going to give me. For whatever snarky retort you'll throw at me that day. Arguing with you is the highlight of my day. It shouldn't be. I can't understand it. It frustrates me. But it's happening, whether I like it or not."

I frowned, blinking sleepily at him. "Why are you telling me this?"

He gave me a sad smile. "Because you won't remember it tomorrow."

"Give me… some credit." I yawned again. "I… might." But the tainsberry was making all my thoughts sluggish. I hardly knew what we were even talking about anymore, just that my default state was to disagree with him.

He only shook his head, a smile still on his lips.

I tried to take a mental snapshot of him, just like this. Because tomorrow, we'd be back to fighting, and all he'd do is stare down at me and scowl. "I like it when you smile. Makes you look nice. Less scary."

"You think I'm scary?"

"Sometimes. But then again, I'm scared of everything these days."

"You do a good job of hiding it."

"I've developed a defense mechanism crafted solely of spite, sarcasm and sass."

"You'll have to teach me some day."

"Won't be alive that long."

"Right." There was sadness in his voice, and I wanted to open my eyes to look at him. But sleep was pulling me in a different direction.

"I have questions for you," I murmured, the thought striking me randomly. I couldn't remember the questions. Something about the Trials and… a curse.

"Ask me tomorrow," he said.

I would. I'd ask tomorrow.

CHAPTER 14

My head throbbed with a fiery vengeance that three glasses of water could not slake.

A soft knocking issued from the door. I groaned, partial memories of the previous day slamming into me with alarming ferocity. I was alone in my room. The last thing I remembered was Kilian tucking me in and a hazy conversation before sleep caught me. I wasn't ready to face him just yet. I wanted to curl up into the fetal position and be left alone forever.

The door cracked open an inch, before I could tell whoever it was to go the fuck away, and Lana stuck her head inside the gap.

"Oh, thank the gods, it's you," I said, peeking over the covers at her. "Come inside and lock the door behind you." I wanted no more uninvited guests.

Lana hurried inside and flopped onto my bed. She gave me a sharp look.

"What?"

"Don't *what* me. You're my closest friend in here. You've been judging me for weeks for wanting to sleep with Septimus, but here you are, clearly shacking up with Kilian. And don't even try to deny it. I saw how the two of you were looking at each other yesterday. Look, I can't blame you. He's so hot he makes lava seem cold, but you have got some serious explaining to do."

"I'm not shacking up with anyone," I grumbled. Although, I had to admit she had a point. I had no right ever judging her for having feelings for an elven. The medal for biggest hypocrite and shittiest friend went straight to me.

"Except for Ayden? Moric's instructor? What is going on with you?"

I sighed. If there was ever a time to come clean to Lana, this was it. So, despite the pounding in my head, I told her everything. From the second unofficial challenge when I had confronted Kilian in his bedroom, to our late-night conversation in the mess hall after the first Trial, my training session with Septimus yesterday, when he had revealed the true motive behind the Trials, and Elena.

When I was done, Lana released a breath. "I don't know what to think about all of this. Firstly, the Trials. Septimus hadn't mentioned anything to me." She shook her head in disbelief. "On the one hand I can understand wanting to break their curse, but the cost of thirteen mortal lives every decade doesn't justify that. Secondly, this thing with Kilian needs to be addressed. You can't keep running around kissing random elven just because you're hurt that he had feelings for this Elena girl decades ago."

I clicked my tongue. "You make it sound like I'm an insecure teenager. I don't care if he had feelings for her." Although, irrationally, it did bother me. "I just want to know if he plays this same game with his candidates each time. I don't want to be another mortal added to his list of conquests."

"I can't answer that. You're going to have to ask Kilian."

"I can't do that," I muttered. "It'll sound like I care."

"But you *do* care."

"Yes. But he doesn't know that I care."

Lana raised her brows. "Lirah, you removed your protection charm the second Calendula told you it belonged to his ex-lover. Then you proceeded to drink almost the entire day away and make out with a random elven. I hate to be the bearer of bad news, but he knows you care."

"It doesn't matter anyway," I said in a small voice. "It doesn't change anything. I'm still a pawn in this game, my life reduced to nothing but the hope of some obscure ability to break a curse. He doesn't care for me beyond that."

"I don't know what he feels," Lana said. "But I do know that he left Greyhaven the second he found out we were missing. I know he was waiting for you at the archway after the first Trial. I know that he nearly killed Ayden for kissing you. And, if none of that matters to you, I also see the way he looks at you. Maybe you're right, and it's all a ploy for the sake of breaking his curse, but then again, he'd have to be one hell of an actor for that. You told me he said you might like him if the situation were different, right? If he didn't care beyond the Trials, why would it bother him whether you liked him or not?"

I stared at her, processing her words.

Lana patted my knee. "But anyway, moping around isn't going to get us anywhere. We have two days before the second Trial. I say we gather Moric and head toward Pyxis, because I managed to seduce Septimus into giving me a clue about it. One word: ghouls."

"I didn't even know ghouls existed," Moric said, thumbing through a large tome. He sat in a wingback chair on the fifth level of Pyxis, still looking as tired as he had the other day at lunch.

We had passed Rayna's group on the way up. Seeing them brought me a wave of nausea – they were the only squad still wholly intact. They hadn't lost anyone to the Trials yet.

I turned back to the book on my lap, trying not to think about how different things had been the last time we had all come together for research.

"There's surprisingly little knowledge on them." Lana chucked the book she had been reading onto the pile we had declared useless and pulled another one onto her lap.

Septimus had told me the second Trial would be 'one of wit and quick thinking'. Were we supposed to outwit our way from being ghoul fodder? And if so, *how*?

"They're mentioned briefly in this one." I gestured to my current read. "The first record of one popped up in the fourteenth century, from a man named Vlad Kobinsky who found one in his attic."

"I saw that as well," Lana said. "They've got a really spotty record throughout history, showing up in the strangest locations. Look at this one, found in a barn. A *barn*, of all places."

"What do they even eat?" Moric asked.

"Human flesh," Lana responded, without looking up. "Seems about on par for the second challenge, doesn't it?"

"Gods above," Moric breathed. He took another book from the pile and began frantically reading.

I perused an old newspaper article that had been copied and superimposed onto a page of the textbook before me.

The entire town gathers in the square to mourn the loss of thirteen-year-old Abby Bayfield. Bayfield was found dead in the early hours of the morning, by her fifteen-year-old brother, Samuel, who claims to have seen a large creature prowling in the area just days prior.

"It was late at night, a few days before I found Abby," Samuel said, in an interview with this author. "I couldn't sleep, so I thought I'd take a walk outside and see the chickens in the coop 'round back. I was returning to the house when I passed by the well, and I saw this large hand – I don't think I can even call it a hand; it was more like a claw, with six scaled fingers and long black nails – coming out. It scared the [redacted] out of me, so I hid. I should have told someone sooner. If I had, Abby might still be alive."

The injuries found on Bayfield are consistent with a six-fingered creature.

Residents are being advised to lock their doors and keep all windows closed until we have further information.

I shut the book.

"Find anything?" Lana asked.

"Just this." I pushed the textbook toward them. The article had left me feeling ill. "I need some air."

Moric and Lana looked up at me as I stood.

"I'll be back in ten minutes. I just need a walk around the block to clear my head."

"Should we come with you?" Lana asked.

"No. I'll be fine."

Moric nodded, returning to the pages of his book, and Lana gave me a soft smile.

I followed the winding staircase back down to the ground floor, passing the scholar in the front as I exited. Cool air greeted me, much to my relief, and I sucked in a few breaths.

A few stalls had been set up in the square today, but I wasn't interested in viewing the items on display. I turned left, leaving behind the scent of freshly baked pastries and fragrant spices, strolling toward what appeared to be an apothecary.

The jars and tinctures that were displayed on the window ledges drew my attention. Objects floated within the containers, suspended in green fluid and, on a shelf beneath them, a row of what looked to be curved teeth were arranged from smallest to largest. I was so engrossed in examining the items that I did not register the shift in energy beside me, until the elven stepped into my field of vision.

Echon.

The gruesome scar that ran along his jawbone was even more prominent up close. The afternoon light cast the planes of his face into harsh angles. Goosebumps rose along my neck.

"What's a fragile thing like you doing so far from Valhan House?" the elven mocked. "Fallen out your nest and gotten lost?"

I resisted the urge to take a step back. It would only prove how much he unsettled me. "I'm here to do some research before the second challenge."

"What research are you doing out here, little bird?"

"I'm not a fucking bird. And I'm obviously not researching out here. I just stepped outside Pyxis for some air. What business is it of yours, anyway? I am free to roam Lomask as I please."

The corners of Echon's lips curled with barely constrained indignation, his fingers twitching at his sides. "You dare talk to an elven like that? How you mortals have grown in courage. There was once a time you worshipped us, like gods."

"Things change when gods turn on you. When they sacrifice you in a ruthless game of survival. When they *silence* you."

Echon's eyes flashed. "You mortals succeeded in the first challenge through mere luck. Well, most of you, of course. Pity your little friend didn't make it."

Rage bottled in my throat, and I stepped toward him, fingers clenched at my side.

Echon tutted. "It's no use breaking your hand again, mortal. You may be under the protection of the Trials, but do not forget that birds who fly too high get their wings clipped. The third Trial waits to conquer you all, and if you do not die during the second challenge, you will most surely meet the sticky end you deserve on Cosanus." He leaned closer to whisper, "I, for one, can't wait to see the look on Kilian's face when another one of his precious mortals meets death."

Echon whistled an upbeat tune as he strode away, hands in his pockets, leaving me white-knuckled as I turned his words over.

As soon as he had left the courtyard, I spun on my heel, marching back to Pyxis with renewed determination. I approached the scholar at the reception, giving her my best smile.

"Could you please point me toward information on Cosanus?"

Echon was a fucking idiot. In trying to scare me, he had given me the one tool for survival: knowledge.

The scholar did not appear surprised by the request, and I understood why when she said, "First floor."

Rayna's group had been conducting research on the first floor. Echon was Rayna's instructor. Perhaps he had let slip the same information to her. I thanked the scholar, hurrying up the staircase to where Rayna's group were sprawled in various armchairs throughout the shelves. I ignored the men, scanning the floor for her.

Her eyes flickered up to meet mine as I beelined toward her and said, "Cosanus."

She sat up straighter. "You've found something?"

"Not quite."

Her brows drew together. "Then why are you here?"

"I know we're not friends," I started. "But I've just had a lovely chat with your instructor outside. He's delightful, by the way. He mentioned that the third Trial takes place on Cosanus. I've never heard of it before. I was hoping you could explain?"

"Gods." Rayna let out a disappointed sigh. "I thought you had managed to find out some information. We've been up here all morning researching and there's hardly any mention of it."

I gave her a confused look. "But the scholar said–"

"Yeah. She also told us to look on this floor. But the books here mainly contain the history of Tarlor. I've gone down to ask her for more specific guidance on where to search, but either she doesn't know, or she's been advised against helping us further." Rayna reached for a tome on the floor beside her, rifling through it until she found the page she was looking for. "This is the only place it's been mentioned so far."

I tilted my head and read the single sentence on the yellowed parchment: "'Before the elven, and long before the creation of the mortals, it is said that a land rich in magic existed, and it was called Cosanus.' That's it?"

Rayna nodded. "But look who that line is quoted from." Her index finger rested beside the name: *Augustine Devior, former scholar of the Great Library of Kraventhorn, current historian and curator of Theology at the Dalhur Institute of Precious Data (DIPD).*

"Thank you," I said.

"Don't thank me yet. We're not friends, but it doesn't mean I want to see you dead. Don't be distracted by the second Trial," Rayna warned. "They want us preparing for it instead of focusing on the third one. That's the one where we're all going to die."

I returned to the fifth floor, the information churning in my head.

Lana and Moric had not changed position since I left, the latter's head still buried in a thick book.

Lana glanced up when I rounded the corner, instantly picking up on whatever apprehension was lurking on my face. "What happened?"

I perched on the armrest of her chair and told them everything Echon and Rayna had said.

Lana's eyes grew wide. "I haven't heard of Cosanus. Have you?"

Moric shook his head, but I could tell he was considering something. "The only person who seems to have any knowledge about it is Augustine."

I nodded. "But he works at the DIPD and most likely lives in Dalhur. We have zero chance of making our way across Lomask and into Dalhur before the third Trial."

Lana stood so quickly the book on her lap fell to the ground. She ignored it, though, wild excitement flickering in her eyes. "We might not need to. Come on."

She didn't look behind to make sure we were following as she hurried across the floor to the winding staircase, taking the steps downstairs two at a time. Her face was flushed as she led us to the bulletin board at the reception, her voice feverish as she said, "I stopped by Pyxis the other day to read up on the Rite, and I happened to see this. Look."

She pointed to one of the black and white leaflets tacked near the top of the board. A photo of a handsome man holding a book filled the square. In neat type above the image, the headline read: *Augustine Devior on his latest book:* Tarlor Through the Ages. And at the bottom: *Join us on the fourth floor of Pyxis, Lomask at twelve pm on the fifteenth day of the ninth month for a special author signing with Augustine Devior, to celebrate the launch of his new book.*

"Lana," I said. "You're a fucking genius."

Calendula was seated on my desk by the time I returned from dinner.

"How much trouble did you get into?" I winced apologetically.

"Enough," the shadow sprite said. "I can't give you any more information about Elena, so don't bother asking. And if you want to go drinking at shady taverns, please take me. I would have happily accompanied you yesterday. You needn't lie."

"I know. I'm sorry." I produced three strawberries, setting them down before her. A peace offering.

I noticed then that she was sitting on a small page that had not been there before I left. "What's that?"

"Oh." Calendula stood, dusting off her dark gown. Silver sparks flickered from her like ash, sifting through the air to land on the page. "It's from Kilian. He asked me to make sure you read it."

"I really don't want to."

"I'll get into more trouble if you don't."

I gave her a defeated look, well aware that she was manipulating me. I reached for the page, dusting the embers off as the sprite nibbled at the first strawberry.

Lirah,
I wanted to speak to you today, but I have been called back to
Greyhaven on urgent business.
I will be back on the evening of the second challenge.
Try to stay alive. There is much we still have to discuss.

Yours,
Kilian.

Yours.
Mine.

I folded the note and slipped it beneath my pillow.

CHAPTER 15

It was nine pm and none of us had eaten dinner yet. Instead, we were all being held hostage in the sparring room, while Septimus had us performing the most archaic obstacle course ever designed. My legs burned and my chest ached. Sweat dripped down Lana's nape as she balanced on a beam ahead of me, her pale hair plastered to her neck.

I swiped my palms against my sparring leathers, keeping my feet planted firmly on the narrow beam I stood on. It couldn't have been bigger than the length of my foot and was six inches wide. My core clenched as I strained to keep upright. If I fell, Septimus would make me start all over again, and there was absolutely no way I was doing that for the fourth time.

Lana sucked in a breath as she hopped to the next beam, and I readied myself for the jump. I bent my knees slightly, channeling focus. I jumped, my left foot landing on the beam. My arms flailed at my sides, trying to stabilize my balance, my right foot dangling behind me. I used it to propel my weight backward, my abdominal muscles tightening as I fought gravity to remain balanced.

The obstacle course had not been designed for the faint of heart and we had been going at this for the past four hours. Everyone was spent. I did not dare risk my careful balance by looking behind to Moric or the others. I knew I would find haggard faces that mirrored my own.

I had skipped lunch earlier in favor of more research on Cosanus and regretted it. My stomach growled embarrassingly loudly.

The second Trial was scheduled for tomorrow. If we kept going at this rate, we were going to be too exhausted to compete by the time morning came.

Lana cleared the last beam with frightening ease, landing on the next horrific part of the obstacle course, and my complete and utter downfall – the spinning wheel.

I had a new tactic for passing the wheel this time, though, having fallen off it three times too many. I propelled myself forward and onto the next beam, my arms righting my balance before I could tip backward. By the time I had straightened, Lana was already past the wheel.

Before I could second-guess my new strategy, I leaped. I kept my eyes straight ahead and not on the rotating wheel beneath me as I sprinted. Miraculously, for the first time tonight, I landed on the other side without falling on my ass. I didn't have too much time to be chuffed with myself though, because the next part of the course required me to rappel myself across a large gap with a flimsy looking piece of rope, which dangled from the ceiling.

I wiped my palms against the side of my pants again, needing them to be bone dry for this part. Fatigue weighed so heavily on me that it was an effort to even keep my eyes open, let alone launch myself across the space. The rope was suspended in the middle of the gap, so I took a few steps back, hoping to make a running jump. I could see Moric from the corner of my eye, hurtling across the spinning wheel. I had to make a move, and now.

I jumped across the gap, hands outstretched and legs kicking at the air to propel me forward. My fingers gripped the tough fibers of rope and my knees slammed against each other as they fought for purchase around it. I swung forward, praying my timing was right, trusting blindly as I let go. My arms reached for the lip of the landing. My fingers brushed air, grasping nothing. And then I was falling.

I landed hard on my hip bone, pain lancing up my side.

Frustration and disappointment tore a hole through my chest, sizzling and aching worse than the fall. I had been so godsdamned close.

"You know the drill, Aldhur," Septimus sang from the sidelines. "Back of the line."

"Fuck off!" I called back. "I'm done with this."

Septimus' eyes narrowed. "You're done when I say you're done."

"Then tell me I'm done. I swear, if I have to do one more fucking lunge–"

A shrill beeping rang throughout the room, cutting my words short. The sound startled Rayna so much that she lost her balance on a beam and clattered to the floor.

She rose to her feet angrily as the sound cut off. "What the fuck was that? It's not fair for me to start over."

Septimus rubbed his hands together, a mischievous glint in his eyes. "You're in luck, mortals. That noise was the sweet sound of the end of the obstacle course."

"Thank the gods," Moric muttered. He dropped down from the rope – my latest downfall – and wiped the sweat dotting his forehead.

Lana swept her hair to one side, panting as she dropped from one of the rungs that had been fitted on the wall for scaling. "I'm starved. I can't wait for dinner."

I dropped an arm to the ground to scoop up my tunic, which I had abandoned around the second time I had had to restart the obstacle course. Lana and Moric had already begun heading for the door when Septimus cleared his throat.

"Not so fast, candidates," he said. "There's been a slight… change in plan. Your second Trial will begin now."

Nine pairs of eyes snapped to him. And then chaos broke out.

"The second Trial isn't supposed to start until tomorrow!" Rayna yelled.

"You can't expect us to compete right now!" one of the more muscular men in her group called out. "We haven't even eaten tonight."

"It's outrageous!" a woman in the first squad shouted. "We were told the second challenge would take place tomorrow."

"And now you're being told it will start tonight," Septimus said. "Things change. Roll with it."

"We're exhausted! You've had us running around this obstacle for four hours," Rayna cried.

Lana shook her head and said, "That's part of the challenge, isn't it? We're tired, we haven't eaten, we're dying to crawl back to our rooms. They want us to feel like this going into the Trial. It's fucking cruel."

Septimus whistled long and loud to quiet the chatter. "You can shut up and listen, or you can all be the ghoul's next meal. Your choice."

There was complete and utter silence.

Sweat rolled down the side of my neck. It was so hot in here I felt like I couldn't breathe.

"You will have the next thirteen minutes to all work together as one team to solve a riddle. If you manage to provide me with the correct answer, I'll let you go up to the mess hall, where a feast has been prepared in honor of the completion of the second Trial – fresh rolls and lamb, cold beverages and crisp, crunchy summer salad. There are even roast potatoes this evening."

My stomach ached like a hollow pit. I knew exactly what Septimus was doing, yet his words conjured up a picture that distracted me so wholly from the Trial ahead that I feared I had lost before it even started.

"If you provide me with the incorrect answer, however," Septimus continued, "I'm afraid the ghoul will have its own second Trial feast."

Moric gulped audibly beside me.

"The riddle is simple, but take some time to discuss amongst the nine of you. All you have to do is let me know how many letters there are in the alphabet. I'll be back in thirteen minutes to hear your answer." Septimus strode toward the exit, shutting the door behind him.

"It's so obvious." One of the men in Rayna's group marched toward the door. "Everyone knows there are twenty-six letters in the alphabet."

"Wait!" Rayna called out, before he could shout for Septimus. "What alphabet?"

The man turned back to her, walking forward slowly. "The Grilish one, obviously."

"But what if they're not talking about Grilish, Caleb? The elven language, Rrasur, has thirty-seven letters."

Caleb scratched the side of his head. "So, how are we meant to know which alphabet he's talking about?"

"We're not," Lana said. "That's the whole point of the riddle. Grilish is the common tongue amongst the mortal isles, but many of them have developed their own native language as well."

"She's right," Moric said. "In Foulkan, Grilish is the dominant language, but the old language of Afsar is still spoken by many. And there are seventeen letters in that alphabet."

I didn't have much to contribute to the discussion. I didn't know of any other languages spoken on Serila. I had only been taught Grilish by Umma and had never heard anyone in the governor's house speak a different language.

"Well, if Grilish is the most common language, I say we use that alphabet as the answer," Caleb declared.

"Caleb." Forced patience filtered through Rayna's voice, and I was sure she'd had a similar conversion with the man before. "Our lives depend on this answer. We have to be sure."

"There's no way to be sure," he retorted. "I'm fucking exhausted. My brain hurts. I don't have the mental capacity to figure this shit out."

"Maybe," Lana suggested, ignoring Caleb, "it's not the type of alphabet we're thinking of. It could be numerical or musical."

"But there are an infinite amount of numbers," a woman from the first group said, and her only remaining partner nodded. "Unless we're talking about numbers on a clock, in which case there are twelve. With musical notes, there are also twelve of those and we know the elven have a particular proclivity for music."

"The natives on Koli speak a language with only twelve letters," a man with round spectacles framing his face said. He was another member of Rayna's group. "I'm from Koli. It's the smallest isle on Tarlor and is said to have been the first island ever created by the gods outside of Dorisport. The native language was a gift from the gods themselves."

"Are we going with twelve, then?" Caleb scoffed like it was a bad idea.

"It seems more likely than going with Grilish," Rayna said. "Grilish seems... too obvious."

The door snicked open and Septimus stepped back inside, looking at us all expectantly. Had thirteen minutes already passed? It seemed far too quick. I swallowed nervously.

"Your time is up," Septimus said. "Have you come to a decision?"

Rayna glanced at us. When no one objected, she stepped forward. "Twelve. Our answer is twelve."

Septimus winced. "So close. Unfortunately, that is not the right answer. There are eleven letters in the words 'the alphabet'."

We gawked at him. Surely he couldn't be serious…

I opened my mouth to protest, but the lights in the room began flickering, dimming to a harsh maroon. Lana's pale hair turned stark red in the glow. And when I looked back for Septimus, he had disappeared. Caleb wrenched on the doorknob, heaving and pulling, but it did not budge. We were locked in.

A soft hissing resonated from the corner of the room. The metal grate near the ceiling began rumbling, and I could not pull my gaze away as dark, wispy tendrils snuck through the gaps. Transfixed, I stared as more black smoke snaked through, twisting and undulating into a thing of nightmares: a gaunt, pulled face with no eyes and only a gaping, sucking mouth. Six clawed fingers each as long as my hand, with taloned nails, dark as onyx. And a body that seemed to be woven of gossamer shadow.

Its mouth snapped open to reveal a black hole circled by rows of razor-sharp teeth. When it spoke in a grating, guttural voice, the sound stirred the ancient darkness inside of me. "It has been a long time since I have delighted in such a banquet. I long to taste the marrow of mortal bones once more."

It hurtled toward us, a creature of claws and teeth. I didn't think. I *ran*. But the entire room had been obstructed by the obstacle course, and there wasn't much space to run freely. I dodged and twisted around beams, not daring to look behind me as I hurried across the first part of the course.

A wide net had been cast along the floor ahead, which had required us to dive beneath and crawl our way across. I sprinted over it now, slipping and sliding against the polished wooden floor. My foot caught in one of the holes and I flailed forward.

A scream wrenched through the air, and I made the mistake of looking back.

A woman from the first group was on her back, legs kicking out as the ghoul pounced on her. Its claws, which had seemed almost incorporeal previously, solidified as they raked down the woman's side. Blood gushed onto the floor around her. The ghoul lowered its head, teeth protruding as its mouth gaped larger and larger.

Out of the corner of my eye, Lana's wrist flicked expertly. A dagger whizzed through the air. The silver blade rotated once, then twice, before plunging right through the ghoul and clattering to the floor. It was as if it had gone through smoke.

The ghoul did not look up or pause in its assault. Its teeth continued to extend, and it began tearing at the woman's flesh. Her screams ricocheted along the walls, piercing and bloodcurdling. Moric, near the edge of the room, doubled over, retching. Only bile came out but the sight of it was enough to trigger my own gag reflex.

I didn't know what was more nauseating, the woman's screams or the harsh silence when they ceased. Lana's dagger had done nothing to the ghoul. How were we meant to kill something that a weapon had no effect against?

Unless we weren't meant to kill it. Maybe it had been sent here to just kill us all.

Fear gripped my heart. I couldn't think like that. Kilian had told me to stay alive. He wouldn't have told me that if there was no way to do so. My brain kicked into overdrive, thoughts whirring as I recalled everything we had read about ghouls. They had been found predominantly in barns and attics. Samuel Bayfield had found one in a well in the dead of night. Why?

The maroon lights flickered up ahead. They had dimmed them before the ghoul entered. They needed it to be dark. That was it! It must not like light.

The sparring room was windowless. I turned to the only person I knew would have some form of light on them.

"Rayna!" I shouted. "Rayna, your lighter!"

At my words, the ghoul's head snapped up, the hollow sockets where its eyes should have been swiveling in my direction. I stumbled backward into the rope that dangled from the ceiling. The ghoul drifted away from its kill, the woman's body a butchered corpse I could not stomach looking at.

Its head cocked in my direction as it floated toward me, unhurried. It knew I had nowhere to go. The gauzy ends of its body trailed along the floor, dragging a smear of blood in its wake.

"Lirah, catch!" Rayna yelled.

I watched as her lighter arced through the air. I held out a hand, catching it fluidly. Still, the ghoul approached.

It grew closer with each breath, and my body shook with apprehension. But I gritted my teeth, thumb poised above the striker.

The ghoul's mouth was a gaping maw, teeth clotted with blood and stringy flesh. It was ten feet away. Then five. I could smell the death and decay clinging to it. I swallowed against the urge to vomit. The air rustled as its folds swayed in midair, a blood-slicked claw stretching out to greet me.

Not yet.

I didn't want to give it a chance to escape. I needed it *just* a little closer before I lit it on fire.

Someone called my name, but I didn't dare break focus. The ghoul met me, its ghastly face hovering inches from mine. A dark nail traced lightly along my cheekbone, and it breathed deeply, its mouth sucking at the air. In a raspy, guttural voice, it said, "You smell deliciously... familiar."

The nail dug against my cheek, swiping down with such alarming swiftness that I felt the warm blood trickling along my jaw before the sharp sting of the cut. The ghoul drew its claw to its mouth, a black tongue darting out to lick at the blood gathered there.

"And your blood is perfectly aged."

I remembered the lighter in my hand and struck the wheel. Nothing happened. I struck it again, but only air fizzled. I let loose a scream of frustration as the ghoul drifted back a few feet.

Wait. Where was it going? With each passing second it floated away from me and my chance of destroying it diminished.

"Not all blood is meant to be consumed," the ghoul said, turning its attention to its next target. Moric cowered near the wall, scrunching into a ball as the ghoul inched closer.

I didn't understand. Why was it not attacking me? What was it talking about? But there was no time to unravel those riddles now. I had hesitated far too long, and now Moric was in danger.

I struck and struck at the lighter, but it was no use. I tossed it to the ground, my hands ripping through my hair.

The ghoul slunk to the corner of the room, its feathery ends rustling like dry leaves as it prowled toward Moric, its mouth snapping open wide enough to swallow a person whole.

My insides clenched. I wouldn't be able to bear it if the ghoul laid one scaly claw on Moric. He and Lana had become more than friends to me. They were family.

The lighter was a dead end.

But… that was not all the light we had.

My gaze snapped to Lana. Lana, who had emitted a strange, golden light in the tunnel network during the first Trial, having drawn it from her link to Septimus.

"Lana!" I yelled. "It hates the light. Use your magic!"

"No fucking pressure," she called back, scrunching her eyes in concentration.

A second passed, and then another. Nothing was happening. The ghoul had almost reached Moric.

The faintest glow shone across Lana's skin, but it wasn't enough. Not nearly enough.

I closed my eyes, focused on steadying my shallow breaths, tried emptying my mind. And for the first time, I purposefully reached for the link.

Lirah, a faint voice on the other end. *What do you need?*

Light. I need light.

My fingers tingled, a spark jolting through me like I had just been shocked by something metallic.

Current zapped through me, scorching my flesh and boiling my blood. From my splayed fingers, lightning erupted.

Blue streaks slammed around me, branching out in every direction and illuminating the room, charring the ground as each strike landed with vicious speed.

And between the veins of electricity, I could see that Lana was glowing, brilliant and golden. Her light formed a protective bubble over her and all the other candidates. It didn't touch me, though. Bands of shadow lashed out, swirling in an amorphous cocoon and protecting me from the lightning showering the room.

The ghoul hissed, and through the shadows I watched it crumple in on itself. Its wispy body shifted, shrinking as the ghoul slammed against the wall, its claws raking out to shield its face, the pits of its eyes and mouth. It scurried up the wall, slinking back toward the grate, where it slid through the holes, nothing more than vapor and air.

I gasped as the magic flowing through me ceased abruptly, stumbling back a few steps from its sudden absence.

Orblights flooded the room, the shadows surrounding me vanished and Lana's light winked out. She swayed and Rayna's arms jutted out to catch her before she could fall.

I ran a hand across my forehead, wiping at the sweat the sizzling current had left behind, and blinked against the harsh white light as the door to the sparring room swung open and Septimus and Echon walked in. They surveyed the room, the charred ground, the mutilated remains of the woman whose name I did not even know.

"You're free to go," Septimus said. I did not miss how his eyes scanned Lana. "If you're injured, the med hall is open. To all who remain, congratulations on passing the second Trial."

But I didn't feel triumphant as I walked toward the door. My brain felt like it was on autopilot, unable to process the events of the last hour. The skin on my fingertips were burned and tender, and my cheek throbbed from the slice through it, but I would not go to the med hall. Not tonight. I did not want these wounds to heal. I did not want to forget.

There would be no celebrations tonight.

CHAPTER 16

I arrived to breakfast the morning after the second Trial to find the seven other remaining candidates seated in one large group. With so few of us left, it didn't make sense for us to stay separated. Not when the first squad had only one remaining survivor: a young woman, whose name I found out was Keila.

Rayna's group was still the only team not to have lost a single member. The men in her squad comprised Caleb, the spectacled man from Koli who introduced himself as Mattieu, and a third man by the name of Nox.

Lana, Moric and I spent the rest of the day running laps and sparring.

At dinnertime, I saw that not much in the way of seating arrangements had changed. Moric sat beside Rayna, looking even worse than usual. Although the ghoul hadn't attacked him yesterday, I could tell the entire ordeal had shaken him. After training all day, I felt weary, my brain like soggy parchment.

It also probably didn't help that I hadn't slept a wink last night after the challenge. Each time I closed my eyes, I saw the ghoul. I smelled its putrid breath. And I wondered why it had spared me.

I'd told Calendula what the ghoul had said to me, but she didn't have much insight. "Perhaps it didn't like the taste of your blood. Some ghouls prefer younger blood," Calendula had said.

"I'm twenty-three. How much younger does it want?" I had replied. "Besides, it said my blood was 'perfectly aged.'"

Calendula had shrugged dismissively. "What does it matter? You're alive."

But it did matter. Something felt off. And I couldn't shake the feeling.

"Lirah," Lana said, snapping me out of my reverie. "You should eat. Your food's getting cold."

I hadn't been eating properly, not since Anama had died. Even that felt like eons ago, the older woman's face a distant memory against the backdrop of last night's fresh death.

I speared a piece of honeyed carrot on my fork and brought it to my lips.

"We should start preparing for the third Trial," Lana murmured between bites of steak. "If last night taught me anything, it's how woefully unprepared we are."

"It just feels like no matter what we do, it's never good enough. We get into the challenge and chaos reigns."

"I don't know." She shook her head. "The research helped. If Rayna's lighter hadn't run out of fluid, your initial plan would have worked. You figured out a key weakness of the ghoul. Don't discredit that or yourself. Anyway, I suppose there's not much we can do in preparation of the challenge until tomorrow."

Tomorrow. When we would attend the author signing, hosted by Augustine Devior. Hopefully, he would have answers for us.

My stomach twisted nervously, but I ate the rest of my food and by the time the end of dinner bell chimed, my plate was empty. I felt restless. I didn't want to go back to my room just to lie in bed and turn over the events of last night's challenge, or consider how little we knew about the third one. I wanted a distraction. And I knew exactly where to find it.

I muttered a quick excuse to Lana before crossing the mess hall to where Septimus stood, speaking with Ayden. Ayden's green eyes flickered to me, and I could have sworn fear crossed his perfect features. He said something to Septimus that caused the golden-eyed elven to glance over his shoulder, and then Ayden was hurrying out of the mess hall.

"What's with him?" I asked.

Septimus grinned. "He's scared."

"Of me?"

"Of Kilian."

"Oh. Is he back from Greyhaven?"

"Yeah. He was a bit delayed, but he got back an hour ago," Septimus said.

I felt it then, the quiet wrath I was slowly becoming accustomed to. It burned in the back of my throat, along my fingers and deep inside my chest, consuming me in the most delicious way.

"Thanks," I said, backing away.

"You don't even know where he is."

I didn't respond. I was already rushing out of the mess hall, my feet tripping over one another before reason could overrule insanity. Before I could remind myself exactly why this was a supremely bad idea. I followed the steady stream of anger, tugging on the link all the way to the fifth floor. When I stood outside his door, my breaths ragged from having run upstairs, I lifted my hand to knock.

The door swung open before my fist made contact.

Kilian stood in the doorway. He was dressed for war. A broadsword was strapped to his side and a bandolier hung across his chest, several onyx-hilted daggers gleaming in their sheaths. It looked like he had run his hands through his dark hair several times with how ruffled it was. His eyes were silver moonlight. I could stare at them for hours and still miss them the second I blinked.

He was fucking devastating.

"You're hurt." He reached out to touch my face, his thumb gingerly brushing the thin cut on my cheek.

"Hardly." The word was a whisper of all the things I wanted to say, but just couldn't. His hand dropped back to his side as he studied me, waiting.

Now that I was here, I found myself stalling, avoiding the real reason for my visit. My gaze skimmed his gear. This close, I could see the elven inscriptions etched into it. "Why are you always dressed for battle? No one's going to attack Lomask."

"You never know," he answered. "It's good to be prepared for anything."

I didn't even know *who* would attack. Certainly not the mortals; that was a losing battle before it even began. Maybe the lower elven, in Greyhaven? My knowledge of elven politics was dismal.

"Why?" he asked. "Does my attire bother you?"

"Why would it bother me?"

"Everything about me bothers you."

"I find your dressing to be the least offensive part compared to all your flaws."

The corners of his lips quirked, amusement in his eyes. "Of which there are many."

"Naturally."

It didn't matter though, how many flaws he had, or how fatal they were. I still found myself standing here, outside his door. It was like trying to change a prophecy that had already been engraved in stone.

He leaned against the doorframe. "How was the second Trial?"

"Awful," I admitted.

"You called on the link." There was a hint of approval in his voice.

I shrugged. "It was either that or watch my friends die."

"You've used it twice now. I don't doubt you've noticed what a useful tool it can be. I could help you practice, if you'd like." A suggestion. Not a forceful command.

I glanced away, glanced back. "I'm doing fine with it as is."

"Right. But you're sloppy. You have no sense of aim, no precision. It's a wonder you didn't hurt anyone last night."

I bit my lip guiltily. He was right. If Lana hadn't cast a bubble around the others, I could have seriously harmed them.

Fine. Maybe I did need to work on it, but I didn't need to do it with him. "I can practice on my own."

"Sure you can," he said. "But you'll learn twice as fast with guidance."

"I'll be fine. I can train with Lana. She's been learning from Septimus."

"You don't want to train with *me*," he surmised.

"I don't want to spend any amount of time with you."

"Then what exactly are you doing here?" Not accusatory. His voice was gentle, questioning. The first time I had seen him at the governor's house I had thought there was nothing soft about him. But when he looked at me now, the ice in his eyes melted.

And as usual, he'd won our imaginary game, because why *was* I standing at the threshold of his bedroom?

I knew I needed answers to all my questions – why the ghoul had spared me and why he had been cursed, first and foremost – but they shriveled up and died as I gazed up at him. I was so fucking tired of thinking. Of constantly strategizing how best to survive. Of death and pain stealing every waking moment.

I settled for a pathetic, "I don't know."

"You don't know?"

I shook my head.

A soft smile curled the corners of his lips, and I forgot everything. "Are you sure?"

"Categorically." I wet my lips and his eyes tracked the movement.

"Do you want to come inside?"

"No."

"No?"

"If I come inside… I don't think I'll want to leave." The admission was more vulnerable than I wanted it to be.

He straightened, eyes darkening. "What do you want, Lirah?"

I paused and he stepped over the threshold. The power emanating from him enveloped me, dark and crushing. Beautiful in its terror.

"What. Do. You. Want?"

What did I want? I wanted everything to return to normal. I wanted to wake up in the morning and know Umma was alright. I wanted my life to not be in danger every single week. I wanted to know that Lana and Moric would be safe. I wanted to expunge the feeling of hate and anger and *grief* that wrecked me every day. I wanted to forget the Trials, forget everything.

And the only person that could give me that – who could make me forget – was the elven standing before me. The one who had caused all this pain and misery in the first place.

I wanted to be selfish. To take something *I* wanted. Even if it was something I should not, it didn't change the frustrating fact that I still wanted it.

I peered up at him and breathed, "You."

"Don't say that if you don't mean it."

I swallowed, placing a hand on his breastplate. "I want you."

Desire and ravenous hunger pulsed through me. He trailed his hands along my arms, sketched the curves of my waist and I *shivered*. His fingers traced my hips and then my feet were off the ground. I straddled his waist, my gaze level with his at this angle.

He did not break eye contact as he carried me across the threshold and into his bedroom, kicking the door shut behind him. He pressed me against the closed door as my feet sank back to the ground. His lips dipped to my neck, and I tilted it, giving him better access as he drew a line down my throat, his cool breath skating along my skin.

"You have no idea how much I want you to never leave this room," Kilian murmured against my collarbone.

"Then show me," I rasped.

I felt him smile against my throat. "You're so fucking sassy. I wonder how you'll argue with me when your mouth is otherwise engaged."

"You'll never know if you keep talking–"

His mouth claimed mine in a brutally decadent kiss. I gasped as my lips opened for him, his tongue sweeping against mine in slow circles. One hand palmed my waist as his fingers sank into my hair, cradling the back of my head against the door. Every lick of his tongue against mine, every inch of pressure against my body felt intentional. Purposeful. Kilian Valhan kissed like the world was ending tomorrow. And I suddenly understood the difference between a pleasant kiss and a world-shattering one.

This did not feel like it had with Ayden. I felt this kiss in every charged atom of my body. It was safe and warm and undeniably right. He tasted like snow and air, and I couldn't breathe fast enough.

"I want this off." I unhooked his bandolier, and the weapons crashed to the floor between us, but I didn't care. My fingers reached blindly for the buckles on his breastplate, deftly unclipping them. I ran my hands up the sides of his neck, sinking my fingers into his hair like I had so desperately wanted to in the tavern. I tugged at the silken strands and he groaned like I knew he would, my mouth absorbing the sound.

I did it again. I wanted to know what other sounds he was capable of making. I wanted it all.

Kilian rocked against me, and hot, aching desire shot through my veins. He grabbed a fistful of the loose-fitting tunic I'd donned over my cuirass in lieu of a long-sleeve. "I hate this tunic."

"Then burn it." I lifted my arms as he pulled it off, exposing my arms, my neck, the gear I wore beneath.

"This fucking corset will be the death of me." Kilian broke our kiss to stare down at it.

My chest was heaving like I had just run a marathon, and I felt lightheaded from the kiss. I didn't have the heart to correct him on the difference between a corset and a cuirass. To be fair, this one did have laces in the front instead of buckles.

The dizziness became progressively worse as Kilian dipped his head to kiss the swell of my breasts. His tongue trailed idly along the curves and back up to my neck, where he sucked the skin until I gasped.

"Do you know how to undo it? The gear," I managed to get out.

His eyes snapped to mine, and there was dark humor in them. "Don't insult me. Although, I don't think I have the patience to untie this one. You're not too attached to it?"

I shook my head once and he grinned. He reached for a short blade sheathed at his side, bringing the sharp tip to the seam of the cuirass. He carefully cut at the laces, the knife slicing through the material quick and clean. And when he was done, he threw the dagger aside and peeled it right off my body.

He drank me in. I was surprised to find that instead of feeling self-conscious, I felt *seen*. "You're so beautiful."

His head dipped once more and my eyes shuttered, as I surrendered to the wave of raw hunger. Every touch was electrifying. My body felt like it was on fire. I dropped my head against the door as Kilian's hips rolled against mine. All his rage and all of mine combined into a supernova. The throbbing in my core was building, kicked into hyperdrive. I threw my hands against his breastplate again, finishing what I had started. The armor crashed to the floor, leaving only his loose undershirt in place. I reached for the hem, tugging.

I pulled, but the shirt didn't budge from where it was tucked into his pants. Frustrated, I ran my fingers along the seam of his leathers and he pushed against my hand. I stroked again, softer this time, and he pressed his lips to my neck, muttering my name. My fingers worked the top button of his pants and then the zip. I felt the soft cotton band of his underwear and then the tip of him.

I slipped my hand beneath his underwear and Kilian swore. I grasped him tentatively. Sliding my hand across the velvety flesh, I marveled at his length, the wet bead that formed at his tip, the soft moan that rent from him as he thrust forward in my hand.

I was doing this. Never had I felt more powerful than I did now, with my fingers wrapped around Kilian Valhan as he came undone. For me. Thunder rumbled and lightning crashed through the window outside. Darkness, heady and fragrant, cloaked me, its kiss the most sensual death.

His hips rocked faster, and I stroked harder. I wanted to taste his skin, swirl my tongue around–

"Don't think those things," he said. "I swear the thought of your lips around me is enough to make me–"

I squeezed him and his eyes grew wide. "Did I ever tell you how fucking invasive this link is? I can't even think about sucking you off in peace."

His lips were on mine then, a clash of teeth and tongue. There was nothing measured or practiced in this kiss. I felt his muscles tensing and his spine straightened as he tipped his head to the ceiling, exposing the broad column of his throat. I kissed it, sweeping my tongue over his pulse.

Kilian came, his hips thrusting hard against me. Darkness swathed the room, and through the windows, purple lightning danced along the summits.

He dropped his head to my shoulder, his chest heaving.

He was so fucking beautiful. Every inch of him, from the delicate tips of his ears to the inky curls spilling against my skin and the hard, unyielding lines of his muscles. I wanted to be the one to make him lose control like this every single night for the rest of my life.

It was probably what Elena had wanted as well.

Until she had died in the Mortal Trials.

Just like I would.

I wondered who would come after me.

And just like that, the magic spell was broken. I shoved at Kilian's chest, unwrapping myself from him. Tonight had served the exact purpose I had wanted it to. It had allowed me to momentarily forget the horrors I had endured these past few weeks. Horrors caused by the male standing before me, looking at me with confusion.

I bent to fetch my tunic, slipping it over my head. The gear was destroyed beyond repair. I did not care. Let him keep it as a souvenir of this decade's mortal.

"What are you doing?" he asked, stepping forward as if to reach out for me, but I dodged expertly.

"This was an excellent distraction, but it's been a long day," I said.

His eyes narrowed, brows drawing together as anger stirred in my chest, chasing the haze of lust. "Distraction?"

"Yeah." I pulled my hair into a knot atop my head, checking my leathers to make sure all buttons were firmly secured. "I've had a shit day. And you've made it clear that I'm not allowed to fuck around with anyone else, so here we are."

The feeling of sleepy satedness that had lurked in the back of my mind vanished in a wink, replaced by stone cold wrath. "I don't believe you. How many times do I have to tell you that the link is reciprocal? I can feel how much you want me. *Only me.*"

"So?" I shrugged. "I can want to fuck you but still hate you. There's nothing more to it."

Kilian grinned then, like he knew something I didn't. A slow, feral smile that sparked the silver in his eyes. "You're a terrible liar, Lirah. But it's okay. I've got time to prove it to you."

"Prove what?"

Kilian twisted the doorknob, holding it open for me to exit. "That this is not just a distraction. You can lie to me all you want, but don't lie to yourself. I have a meeting tomorrow morning in Dalhur, but I'll be back around lunchtime for our training session."

"We don't have a training session tomorrow."

"We do now. I want to get to the bottom of whatever's churning around in that mind of yours. And the best place to do that is the sparring mat. Bonus points if you don't wear underwear." He winked.

I ignored the pounding in my heart and the tightening of my core. The only thing preventing me from begging him to kiss me senseless once more was my pride, and even that was wavering.

"Be careful what you wish for," I threw his words back at him with contempt before stalking out the room, aching and desperate for more.

CHAPTER 17

I stood outside Lana's door for a good minute before it opened, just a crack. Enough to reveal mussed hair and bare legs. Her skin glowed as she blinked sleepily at me.

I narrowed my eyes at her. "You had sex last night."

Lana shushed me, slipping outside to stand in the hallway.

"Is he still in there?" A grin plastered itself on my face at the panic in her eyes.

She swatted my arm, whispering, "Yes. What do you want?"

I laughed. "I just wanted to make sure we're on track for our plan later."

Lana groaned. "It's six thirty, Lirah. Yes, we're on track for our plan at *twelve*."

"Alright, alright." I held up my hands in surrender. "I'll leave you to it then. Enjoy all the sex."

Lana flushed beet red before slipping back into her room.

Calendula floated at my doorway, daintily, her wings stirring gently against the air. She reminded me so much of Kilian that it hurt looking at her. The events of last night irked me more than they should have. Despite brushing my teeth for a full five minutes this morning and having an extra-long shower, I could still taste him on my tongue. I still felt him in my bones.

"What plan is this?" the shadow sprite asked.

I flipped my palm over for her to rest on it as I made my way past the dorms, to the staircase that would lead me to the mess hall. "We're going to speak to Augustine later. He's doing a signing at Pyxis. We're hoping he might have some information on the third Trial. You don't happen to know anything about Cosanus, do you?"

Calendula sighed. "I've already told you. I've been sworn to secrecy. It's an oath stronger than even the link you share with Kilian. I do think that speaking to the historian will be beneficial, though."

I gave her a resigned look, continuing up the stairwell until the mess hall came into view. The breakfast bell would not ring for another half-hour, but it appeared Rayna was an early riser. She sat at the table, an empty plate before her.

I stared at her for a moment, the way her shoulders sagged forward, the frown on her lips, her deadpan gaze at nothing in particular. Her youth was barely visible beneath the weight of stress and exhaustion.

I drew up the chair beside her and her eyes flicked to me.

"Never seen you up this early before," she said by way of greeting.

"Sleep is a luxury these days."

"Tell me about it."

"Your group's still whole," I said. "That's impressive."

"It's dumb luck," she muttered. "I could have died so many times, and I keep seeing the alternate outcomes – the ones where I didn't survive – in my head."

"My brain is my own worst enemy sometimes as well." I couldn't give her some motivational speech on how to rewire her thoughts when I didn't know how to do it myself.

There was clarity in her eyes when she looked at me. Certainty when she said, "It's only a matter of time before our luck runs out. We are going to die here."

A cold, hard fact.

"Maybe not." I hated how much hope was in my voice. It would make the inevitable disappointment hurt that much more. "Augustine Devior will be at Pyxis today. He might be able to give us some information on the third Trial, on how he passed the Rite. We're leaving the house at eleven thirty, if you want to come."

Rayna nodded slowly, still unconvinced. "Thanks for letting me know. Do you think he'll be willing to speak to us, though?"

"Why wouldn't he be?"

She shrugged delicately. "No one really seems to be in much of a rush to help us out."

"You're right," I said. "But it's worth a shot. We're meeting in the courtyard if you decide to join us."

I stood, my muscles groaning as I did. I needed to stretch or go for a walk. Anything that didn't involve sitting around and waiting for eleven thirty. I was too restless and impatient this morning.

Exiting the mess hall, I took the steps down to the courtyard. It was early enough that the elven who usually brought the daily food deliveries still carted trays of vegetables inside the house. I passed them, heading toward the archway.

Cool wind whipped loose strands of hair across my cheek, and I lifted a hand to push them back. A soft touch caressed my exposed neck, and I whirled around, my hand reaching for the dagger I now kept pocketed at all times.

"Are you planning on using that against me?" Kilian murmured. He stood a hairsbreadth away, and I cursed myself for being so oblivious that I had not noticed him trailing me through the courtyard. The problem was that I felt him all the time. Even when I didn't want to. It was getting difficult separating his emotions from mine. Lately, they felt one and the same.

"If I need to, yes."

"So vicious." His lips quirked in a smile that made my heart flutter dangerously.

I banished thoughts of the previous night to the darkness, forgetting that everything that dwelled there belonged to him. "What are you doing here?"

His brow lifted. "In the courtyard of my own house?"

I rolled my eyes and he grinned.

"I told you last night, I have an appointment in Dalhur this morning. Or did that slip your mind?"

"My apologies. I guess your whereabouts just aren't that noteworthy to me."

Dark amusement flashed in his eyes. "I do wonder, are you ever going to tire of this charade? It must be exhausting pretending you don't care."

It *was* exhausting. And there were far greater problems in my life than whether Kilian Valhan knew I liked him, but he was an easy target for my rage, and I think he knew that too.

Allowed me to channel some of my blistering anger onto him so it didn't boil me alive.

"Tell me, is this the first time someone hasn't been interested in you? Is that why you're struggling to accept it?"

He laughed then, and it filled the cold courtyard with warmth. "I'm struggling to accept it because just last night you were sending me all sorts of different signals. I think you're just scared to admit that you like me. Because that conflicts with everything you think you hate."

I injected boredom into my voice as I said, "You would think with how busy you claim to be, you'd have more pressing things to do than make up scenarios in your head."

"There's nothing I enjoy more than making up scenarios. All of them involving you," he said softly, in a way that had me picturing scenarios of my own. Him, no clothes, lightning flashing outside the windows.

I hated how effortlessly he dug his way beneath my skin, but gods, did it make me feel alive.

"You should get a move on to your meeting," I said, forcing ice into my tone. "Unless you'd like to prove you can last longer than twenty seconds?" It was meant to be a barb dipped in venom but came out far more suggestive.

His grin vanished, replaced by something wild and starving. He lowered his head, lips angling millimeters away from mine. I sucked in a breath as he whispered, "In fact, I would like to prove that. Will you let me?"

I shivered at his request, aching for him to close the distance between us, but he pulled away, leaving me breathless.

"I'll see you after lunch, Lirah. I can't wait." Kilian tossed over his shoulder as he disappeared past the archway.

By the time eleven thirty rolled around, I was an anxious wreck. After my encounter with Kilian, I had paced the length of the courtyard, taken a brisk hike up the slope of the summits to the spot Septimus had shown me, watched the sun journey across Lomask and then returned to Valhan House to pester Moric for an hour.

He was sufficiently annoyed with me by the time we made our way to the courtyard to meet Lana and Rayna.

"Remind me again why you invited her?" Moric grumbled. He clearly still held a grudge against Rayna for whatever she had done to him during that first unofficial challenge.

I looped my arm through his. "Because she's the entire reason we're going to speak to Augustine. She has a right to join us."

"She can go on her own," he protested.

I clicked my tongue. "We're down to the final eight. Harboring hate won't get us anywhere. We should be working together to pass the final Trial."

Moric muttered something incoherent but did his best to plaster a smile on his face. Rayna and Lana stood near the archway, both dressed in sparring leathers.

I gave Lana an apologetic look as I neared. "Sorry about this morning."

She waved me off. "I need to update you later."

"*Please*. I need all the details."

She smiled, her entire face lighting up. Moric was right. Hate-sex really did do wonders for the skin.

Pyxis was swarming with elven by the time we entered the library. Many milled around the reception, some studying the books that lined the staircase. But most were already seated up on the fourth floor, where an area had been designated for the signing. Plastic chairs littered the space and a podium stood at the front, a microphone affixed to its end. Thick books towered on every inch of the table to its right, behind which Augustine Devior sat.

The male was as handsome as the photo on the bulletin board had suggested. Despite knowing that he was older than seven decades, he didn't look a day over twenty-seven. His pale hair was slicked to the side, blue eyes assessing the gathering crowd. He adjusted his lapel and stood, crossing to the dais.

He leaned forward slightly, his mouth close to the mic. "Testing, one, two, three." The deep timbre of his voice echoed through the library, and he pressed a button at the base to decrease his volume. "Welcome and thank you for coming."

Lana tugged at my elbow, pulling me toward a seat in the back row.

"As many of you are aware," Augustine said, "I have been a scholar my entire life. This book–" He looked fondly at the stack on the desk, "– is a culmination of my life's work. I can't begin to describe how grueling it has been, poring through research and tracking down firsthand accounts of historical events. Not to mention the many sleepless nights spent wondering whether this would all be for nothing."

Lana coughed and rolled her eyes.

Augustine continued, "I questioned my line of work several times, but the scholar in me refused to give up. I knew I had been created for this purpose, to share knowledge and impart wisdom, for who are we if we do not know our own history? How can we seek to be better than our predecessors if we do not know which mistakes we should not repeat? And how can we know where we are going if we do not know where we came from? These are the questions I set out to answer when I sat down to write this book. It has been a labor of love and a true test of faith, but I am so pleased to stand before you today to present *Tarlor Through the Ages*. I'll open the floor up to any questions before we commence the signing."

Hands fluttered through the air and chatter broke out amongst the crowd as they pelted question after question at him. He greeted and addressed each one with dexterous ease.

Lana leaned over to whisper, "Sounds a bit full of himself, doesn't he?"

We waited as Augustine patiently worked through each question lobbied his way. And then the signing portion of the event began. It was clear this was what most had attended for. A long line stretched halfway down to the third floor, and we leaned back in our seats, prepared for the wait. Moric burrowed into his chair, eyes drifting shut. He started snoring softly a few moments later. I was relieved he was finally getting some sleep.

Rayna stood.

I looked at her. "Where are you going?"

"To the first floor. We should probably show Augustine his quote on Cosanus, in case he pulls the old 'I don't know anything about that' spiel."

"That's a good idea."

With Rayna out of earshot and Moric fast asleep beside us, I turned to Lana. "This morning. Spill."

She blushed prettily. "There's not much to tell. I just got tired of wanting Septimus. After the second Trial… Everything just feels so precarious, you know?"

"I understand."

"What about you? Did you manage to sort things out with Kilian?"

"No," I answered quickly. Too quickly. Trying to recover, I said, "I mean, not yet. We've got a training session after lunch, so maybe we'll get to speak then."

She nodded. "I have a feeling that things are going to move pretty fast after the third Trial. I've been doing some reading on the Rite, and it's heavy stuff. After the final challenge, there's really no reason to delay. I expect it'll happen a day or so after, just to give our bodies some time to recoup, if needed."

"With how the other Trials are going, I definitely think a recoupment period will be necessary. What did you find out from your research?"

"Not a lot, honestly. There wasn't much information on the way in which it's performed, but more on the effect of it. A lot of mortals don't pass the Rite because our bodies just aren't genetically compatible with the energy current. It changes the entire composition of our bodies not just on a structural level, but on a cellular one. And a lot of mortals can't handle that transition. None of them have, in fact. Except Augustine." Lana's blue eyes slanted to the male seated behind the desk, happily chatting with the elven female before him.

"Curious indeed."

The line was considerably shorter now, with only a few elven still waiting. I placed a gentle hand on Moric's shoulder, rousing him. He jerked up with a start, eyes wild, and I knew he had been having a nightmare.

I gave him a soft smile. "We're going to join the line now."

He nodded, checking the corners of his mouth for drool.

There were three people ahead of us by the time Rayna returned. We slowly shuffled forward with each new autograph signed, until we stood directly before Augustine.

The male blinked up at us. "You're… mortal."

"Yes," I said. "We're competing in this decade's Mortal Trials."

He seemed flustered as he reached for one of his books, thumbing it open.

"Oh, no," I hastened. "We're not here for autographs. Not that your work isn't tremendous. It's just…" I glanced at Rayna, who took this as her cue to shove the volume she had fetched from the first floor beneath Augustine's nose.

"We've been told our third challenge takes place on Cosanus. The only bit of information I could scrounge up on it was this single sentence, written by you, nearly a decade ago." She pointed to the line on the bookmarked page.

Augustine paled. His square reading spectacles had slid down his nose and he pushed them higher before examining the inscription. "'Before the elven, and long before the creation of the mortals, it is said that a land rich in magic existed, and it was called Cosanus.' Yes, I wrote this."

"Are you able to give us any more information on Cosanus? Anything you can think of might be helpful for the Trial," I pressed.

Augustine set the book on the table and removed his glasses, pocketing them. He surveyed us for a moment before he said, "The Mortal Trials are different each decade. I can't say I've ever spoken to any of the candidates that came after my decade to tell them this, but I think it's important to note. What I'm trying to say is that I won't have any knowledge of what is going to happen during your third challenge."

"That's fine," Lana said, "But do you know what Cosanus is?"

Augustine looked offended. "Of course I know what Cosanus is. We're standing in it right now."

I gazed around the fourth floor, shocked. "Pyxis?"

"No, silly girl." Augustine waved his hand through the air. "The entirety of Lortan is Cosanus. Or, it used to be, millennia ago. When the fae still roamed."

I remembered reading about the fae in a textbook, seated across from Anama, as I researched the history of Lortan. It seemed like a lifetime ago. But nowhere had that book mentioned Cosanus.

"I know the story of the fae," I told Augustine, determined to prove that I was not as silly as he thought. "I know that Winipyr, goddess of life, created them first, but their rebellion ensured their swift destruction."

"Certainly," Augustine agreed. "That is the version of history we have been taught."

"Is there another?"

Augustine templed his fingers beneath his chin, looking contemplative. "Well, Cosanus was the land of the fae. Once the fae were exterminated, the land was still ripe with magic and so, Winipyr, seeking to rectify her error, molded the elven and gave them a home on what was once Cosanus. A name change later, Lortan was born."

Maybe I truly was silly, but I was not following. "If Cosanus no longer exists – if it is now Lortan – and Cosanus has been all but forgotten by the history books, why was I told that I would meet a sticky end on Cosanus specifically? Why not leave it at Lortan?"

A spark of curiosity gleamed in Augustine's eyes. "That is, indeed, a good question."

"You know something," Lana said, her eyes narrowing on Augustine.

The elven held out his palms in a supplicating gesture. "I promise, I don't know anything for sure. It's all just unfounded theories. Scholar's brain. It's a bad habit I can't seem to kick. I'm always considering the why."

"What unfounded theories?" Rayna's tone brooked no nonsense.

Augustine pursed his lips. "Well, more like a wandering thought. One I've had before, but seems more... rooted now."

He was taking so long to spit it out, I wanted to reach across the table and shake the words out of him. But controlling myself, I left my hands loose at my sides, waiting for Augustine to continue.

Finally, he said, "You see, I've been pondering for some time what might have happened to the fae that were exterminated. It is said that Azrael bore swift winds and tidal surges down on them, clipping their wings and drinking their power. And when he was done, nothing remained of the creatures who once ruled at the helm of the gods themselves. But I don't know if I quite believe that version of history."

I shook my head slowly. "You think the fae still exist somewhere? Somewhere on Lortan?"

Augustine shrugged. "Like I said, it's all unfounded. But if you were told your challenge takes place on Cosanus, I'd be hard pressed believing that was a mistake."

My head was reeling, my thoughts spinning in directionless waves. It simply couldn't be.

"Surely we would know if the fae still existed," Rayna scoffed. "One would think they wouldn't be sitting around, content with the elven presiding over what was once their land."

"Of course," Augustine murmured thoughtfully. "Unfortunately, I do not have any further light to shed on the topic. As I've mentioned, this is just wild speculation and completely up for debate. A historian must, first and foremost, gather accurate data before making definitive conclusions. If history intrigues you, I'd be remiss not to refer you to my latest book, *Tarlor Through–*"

"How did you pass the Rite?" Lana blurted out, interrupting him.

A flicker of annoyance flashed through his blue eyes, and he clicked his tongue. "That's a highly personal question."

"You'll forgive my friend," I said smoothly, trying to keep the peace. From hearing Augustine speak for the past hour and go on to schmooze his guests, I had gathered a picture of the male before me. He was eloquent, professional and clearly very passionate – borderline vain, in fact – about his line of work. "I'm sure you understand what it's like. We've all got family we'd like to go back to. And we understand that a scholar of your caliber would have the appropriate respect and deference for our pursuit of knowledge."

His eyes softened. "I do understand. However, I do not think the answer will be very beneficial to any of you. It is not something you can easily control."

"Tell us and we will decide whether it's beneficial or not," Rayna snapped.

Augustine sighed. "I'm afraid it will help no one. The Rite is not a challenge. It is a mechanism designed to test a mortal's genetics. It changes one on a molecular basis. If your body isn't equipped, the surge of power will kill you."

"Well, can we *try* to equip our bodies?" Rayna pressed.

"There are methods that can be learned, but I'm afraid they take years of practice." He grimaced, the implication in his words plain. We would not have years. We barely had days left.

I waited for him to elaborate, but he didn't. After a spell of silence, it seemed our time with him was up.

Rayna sneered, annoyance curling her lips. "Let's go. This is pointless."

"You're nice kids." Augustine looked sadly at us as we turned to leave. "But there's nothing you can do to prepare for it. Enjoy the rest of your days in Lortan while you can. The Rite rarely leaves survivors."

CHAPTER 18

"You're late," Kilian said as I crossed the courtyard.

I bid farewell to Lana and the others before striding toward him. "I've been busy."

He wasn't dressed in the battle armor he had donned this morning, opting instead for sparring leathers and a dark shirt that hugged the dips and contours of his muscled frame. "Harassing Augustine? I'm well aware. Calendula told me."

"I figured she might. Anyway, it's not a secret. Echon let slip that the third challenge is taking place on Cosanus. I saw the opportunity to find information and took it."

Irritation flashed through Kilian's eyes. "I wasn't aware Echon had spoken with you. What did Augustine say?"

I shrugged. "Just a bunch of crackpot scholar theories."

His eyes narrowed.

"If you've got any information pertaining to the third Trial that you'd like to share, now would be the time." I knew it was futile, but it was worth a shot.

He sighed. "I'm trying to help you *prepare* for it. Which brings us to today's session. I thought we'd do things a bit differently. Away from the house for a change, so we can train and talk."

I scrunched my nose. "Talk? About what?"

"Us."

I let out a harsh laugh. "There is no us. There's you. And then there's me. And I've got a Trial to prepare for. One my fragile mortal life depends on. I don't have the capacity nor the inclination to talk about *us*."

"Well, lucky for you, you won't have to do much talking. You can run laps and train. All whilst listening."

"We're not sparring?"

He shook his head. "There's a park nearby. We'll train there." He started toward the archway, angling his head to look at me. "Are you coming?"

I hesitated. After what had happened between us last night, and what seemed to always happen when I was near him, I didn't trust my body to not do something reckless that my heart would later suffer the consequences of. It was much easier to shut him out. To remain cruel and callous and unfeeling.

"Lirah," Kilian said, the softness back in his voice. "Please come."

I don't know if it was the gentle, almost reverent way in which he said my name or the fact that he said please, but I forced my legs forward, falling into step beside him. Kilian did not strike me as someone who ever asked so nicely.

He led me out the archway and along the cobblestoned path. We passed a signboard, written in the elven alphabet I now knew was called Rrasur, turning left. Up ahead, I could see the beginning of what looked like a park. Wide, open land stretched for miles, the grass green and neatly trimmed. A sprinkling of snow had melted, leaving drops of dew glistening on the blades. Tall trees and shrubs were scattered sparsely across the ground, lending shade against the warm midday sun. A running trail curled through the field, sloping toward a small, secluded lake where ducks idly floated. As we approached, I saw tiny goldfish flitting beneath the glossy surface, their scales sparkling in the catch of light. Kilian took a seat on a bench before the lake, scanning the ducks swimming by.

He looked so completely out of place there in full sparring leathers, the sunlight glinting off his hair turning it blue black.

"Do you… come out here often?" I asked.

Kilian shook his head. "I rarely have the time."

He looked more at peace than I had ever seen. His posture was relaxed, arm slung across the back of the bench, legs crossed at the ankles. For once, his muscles did not radiate tension, his eyes devoid of their usual wrath. And when I brushed tentatively against the link, I found a quiet calm.

His gaze slid to me, standing at the edge of the lake. "Take a lap around the park to warm up. When you get back, I'll run through a few core strengthening and endurance exercises with you."

"Okay."

I did a quick stretch, pulling at my quads and hamstrings, and then my calf muscles. I tied my hair in a high ponytail and rolled the sleeves of my tunic up before setting off in a light jog.

The trail was surprisingly quiet, and I didn't see another elven along the path. It led me on a winding run through the park, past pine trees from which blue robins darted to and fro, carrying twigs and other bits in their beaks. When I returned to the lake, I saw Kilian had not moved an inch. He looked up at me as I slowed to a stop. I swiped at the light sheen of sweat on my forehead and tried to stabilize my breathing.

"Ten minutes," Kilian remarked. "You need to work on cutting that down."

"I didn't know I was being timed. You said it was a warmup exercise."

"And I'm sure that the next time you're being hunted down by a creature who wants to kill you, it will understand that you haven't warmed up yet."

I rolled my eyes. "What's the next exercise?"

"Core strengthening. I assume you've done a plank before?"

I hadn't, but I knew what it was. "Obviously."

I settled on a grassy spot a few feet away from the lake and positioned myself on my forearms and the balls of my feet. It was surprisingly easier than I thought it would be. "How long do I have to stay like this?"

"Hmm, let's say, the length of time it took for you to warm up." There was amusement in his voice. "And you're doing it wrong. Your back needs to be lower. Lower."

Kilian groaned in frustration, and I could see his boots striding toward me. He dropped one knee to the ground beside my head, his hands tracing the curve of my lower back, and I couldn't concentrate on anything but the feel of his hands on my body. He pushed gently, leveling me until I was perfectly parallel with the ground.

That's when I realized that planks were the most torturous exercise on the planet.

"Keep your core tight," Kilian's voice was a whisper at my ear, and I trembled.

I blew a steady breath from my lips, holding the position for as long as I could. But with each passing second, my muscles vibrated harder, until I couldn't take it anymore. I flopped onto my back, my chest heaving as I stared up at the cloudless sky.

Kilian sat on the ground beside me, shaking his head. "One minute. That's pathetic, Lirah."

"Fuck off."

He chuckled. The sound was rich and dark, and I angled my head to look at him.

The meeting with Augustine still weighed heavily on me. One run and a plank was not enough to shake off the feeling of hopelessness left from that conversation.

"We thought… We thought Augustine might be able to help us prepare for the Rite. But he basically told us we were going to die. I've known about the Trials nearly my entire life and how supremely unlikely it is for anyone to survive, but… I don't know." I blew out a breath. I didn't even know why I was telling him all this when he didn't care. "I guess I was just hopeful. Not even just for me. I want to survive, but I want Lana and Moric, the other candidates, to live as well."

"Augustine didn't tell you anything about the Rite?"

"He said there were methods to equip our bodies. He didn't bother explaining, basically said we won't master them in our remaining time here. Quite honestly, I'm wondering at the point of competing in the third Trial if I'm just going to die during the Rite." It was morbid and depressing, but true.

"Augustine is right," Kilian said. "There are things you can do to prepare for the Rite, to increase your odds of survival, but even then, it's not guaranteed. And it takes a lot of practice."

I raised up on my elbows to look at him better. "How do you do it?"

"The current that passes through you during the Rite can be managed if you have an adequate outlet for the excess. It'll be a different method for everyone, depending on the power they've been gifted, but in theory, if you have a good grasp on the magic drawn from the link, you can use it to expel the surplus current. You'd have to let some of the current through in order to effect the change from mortal to elven, but the rest would need to be expelled before it kills you. That's the general principle."

"If it's a current..." I thought out loud. "Will it affect me? I've wielded your lightning before and it hasn't majorly harmed me."

"The current during the Rite is vastly different to mine, and a far higher voltage than anything you've managed. It will be too damaging for your body, unless you're able to expel some of it."

"Why isn't this more widely known?" I asked. "If there's something we can do to prepare for the Rite, we should have been told from the start."

"You weren't told because it's not a guaranteed way to pass the Rite. The type of skill required to discharge the extra current takes more practice than you or anyone else will have time for. We try to train you in both magic and combat. It's never enough," Kilian said. "You think we haven't tried training mortals on how to expel the surplus current? For the first few decades, all we did was train them. And you know what happened? Everyone still died. We don't tell you because hope is dangerous, Lirah. When you hope, the disappointment is even more heartbreaking."

"But there's a chance, right?" I pressed. "Minute, but still possible. Right?"

"Yes," he murmured. "There's a chance. I want to train you. I insist on it. But you need to understand that there's an even higher chance that the preparation still won't be enough."

"I understand that."

"Are you sure?"

"Yes. Show me what to do."

He took my hand. Warmth radiated from the point of contact and my stomach somersaulted like I was in free fall.

"Septimus taught you how to clear your mind?" he asked.

"Yeah. I was able to summon a ball of darkness for a few moments."

His eyes snapped to me. "Darkness?"

"Yes. Why? What's wrong with that?"

He shook his head, but he looked unsettled. "Nothing. It's just... an unusual manifestation of my power."

"Why are you surprised? You told me to use it in the cave during the first Trial."

"No. I didn't."

"I heard your..." But *had* it been Kilian's voice I'd heard? To be fair, I hadn't been the most clear-headed in the first challenge.

"I spoke to you before you went into the cave, but not while you were in there. I felt your pain when the creature attacked you and then the link went silent. Remember?" Kilian was giving me a strange look, like he was trying to figure something out.

"Maybe I'm mistaken." I gave an airy laugh, hoping it concealed my unease. Perhaps it had been the same voice I'd heard on the summit, when practicing with Septimus? But if it wasn't from Kilian, then where did it come from? I was too disturbed to think more on it and Kilian was eyeing me like I was mad. "*Anyway*. You were saying?"

He was still looking quizzically at me, but he said, "I'm going to send a small shock through you. You're going to draw on the link. Since you've handled shadows before, I'd suggest using that to smother the current."

"Is it going to hurt?"

"It shouldn't, if you diffuse it correctly."

I inhaled deeply, letting my eyes drift shut. All it did was heighten my other senses. And he invaded each and every one of them. His hand, callused against mine. His scent. The power radiating from him. It made thinking of anything else *very* difficult.

A tingle jolted through my palm, and my eyes flew open in surprise.

"You're not concentrating."

I frowned. "That hurt."

"No, it didn't. You need to focus."

Focus. I needed to focus. My life was quite literally dependent on me learning this skill. Mine and the other candidate's lives. I had to pay attention so I could tell them all how to do it. I needed to not imagine his hand sliding up my arm and trailing down to my waist. If he might pull me onto his lap after and let me straddle him. How he'd feel beneath me. If he'd suck on my pulse point until–

"Fucking hell, Lirah. You're going to kill me."

"I told you we shouldn't practice together," I said churlishly.

"If you could keep your thoughts out of the gutter, this would be a lot more straightforward."

"Maybe you should stop breaking into my head and let me concentrate."

"Maybe if your thoughts weren't so fucking loud, I'd be able to ignore them."

"Maybe–"

"*Shut up.*" His hands were on my waist then, and he drew me toward him so quickly I hardly registered the movement. My knees fell on either side of him, and he closed the gap between us instantly. His lips were on mine, unhurried. A gentle reunion after last night's hasty departure.

"Don't tell me to shut up," I muttered, running my hands through his hair.

"Never shut up." He pulled me against him, deepening the kiss.

I rocked my hips against his and he groaned into my mouth. He dropped his head to my neck, his tongue laving over my pulse, better than anything I'd imagined.

"This isn't the sort of practice I thought we'd be doing today," I gasped.

"Tell me to stop."

"Never stop."

"I need to teach you how to channel the magic."

"Teach me tomorrow."

"There are important things we need to speak about before I do the things I want to you," he murmured against my skin, his nose tracing the curve of my jaw.

"More important than this?" I punctuated my question with another roll of my hips, my fingers twisting around strands of his hair.

"I wanted–" He pressed a kiss to the corner of my mouth, "–to clear the air between us."

"Consider it cleared," I responded definitively, unable to remember why I was supposed to *not* be enjoying this.

He drew back with surprising self-restraint for someone who couldn't seem to keep their tongue off my neck seconds ago. "We need to talk."

I sighed heavily, leaning back slightly but making no effort to remove myself from his lap. "Fine. The floor is yours."

He stared at my wrist. "You haven't been wearing your protection charm."

I huffed. "Not this again. I told you. I'm not interested in wearing a relic that belonged to your ex-lover."

"I didn't take you for the jealous type."

"I would have to *care* to be jealous. And I don't."

He eyed my body, the point of contact where our hips met.

I gave him a sour look. "We don't need to talk about this. I get it." I gestured between the two of us. "This is a temporary thing. Next decade, you'll find another mortal to play with, but forgive me if I don't want the hand-me-down jewelry as well."

"You're so dramatic." He rolled his eyes. "I'm not going to sit here and pretend I didn't care for Elena, because I did. I met her during the third decade of the Trials. She came from Kraventhorn. She was quiet, but she had a fierce passion for the rights of mortals. And when she spoke, there was fire in her eyes. She made you want to listen."

His words felt like glass against my skin, rubbing and chafing to the quick. "Why are you telling me this?"

"Because I want to tell you the truth. It's the only way we're going to move past this. I gifted Elena the protection charm because I hoped she would make it through the challenges and pass the Rite. But she didn't. When she died, I grew... cold and detached. There were no mortals after her. I dissociated myself from the other candidates, decade after decade. I didn't want to know about the lives we had taken them from, the homes we had destroyed, what kept them up at night. And with each passing decade, I grew harder. I cared less. Until... I met you."

I could only stare at him, transfixed.

He brushed a lock of hair behind my ears, fingers catching around a curl. "You're stubborn and rude and swear like a sailor, but I can't stop thinking about you, Lirah. I can't stop looking for you, waiting for you to spare me a glance, even if it's only to scowl at me. I want to hear your voice, even if you only use it to curse me. You're always there, like a tune I can't get out of my head. I feel you through the link every second of every day. I feel your pain and your grief. I feel the love you have for your friends. How much you miss your mother. How much you hate what I've done to you. And I hate myself for it too. It is the worst torture."

I stared into his eyes, the weight of his confession burning a hole through my heart. My treacherous heart, which thumped and galloped so furiously I thought it might explode.

He loosened a ragged breath, like his words had taken something from him. "I needed you to know that you are not just another mortal, or some sort of distraction. Not to me. You have crawled beneath my skin, and I cannot dig you out. It is most inconvenient."

His words clawed at something ancient inside of me and my chest felt like it had split, buttery light leaking from the cracks. "But I *am* just a mortal," I whispered. "And even with the training, passing the Rite is not guaranteed..."

Pain flashed across Kilian's eyes, and I felt it acutely. A sharp stabbing that gutted and wrenched. A blade twisting deep in my chest. "You once said I do not have humanity because I am not capable of feeling or caring, but you were wrong. When the Rite comes, I will be grateful to have known you. And the only thing I will regret is not telling you how I felt sooner."

My eyes shuttered, frustration ripping through me at the impossibility of the situation. "Septimus told me about the curse."

Panic flared through his eyes and his mouth twisted into a grim line. "Can no one keep a fucking secret these days?"

I didn't smile. "I know you're trying to find an elven capable of restoring your powers, but how can it be worth this cost?"

Kilian's lips pressed into a thin line. "I came here today intending to give you the whole truth, but there are some things you won't be able to understand, Lirah. Not right now, at least. I know it's a lot to ask, but can you trust me enough to settle for as much as I can tell you?"

I swallowed. It didn't sit right with me. The secrets and mystery surrounding it all. How could he intend to be honest, while still concealing part of the truth? A very important part. One that defined how I viewed him.

"No. You haven't earned my trust yet. People have died here. They're still going to die. You're asking me to forget–"

"I'm not asking that. But there are things bigger than you and I. And the greater good of humanity relies on the restoration of my powers."

"Humanity? Septimus didn't mention anything about that. He just said you pissed off someone and they stripped your powers."

"That *is* what happened. But I didn't act on a whim. There was a plot I'd overheard, crafted by someone I hope you never have to meet. A plan with disastrous consequences... The humanity-destroying kind. One that makes the loss of thirteen mortals every decade look like nothing, harsh as it sounds. And I was the only one able to stop it. Septimus and Syrina, they helped. Except, we only managed to execute half of the plan before we were caught and stripped of our powers. The Trials... they're not for sport or entertainment, glory or fame. They're a necessary means to an end. A careful method to select the strongest: those most suited to pass the Rite. We're searching for someone with a particular skill to break this curse, so I can finish what I started."

My questions multiplied with each sentence that left his lips. If what he was saying was true... If humanity really was at stake, hinging on the outcome of the Trials, our roles were far larger than I'd ever imagined.

And Kilian... What did that make him? It challenged everything I thought I knew about him.

"I want to help you," I said. "Tell me who did this to you. Tell me so I can try to help."

"I've already said too much, Lirah. It's not your burden to bear right now."

"But it's yours? How can that be?"

"It's complicated. And now isn't the time to discuss it." His jaw was set, stubborn determination in his eyes. "I know you want to help. But you can do that by staying alive. By completing the third Trial and passing the Rite. It's wishful thinking, but maybe you'll be the one to break the curse after all."

I wasn't getting anything else out of him today.

I sighed. "Alright."

"Alright? I'm not used to you agreeing with me. It feels like you're speaking a different language."

"I'm only agreeing for *now*. But you can't keep me in the dark forever. And I have demands."

He caught my wrist, bringing the inside to his lips. "List them."

"I want to know about the third Trial."

He hesitated. "Are you sure? It could cause unnecessary panic."

"Or help us prepare," I shot back. "And I want the entire group to be trained on channeling in preparation for the Rite."

"Lirah. It's highly unlikely that, even with months of practice, every candidate would be able to channel well enough to pass the Rite."

"A chance is still a chance, no matter how small. Let each person decide for themselves whether they want to take it."

He nodded slowly. "Okay. We'll start tomorrow."

"Okay."

It was a weird thing, being in agreement with him. I was certain it would not last long. My fingers grazed his forearm, and he tensed ever so slightly. I let them trail up his arm, marveling at the contours.

I glanced up at him. "I lied. I don't really hate you. Not for a while now."

"I know." His hands wrapped around my lower back, and he pulled me closer. "I've never been so bewitched by such a dreadful liar."

The corners of my lips twitched. "I wonder what that says about you."

"Certainly that I have excellent taste."

His lips pressed against mine in a soft, slow kiss. His fingers sank into my hair, caressing my nape.

He drew back only to say, "I have something I need to prove. I believe the record was... twenty seconds, right?"

A mischievous glint appeared in his eyes, and my core went molten.

"More or less." I lifted my arms, and he pulled my tunic off, I lay flat on the ground as his fingers moved deftly along the ties on my gear. "No blade this time?" I teased.

But there was no amusement left in his eyes, only voracious want.

He undid the laces of my cuirass with ease. I didn't care that he was undressing me in the middle of a park in broad daylight. But as soon as the thought crossed my mind, a blanket of shadow caressed me, blocking out the sky above.

It was just Kilian and I in a pocket of darkness, only faint light streaming in from high above.

"This," Kilian said, his fingers splitting the gear apart, "is *only* for me."

He ran a hand down the plane of my stomach, and I whimpered. I wanted his hands on every inch of my body, rough and unyielding, not the gentle, whisper soft caress he was trailing along my skin. I wanted his length pressed against me, and to feel the hard lines of his body flush against mine. I wanted him to rock against me the same way he had done last night, with hips and teeth and rage. I wanted him utterly and completely. So much that the revelation scared me.

He pressed a soft kiss to the hardened peak of my nipple, his hand continuing its sweep across my stomach. His fingers unhooked the button at the top of my pants, and he unzipped the closure with maddening slowness. I didn't know what to concentrate on: his tongue as it dragged lazily across my neck or the hand tracing the seam of my underwear. He slipped a finger below the cotton band, stroking the skin just beneath.

He was barely touching me, but it felt like I was going to explode. My body was taut, my muscles quivering in anticipation.

"Are you planning on doing something worthwhile, or do I have to do it myself?" I bit out.

Kilian's answering laugh rumbled across the darkness, and I felt his smile press against my neck. I wanted to pull him away just so I could look at it, but I couldn't bear the thought of his lips parting with my skin. He dragged his teeth along the column of my throat in an arc that alone made me see stars. His lips pressed to the corner of my mouth, and he said, "So impatient."

I panted as his fingers dipped lower, drawing small, idle circles with each inch they descended. Until finally... *finally*...

Soft pressure glanced against the most sensitive spot on my body, and my eyes slammed shut, my neck stretching so that my mouth could slant against his. He met my urgent kiss, stroke for stroke, while his fingers continued their ministrations. It was not nearly the kind of pressure I craved though, and my hips rolled against the palm of his hand, needing release.

Kilian held me down with that same palm, his grip a stone vise, and I writhed beneath his hold. He tutted against my lips. "Good things come to those who wait."

His fingers traced the shape of me, running down my core and then right back up. He slid a finger inside of me, and then added a second. I wasn't going to make it. Not to the third Trial. I was going to fracture into a million tiny pieces of starlight.

And then, without warning, he wrenched his fingers out of me, dragging them back across my stomach. I nearly screamed at the loss of contact. He tore his lips away from mine. Staring down at me, he drew his fingers to his mouth and licked them clean.

"You'll forgive me," he said, his voice rough like gravel, "if I want a second taste. Lift your hips for me."

He pulled the waistband of my pants and underwear down in one swift move, and then paused as he stared at me, swallowing hard.

Everything inside of me was hot and aching, my entire body quivering. "Can you stop gawking and fuck me?" I didn't have time to ask nicely when I was wound tighter than a coil.

It seemed to jolt him out of his stupefaction. "There's that sailor's mouth I so enjoy."

Kilian placed his hands firmly on my thighs, holding me down as he positioned himself before me. I sank my hands into his silken hair. It was all I saw before the first swipe of his tongue against my folds, and my vision turned black.

He suckled, his tongue circling me with lethal precision and tantalizing accuracy. His fingers stroked my entrance and then they were back inside me, rolling and curving along a spot that made me gasp for air.

The feeling was choking, the sensation overwhelming. My skin was on fire, fresh hunger coursing through my veins. I ground my hips against him, but his grip on my thighs was firm, limiting my range of motion. I was going to scream if he didn't pick up the pace.

"Kilian," I rasped.

He lifted his head, lips glistening, silver eyes meeting mine. "You've never said my name before."

That was ludicrous. I'd said his name plenty of times... in my head. Never out loud to him.

"If I say it again, will you let me come?" I squirmed beneath him. "*Kilian.*"

He shivered. It was quick soft vibration of his skin against mine, but unmistakable. His expression morphed into one of pure, unfiltered need, a savage gleam in his eyes. His mouth was back on me.

"One." He spread my legs wide.

"Two." His tongue swept clean along my center.

"Three." He plunged two fingers inside of me.

"Four." His teeth grazed me, his tongue darting out to soothe the sting.

"Five." He gave me exactly what I needed.

His fingers set a fast pace, his tongue lapping against me, and my muscles quaked. My back bowed straight off the soft grass as blinding pleasure ripped through me. I was falling and flying, hurtling toward nothing, pure ecstasy singing in my soul as he kept the same hard rhythm, allowing me to ride out my high. I screamed his name as I came apart on his lips.

He grinned up at me with feral satisfaction.

"Five seconds. You just beat my record."

I wanted to hurl some witty retort back at him, but I was so sated I could barely keep my eyes open. I reached for him, but he pulled away, reluctance shining in his eyes.

"Not today, Lirah. We should get you back to the house and cleaned up before supper. Rite training starts tomorrow. You should get a good night's rest."

"You haven't told me about the third Trial yet," I said through a yawn.

"Tomorrow," he said. "You're exhausted. I can feel it."

I *was* exhausted. And I had been up at an ungodly hour this morning. I could use a bath, a hot dinner and a seven-to-eight-hour sleep.

I re-laced my cuirass and grasped my tunic, my movements sluggish as I pulled it over my head. I slid my pants back up my shaky legs. Kilian hooked a finger in the band where a belt might go, dragging me toward him. His hands fell to my waist.

I watched as he buttoned my leathers and zipped the closure back up. He leaned down to press a soft kiss against my head, and I breathed in his scent, letting it flood through me.

Something vital and raw had shifted between us today. I could feel it through the link. In the current of power echoing around him and encircling me.

It was a distressing peculiarity to note that I no longer loathed Kilian Valhan. An oddity to acknowledge that all the energy spent despising him had been a complete and utter waste. That after trying my very best not to, I'd still somehow fallen for the enemy.

And maybe... he wasn't really the enemy after all.

CHAPTER 19

"You're not paying attention." Kilian scowled at me across the sparring mat.

I tore my gaze from Lana beside us. She had, quite literally, been engulfed in golden light just a moment before. Septimus had rushed to absorb some of the overflow magic, helping her to the ground to rest for a moment. Even now, her skin still had a luminescent sheen to it.

The other candidates were in various stages of practice with their instructors as well. The sparring room was set in a simulation of the Rite. Every so often, a current branched out and we were supposed to draw on our respective links to diffuse it.

I glared right back at Kilian. "I am checking on my friend. Can you relax?"

"Septimus is supervising his candidate. He has it under control," he said through gritted teeth. "You're too focused on everyone else's progress instead of your own. Do you want your friends to live while you die, Lirahna? Because that's what will happen if you do not *pay attention*."

I raised a brow, amused by his use of my full name. "Overreact much?"

"Over–? I have half a mind to let you flounder your way through the Rite and see for yourself whether I'm 'overreacting.'"

"Why don't you then?" I jibed back.

"Because then you'd be dead. And for some reason I still can't comprehend, I'd be sad about it."

I rolled my eyes.

"You know, you should really host a seminar on how to provoke people. You're certainly overqualified to teach others," he muttered. "Now, will you stop driving me insane and *please* concentrate?"

I glanced at Lana, who was sipping on a blend of electrolytes and water, the glow slowly fading from her skin. Septimus hovered over her protectively.

"I'm fine, Lirah," she called, noting my concerned stare.

"If you need to rest–"

"I'm alright," she insisted.

I turned back to Kilian. "Fine. But I wasn't listening to you the first time you explained it. Can you tell me again?"

He sighed heavily, like I'd just told him we were under enemy attack instead. "When did I lose you?"

"Er... At the beginning?"

He consulted the ceiling like it held the answers to life's great mysteries. With patience he dredged up from the gods knew where, he said, "The magic manifests through the link in different ways for everyone. I'm able to manipulate it into various forms through years of practice, but my favored form is lightning. You're able to use it to summon darkness as well. There may be more you can do with it, depending on how well you hone the skill. Still following?"

"Yes. I used it in the cave network during the first Trial to help me see. What else can I use it for?"

"Anything, really, within the parameters of the power since it's only a grain, and you wouldn't be able to handle much more as a mortal. It can be used in combat as a strengthening tool or, in terms of the Rite, to diffuse power. It's just a matter of intention, instruction and focus. Each interaction you've had with it so far has been through your instruction. Whether consciously or subconsciously, you've been manipulating it to do what you want."

"So, if I intended to use it to knock you to the ground, I could do that?"

"If you happened to catch me off guard, which wouldn't happen, then sure."

"Hm. Interesting. Show me how."

He ran me through a few breathing exercises, meditative methods to declutter my mind and focus internally. I brushed against the link, pulling on it until something unspooled inside of me.

Show yourself, I commanded.

A deep, velvety voice that belonged neither to Kilian nor I whispered in the back of my mind. It was the same one I had heard when training on a wintry mountain with Septimus. A voice I had mistaken as Kilian's in the tunnel network during the first Trial. I was now certain it was an entity of its own.

With pleasure. What shall we destroy first, wicked?

I tore my eyes open to find the manifestation of power, a sphere of darkness floating between us. Whatever this shadowy orb was, it was *definitely* talking to me. Or maybe the Trials had broken my mind, and I had gone crazy a long time ago.

I stared at it, hardly daring to breathe as it undulated lazily, its edges hazy.

I grow weary of your indecision, it drawled. *There are enemies in the north. We must act swiftly. Let me loose, set me free, allow me to feast.*

My eyes widened.

"You're doing great, Lirah," Kilian said, clearly oblivious to the demonic voice that only I could hear.

"What do I do?" I hissed.

"Direct it. Guide it. It will listen to instruction."

I could feel the power pulsing from it, convinced it would obey no one, much less me. It terrified me. Half of my fear stemmed from the actual power that just casually lurked inside me, the remainder from being branded psychotic if anyone knew it conversed with me.

"You can do it," Kilian encouraged. "I'm right here. It'll be okay."

Hesitantly, I willed the sphere to move, my gaze flicking across the space. To my surprise, it did. It occupied the area on the right of Kilian, swirling in an amorphous wave before I sent it to the center once more.

Shall you have me perform party tricks for the rest of the day? it mused. *How insulting.*

"Let's try it with the current," Kilian said. "I'm going to send a shock through you. You'll need to instruct the magic to smother it."

The darkness made a noise which sounded an awful lot like a yawn. Was it *bored*?

Yes, it answered. *I desire a far more substantial meal than electricity. Blood and bones will suffice.*

A tingle buzzed along my fingertips, running down the length of my palm and the darkness vanished in a wink. It was barely a thought, more an acknowledgement of the current zipping through me. But then it was gone – disappearing with the shadows.

"Did I do it?" I breathed, relieved the disembodied voice had quietened.

My mind was relaxed, the calm of a still sea.

Kilian gave me an impressed look. "Yeah. You did it."

I scraped my nails along my palms, staring down at them in wonder. "Let's try it again."

Three nights later, Kilian found Lana, Moric and I alternating between training and practicing magic in the sparring room.

Lana had grown comfortable with summoning a beacon of light without having it swallow her completely. But Moric was still struggling somewhat with his grasp on Ayden's magic.

Earth magic was temperamental, he told us. Whenever he tried diverting the current in each simulation run, he ended up sprouting roots across the ground.

We still had time, Lana and I assured him. But it was more to soothe his anxiety. The truth was we were swiftly running out of it. The third Trial was in one day. The Rite would follow shortly after.

Optimism felt like an elusive dream these days, and I was cautious of where I placed my hope, but we had more of a chance than we'd had last week, and for that I was grateful.

I still hadn't told anyone about the dark voice inside my head; the one that always longed for battle and bloodshed. It had begun emerging more frequently but, truthfully, it was growing on me. I didn't know what that said about my frame of mind.

My gaze met Kilian's as he strode across the room, dressed for war.

"Where've you been?" I asked. I hadn't seen him all day. He'd been absent from our training session earlier as well.

"Greyhaven, resolving a strike."

"A strike?"

He waved a hand. "It happens every so often. This time it was over fair wages down at the quay. I had to diffuse it."

It sounded so… normal. We were fighting to see the next day but on the rest of the isles, life continued. But from what Kilian had told me about the real purpose of the Trials, it seemed that way of life was also at stake.

"Anyway," Kilian continued. "I've been meaning to find you to talk."

"In private?" I asked, glancing at Moric and Lana, who weren't even pretending not to eavesdrop.

"No. It's fine. I'm sure it'll come out anyway, so I might as well tell you all. It concerns the third Trial."

Lana dropped her practice dagger and crossed her arms, waiting.

"You're aware that the fae that once ruled Lortan?" Kilian asked.

"Yes. Azrael destroyed them." I couldn't help but play Augustine's words back in my head: *That is the version of history we have been taught.*

Kilian shook his head, regretfully. "The fae weren't destroyed. Not all of them, at least. A few remain in a sealed-off portion on Lortan. On what is still Cosanus. Only elven with special clearance for the Mortal Trials know this."

My eyes grew wide, my jaw dropping open. Moric took a step back, as if trying to put distance between himself and whatever was about to come next.

I had thought Augustine's theories were fanciful at best, mad at worst. For the fae to still exist, to be sequestered on this very isle, their entire history warped, and no one outside of the Mortal Trials knowing about it…

"How? Why? *How?*" I repeated.

"It doesn't matter. What matters is the third Trial takes place on Cosanus. And your objective will be to find the cave in there that houses the remaining fae. We think there's a weapon hidden with them. You'll need to bring it back," Kilian said.

"You *think*?" Lana scowled. "Gods above. If you hadn't already sent us into a monster's lair in the first Trial, I'd think you were joking."

But Kilian was not the joking type. At least not about something like this.

"What does the weapon do?" I asked.

He stared levelly at me. "I hope it'll save the world."

Moric glanced between the two of us. "One of you needs to explain exactly what the fuck is going on."

I still needed to tell them everything Kilian had shared about the Trials that day in the park. "Later. I'll brief you both later."

Kilian carried on, "The fae were left in Cosanus before it was sealed off from the remainder of Lortan, and no elven can cross to retrieve the weapon." He gave me a pained look. "It has to be you."

I had so many questions and unknowns that my head felt like it might explode. So I considered what I *did* know. There was a plot underway which would have a grievous impact on humanity. Kilian was trying to prevent it from happening. But he was cursed, stripped of his full powers, and waiting for someone to come along who would be able to break it. And somehow, this weapon would help.

"I know it's a lot to digest, and I want to answer your questions, but as a priority there are things you need to be briefed on. Cosanus is a hostile environment," Kilian warned.

"No shit. I would have never guessed," Lana muttered.

"The only way to get there is through a scry," Kilian said.

"I've heard about scries," Lana interjected, and Moric nodded. "We have one in Dorisport."

Kilian nodded. "There's one on each isle. But they're temperamental things. You have to input the precise co-ordinates of a corresponding scry or else you'll end up stuck somewhere in the plane between."

I shivered, the thought making me feel claustrophobic.

"We use the scries often on official business to the mortal isles, the monthly occasion to drop magic into the soil or to negotiate trading agreements. Have you ever seen one, Lirah?" Kilian asked.

I shook my head.

"It's a portal, fueled by upper magic," he continued. "But they only work if another scry has been set up at the location you're trying to enter. And it's the fastest way to get to Cosanus. It'll drop you right outside the boundary. Then you'll have to cross over yourselves. What do you know of the world before the elven and mortals?"

I glanced at Moric and Lana, anxiety settling inside me. They gave me blank looks which I was sure matched my own. "Nothing."

"Right, okay. When the fae ruled, the land was very different. Where mortals and elven find sustenance in food and water, the fae nourished themselves with magic. The land – Cosanus – was rich in it. But it wasn't the type of magic we know these days. The gods tamed it with the introduction of the elven afterward, but before that, the kind of magic on Cosanus was raw and wild, completely unchecked, and the fae grew drunk on it. You know of their rebellion against the gods which prompted their destruction?"

Three nods.

"They betrayed the gods. They stole weapons of great importance. One has remained missing for a very long time, and we have reason to believe it might be on Cosanus. Scries cannot be set up within Cosanus. We've tried before but our current magic doesn't react well to that environment. So a portal was set up just outside, right on the edges of the salt-lined boundary delineating the end of Lortan and the beginning of their land. That's the furthest an elven can go. We can't cross the boundary. The salt – it's not ordinary dinner-table seasoning. It comes from the mountain Caspir, directly from the land of the gods."

"Is that where the stupid rumor that elven can't cross salt comes from?" Lana muttered. "It would have been helpful knowing what *type* of salt before we wasted so much of it on Augustine."

"This is… a lot to process," Moric murmured. "Much more stressful than wasting salt, Lana." Sweat had begun dotting his brow.

I couldn't understand why Cosanus still existed, or why certain fae remained upon it. Azrael was supposed to have destroyed them all for their rebellion. The God of Death did not strike me as merciful and so there had to be a reason they were spared. But either way, the gods were divine. Azrael's actions couldn't be questioned. To do so was treasonous. And I was not in the business of angering the God of Death when my life hung so precariously in the balance.

"If the elven cannot cross, does that mean the fae cannot either?" I asked.

"Yes. Cosanus itself has been purged of magic, but the land is constantly craving it. You've each got a grain of magic from the link. The land will want it. We estimate you can go undetected for about an hour before the land begins leeching from you whatever power it can. It won't stop taking until it kills you. So you'll need to get out before then. Whether you've found the weapon or not, once the hour is up, you have to be back on Lortan."

"Forget the land, what about the *fae*?" Moric's voice hitched a decibel higher.

"There's no magic for them to consume on Cosanus. My best guess is they've entered a sleep-like stasis in their cave," Kilian said calmly.

"Your best guess," Lana echoed dully.

"How will we even know where to look? Do you have a map?" I asked.

He grimaced. "No. The exact coordinates are unclear. Which is why we'll have to split you up on different points around Cosanus. You'll each enter in pairs so you can cover more ground before the hour is up. The teams have already been set by Echon."

I stared at him in disbelief. It was an impossible task. A dangerous one, made almost entirely of conjecture. And to add wood to the pyre, he was telling us that the elven who hated my guts had set the pairings? I felt faint.

"Do you have *any* good news for us?" Lana asked weakly.

"Your sprites will be able to join you on this Trial," he offered. "It's a weird glitch in the rock salt we discovered recently. Technically, they shouldn't be able to cross, given their relation to the fae, but the salt doesn't register sprites. We think it has to do with their size. They don't emit as much energy as an elven or fae. We're still conducting studies on it." All of this was added as an aside and Moric shook his head in disbelief.

"That doesn't help," he wailed. "We still have to face the creepy fae and hope to all the gods they don't eat us alive."

"I'm ninety-nine percent sure they're asleep," Kilian said. "And don't underestimate your sprites. They might be of more use than you think."

"Still doesn't make me feel better," Moric said.

Kilian was giving me a worried look. "I know this is far from ideal, but the weapon... We wouldn't send you in there if it wasn't important."

I swallowed past the hard lump in my throat.

"If you pass the Rite, I swear I'll explain everything," Kilian said. "It will all make sense, I promise."

If we even made it to the Rite.

If the fae or the land itself did not kill us first.

"You just need to trust me until then. Can you trust me?" This wasn't a question aimed at the others. Kilian was asking *me*.

I stared up into silver, imploring eyes, trying to quell the panic rising inside my chest. I wanted to trust him. I really did. I wanted to believe that he would not risk my life, the lives of my friends, on a whim. He had advised us on the third Trial and was preparing us for the Rite, but other than that he wasn't giving me much to hold on to other than his words. And I couldn't help but feel my days would come to an end before I could give an honest answer to his question.

After all, promises meant nothing if you did not live to see them fulfilled.

CHAPTER 20

A great feast had been spread along each of the tables in the mess hall, but no one ate.

There was a soft scuttling as a rat scurried across the floors. I watched as it wended its way past the legs of the table where Kilian sat beside Septimus.

He looked at me, his face blank. But through the link, gentle sorrow scraped across my mind.

Are you okay? he asked.

Considering the third Trial is in an hour, just dandy.

Eat something.

So I can vomit when I cross the scry? No, thanks.

Right before the feast, Echon had briefed us all on the Trial and announced who we'd be teamed up with. I had the particular joy of entering Cosanus with Caleb, the Grilish alphabet expert.

Lana would enter with Rayna.

Moric with Keila.

And Nox and Mattieu would round up the group.

Food made my stomach churn and my mouth dry. I was nauseous and lightheaded. I stood quickly, and Lana looked up at me.

"I need some air," I said.

"I'll come with you." She set her clean fork on the table.

"Me too," Moric muttered, pushing his plate away.

I didn't look at Kilian as I left the mess hall.

I stepped onto the balcony just outside, leaning my arms against the railing for support and looked up at the cold night sky. Starlight winked bright and blue, scattered in constellations that had always fascinated me.

The door snicked shut as Lana and Moric joined me at the railing.

I pointed up at the sky, at a cluster of stars that looked like a network of veins spiraling from a tight core. "That one's named after Roriola, the Goddess of the Hunt," I said to them. "They say she sleeps somewhere far away, imprisoned for betraying one of her own."

Lana tilted her neck skyward. She carved out a sharp, whiplike curve through the sky. "I know that one. Kadax, the God of Cruelty and Malice. They pray to him on Dorisport, even though he sent plagues and forest fires in the past."

Moric sighed softly. His hand swept across the northern sphere, where the stars scattered in a straight line, arching near the point to split into two branches like a wishbone. "That one's Adonitis, God of Luck and Fortune. May he be with us tonight as we cross into Cosanus."

I reached out to link hands with my friends, not daring to point out the constellation that drifted above us forebodingly, shaped like a beautiful spiderweb, stars dotting each corner like gleaming strands of silver silk. Azrael, the God of Death.

We stood like that for a while, until the door cracked open behind us.

Septimus stood at the threshold, his eyes only on Lana. "It's time, sunshine."

I grasped my friends' fingers, squeezing tight. I turned to Moric first. I refused to cry as I looked up into his handsome face, hazel eyes dark in the moonlight. "Be safe. Keep watch. Come back."

He pulled me in for a quick embrace and pressed a kiss to the top of my head before pulling away to hug Lana. "I won't say goodbye," he said. "But... if something happens to me..."

"Don't," I said.

He gave me a stern look. "If something happens, will you make sure my brother's taken care of?"

I nodded, my lip wobbling. Something about this last Trial felt so... final.

Moric turned before the tears welling in his eyes could spill. He brushed past Septimus and hurried back through the mess hall.

Lana took a step toward me, and I held out a hand. She clasped it, pulling me close to her. She wrapped her arms around my neck.

"I love you," she whispered.

"I love you too."

We broke apart, and she wiped a hand across her glistening cheek. I bit my lip hard enough to draw blood. *I will not cry.*

I slipped through the door, leaving her and Septimus on the balcony. When I glanced back, his hands were on her waist, no amusement in his eyes, only gentle yearning and desperate sadness. He stroked a thumb across her cheek, lips brushing softly against hers as fine summit snow wreathed them. The door softly shut behind me. I moved sluggishly through the now deserted mess hall and downstairs.

Kilian waited for me in the courtyard, Calendula perched on his forearm. Silver snow coated his dark hair. He looked like a fallen angel.

The scry had been set up at the arch. It was a wide doorway with a solid base, and was big enough for two people to step though at once. It glowed blue, its insides swirling with brilliant streams of light and gossamer threads. The other candidates stood with their instructors and sprites nearby, but I paid them no attention as I crossed to Kilian. I stared up at him, a wordless conversation passing between us.

Calendula flitted off him as he drew his arms tightly around me. My hands went to his neck. His lips pressed against mine tenderly, like we had all the time in the universe. Trust Kilian Valhan to kiss me like my entire world wasn't about to end.

He kissed me so thoroughly, so languidly, it left me breathless. But I needed his lips on mine more than I needed air. When he eventually broke away, he stared down at me, fierce intent in his eyes.

"Come back to me. Promise it." There was urgency in his voice. Terror too.

I swallowed. "I can't promise that."

His eyes shuttered. He dropped his forehead to mine, breathing hard. "Remember everything I told you. Keep your eyes sharp. And you make sure you're out of there before the hour is up, Lirah. I mean it."

I nodded. "I'll remember."

"There's still so much you need to know. Come back so I can

tell you."

I looked across the courtyard, to where Moric and Keila now stood directly before the scry. It hummed gently, a dazzling aquamarine glow pulsing from it. It was time.

"I have to go," I told him.

He pressed his lips feverishly to my forehead before clutching my hand and leading me to the scry. Calendula soared ahead, her wings tucked close to her body as she flew in a tight line.

I watched as Moric and Keila stepped through together, the light twisting and undulating around them with a milky haze. And then they were gone. Caleb stood a few feet from the scry, a sour look on his face. A woodland sprite sat on his shoulder, her entire body trembling.

"Are you ready, Aldhur?" Caleb asked.

"As I'll ever be."

He gave me a sharp nod and strode forward.

Calendula floated to my shoulder, and I twisted my neck to look at her. "I thought you didn't like the shoulder perch?"

"I understand tonight is tough for you." She sniffed. "I'm trying to make things easier."

I smiled. "Did anyone ever tell you you're the greatest shadow sprite a girl could have?"

Her chest puffed out proudly and her cheeks tinged gray. Gray. She was *blushing*.

I faced the scry, stepping up to the solid dais beside Caleb. Heat roiled in waves from within, warm against my cold skin. Tendrils of blue light snaked out, and I wondered whether it would feel as it looked, like stepping into clouds and nothing.

Kilian punched in a set of coordinates on a keypad affixed to the scry, and its whirring increased in tempo.

I looked over my shoulder to where Lana was entering the courtyard, hand in hand with Septimus. Rayna waited for her with Echon, just before the arch. Kilian took a step back from the scry, mouth set in a grim line.

Perhaps it was the ache in my chest, or the pain in his eyes, but words tumbled from my mouth. The promise I was not sure I could keep: "I'll come back."

With the image of him branded in my mind, I stepped through.

CHAPTER 21

Stepping through the scry did not feel like stepping into air. It was hot and muggy, like wading through thigh-deep water. Or gelatin.

It was over in a few seconds. The scry grew silent behind us, its insides dulling to a dark gray. The portal would reopen in exactly an hour. Time was already running out. Calendula shivered gently on my shoulder, and I knew it was not from cold.

The stretch of land Caleb and I stood on was warm, unlike the cool air at Valhan House. It reminded me of the summers on Serila. The grass was patchy and dry, as if it hadn't seen rain in a very long time.

When I looked out, I could see nothing but empty land. There were no other candidates in view. The scry had deposited them further along the boundary.

As for Caleb and I, we stood quite close to Cosanus. I could see a thin line of salt yawning across the dry grass for miles.

"We should just stay out here and wait for the hour to pass," Caleb said.

We *could* do that. It wasn't like there was anyone out here to make sure we crossed over into Cosanus and endured whatever horrors were waiting on the other side. Maybe the others would stay on this side of the border.

But I couldn't. This Trial – finding the weapon – was important.

"You don't have to come." I shrugged. "But I'm going."

I took a step toward the salt and Caleb groaned. "I can't just let you go in there alone."

"Then come with but decide quickly. We're running out of time."

He made an irritated noise and then I heard his hurried footsteps behind me as I crossed over the boundary.

As soon as I did, it was clear I was no longer on Lortan as I knew it. Sweat pricked on my nape. The field of grass had disappeared. What stretched before us now was scorched ground, a desert of cracked soil, uneven with dips and swells, some far higher than others. Though the moon hung low overhead, the heat was sweltering. Dusty sand stirred in a warm breeze, billowing across the top of my shoes, and I blinked against the small grains in the air.

"We're here now. Which way should we go?" Caleb scanned left then right. There was nothing but abandoned land as far as I could see.

"Can you feel anything?" I asked Calendula.

The tiny sprite shuddered. "There is nothing left."

But the night sky was out, the stars in full, unimpeded view. I looked up toward the gentle curve of Mahleia, the northernmost star. "Let's carry on straight ahead and see what we find."

Caleb set a hard pace, his strides long and measured – but I had been training for this too. Running each day and building my strength so that I could keep up. Calendula's foot bobbed nervously at my clavicle, and I whispered, "Are you okay?"

She made a faint noise that was halfway between a yes and a no. "There is so much death here. I can feel it."

The land certainly looked dead, but aside from that there were no rotting carcasses or skeletal remains visible.

In fact, our surroundings had not changed much in the minutes we had been walking. Only a few rocks had cropped up, jutting out of the ground like monoliths. Every so often, we stumbled across geysers. I steered clear of one now as it rumbled menacingly, and hot water jettisoned out of its tip in a quick stream, filling the air with steam. The ground fizzled where the water splashed, searing the earth. Sweat streamed down my neck.

Then there was silence. There were no insects or other animals, no vegetation that I could see. It was as if the land had wholly swallowed all traces of life. Even if something wanted to grow here, I had a feeling the land would not let it.

"This is pointless," Caleb muttered as we passed yet another stone that looked similar to one we'd seen moments earlier. "Wandering around a desert, looking for a cave and some mystical weapon. You do realize that the farther we go, the longer it will take to get back to the border, right?"

I glanced down at the watch strapped to my wrist. We had been walking for fifteen minutes now, which did not leave us much time to find a weapon and return to the scry before the land cracked one sleepy eye and consumed us too.

"I know that. But we have to try. Maybe we should climb one of the higher banks to see our surroundings better? Let's also keep watch of the time and when it hits the halfway mark we'll start to head–" I paused. "Can you hear that?" I cocked my head to the right as music – no, not *music*, voices called out.

A cacophony of them, all overlapping, all crying and screaming at once. It was too much. I grabbed my head, dropping to one knee as I struggled to focus around the sound.

Caleb clutched my wrist, his face angling in front of mine. "What is it?"

I grit my teeth. "Voices. So many voices!"

"I can't hear anything!"

"It's the death." Calendula hovered in midair, then dropped to my knee. "Breathe, Lirah. Push through it. You need to follow it."

Follow it? I wanted to run a hundred miles from it.

The sound grated against my eardrums like a high-pitched staccato, but mournful. *So* mournful. The last note sounded like it was drawn by a violin.

The noise gave way to a fervent muttering, a thread of words spoken over and over, but at least the screaming had ceased.

"Your nose," Caleb said in horror. "It's bleeding."

I lowered a hand to it, dragging my fingertips across my skin to find it wet. The blood glistened beneath the moonlight.

"I'm okay." I caught my breath for a minute and when the ground stabilized beneath me, I allowed Caleb to pull me back to my feet.

"What happened to you?" Caleb asked.

"I don't know." I glanced around, the voices still playing in a loop in my head, urgent and panicked, in a language I didn't understand. But from their tone, I knew it was a command. They wanted me to do something.

"It's this way." I stumbled across the plain, in a more western direction, where the earth sloped into a steep skyward curve. Following the sound like I followed the link, I allowed myself to be tugged by the crescendo of voices. It was almost unbearable. I couldn't *think* around it, and still they spoke, words that were guttural and melodic at the same time; strange sounds overlapping in different pitches with one another.

"Don't you think it's weird you're hearing things *I'm* not?" Caleb called from behind me. "That it might be a trick?"

"A trick from who?" I was breathless as I climbed the hill, nearing the top.

"I don't know, maybe this evil fucking place we're in?" Caleb grunted as he trailed after me.

I shook my head as the voices continued fervently, like they were trying to tell me something.

At the peak, the plain stretched out in uninhibited view. And visible with it was a cave-like structure. It was as wide as it was tall and seemed to be made of many small stones, all welded together to form a large circle.

"There it is," I said, relief wending through me as I slid down the slope. Scuffling sounded behind me from Caleb.

"What does it mean?" I asked Calendula as I strode toward the cave. The very ground thrummed as I neared it. I recognized it for what it was: energy, unlike anything I had ever felt before. Radiating from within the monolith was death. Glacial, ruthless death.

I repeated the chant; the words being yelled at me.

Her face went pale gray. She whispered, "Keep away. And never return."

"That's encouraging," Caleb muttered.

A large black mouth gaped open like it wanted to devour us. Another salt line ringed the base of the cave, fencing it off.

"Fuck." Caleb's eyes tracked the salt. "They really don't want the fae getting out."

A shiver skittered down my spine. No one would save us. If we died here, Kilian would not even be able to cross into Cosanus to retrieve our bodies.

"We should go back," Caleb said, his voice wavering. "I have a *bad* feeling about this."

I did too. A gut-gnawing, sinking feeling that nothing good was going to come of entering this cave.

The voices... I'd thought they were commanding me toward the cave. But they were warning me away. They went silent now, as if they had done their job and now waited for me to make my own decision.

I looked at my watch, chewing on my lip. "We still have time."

"Gods above, of all the people I had to get paired with for this challenge, I had to get the one who *wants* to go into the scary cave filled with ancient monsters," Caleb complained.

"You don't have to come," I snapped.

"If you die in there, I'll have to explain how it happened to your terrifying instructor, and then he'll probably kill me anyway," he grouched. "Let's just get this over with."

Caleb reached into his pocket and drew out a small globe. It glowed a bright silver. "Orblight," he explained. "I nicked it from one of the sconces in Valhan House."

I was reluctantly impressed. How clever for someone who'd insisted on the easiest solution for Septimus' alphabet riddle.

I unsheathed the dagger Umma had gifted me so long ago. It brought me a small comfort. Rubbing my thumb across the ruby hilt, I thought of home. Home, which no longer felt like Serila, but like a girl with cornsilk hair and fierce loyalty, a soft boy who loved his brother, and a pair of silver eyes that haunted me.

I stepped across the boundary. Calendula's wings fluttered, timed perfectly with my own racing heart. The light from the orb illuminated the rocks around us and the parched ground ahead, casting everything in an incandescent sheen. Goosebumps prickled my skin as new shadows were thrown into light, each step bringing us closer to the unknown. We followed the curve of the wall until the stones sliced open, revealing a cavernous space. What was set inside turned my saliva to sawdust.

In the glow of the orblight, a long banquet table swam into view. Food, which had long since rotted and turned to powder, littered the surface of the table. And among it, discolored in the light, was bone.

But the most horrifying thing in the room were not the tiny fragments of bone filling each plate, but the thirteen massive creatures that sat, unmoving, in chairs before them. Each one was as large and tall as Kilian, their faces withered and sunken. Veins protruded from their stretched skin, pale and grey. Leathery, paper-thin wings sprouted from their backs, shrunken and decrepit as they hung on the floor, centuries of sand and dust coating every inch of them.

The remaining fae. All that existed of the primordial creatures who had seen the beginning of our world.

They looked like statues, carved from ancient stone. Their eyes open and unseeing, glazed over from years of desiccation. They were not dead though. They were meant to be immortal. There was just no magic left for them to feed on. They had entered a stasis, just as Kilian had predicted.

I swallowed as I stepped forward, my eyes scanning the rest of the space for any sort of weapon. I wasn't sure if Calendula was even breathing, face-to-face with her prehistoric ancestors.

"We need to search for the weapon," I whispered, but the words sounded loud and harsh in the absolute stillness.

Caleb nodded, moving carefully around the table, giving the fae a wide berth. His sprite flitted from his shoulder, landing softly on the table. She picked her way daintily across the plates, searching. Calendula's wings fluttered ahead of me.

"Don't go too far," I murmured.

The shadow sprite dipped inside a dusty vase in the middle of the table, her resounding sneeze echoing through the cavern.

I shot a wild look at the fae, but they remained motionless.

I probed through the ether for the voices that had warned me away so desperately, but nothing reached back. Dropping to my knees, I dipped my head beneath the table, but only dry sand and faded bone was visible. Caleb's shadow was moving around, taking the orblight as he went. The light flickered and danced, and the shadows inside of me thrummed.

I moved away from the table, convinced there was no weapon hidden beneath and instead focused on the fae seated around it. The one closest to me looked female. Her thin hair had separated in clumps on her skull, leaving bald patches behind, but I could tell she had once been beautiful. She had a heart-shaped face and large, glazed-over eyes, her full lips parted as if she were about to speak. She wore a rose-colored gown, with a low neckline that hung limply off her too-thin body. The grey veins snaking along her forearms made her look dehydrated and malnourished.

I examined the male beside her. He was broad-shouldered and twice as big. A cut ran across his left eye to his chin. Several onyx rings gleamed on his fingers.

The fae opposite him was tall and lean. He stared ahead sagely; his jaw was relaxed but his posture rigid. How a soldier might hold himself. He looked calm, in the way one might when they've accepted death. I scrutinized his face. I had the strangest feeling I'd seen him before, but as soon as I tried chasing the thought, it vanished.

He wore a sleeveless chain-link tunic above an open necked shirt, exposing the hard column of his throat. A delicate silver chain wound around his neck, its pendant resting against his breastbone. Shaped like a dagger, it was large and looked heavy, and at its hilt…

It couldn't be.

I held out the dagger Umma had given me, placing it near the one on the fae's chest, comparing them side-by-side. His tunic concealed most of his dagger, but its hilt peeked through the mesh, the stone in the center a polished ruby that, after all these years, had not dulled in shine.

They were the same.

Why were they the same? What were the chances of me entering Cosanus, finding a cavern filled with sleeping fae, only to find an exact replica of the dagger Umma had gifted me at the very start of all this?

It couldn't be a coincidence. There was something here, something more to this, something that somehow connected me and my dagger to the weapon around the fae's neck.

This had to be the weapon we were looking for. I was certain of it. I only wondered why Kilian had sent me in here to find it, when I'd had its twin all along. But that was a question I'd have to ask when I saw him again.

I looked down at my watch. Forty minutes had passed.

"Caleb."

He turned from where he stood, orblight in hand as he peered down at the contents of a long-forgotten serving platter.

"This is it. Come help me take it off."

"Are you sure?"

Now wasn't the time to explain to him why I had no doubts this was exactly what we were looking for. "See any other weapons around here?"

"No." Caleb set the orblight on the table, his hands fluttering around the fae before giving me a lost look.

I huffed a sigh. "Hold out his armor so I can pull the chain free."

Caleb grimaced as his hands brushed the fae's tunic, eyes wide with fear and never leaving the male's face. There was no clasp to the chain, so it had to be pulled over his head. This close, I could feel how cold and hard the fae's skin was. Like the blood had congealed and solidified in his body, turning his skin to granite.

I tried grasping the chain, but it was as if the links were fused to the fae's skin. Like it had gotten stuck there as he had solidified.

"What's going on?" Caleb whispered.

I didn't dare breathe, not this close. Not when I had smelled the death clinging to the fae. I tried again, but I couldn't get a grip on the chain.

"Cut it free," Caleb urged.

I angled my own blade to the fae's skin, trying to dig the tip beneath it, terror coursing through me all the while. The silver scraped across flesh turned stone, but there was no way for it to slide beneath the chain unless I sawed through it. Even then, we didn't have the *time* for me to make my way around the entire thing. Panic bubbled inside of me, cresting into a scream I was too afraid to let loose in the eerie cavern.

Sweat dotted my palms, and it took me a second to realize it wasn't just because I was overheating with nerves. My dagger was slowly warming, searing my hand with heat. The blade turned orange where it met the fae's skin and I wrenched it away. It fell to the ground with a thud, sand pluming in its wake. Caleb jerked backward, his boots knocking the chair behind him.

I didn't understand what was happening, but Calendula did.

For the first time since I had known her, the shadow sprite swore. Out of the corner of my eye I saw the smallest finger on the fae's right hand twitch.

There had to be magic imbued in the blade. Because the fae before me had begun to breathe. Ragged, gasping breaths sounded as he sucked in lungfuls of air.

As he breathed, the chain around his neck rustled. Without thinking, I reached for it again, pulling hard. It gave way easily this time, the magic seemingly unsticking it from the fae's neck. I pulled it over his head even as his hands slowly reached for me, fingers stiff and unbending. He was sluggish and clumsy, awakening from his slumber, but I doubted it would last for long. I stepped back quickly, horror eating at my heart.

The fae blinked, onyx leeching into what were once stone-grey eyes. His wings rustled half-heartedly, stirring the dust on the floor. His skin was deathly pale, veins still hard and protruding.

I was frozen in place, my heart thumping against my ribcage like a war drum, so loud I was sure the fae could hear it. Caleb stood, also immobile, near the edge of the table, his sprite between the dinner plates. The fae turned his head toward me in a sickeningly slow arch that made the bones in his neck crack. His lips parted and the low sound he uttered was so primal and throaty that it stirred something in the deepest recesses of my soul.

The next few moments seemed to happen in slow motion. The fae rotated his wrist, congealed blood squelching as he clenched and unclenched his fingers. In one swift motion, he whipped his hand out, reaching for Caleb's woodland sprite. He grasped the sprite with long fingers and black nails, drawing her toward him.

The fae's mouth snapped open wide, and his teeth closed around the sprite's head. There was only the shocking crack of bone and the wet smacking of his lips as the sprite's head separated from her body, blood and strings of gore pulsing from where her neck used to be.

Caleb let out a shriek of pure terror. Some color had returned to the fae's skin now, and there was a vibrance in his eyes as they snapped toward Caleb. The legs of the chair scraped back, and my heart dipped, stopped and restarted all at once when I realized that the fae was rising, bones clicking and snapping from years of disuse.

The neurons in my brain began firing all at once. I snatched my dagger from the ground, sheathing it quickly, and slipped the one I had taken from the fae around my own neck. It fell against my chest with a heavy thud and the fae swiveled his head toward me.

Fuck.

"Run!" I yelled.

Calendula whizzed past me, not needing to be told twice. I didn't look at the fae, or the remains of the woodland sprite, or even Caleb. I turned on my heel and fucking *ran*.

I didn't need to look behind me to know I was being chased. Wings rustled and scraped along the ground. The noise the fae emitted was so ancient and malevolent, it made me want to drop to my knees and puke. His hunger and rage ripped through the cavern, the energy so fierce and powerful. My legs burned but I continued sprinting, following the curve of the wall until a warm breeze greeted me and I saw the exit, the salt boundary beyond glistening in the moonlight.

The orblight flickered once and then disappeared. I heard the glass smack and crack, before chancing a look over my shoulder. Caleb had tripped over a root, his hand outstretched toward the smashed globe. I turned back. Gripping his hand, I heaved him up and yanked him across the boundary. I collapsed on the dirt, panting, as the fae came flying into view behind us.

The veins in his neck had softened slightly and color had returned to his face, flushing his cheeks with a faint pink tinge. He was a marvel to behold. Terrifying in his beauty. Large, leathery wings unfurled behind him as he licked the blood off his lips.

Onyx eyes pierced straight through me. "I have waited many years to destroy your kind," he said, voice harsh. He looked down at the salt line before him with distaste curling his lips. "I can wait a while longer."

Caleb yanked on my arm, but I ignored him. Calendula stirred the air around me, wings flapping anxiously.

Bold with the knowledge that he could not cross, I stood. "Why do you want to destroy us? We have done you no harm."

A cold, cruel smile touched the corners of the fae's lips, and he spoke in that commanding, primeval voice. "You do not know? How foolish you have allowed yourself to become."

I stepped forward, despite Caleb's insistent tugging, but the fae was moving, back into the depths of the cave. Darkness swallowed him instantly.

"Wait!" I shouted.

The rustling faded to a soft slither as the fae disappeared. Hollow, abject disappointment struck through me. Caleb succeeded then in spinning me around to face him.

"What?" I half-shouted, frantic with adrenaline, questions burning through me like acid.

"We need to go. The hour is nearly up!"

I looked down at my watch. Ten minutes left. It wasn't enough time.

We took off in a blind sprint, scrambling back up the hill. The dagger clanged against my chest with each stride toward the scry. I slipped at the peak, skidding down the slope and into the flatter part of the plain. I didn't allow myself a moment to catch my breath before hurtling after Caleb, gaze swinging between the land and the stars ahead, making sure we were going in the right direction. When we crested a mound and I saw the brilliant blue light of the portal up ahead, I nearly sobbed with relief. But there wasn't time to cry; we had to keep going. There were only three minutes left until the land discovered us and took whatever energy it could.

My lungs protested and my throat was parched, but still I ran. The ground rumbled beneath us and Caleb faltered ahead, tripping over his feet. A massive gurgle came from below and the ground fissured, soil cracking and warping. Boiling water spurted from the slivers in a rapid stream, so hot and close it felt like my skin was melting right off. I instinctively shielded my face with my arms, my knees dropping to the ground.

"Get up!" Calendula screamed.

But I couldn't. My arms and hands were raw, the skin around my eyes so sensitive. When I blinked, all I saw were waves of silver and gray. Strong hands grabbed me beneath my armpits, yanking me to my feet, and I blinked again. Caleb's face was blurry as we ambled across the desert, my weight leaning heavily against him. We were too late. Our time was up and the land was waking. I was only slowing him down. He had to leave me. The both of us didn't have to die in here.

I shoved weakly at his arm, wincing at the sharp pain that shot through my body. "You have to go. I'll be right behind you."

Caleb paused for just a second, and I knew he was considering it.

"Go!" I insisted.

He took off as I wheezed. I wiped a hand over my brow. I knew the sticky substance there was not sweat, but peeling flesh. Through my hazy vision, I saw blood coating my fingers.

Calendula was yelling at me to run, but I barely heard her. I could hardly hear my own thoughts through the blood pumping in my ears. My legs moved forward, slow and lethargic. I considered crawling the rest of the way.

The ground lurched beneath me once more, thrumming with energy it could only be taking from us. The hour had to have passed by now.

It was stiflingly hot on Cosanus, but a chill swept through me. It was a foreign sensation, sharp nails dragging across my chest, splitting me open so the land could drink from me.

The sky lit, a brief flash of brilliant light that pained my eyes.

The scry. Caleb had surely made it out. He would tell Kilian what happened.

I suddenly remembered the dagger.

I hadn't given it to Caleb. Kilian *needed* the dagger. I let loose a ragged scream.

I had to make it past the boundary. I had to give him the dagger if that was the last thing I did before my body failed. Each step felt like I was walking on glass. Sand grated against my eyeballs, blurring my vision, but I forced one foot in front of the other. The air was thick around me. I could barely breathe. I stumbled forward, falling on my hands and knees. Grains of rough sand ripped through the exposed flesh on my palms, burning as if I were holding my hand above a flame, but I inched forward, desperate and praying to whichever of the gods were listening.

Salt.

The thin white line yawned before me and I cried, a gasping choking noise as I shoved myself forward, the salt stinging each wound simultaneously. I rolled across the line, back into Lortan, just as the ground splintered and another shot of sizzling water spurted right behind me from deep below.

The heat was unbearable, the steam so excruciatingly painful that all I could do was curl into a fetal position, allowing my back to take the brunt of it. The leather of my pants seared into my skin; I screamed but there was nothing except empty field to hear me. I couldn't remember what it felt like to *not* be in pain. It was all I could think about, all I could feel. There was only agony and the teasing lure of oblivion if I just allowed death to take me. But Calendula was there, her voice a lifeline.

"Lirah, you must get up!"

I wanted to tell her I couldn't, but I was so exhausted.

My body no longer worked. The flesh had melted right off it, leaving charred muscle and skeletal remains behind. I could hardly see through the blood and sand in my eyes.

Still, Calendula urged me, "There's a scry opening! Just up ahead. You have to survive. *Please*, survive." Her voice in my ear was urgent, her plea a broken whisper.

The last of the heat evaporated into the air, and I forced my eyes open, my lids scraping like sandpaper against the sensitive, innermost gel.

I blinked through the grit, just able to make out the shadowy shape of an arch, blue light filtering through it.

Gods, it would be so easy to close my eyes again. I longed to slip into nothing. A place where pain did not exist. There would be no Trials, no Rite, no more death and loss. Just peace. I considered it. Considered all I would be trading in. I'd never hear Lana's laugh again, or Moric teasing her over her infatuation with Septimus. I thought about my room in Valhan House, which would be stripped bare of all traces of my stay in it. My mother breaking down with the news. I thought of Lana's hand in mine over a grimy table in a tavern not so long ago. Kilian's hands on my waist, lips on mine. His voice at my ear. I could almost hear what he'd tell me.

It would *be easy. But it's a coward's way out. You are many things, Lirah, but a coward is not one of them.*

Trust Kilian to ruin my plans for a peaceful, early retirement without even being here.

I sucked in a breath. I was dying, could feel each precious gasp for breath rattle my lungs. But there was a single thread which I was hanging on to. It shimmered bright and golden, refracting into brilliant shards that reflected the faces of everyone I loved.

I was not ready to give up. I wanted to live. To hug my friends, even if it was just once more. My muscles trembled as I crawled toward the scry, skin tearing on my forearms as I dragged my body forward. I grunted, expelling all the air in my burning lungs.

Calendula gripped my belt-loop. I heard her tiny wings fluttering as fast as a hummingbird's as she tried tugging me along. I reached one blood-slicked hand out, fingers scraping the side of the scry. In one final push, I heaved forward. And then I was falling. Falling… falling… falling through the scry's murky depths.

Starlight and inky darkness pooled around me, and then blessed, cool air enveloped me.

I stared up at the night. The stars were fuzzy, their light distorting into a million dazzling streams across the sky. My thoughts cleared in one startling moment of clarity as I wondered why, if Kilian had re-opened the scry, he hadn't just come through it to fetch me himself. Dread sank talons inside me as an indistinct face came into view.

His voice was rough and unfamiliar as he said, "Who the fuck are you?"

My lips parted to answer but darkness clouded my vision. And then my wish came true, and finally there was nothing.

CHAPTER 22

I knew I was awake because everything hurt. My skin chafed like it had been rubbed raw with a grater and my throat burned drier than a desert. My eyelids were heavy, but they opened to reveal a thatch-roof ceiling. Soft light leaked through the straw. I tried lifting my arm, but something rustled when the limb moved.

I tilted my head, glancing down to find dark leaves wrapped around every inch of skin I could see. The bed I lay on was straw and hay. Uncomfortable, but beggars could not be choosers.

A male tended to a pot over a flame near the entrance of the hut. "You're awake," he said, with his back toward me.

"Where am I?" I croaked.

He turned to look at me. His pointed ears told me he was elven. His face was averagely handsome, with a rugged beard and dark eyes which assessed my bandaged arm. "Don't move those. Your skin has just started to heal. I don't want it pulling off again."

He slipped a pair of mitts over his hands before lifting the pot off the flame. He moved to the left where my field of vision didn't quite stretch and then came back into view, striding toward me with a porcelain bowl in hand. He took a seat on a rickety looking chair beside my bed – if I could even call the thing I slept in a bed – and spooned some of whatever was inside the bowl. He held the spoon to my lips, and I eyed it cautiously.

He rolled his eyes. "It's safe for mortal consumption. If I wanted to kill you, I'd have left you bleeding outside. Now drink."

I parted my lips, and warm broth filled my mouth. I sucked on the spoon as the elven drew it from my lips. I was so thirsty. So hungry. So sore. So curious.

I didn't know which need to address first. I settled for taking the next few spoonfuls of broth, gulping greedily, before asking again, "Where am I?"

He dipped the spoon back into the bowl. "Greyhaven."

Greyhaven?

"How did I get here?"

"You came through the scry. Don't you remember?"

As soon as he said it, the memories hit me all at once. Cosanus. The fae. Caleb. The scry. Calendula. Where was Calendula?

"My sprite!" I tried sitting and regretted it immediately. I could feel my broken skin stretch and crack beneath the leaves, and a wave of dizziness consumed me. "Where is my sprite?"

The elven set the bowl on the floor and placed gentle hands on my shoulders, laying me back down. "There was no sprite with you. But I do have some questions of my own. You're mortal."

"Astute observation," I muttered. "That's not a question."

"Let me rephrase. What was a mortal doing on the borders of Cosanus?"

My eyes locked with his. "How do you know about Cosanus?" Kilian told me only the elven with special clearance for the Mortal Trials knew about it. Unless this male was somehow involved?

He leaned back in his chair, crossing his ankles casually. "I'm a bit of a scholar. One of the few who believe the fae still exist. I've been examining the borders of Cosanus for well over a decade now, trying to find a weak spot. A way in. Wasn't it a surprise when I opened the scry, intending to resume my work, only for you to amble in all bloodied? So, I'll ask you again: what was a mortal doing on the borders of Cosanus?"

This male knew about the fae. He knew about Cosanus. He wanted to get *inside* Cosanus. Why anyone would want to go into that demonic place, I had no idea. The land would devour the elven's magic. It would drink him like wine. And then the geysers would melt the flesh off his bones. And the aching sun would bleach his bones white. And eventually they would turn to dust and ash on a warm wind.

I swallowed and decided on a half-truth. "I was sent in to survive for an hour. It was the third challenge in the Mortal Trials."

"Ah." He leaned forward, intrigue lining his face. "And what did you find?"

Just a cavern full of dried-out fae, before accidentally waking one, then watched as it ripped a sprite's head from her body and barely escaped with my own life. All for a dagger.

The dagger.

The leaves rustled around my arm as I reached for my neck.

The elven's gaze went to the hollow dip in my throat, and he clicked his tongue. "The blade. Of course."

"Where is it?"

"I'm curious, did you find the fae?"

"The fae don't exist," I snapped. "I was sent to retrieve the dagger. If you don't give it back to me, I will have failed the Trial."

"If the fae don't exist," the male said evenly, "then who put the dagger there?"

My mouth snapped shut.

"You should rest," he said. "Your injuries are serious, and I'm no healer. The mud leaves will help, but they're slow acting. You should feel better in a few days."

"*Days*? How long have I been asleep for?"

"Little over a day."

Little over an entire day. Calendula was missing. And Kilian had not found me.

I reached for the link, but there was nothing. Only unending silence.

What if Caleb had not made it to the scry in time? I hadn't actually seen him cross the boundary. The scry had simply lit. It didn't mean Caleb had exited through it. What if Kilian thought I was dead? He would have no way to know for sure, but the aching silence in the link would certainly give that impression.

My saliva turned sour and hot tears pressed against the back of my eyelids as I shut them against the sunlight streaming through the roof. I let the darkness wash over me once more.

When I next woke, it was no longer day. Navy sky peered down at me from the gaps in the thatch. My skin itched furiously, and I reached for the leaves, grateful to find that my fingers no longer felt like someone was slow-roasting them.

"Don't touch it," my nameless savior called. I rose on my elbows, much slower this time to avoid the dizziness. He sat near the entrance of the hut on a small wooden bench, studying something in front of him.

"It's itchy."

"It's supposed to be. Your skin is regrowing."

I slid against the bedframe, dropping my head against the backboard as I peeled the top layer of one of the leaves away from my arm. The skin was indeed healing, but not well. It was mottled and patchy, raw in some places and plasticky in others. I stuck the leaf back down.

"How long has it been now?"

"Since I found you? Three nights."

The words clanged hollowly in my chest. Kilian had thought me dead for three nights.

"You have a scry," I said. "Send me back to Valhan House. I have to participate in the Rite."

It would be happening any day now. Lana and Moric... I lifted my hand to my mouth. I hadn't even thought about them. I didn't even know if they had survived the Trial.

They had to have, I decided. There was no way I would allow myself to think otherwise. Not stuck here with nothing to do but consider the worst possible outcome.

"It doesn't work like that," he said calmly, like I wasn't a second away from hyperventilating. "For a scry to open, it needs to have a beacon point on the other side. I've never been to Valhan House, so I've never set one up there."

"That's fucking helpful," I muttered.

He shot me an annoyed look. "I literally saved your life. I think I've been plenty helpful. So much so that one might expect a thank you. When you're strong enough to walk, by all means, leave. But for now, the only place it looks like you'll be going is back to dreamland."

"Thank you."

He grunted in response and jerked his head to the chair beside me. "There's soup. It might have gone cold."

I reached for it, suddenly ravenous. It was cold, but I didn't care. I ate so quickly I felt sick. As I ate, the elven shifted in his seat, revealing my dagger and the one from Cosanus on the table before him. He seemed to be evaluating the pair. Curiosity burned through me just as it had when I'd noticed the similarities for myself.

Setting the empty bowl back on the chair, I asked, "What are you doing with those?"

He looked at the blades. "I'm trying to figure out what magic they contain. It doesn't look like upper or lower magic."

That didn't make sense. "If it isn't upper or lower magic, then what is it?"

He gave a low chuckle. "That's what I'm trying to find out."

I settled back on the bed, careful not to disrupt the mud leaves as I rolled to my side to keep an eye on the elven. I watched him until my eyes grew heavy again. I yawned as I said, "I don't know your name."

Right before I fell asleep again, he murmured, "It's Aaron."

A loud clattering jerked me awake and my eyes flew open, then immediately shut again as a ray of sunlight pierced them. I blinked quickly, pushing up onto my elbows. I had to be dreaming, or the leaves were making me hallucinate, because Kilian stood in the doorway. He looked so out of place amidst the thatch and wood that I almost dismissed it as a delusion.

Until Aaron toppled from his bench.

Kilian did not give the elven so much as a glance before striding toward me, fingers outstretched to cup my face. His touch was featherlight, and I knew I was not imagining the cold steel flashing in his eyes. I felt like sobbing. I had never been so relieved to see Kilian Valhan in my entire life.

"Are you okay?" he asked in that soft voice he used only when he spoke to me.

My chin dipped in a nod. I looked at Aaron, who was rising shakily, fingers gripping the bench tightly.

Kilian's lips curled menacingly as he stared at the other elven. "Did he hurt you?"

"No," I choked out. "No. He saved my life."

Kilian's gaze softened an inch, but the look of icy wrath on his face did not change as he assessed the leaves covering my body. "This is why the link was silent," he muttered. "Mud leaves. Can you walk?"

Aaron cleared his throat. "She really shouldn't. She's suffered multiple third-degree burns."

"Then I'll carry her," Kilian said roughly. He scooped gentle arms beneath my legs and waist, drawing me into his chest. I wrapped my arms around his neck and buried my face against his shoulder, breathing him in. He felt so warm and safe, and so much like home that I trembled. All the fear and pain I had felt the past few days tumbled to the surface, and I held onto him like a lifeline.

Kilian ran a soothing hand across my hair and pressed a quick kiss to my temple, then turned to Aaron. "Thank you. Whatever you need, Valhan House will oblige."

"The blades," I murmured against Kilian's neck. "The weapon."

Aaron stared down at the ruby-hilted daggers, hesitation curling his lip. "I'd like to keep them. To study them."

Kilian glanced above the elven's head, to a whiteboard I'd missed from my vantage point at the bed but could now see quite clearly. It was filled with notes and drawings, red string linking different points, and a map of the boundary separating Cosanus from Lortan, with various checkpoints marked out.

"It's not yours to keep," Kilian said. "And I don't advise you to continue searching for a way to cross the boundary. There is nothing but death waiting on Cosanus."

Aaron's mouth set in a grimly determined line, like he didn't much care about the supposed threat of death. His eyes remained focused on the daggers, clearly unwilling to part with them.

"They won't help you cross over," Kilian said, eyes falling to the blades. "They don't serve that sort of purpose."

"What purpose do they serve, then?" Aaron asked, unable to help his curiosity. I wanted to know too.

Kilian narrowed his eyes. "It is not your business. Give them to me, or I will take them from you."

"Don't be rude," I chastised weakly. "Aaron saved my life."

"And I am grateful for it, but if he wants to keep his, he will not delay us any longer." He looked down at me. "You're injured."

Aaron gave the daggers one final wistful look, but at the menacing glare Kilian shot his way, he hastily thrust them toward us, muttering, "I don't want any trouble. Just go."

Kilian adjusted me so that he could sheath the blades in the bandolier across his chest and I murmured a quick, final thank you to Aaron before we left. Kilian's arms were strong around me as he took me away from the hut, from Aaron, from the closest encounter I had ever had with death.

"You came for me," I whispered when we were out of earshot of the hut.

He peered down at me, eyes glowing once more. "Of course I did. I'm just sorry it took so long. As soon as Caleb came back without you, I tried reopening the scry, but I told you how temperamental it is. It didn't allow me to input the coordinates fast enough. And when I eventually did manage to open it, you weren't there. I spent days searching the border for you. I thought you hadn't managed to cross. I nearly went out of my mind." I felt his throat bob hard as he swallowed.

I stroked the side of his neck, more to remind myself that he was real. He was here. "How did you find me?"

"Calendula."

The single word was enough to make me shudder in relief. "She's okay?"

"She's resting at the house. She flew nonstop across the Green Sea, from Greyhaven to Lomask to tell me what happened. Where to find you."

I stopped breathing entirely. "She did what?"

"She flew an ocean for you."

Emotion choked my throat and tears pressed against the corners of my eyes. Sprites could barely fly for a few hours before sleep took them. Their bodies couldn't handle the exertion. For Calendula to have crossed the Green Sea, it must have taken her days of continuous flight. "That's impossible. How did she do it?"

"She drew on our oath. The power that flows through me also flows through her. It's old magic."

"But she's alright?"

"Yes, Lirah. Are *you* alright?"

"I'm fine." My skin still itched, but it was more uncomfortable than it was painful. Nothing compared to a few days ago. "The geysers got me."

"Conserve your strength," he murmured. "You can tell me all about it once I've gotten you back to the room and given you a healing tonic, a hot bath and some food."

"The room? We aren't going back to Valhan House?" In fact, we had been walking a while now, with seemingly no direction.

He shook his head. "The beacon point for the scry is in central town. Once you've healed and had a good night's sleep, we'll make our way back to Lomask."

I nodded and rested my head on his shoulder again, allowing the relief and surety of him to wash over me as we walked.

The room turned out to be inside a cozy inn, nestled on the outskirts of a lush garden. Kilian paid no mind to the housekeeper at reception as he bustled toward the staircase. He hadn't so much as broken a sweat carrying me from Aaron's hut to the inn and up several flights of stairs to the room.

"Do you come here often?" I asked.

"I have a standing reservation for when I attend Greyhaven on business." He strode into the room and set me down gently on the large bed. The room wasn't anything to write home about. Just the bed, small cabinet, white sheets and a desk set against the opposite wall beside another open door. I could make out a porcelain sink and the edge of a clawfoot bathtub just beyond. Floating shelves were affixed above the tub, an array of bath salts, soap and sponges lined neatly atop them.

Kilian rummaged in the desk, drawing out a small vial with clear liquid inside. He handed it to me. "Drink this."

I brought it to my nose, sniffing delicately. There was a slight hint of licorice and rose. I raised it to my lips and drank. The liquid traced a fiery path down my throat and I coughed. Kilian dropped before me on his knees, gently pulling at one of the leaves stuck to my bare leg. It fell away, revealing unmarred skin.

"That's amazing," I breathed.

"Midius' emergency tonic," he murmured, running his hands up the length of my calf to the next leaf that wrapped around the back of my thigh. He freed it, tossing it to land atop the other. "Don't get me wrong, I'm grateful for the elven who found you, but I want to murder him for taking your pants off."

I huffed a breathy chuckle, his knuckles brushing the sensitive skin behind my knees. The simplest touch from him set me alight. The sight of him, on his knees before me, sent thoughts racing through my mind. But I was also aware that I had spent an hour running through Cosanus, nearly been eaten by a fae, had the skin on my body melt off and regrow, and had not bathed in gods only knew how long.

I placed a hand on his to stop him from pulling off the next leaf that covered my upper thigh. His hand stilled immediately, silver eyes flickering up to meet mine.

"I need a bath." I smiled softly.

He stood and crossed to the ensuite. I heard water running a second later. He stuck his head out the door to ask, "Lemon or lavender?"

"Lavender." I peeled the remaining mud leaves off my body and strode to the bathroom. When the last one had left my skin, the link crashed through me with such force I had to grip the edge of the bathtub to steady myself. The steam from the tub wafted up to greet me, and I focused on the swirling tendrils as I breathed through the tidal wave of emotions.

Sharp agony sliced through me, pain that wrenched a jagged arrow right through my heart. No, not pain. Relief. Relief so pure and unfiltered that it hurt.

Kilian's hands wrapped around my shoulders, and he rubbed soothing circles along my back. "What's wrong?" he asked.

"The mud leaves," I murmured. "I can feel you again."

I turned to look up at him, but he only stared back.

"Now you know how grateful I am that you're alive. These past few days…" He ran a hand through his hair, his gaze going to the ceiling, then back to me. "Lirah, I thought I'd lost you."

If I hadn't believed his admission that day we'd trained in the park, the absolute relief pouring from him was confirmation enough.

I wanted to kiss him. But I was also painfully aware of how utterly gross I felt.

"Bathe. We'll talk after," he said, sensing my reluctance.

When I emerged from the bathroom sometime later, I found Kilian at the desk, examining the daggers.

He looked up as I entered, wrapped in a thick towel, wet hair hanging down my back. "Feel better?"

"Loads."

"You should eat something." He gestured to the bed, where a spread of meat, cheese and bread had been arranged with mini tarts and scones to the side. I reached for a tart – strawberry, judging by the slices artfully arranged atop what looked to be custard.

Halfway to raising it to my lips, I paused. "It's not elven, is it?"

"Of course not. I didn't spend days praying you were alive only to allow you to be poisoned by a pastry." He was still staring intently at me, like he expected me to vanish if he blinked.

I bit into the shortcrust, delighting in the sweet custard and tangy strawberry. "I think this is the most delicious thing I've ever eaten."

I held it out to him, surprised when he actually obliged, biting into the corner.

He chewed thoughtfully. "It's not terrible. I've had better."

I popped the remainder into my mouth. "You're such a liar."

"I'm not lying." His hand circled my wrist, and he drew me onto his lap.

My legs fell on either side of the chair.

He brushed a wet lock of hair behind my shoulder. A drop of water slid down my arm and he met it with his tongue. He looked up at me, through dark lashes. "You're far tastier than any tart."

I linked my fingers around his neck. "Maybe you just haven't eaten many tarts."

"I've had plenty," he murmured.

He kissed me and I felt the full range of his emotions.

Rage, as he pulled me closer, fingers sinking into my hair.

Sorrow as his lips moved gently, devoutly, against mine.

Relief, as he sighed into my mouth, whispering my name like it belonged to a deity he was about to pledge fealty to.

I wanted nothing more than to continue kissing him. To let my hands skate over his shoulders, for the clothes he wore to disappear, but I couldn't switch my brain off. The thoughts I had been trying not to let consume me over the past few days re-emerged with ferocity.

I pulled away slightly, "Lana? Moric?"

Kilian's hands stroked my arms. "Safe. Keila, Nox and Mattieu did not make it, though."

There was relief amidst the ache for the other candidates. "What happened to them?"

"Rayna convinced Lana not to enter Cosanus. Moric and Keila did enter but didn't make it very far before stepping into sinking sand. Keila was too far in. Moric wasn't able to pull her out."

"Gods." My eyes shuttered as I imagined how traumatic it must have been for the both of them.

"As for Nox and Mattieu, neither returned. I searched the border for days, they weren't anywhere."

Which had to mean they had either fallen prey to the geysers, or they hadn't made it back to the boundary within the hour and the land had drained them of all magic and lifeforce.

"We have elven still searching the border," Kilian said. "But when Calendula found me, I left them there to fetch you. Although, unless they also fell into another scry, there's no likelihood of survival."

An anvil weighed me down and I nodded.

"Do you want to talk about it?" he asked softly. "The Trial?"

The memories flashed through my mind. An eerily still cavern, thirteen desiccated fae, sweat rolling down my neck, the heat of a dagger being siphoned of magic, a sprite's head being torn from her neck.

How foolish you have allowed yourself to become.

I glanced down. "It was terrifying. I don't think I've ever been that scared before. The fae… one of them woke. He spoke to me. Like he knew me."

He nodded. "Caleb and Calendula briefed me."

"And the land, I felt it split me open. Did it…? It can't have taken all the magic from me; I still feel the link."

"No, you crossed over in time. There's still trace elements of magic left in you."

"I just don't understand any of it." I dropped my gaze to the daggers gleaming side by side. "Why is it that a weapon worn around the neck of a fae is a twin to the dagger my mother gifted me?"

"It's not a twin, technically. It's part of a larger set. Thirteen, to be exact. You brought this one with you from Serila."

"Yeah. My mother gave it to me right before you took me. There were seven others just like it in the kitchen."

"I know. I went back and found them when I noticed yours, the day after we took you."

"You went back… to the *governor's* house?"

"Yes. I needed to make sure the one I'm searching for wasn't part of that lot."

"Okay, but what's the connection? Why would a weapon – a very important one, I gather – be in a kitchen of the governor's household?"

"Some of the set were stolen by the fae a long time ago. I can only assume the possession changed hands a few times after, got lost through the passage of time. Some ended up in Serila, one on Cosanus, who knows where the remainder are." He shrugged. "The Serilan governor always had his hand in the black market. Probably didn't even know what he was buying."

I leaned back, exhaling in the direction of the blades. I eyed Kilian. "Still not going to tell me what makes them so special?"

A troubled look flashed over his face, his eyes darkening as he stared at an empty spot above my shoulder.

I cupped the side of his face. "Hey. Where'd you go?"

He shook his head, the storm clouds parting as if they had never been there. "You should get some rest. We can talk more in the morning."

I sighed, shaking off the sorrow and stress, the endless questions and confusing answers that gave me a headache the more I thought about them. Resting sounded good. The Trials, the puzzlement and pain surrounding it, would still be here for contemplation tomorrow.

My gaze slid to the bed. "There's only one bed. Where will you sleep?"

He rolled his eyes. "You're concerned about propriety *now*?"

I huffed a short laugh, extricating myself from him. "I suppose not."

"Here." He strode to the cabinet, drawing out a white button-down. "It's all I have on hand. Although, I wouldn't be opposed to you sleeping in nothing at all, if you'd prefer."

I snorted, yanking the shirt over my head and letting the towel drop. "Bet you'd love that."

"I really would." He moved the food tray and held the covers open. "But it won't happen. You've got a thing for making me suffer."

I cast a smile at him as I got into the bed, watching as he kicked off his boots and unbuckled his bandolier. His breastplate went next, falling to the ground, and then his shirt. I hadn't seen him shirtless since the day I trashed his room. That felt so long ago.

He was all golden skin and battle scars. I wanted to kiss each one. Longed to know the stories behind them. More than anything, I wanted him to open up. To tell me the whole truth, leaving no gory, messy, shameful part behind. He was always asking me to trust him, but he needed to trust me too. Enough to let me know him. I wanted to tell him it was okay to show me whatever darkness lived inside of him. That there could be no light, no stars, without it.

But then he was pulling off his pants and slipping into the bed beside me and the moment passed. He drew an arm around my waist, pulling me closer. I breathed him in, reveled in his warmth, the acres of skin I couldn't help running my hands over.

He pressed a kiss to the crown of my head and my eyes shuttered.

"I'm never letting you go," he murmured tenderly. Repeatedly. As if he was speaking to himself, making a promise only he could keep.

It was right then – wrapped in his arms, his whispered words gently lulling me to sleep – that the realization hit me. Like the sharp rays of the sun, half-hidden behind a cloud which had suddenly parted, clarity dawned.

I had fallen in love with Kilian Valhan, and there wasn't a godsdamned thing anyone could do about it.

CHAPTER 23

Cold, gray hands reached for me, long fingers clasping around my neck. Onyx eyes filled with brutal death held me prisoner. Hot breath skimmed my face. It smelled of rot and decay. Icy terror gripped me, and I could not move. My fingers spasmed, my chest constricting painfully.

How did he cross the salt boundary? How did he find me?

The fae rasped, "Did you think rock salt could keep me from you? Your last breath will be *mine!*"

Long nails dug into the skin at my neck, drawing blood. I screamed and the fae laughed, his face callous and cruel.

"Lirah." Pallid, glacial skin was replaced by warm fingers and bright eyes. Kilian's face hovered inches above mine. He pressed a kiss to my temple, drawing me into his strong arms. I heaved a shuddering breath, the stench and sight of the fae still clogging my senses.

"You're okay," he murmured against my hair. "You're okay."

I shut my eyes tight, allowing Kilian's scent to wash over the putrid aroma. We were tangled in a mess of limbs and sheets. His body pressed against every inch of mine. Light peeked through the shutters at the window; I focused on the slivers and Kilian's rhythmic breathing to ground myself in this reality.

"What did you dream about?" he whispered against the shell of my ear.

"Fae." The word made the hair on the back of my arms stand on end.

Kilian ran a hand along my arm. "Do you want to talk about it?"

I shook my head. No. I did not want to relive the dream; I wanted to forget the entire experience on Cosanus.

"Okay." Kilian grazed his lips against my head, his hand rubbing comfortingly along my back. "It's going to be okay."

But it wasn't. Nothing was going to be okay. Sure, the third Trial was over and the fae were still imprisoned on Cosanus, but I had to survive what came next: the Rite. Kilian seemed to sense the shift in my energy. He pulled away, peering down at me.

"What are you thinking about?"

"The Rite."

And with those two words, his energy changed too. His eyes shut, spine tensing. I felt quiet rage through the link. "I've been thinking about that a lot recently. You don't have to do it. I won't make you."

I blinked. "What do you mean?"

He swallowed hard, his eyes intent. "I don't want to lose you."

I sat up to survey him. "We've been training. There's a chance."

"It's not high enough. And after what happened on Cosanus, there's only trace magic left in you. It's not a chance I want to take."

"It can't have all been for nothing. I can't have endured three Trials only to stop at the final hurdle. What about the Mortal Trials being bigger than the both of us? What about your curse and the humanity-destroying plot you need to prevent?"

"There's no guarantee you will be able to break the curse, even if you pass the Rite. Augustine wasn't able to. It's a gamble, and you're too valuable to bet."

"You can't just decide this now. It's too late."

"It's not. You have your whole life still ahead of you. I'm not taking that away."

He couldn't be serious. "So what? I'm just supposed to sit here and let my friends compete? Watch them die? Grow old in Lortan and eventually die myself? Because that is what will happen either way. We'll just be prolonging it. If I stay here, as a mortal, I can never set foot outside Lortan. I will never see my mother again."

"Your mother is well taken care of. I saw to it before we left Serila."

I stiffened. "What? How? Echon cursed her. She's voiceless."

He shook his head. "I undid the curse and nearly stuck a dagger in Echon before we left. It was after Septimus knocked you out. She's been living on Ascan for the past month, in a house I registered in her name. Like I did for all the families of candidates. I assure you, your mother has access to whatever she may need."

I heard his words, but my sluggish brain was struggling to process them. "You're telling me... she's fine? You gave her a house and her voice back?"

His brows knitted together. "Of course. The candidates competing in the Trials sacrifice their lives. The least I can do is try to compensate their families. Not that it will ever equate to the loss."

Tears were in my eyes, and his face grew blurry.

"Fuck, Lirah." He reached for me. "I didn't mean to make you cry. I'm so sorry to have forced all this upon you. You don't know how much I regret taking your choice from you. I'm trying to give it back to you now."

I dragged my fingers across my wet cheeks, shaking my head. "There's still no choice. I have to do this. I've come too far not to."

He grasped my hand, pressing it to his lips. "Don't."

I began shaking my head and he said, "You don't understand. I *can't* lose you. I... I cannot think when I am near you, and yet nothing makes sense when we are apart. I look for you in shadows and crowded rooms. I hear you, I feel you, even when you are not there. I have lived for a long time, Lirah, and hardly anything scares me anymore. But you... When you didn't come back after the Trial, I realized just how terrified I am of losing you. I understand you're mortal, and eventually the day will come when you leave me, but I am selfish. I want as many days with you as I can get before that happens."

"Kilian... You told me the greater good of humanity is at stake here, and while I don't fully understand that, I think I know you well enough by now to know you wouldn't have done all this for no reason."

"I'll let humanity burn sooner than lose you."

I blinked. "You don't mean that."

He let out a harsh, ragged scoff. "You still don't get it. You need me to spell it out for you? Fine, I will. I am madly, stupidly, *desperately* in love with you. I'm so fucking in love with you it hurts. It's enough for me to tell the world to fuck right off. It's taken too much from me already. It won't take you as well. I will not let it. Do not ask me to do that. Please. *Please*, don't ask that of me."

The raw confession ached. It tore at my heart until it was a piece of stringy flesh and blood.

I angled to face him fully, lifting up onto my knees and placing my hands on either side of his face. He gave me a pained look, and I dragged my thumb over his brow, smoothing out the creases. "I love you too. But you already knew that, didn't you?"

His eyes shuttered briefly, and he nodded.

"But do you know how much?" I pressed a kiss to his lips, the barest touch. "Catastrophically," I whispered. "Apocalyptically. That means that no matter what happens, even at the very end of the world, in every lifetime that may come after, I will find you. I know what I'm doing. You didn't give me the choice to compete in the Mortal Trials, but you've given me the choice of becoming elven now. And I choose to take the risk. If I don't try, I'll regret it forever."

His hands came to my waist, and he tugged me onto his lap. He pressed his lips to mine, and I let my eyelids close. It was so soft, so deliberate, it almost felt like a goodbye kiss.

His fingers drifted down my spine, catching at the hem of my shirt and he began tugging it up. I lifted my arms, letting him pull it off.

He tossed it off the bed and then his hands returned, callused palms scraping along the sides of my body. I ran my hands across the planes of his shoulders, dropped my head to kiss his collarbone. My touch mirrored his own – gentle, loving, reverent.

He was hard beneath me, and I shivered at the building ache, the desire that consumed me so wholly it was scarier than any Trial I'd faced.

I leaned back to tug at the band of his underwear, my finger running along his navel, and he inhaled sharply, lifting his hips enough for me to pull it down. When it was off, he settled me against him again and I bit my lip at the sensation.

He ran a thumb across my lower lip, freeing it from my teeth, and then his mouth was on mine again. Not soft this time, but a brutal claiming. A devouring of souls. There was no beginning and no end to this kiss. I rolled my hips, sliding along him, swallowing his groan.

He tore his lips away to look at me. "In case you're wondering, I take the preventative tablet, but we don't have to– if you're not ready–"

I brushed a curl off his forehead. "I'm ready. Unless *you* don't want to?"

He scoffed. "If there's any part of you questioning that, then I haven't done my job right."

"It's not supposed to be a 'job,'" I said.

"Will you ever stop arguing?"

"Some might call it banter."

He laughed softly at his words, thrown back at him. "You know, it stuns me how much I love you." His lips ghosted across mine. "Shall I show you how much I want to do this?"

I melted at the darkness, the hoarse ache in his voice. I lifted my hips. "Show me."

He positioned himself at my entrance and I bit down on his shoulder as he lowered me onto him, the fit agonizingly perfect. He paused, allowing me to adjust and to catch my breath, before lowering me all the way to his base.

I let my lips trail across his shoulder, to his neck, and he dropped his head, hands roaming my back, sinking into my hair.

"Lirah…" My name sounded like a prayer on his lips.

He didn't move for a second, his muscles tense like he wasn't quite sure what to do, but then I rolled my hips against his and he seemed to remember.

Quick as a flash, he flipped me over, the movement stealing my breath once more. He settled between my thighs, and I hooked my legs around him. I hadn't realized how much I needed the pressure of his chest against mine until it was there, or how much I'd wanted him to take charge until he did. His tongue was at my neck, arms bracketing me as he moved in a rhythm that had me seeing stars.

I dragged my nails down his back at the exact moment his control slipped. He withdrew completely and then slammed into me, rough and hard. At the bounds of the link, there was no rage, only blinding pleasure. If I'd ever wondered before what it meant to be entwined with someone body and soul, I now knew definitively.

He grabbed my hand, fingers intertwining with mine as he held it in place above my head.

"Kilian, I'm going to–"

His other hand reached between us to the apex of my thighs, and his thumb stroked decadent circles in time with each hard thrust. It was over before it had even started. Cause of death: Kilian Valhan.

I splintered into a million pieces, the world fracturing and reforming in a matter of seconds, but still he rolled his hips against me, his pace unfaltering.

I pressed my lips to his throat, scraping my teeth against his pulse point. I bit down. His muscles tensed and darkness lashed out in waves. Thunder crashed and boomed in the distance as he finally, *finally*, let go. I stared up at him, realizing with somewhat alarming clarity that the brightest stars were not in the night sky. They were in his eyes. He was made of darkness and starlight, pure energy and raw power. And he was mine.

His chest heaved and he dropped his forehead against mine, as if to agree: *I am yours.*

"How can you expect me to let you compete in the Rite?" He sighed. "I understand my role in the Trials has been cruel, but this is diabolical of you."

"I'm not trying to punish you." I ran my fingers over the bite mark I'd indented into his skin. "I want to make it through the Rite so we can do this every day. Forever."

"I can't convince you otherwise? I won't be able to help you during the Rite. I can't control it when it starts. Once you're in there, the process can't be halted. If your body rejects the current…" Anguish laced his words, and I felt the sting ricochet through me.

"I understand. I've made my decision. Can you respect it?"

A heavy breath ripped through him. "I don't like it."

"I know."

He gave me a grim look. "It's been days since you've been away. The Rite is tonight."

Tonight? Fresh panic clawed at my heart, but I tamped down on it. I didn't want Kilian to know just how fucking scared I was.

I pressed a quick kiss to his lips before slipping out of his hold.

He reached after me. "Where are you going?"

Empty sadness radiated through the link, drenching me in hollow, aching despair.

"To get ready. I've got a big day ahead of me." I winked, hoping that he would not sense just how false my bravado was.

Valhan House was a melting pot of activity by the time we returned. The elven, it seemed, were all preparing for the Rite. Not Syrina, though. She was at the arch, arms folded as she stared into nothing, when we returned through the scry.

She gaped at me and then rushed forward, scooping me into a hug. I blinked and slowly hugged her back. I had only spoken to her once before, but she held me like we were old friends. When she pulled back, she looked at Kilian. The pair seemed to be having a wordless conversation, conveyed only by looks.

Finally, she said, "I'm really glad to see you again, Lirah."

"I, uhm… I'm glad to see you too."

Syrina murmured something about waiting for a delivery and then strolled off past the archway. I gave Kilian a quizzical look. "What was that all about?"

"Syrina was worried when you didn't come back," he said simply.

"Oh."

"Come on, let's get you inside. It's freezing out here."

Kilian parted ways with me on the third floor, claiming he needed to find Septimus to assure his friend that he had not razed Cosanus to the ground in search of me. He kissed me softly before leaving, and all it did was make me want him more.

Lana and Moric were in the sparring room, meditating of all things. But when Lana saw me, all quiet and calm vanished. She leaped up, sprinting to pull me into her arms, Moric right behind her.

I clasped my friends tightly as they peppered me with question after question.

I told them everything. From the fae, to the geysers, to Greyhaven. They listened with wide eyes and open mouths.

"We thought you'd died. I've been a wreck," Lana said, and indeed, her eyes were red and rubbed raw. "Was it terribly scary in that cave?"

"Yeah." I couldn't lie to her. Not about that. Aaron had a complete death wish if he actually wanted to see the fae up close and personal. "Caleb's sprite... what the fae did to it... it's unspeakable."

Lana swallowed, her eyes skittering to Moric then back to me.

"What?"

Moric shuffled, uncomfortably. "Caleb told us... He said you spoke to the fae."

"The fae spoke to *me*," I clarified. "Caleb heard exactly how much the fae want us dead. What we did to them to warrant their violence, I don't know."

"Is that what the fae told you? Because Caleb didn't understand what he said. He said he spoke a different language. That you did too."

"What? We spoke in Grilish."

"That's not what Caleb said."

"Well, Caleb was out of his mind. He'd just seen his sprite get eaten." I only knew Grilish. There was no way I had understood and spoken another language.

Moric and Lana nodded their agreement, but they did not look convinced. I didn't know what else to say, so I made up an excuse and slipped out of the sparring room, the weight of their gazes boring into my back as I exited.

I banished all thoughts of the fae and the third Trial as I walked to the dorms, intending to find Calendula. I owed the shadow sprite so much more than I could ever put into words.

Calendula was snoring softly on a hammock of her own making when I stepped into my room. She stirred when the door closed, blinking sleepily up at me.

"Lirah?"

"Hey." I smiled softly.

"Kilian found you, then."

I sat on the bed beside the desk. "Thanks to you. Calendula... I don't think I'll ever be able to repay you for what you did."

She waved a hand idly. "It was nothing."

"Kilian told me you flew the Green Sea. That is no ordinary feat."

"I am no ordinary sprite. Need I remind you, I am descended from Mirau Titan. Of course I can fly the Green Sea."

"Regardless. Thank you. I know you've grown tired of forming bonds with mortals over the decades, but I'm so grateful for what you did for me."

Calendula sniffed delicately. "I guess I don't want you to die."

A smile tugged at the corners of my lips. That was as much emotion Calendula would bestow upon me. But I knew she would not have flown the Green Sea if she did not love me.

"The Rite is tonight," I said. "If I don't make it, I don't want you to be angry."

Calendula rose from her hammock and puffed her chest out, the folds of her midnight dress ruffling. "But I will be. I did not fly the Green Sea for you to die, Lirahna. You *will* survive." And there was such command in her voice that, despite the overwhelmingly awful odds, I believed her.

I would do my best. For Calendula.

For Kilian.

And for me.

CHAPTER 24

The sound of beating war drums met me before Kilian did. He rounded the corner as I slipped out of my room. I was dressed warmly and armed to the teeth, although I most likely would not need blades where I was going. My hair was braided into a tight crown around my head, and I had said my goodbyes to Calendula. I was ready.

"Sounds like we're going into battle," I said.

"You are." He fell into step beside me, following me to the staircase. "You know, you can still change your mind."

I looped my fingers through his, bringing his knuckles to my lips. I didn't know how I had not spent every waking minute in Valhan House touching him, holding him, learning the divots and hard curves of his body. I wanted him tonight and for the rest of our lives. "We've discussed this."

"Humor me." He stood one step below me. One hand dropped to my waist, the other slid softly down my neck. His lips dipped to trace the same line down my neck and my toes curled in their boots.

"We don't have time for this," I choked out, even as my hands reached for his hair.

"I know," he murmured. "But I'd be remiss if I let you go to the Rite without a proper sendoff."

He pressed my back against the railing, and I let out a soft gasp as his mouth claimed mine. He was warm against me, and when his tongue brushed the seam of my lips, I opened for him. He kissed me languidly, like the Rite was not due to start at any second, his tongue idly trailing across mine, scraping along the roof of my mouth and across my teeth. There was no area of my mouth he left unexplored. I was panting by the time he pulled away.

I couldn't help but brush myself against him again. I wanted to kiss him beneath the starlight and hold him in the early hours of the morning. I wanted his body wrapped around mine each night and to hear that he loved me each day.

I wanted time. Time we did not have.

So instead, I pressed my hand to his cheek, ran my thumb across his cheekbone and watched as the steel chips in his eyes softened. He caught at my wrist and brought the inside of it to his lips. It was such a tender, loving kiss that my heart yearned for more.

"You will complete the Rite. And you will return to me," he ordered.

"Azrael himself could not keep me from you."

A soft, sad smile touched his face, and I committed it to memory as he relinked our fingers and led me downstairs.

With each step, the sound of the drums grew louder, until it reverberated along the corridors of my brain. The other candidates were already lined up in the courtyard, their instructors beside them. As soon as Kilian and I joined the queue, we began to move.

The night sky was still and the flurry from the summits had ceased; for once, the constellations were perfectly visible up ahead. It was cold, but I welcomed the fresh air. It reminded me that I was alive.

"Where is the Rite taking place?" I asked.

Kilian sketched out a curve along the summits, and I could see tiny lights strung up in a winding path all the way to the top of a peak.

I raised my brows. "We're hiking?"

"What? Did you think the Rite consisted of drinking hot cocoa and watching the stars?" He gave me a sardonic look, and I rolled my eyes.

Caleb and his instructor led the group. Lana was behind them with Septimus, his head bowed toward her as she spoke softly to him. I kept my gaze firmly averted from Moric and his instructor, Ayden, who I had not spoken to since that day in the tavern. Rayna strode ahead of me with Echon, pointedly ignoring everyone else. She looked tired, and rightfully so. The Trials had taken a lot from us all, and it was patently obvious how small our group had become since the first challenge. Only five of us would enter the Rite. And none of us might leave it.

I squeezed Kilian's fingers as we began ascending the mountain. I was pleased to find that my muscles welcomed the exercise. Somewhere between the weeks of grueling training, running, and fighting at every turn to stay alive, my body had grown accustomed to life on Lortan.

The lights – orblight, I realized – were strung up at regular intervals, marking every hundred yards. At the six hundredth marker, I ate my earlier words as my calves began to cramp. But it wasn't much further to the top. I could see the final orblight from the back of the line. Lana and Septimus were already passing the third-to-last one.

"I can't accompany you across once we reach the top," Kilian murmured beside me.

I shot a look at him.

"There's a border of obsidian sand fencing off the portion of the summit where the Rite takes place," he explained. "It'll test your strength, your resilience, as you cross. If it deems you worthy, you'll find yourself on the other side."

"Is it like rock salt?" I asked him.

"Not exactly. Rock salt bars entry and exit for elven and fae, permitting only mortals and sprites. Obsidian sand is one-sided. Only a mortal can enter. And only those who possess upper magic can exit. It's designed so that no elven can interfere in the process. Once the Rite starts, there's nothing I'll be able to do. You can only return if you transform."

I pressed my lips together. "Right."

We crossed the penultimate orblight, and I saw Lana at the top of the peak. Her pale hair streamed behind her like a flag. Septimus brushed a gentle kiss to her cheek and her eyes fluttered closed.

This was real. Too real.

Kilian paused, allowing me to continue ahead of him as the trail narrowed. When I crested the summit, the flat mountainous peak came into view. It was a wide expanse of snow, razed even and smooth for the most part, but every now and again, I could see tiny bumps and jagged rocks on the surface. The lighting was too dim for me to make out anything further. I did notice a line of glittering black sand drawn along the snow, though, a luminous sheen glowing off it. It remained unmoving even as a wind rustled past, pulling a few strands of hair loose from my braid.

Thunder rumbled ominously in the distance, and I shivered involuntarily.

"This is as far as I can go," Kilian said, my vision filled by him. He brushed a hand across my cheek. I leaned in to his touch. "I won't say goodbye."

"Don't." It was too painful to bear.

"I'll wait for you here. Don't be late." His smile was soft, sad, and I pulled away from the ache in our link. It echoed the sorrow in my heart.

I took a step away from him and it was the most painful thing I had ever done in my life. My chest twinged like it had been carved wide open with each step away from Kilian and toward the sand. But I forced my legs forward, until I stood beside Lana. She reached out to entwine her hand with mine.

We had said our goodbyes earlier in the dorms. The look that passed between us now conveyed only love. Moric slung an arm around me, pressing a kiss to my forehead before doing the same to Lana. He took position beside her, linking his hand with hers.

"Do you remember when we met?" Lana cocked her head toward me.

"Of course. You saved my life," I said.

She shook her head. "Do you remember what I told you?"

I thought back, sifting through my memories, before whispering, "Lirah and Lana."

She looked out at the frozen tundra. "Our deaths will be poetic as fuck." Her words were carried away on a summit breeze.

I hadn't told them about the trace magic remaining in me. I couldn't bear to see the sadness in their eyes as they realized my already slim probability of survival had decreased even more.

Instead, I squeezed Lana's hand, looking over at her and Moric. "Don't say that. We've been training. Just remember what we've learned."

Moric gave a determined nod, Lana a weaker one. I could see hesitation in her eyes. The nerves must have gotten to her. I knew they had continued practicing channeling the excess current while I'd been healing in Greyhaven. I could only pray it was enough to have given them a slight advantage for what we were about to face. I remembered what Kilian had taught me. I knew what I needed to do with whatever magic remained in me. We all just needed to focus, and we would make it through.

"We're the trio. We're going to be fine," I said, as if my sheer will alone would make it true. "We have to be."

And on that final note, I threw one last look at Kilian over my shoulder as we walked across the boundary line. There was a pulling sensation. A resistance band snapping around my body, tugging me back. It was like being cloaked beneath the weight of magic. A heady, dizzying pressure that pulsed against me. Testing. Probing for weaknesses. Pain lanced through me as the magic forced me to relive some of my darkness memories. Being torn away from a voiceless Umma, Anama's death, my flesh melting and burning.

And then it was done. The pressure lifted. I had been deemed worthy – strong enough – to enter the Rite.

I cleared the boundary, and it was as if I had stepped through frosted glass. The elven on the other side disappeared completely. The only thing visible was the flat expanse of land before me and the other candidates. From the traumatized looks on their faces, they, too, had undergone a similar experience.

Moric released a shaky breath. "What happens now?"

Rayna strode forward a few steps. "We wait."

I unclasped hands with Lana, my gaze on one of the rocks a few feet ahead. I walked toward it, toeing it with my boot, until it flipped over. I yelped, jumping back.

Lana came to stand beside me, peering down at what I had thought was a rock. "That's…"

"A human skull," I finished, bile rising in my throat.

"Gods above," she breathed.

"I don't think the gods are going to help us here," I said.

Thunder roared, seemingly directly above us. The sound made my teeth clench. Lightning skittered overhead, and I stared up at the night sky. Felt the building current.

"RUN!" I yelled.

We scattered, even though there was nowhere to go. Just endless, snowy mountain and bare bones from candidates past.

Rayna shrieked as lightning struck down a few feet ahead of her, singeing the ground. Snow fizzled and melted, and a strong electric current permeated the air. Everything felt hazy, the pungent scent of scorched rock and chlorine in the air.

Lighting flashed across the sky in lashes of purple, dancing across the summits. I didn't know if it was me screaming, or if it was Lana or the others. I skidded across the snow, dodging strike after strike and trying to keep my balance. Lightning slashed down in a great surge, and I was knocked backward. From the periphery of my vision, I saw Caleb come to an abrupt halt, as lighting speared through him. The scent of burning flesh seared my nostrils, and I dry heaved, my stomach empty.

There was nowhere to hide. I crouched into a ball, tucking my head between my shoulders, covering my neck with my arms, and muttering a fevered prayer that I could hardly hear over the screams. With each strike, the air vibrated with electricity and the ground rocked. I coughed against the acrid fumes, my lungs burning with smoke and something else. Something powerful.

And then it stopped.

I blinked through the smog, slowly lifting my head.

"Lirah?" Lana called.

I sagged in relief. "I'm fine. Moric?"

"Alive," his voice came.

As the smoke cleared, Caleb's charred body became visible on the ground. Lana, who was closest, dropped beside him. "No, no, no!" she cried. Her fingers skated across his neck. "There's no pulse."

I stared down at Caleb, at a loss. I hadn't known him well, but our time in Cosanus had bonded us. Seeing his body reduced to nothing but burned flesh and bone was unbearable.

I turned away, scanning the others. "Is everyone else okay?"

Rayna's face was dirt-streaked, and Moric and Lana looked thoroughly shaken, but they were still alive.

Moric didn't answer. Instead he said, "Is it over?"

Lana licked her lips, her gaze darting nervously across the sky. "I don't know. I don't feel any different. Do you?"

I assessed my body. "No." The ground trembled, vibrating softly. "Do you feel that?"

Moric dropped to one knee, his hand skimming the snowy surface. "Something's happening."

Electricity thrummed, throbbing like a living, breathing thing, as if the earlier lightning shower had somehow charged the ground. I felt it then, a soft pinprick starting from my toes and inching along my calves. It tickled gently as it skimmed my skin in a warm wave. Smoke rose around us, wreathing me in an opaque cloud, and I couldn't see anyone else, but the others had become deathly silent; they must have felt something too.

I stared down at my hands. Dazzling purple light skipped across my fingers, a light current stinging with each contact made. It hadn't felt uncomfortable at first, but the stinging was slowly becoming painful. Each zap seemed to strike a nerve, and I gasped as a particularly strong one knocked the breath out of me.

This was it. It was starting.

I fell to my knees and rocked back, staring up at a sliver of dark sky as the charge slithered from the snow and into my body. Lightning fizzled along my veins, cooking me from the inside out. Different to Kilian's. Harsher, vicious. Something thumped outside the scope of my vision, but I was frozen in place, my limbs locked. A tear slid down my cheek but even that sizzled and dried in a flash.

The air was cold, but I was so hot, my skin flushed and boiling. It felt like the geysers all over again. Raw, blistering pain sliced through me. Everything itched, and my bones cried out, begging for mercy, but none came. My organs felt like they were collapsing in real time. My lungs couldn't expand fast enough to breathe the vital air that my body needed.

The current was too much.

I was dying.

There was something I was supposed to remember. Something I was supposed to do.

I keeled over, retching for air, but still the electricity radiated through me, throbbing and shoving its way through every atom, every molecule that made me who I was. I was crying, calling out for Umma, for Kilian, for anyone that would make the pain go away.

No one was coming.

I had to do it myself. I breathed through the pain, sucking in rattling gasps of whatever air I could find, and reached for the spool of magic inside of me.

I could sense it, feel it like a glass of water just out of reach, my fingers scraping at the edges. There were only dregs left.

I needed to get rid of the excess current before it burned me alive.

Energy thrummed through me, singing a mournful, terrifying tune. I scrunched my eyes, but I could not expel it. The current had taken up residence inside my body and refused to be evicted. There was nothing in the world beyond the agony.

Still, I reached. The magic was so close, I just needed one, tiny push.

A voice slithered in my ear, dark velvet. *Looking for me?*

"Yes," I panted aloud. "Help – help… me. Please." I needed it to smother the current. I poured every last bit of my willpower into that singular thought, directing it. Shaping it.

My chest split and the slumbering creature inside me cracked one eye open. It greeted me like an old friend, its wrath pouring out to dull the stream lashing across my skin. The current subsided, inch by inch. I whimpered in relief, my limbs sagging with the respite.

It was short-lived. Images flashed through my head, like a slide show on hyper speed. I struggled to press pause on a single one of them. It was all a blurry mess of faces I did not recognize and places I had never been. As quickly as the pictures came, they filtered out in a dazzling stream of light, leaving me clutching at my temples with a pounding headache.

Colors floated in my vision, crystalline and incandescent, as the pain dwindled and my other senses returned. My sight was crisp through the smog left behind by the lightning. I rose on shaky limbs like a new fawn and stretched my hands out before me, marveling at how similar yet different they looked.

My fingers were slightly longer, my legs heavier, and when I ran my hands along my head, they caught on the tips of my ears. The pointed tips. Inside, my chest whirred with a power so vibrant, so fluorescent that it felt like it might rip through me at any second, demolishing everything in its path.

I breathed through the transition, focusing on my lungs expanding and contracting. Even the air smelled better, the night brisk and fresh. Something rustled behind me. I whirled around, my senses on overdrive, only to find… Lana.

She clutched at her chest, eyes wide with panic. I dropped to my knees before her as she wheezed for breath.

"Focus. Fight through it, Lana," I urged, "Breathe and think of home."

I didn't dare touch her as she choked on nothing. She stretched forward, her fingers grasping at the snow, knuckles white, a pale glow coating her skin. She bared her teeth in anguish. I watched in amazement as her body changed, fingers stretching and ears lengthening. Her blue eyes flashed violet, and I shielded my own against the glare of a blazing golden arc. When the light dimmed, I found her eyes had returned to their normal pastel blue hue. Lana stared up at me, shock coloring her face. She was even more beautiful than she had been as a mortal.

"The Rite…" she breathed.

I stared down at my fingers for a second time, still as surprised as she was. "We made it. We… We're elven."

I helped Lana to her feet, holding onto her as she adjusted to the new weight of her bones. She pulled me to her, tears streaming down her face. I held her tightly. She was alive. I was alive. Against impossible odds, we had survived.

"The others?" she whispered. I let her go and we took a few steps to the side, to where we had last seen Moric and Rayna.

They were both sprawled on the snow, unmoving.

I blinked, sure that in a few seconds I would see Moric's fingers twitch, his chest heaving as he rose onto his elbows. I waited, but he remained still. I dropped beside him, my hands roaming across the planes of his shoulders.

"Moric." I shook him.

He did not stir.

"Moric, wake up."

Lana had crossed to Rayna, checking for a pulse. She looked at me and shook her head. It couldn't be.

Moric… Rayna… It just couldn't be.

I shook him again, this time more violently. His neck rolled to the side, hazel eyes staring out unseeingly. Lana collapsed beside me, tears streaking silently down her cheeks. I didn't understand why she was crying. Moric was *fine*. His body just needed a minute to recuperate from the current. The pain had been intolerable. I knew how it felt. His body just needed time.

"Lirah." Lana placed her hand on top of mine, where it rested on Moric's shoulder. "He's gone."

"He's not gone!" I snapped. "Just… give him a second."

Lana swallowed. "He… he struggled with the earth magic."

"No. We've been practicing. He *knew* what to do." I tried to keep my voice steady, but a sob ripped free from my throat unbidden.

I was not going to fail Moric like I had failed Anama. I was not going to let him die. I pushed at his chest, slamming my hands against his sternum. I lowered my lips to breathe air into his mouth and pumped his chest. He grew blurry beneath me, tears obscuring my vision. I wiped them away, hot, metallic anger coating my tongue.

This was not how the Rite was supposed to go. I was supposed to leave here with my friends, or not leave at all.

"Lirah." Lana clutched at my wrist, and I whirled blazing eyes at her.

I wrenched my wrist from her grip. "Why are you trying to stop me from saving him?"

The heartbreak on her face cleaved something inside me. She drew her hand up my arm, pulling me toward her. I let her, my face crumpling as I finally registered just how pale and cold Moric had become. The spark in his hazel eyes had been extinguished. He would never return to Foulkan or make maps for his brother. He would never tease Lana or recite facts about Lortan. He would never leave these mountains. All the pain, all the worries that had plagued him, all his hopes and dreams and every thought he'd ever had, vanished in a wink. Snuffed out, like it had never existed.

And Rayna. Rayna had been so young. She should have had decades more to live. Now, there would be nothing left of her but her bones on this mountaintop, and a memory that would exist only in others.

Life was cruel. It took too much.

Great, heaving sobs wracked through my body as I held onto Lana. She clutched me tightly, her fingers clawing at my cloak as she cried too. We sat for what seemed like hours beside their bodies, grieving the loss.

As the cold crept into our bones, Lana sniffed and said, "We can't leave them like this."

"We don't have tools." My voice cracked.

"Then we'll use our hands."

So we did. We dug snow until our skin frosted with ice burn, and then we continued. I owed Rayna for her hint on the third Trial. And Caleb, for sticking with me in Cosanus, for going back through the scry and telling Kilian what had happened.

Most of all, I owed Moric, for being my friend.

My hands were raw and bleeding by the time we patted the last bit of snow on top of the final shallow grave. But my heart did not feel any lighter.

When the sun began to peek over the horizon, throwing pale arcs across the peaks, I allowed it to wash over me. Prayed it would give me the strength I needed. I had cried so much that my throat felt hoarse and my cheeks stung from the biting cold. I looked to the sky and wondered why becoming elven had not taken away the pain of death and loss, the humanity I'd thought would surely disappear with the transition.

Lana stood, reaching a hand to help me up. I rose beside her, sunlight warm on my face as the new day broke across the summits. Before we crossed the boundary, I gave one final look at the three new graves along the expanse of the mountain, sending a prayer to Azrael to watch over them in death.

CHAPTER 25

Kilian Valhan was a sight for sore eyes.

He stood outside the sand boundary, in the exact same position I'd left him. Septimus was beside him, the skin around his eyes red. When he saw Lana, he let out a hoarse cry, rushing toward her.

"You're okay? You're okay, you're okay, you're okay," Septimus kept reciting as he held Lana.

Kilian stared at me, eyes wide. His gaze rose to the tips of my ears, then dropped along my body, as if scanning for injuries. He took a step forward, halted, and blinked furiously. The way he was looking at me, it was like he was seeing a ghost. He took a step toward me, shock giving way to realization. "Lirah…?" His voice broke.

I ran to him.

He met me, hands gripping the back of my neck as he tilted my mouth to meet his. Everything stilled for one, blissful moment. Even the snow drifting around us paused its descent as we stood locked together. In this moment, there was no pain, no death. It was just him and I, warmth and life and a *future* stretching endlessly ahead.

Slowly, life resumed. Everything felt heightened as an elven. The sound of the birds chirping overhead. The feel of the wind on my cheeks. Kilian's lips against mine. His whole body trembled as he held me, stroking my hair, my cheeks, every inch of exposed skin. He was so gentle, like one wrong move might cause me to disappear.

Sobs came from behind us, and I wasn't sure if it was from Lana or Septimus, or both of them. I couldn't pull away from Kilian to look.

"You… you're alive," he murmured against my lips, almost like he was convincing himself. "I can't believe…"

He shivered, pulling back to look into my eyes, like he needed to see me to know I was there. It felt like a fever dream to me too. His fingers brushed the tips of my ears and he grinned, his entire face lighting up. "Your ears. They're like mine."

I smiled back, but it was a weaker version of his. "The others didn't make it."

He pulled me to him again, breathing me in, fingers still shaking slightly as he ran his hand over my lower back. "There are no words for how sorry I am. Moric's brother will be well cared for. I hope you know that. All the families of the candidates will never want for anything."

I nodded against his chest, but my heart still burned fiercely.

He held me tightly, and I could hear his heart racing, beating like a war had just ended and he had somehow managed to survive.

I reached for the link, but there was only silence at the back of my mind. "I can't feel you anymore. The link…"

"The sacred oath has been fulfilled," he said, "Your mortal life has ended. I cannot feel you, either."

The thought made my chest throb dully. I had hated the link for so long, thought it so intrusive of my innermost thoughts and feelings, but now that it was gone, I felt hollow, like a piece of me was missing.

"Are you hurt?" Kilian asked.

Apart from an overwhelming thirst and my frostbitten fingers, the pain of the transformation had subsided, replaced by a constant, prowling energy. "Not by the Rite. The transformation was rough, but I'm okay. The training – the channeling, it worked for both Lana and I. There haven't been any survivors since Augustine, but what we learned helped. *You* helped." I squeezed his hand.

Kilian's brows drew together. "I don't doubt the training helped, but… I told you, that sort of skill takes many years to hone. Channeling the current wasn't the sole reason you survived."

I blinked up at him. "What? What else could it have been?"

He hesitated. "You must be freezing. Let's go back to the house and get you warmed up before we talk about it. We *will* talk about it," he said, as my lips parted to argue. "But my priority is your well-being." Kilian kissed me on the brow, before grasping my hand to lead me down the trail, back to Valhan House.

I glanced over my shoulder to where Septimus and Lana still stood huddled near the boundary, their heads bent together as they spoke to each other.

"They'll be fine," Kilian assured me. "Septimus will take care of her. Let me take care of you, and then I'll answer all your questions."

Curiosity burned through my veins, but he was right. I needed to soak my aching muscles in a bath. And I needed to eat. I was starving. We descended quicker than it had taken to ascend the trail. My body moved easily, sinuously, with the slightly longer limbs. Even my muscles felt stronger. We entered the house, Kilian pulling me past the dorms on the third floor, to his bedroom on the fifth.

"What about Calendula?" I inquired. I wanted to see the shadow sprite and thank her for everything. To tell her I had passed the Rite.

"She returned home to the Shadow Soil. She was too anxious you wouldn't make it through. She's really grown to care for you," Kilian said. "I'll send her a message, though."

I nodded. I couldn't fault her for leaving. I knew how much she hated being away from her home.

Kilian opened his bedroom door. It was as I remembered it. I stared at the bed. Was this *our* room now? He hadn't formally asked, and I wasn't the expert on elven traditions. I assumed we'd be sharing it from now on, but maybe he hadn't *really* expected me to pass the Rite and now he felt obliged–

"The link's gone, so I won't know what's bothering you unless you tell me," Kilian said.

I realized my brows had scrunched as I considered our living arrangements.

"What a shame," I jibed, "that you can no longer spy on my innermost thoughts."

"It truly is a pity," he said. "I rather enjoyed your thoughts, violent as they were."

I huffed a short laugh. "I was just wondering... where I'd stay now."

"Here, obviously. Unless you don't want to? Your room's still available on the third floor if you'd prefer, I just thought... the hallway will be empty now."

My eyes closed, a hard lump forming in my throat. Moric would no longer be next door to me. And Lana would likely room with Septimus.

"Right. I mean, here's fine. I just don't want you to feel like you *have to*–"

"Hey." He pulled me against him, arms wrapping around me. "I don't want you going anywhere. If I could, I'd keep you in my bed all day."

I smiled against his chest. "All day?"

"And night. I meant what I said yesterday. I love you." He lifted my chin and our eyes met. "Will you remember that?"

I nodded.

He pressed a soft kiss to my lips then drew away, a hand sliding down to grab mine as he led me to the bathroom. He pointed out where the towels, bath salts and soaps were and turned to leave.

"I'll have some food sent up," he said, closing the door behind him.

Alone in the bathroom, I let the water run in the tub. I mixed blue and green salts together, watching as the colors swirled into a pretty teal, before shucking off my clothes and stepping into the bath. I let the water wash over me, sinking low until my entire body was covered. I held my breath, surprised to find that thirty seconds had passed, yet I was still comfortably submerged. It was so quiet, so still, beneath the water. Like life itself was muffled. I could pretend that Anama and Moric, and all the other candidates were alive for one idyllic minute, before crushing reality set in.

I resurfaced. Water streamed off my face, and I slicked my hair back, breathing in the soapy scent to ground me. I scrubbed myself clean and dried off with a fluffy towel before padding into the bedroom. Kilian wasn't there, but the smell of food greeted me as soon as I entered the room, and my stomach clenched.

A fresh set of clothes had been laid out on the bed. I changed quickly before surveying the food. Several bowls were arranged on a tray. I salivated at the contents. I picked up a bowl of what looked like creamy pumpkin soup, bringing the spoon to my lips. I moaned at the taste. It was unlike anything I'd ever eaten before – spiced to perfection, with a hint of cinnamon and something else I couldn't quite place my finger on.

"I thought you only made those sounds for me." Kilian stood at the doorway, amusement lighting his face.

"You wish you tasted as good as this soup," I teased.

He snorted, stepping into the room proper. "It's elven. You've never tried our food before. Doesn't it make that mortal stuff seem horrendously bland?"

I smiled, then remembered that Moric would never get the chance to try it. Fresh grief cut through my chest once more, and I set the spoon down with a clatter. "Are you ready to talk about how I survived the Rite?"

Kilian took a seat on the corner of his bed and ran a hand down his face. "Septimus is speaking to Lana about it now. I thought it best we do this separately."

He was being cagey. I noted how his eyes did not meet mine; they were fixed on a spot on the floor. Anxiety settled in the pit of my stomach.

"You told me Augustine didn't explain much about the Rite to you. He didn't tell you why his body was able to process the current when no one else could?" Kilian asked.

"Yeah, that's right. I just assumed he used one of the channeling methods."

"No… we didn't understand it at the time, but we later found out that somewhere along his family tree, his bloodline had been mixed with that of an elven. Though very distantly related, Augustine was of elven descent. And when the power of the Rite surged through his body, it was that ancient elven blood that stirred awake to protect him."

"But then…" My eyes grew wide. "He was not fully mortal?"

Kilian nodded. "He had mortal parents and grandparents. Even his great grandparents had been mortal. But, yes, there was some part of him that was elven."

"So, what are you saying?" I narrowed my eyes as the puzzle pieces slotted together. "If channeling the current wasn't the sole reason for my transition, am I distantly related to an elven? Is that how I managed to survive?"

"No. I think Lana might be, but not you. I've suspected for a while what you might be," Kilian said this last part softly, like it was an admission he wasn't fully prepared to confess yet.

The little bit of soup I had eaten churned in my stomach. "What does that mean?"

"I think it's time we talked about the daggers. I told you Caleb and Calendula informed me of what happened in the cave on Cosanus. I know the fae rose when the blade touched him, because your dagger, and the one you found on him, are imbued with magic. Magic from the gods themselves. Of course, the fae depleted whatever magic was in the blade around his neck and very nearly drained yours too. I didn't want to tell you straight after the third Trial… Everything was still so fresh and you had been through so much, I didn't want you to feel like it had been a waste, but… The weapon you brought back is useless."

My mouth opened. Closed. I chased different questions, finally deciding which to ask first.

"You told me the fae stole several daggers, that they're part of a larger set of thirteen. Who did the fae steal them from?"

He looked at me like I knew the answer. In a self-explanatory tone, he said, "Thirteen daggers imbued with godly magic. Thirteen gods."

"Don't tell me… The daggers belonged to the *gods*?" I hissed, horrified. My thoughts tripped over each other, spilling out my lips. "Why are you searching for daggers that belonged to the gods? Do you know how dangerous this is?" If the gods were somehow involved in all this, if they were listening to this conversation we were having, there was no telling how they would retaliate over having their possessions passed around amongst thieves.

Kilian sighed. It looked like the words were eating him from the inside out. "It's complicated, Lirah."

"And you said you'd tell me after I made it through the Rite. Lightning tore through my body. I buried my friends just hours ago. I've been turned into a fucking *elven*. You owe me the truth, Kilian. And not the partial truth. The whole, entire thing."

He flinched like my words had hit him and ran his hands through his hair, tugging slightly on the ends, and I wondered just how awful it could be.

"You're right," he said, eventually. "You need to know everything. You asked me, that day in the park, about who had taken my powers from me."

I nodded, urging him to continue. The suspense was eating me alive.

"It was a god," Kilian said in a rush. "Primus, the God of Curses, specifically. I did something that he didn't like, so he exiled me to Lortan with only a kernel of my power."

I paused, absorbing. "Kilian, what did you do?"

He grimaced. "I killed Kadax, the God of Cruelty and Malice."

I wasn't breathing.

"So, you can understand why the other gods would be hesitant to break the curse placed on me. It's the highest form of treason."

"You killed a god," I repeated. How did one even *find* a god to then kill them? And *why*? "How do you even kill a god? They cannot be killed."

The gods were perfectly immortal. It was what made them gods. From everything I read at Pyxis, I knew that when the fae rose against the gods, they had tried to kill them all, only to find that while the gods' bodies would die, their souls would remain intact. Then once a god found a new body to host, they would simply return to their place in Tuscan, the land of the gods, and seek vengeance on those who had tried to slay them.

"That is partly true," he said. "The only way to kill a god permanently is to destroy their soul. And there is only one being capable of wholly annihilating a god."

My mouth went dry. "A… being?"

Kilian said nothing.

"You said… you said you were exiled." My voice quivered. "From where?

Kilian exhaled. "From Tuscan."

"So that means…" I blinked, and when I looked at him again, he had become an entirely new person. A stranger to me. "What are you?"

"You know what I am, Lirah."

"No. No, no, no." I took a step backward, crashing into the food tray. The soup bowl clattered to the ground, puréed pumpkin spilling across the floor.

Kilian stood, but made no move toward me, his arms hanging limply at his sides. "I am Azrael."

"That's… *impossible*."

He scoffed bitterly. "Is it? I killed Kadax, and I'd do it again in a heartbeat. Naturally, that upset the others. But they couldn't kill me. No one can truly destroy another god, except for death itself. Except for *me*. So Primus cursed me, stripping me of nearly all my powers, and the majority voted to exile me to Lortan to live amongst the elven and atone for my crimes."

"But why? Why did you do this?"

Kilian took a step toward me, and I took another back. "I had overheard of a plot between Kadax and Primus – they wanted to eradicate humanity. They believed the mortals were growing restless and would soon stop praying to them. Stop serving them. I tried to convince the others, but there wasn't hard evidence, and I was running out of time. So, I killed Kadax before he could make a move. Primus was… trickier to kill, so I planned to banish him – an imprisonment of sorts." He had a faraway look on his face, distant, like he was remembering a pained chain of events. "But before I could banish Primus, he cursed me. That's why I need my powers restored. It's why the fate of humanity depends on it. They couldn't just stop with the fae," he said bitterly. "I didn't resist then and have regretted my role in it ever since, even after saving some."

"The thirteen fae…" I muttered. "*You* put them in Cosanus?"

He nodded. "I had to destroy most of them, to make it look like I had done the job of quelling the rebellion. The fae… they attacked our home. Their hatred of the gods made them too risky to keep alive, but it's different with the mortals. They've done nothing except lose interest in the gods, which shouldn't be a crime punishable by death. I left the most powerful fae trapped on Cosanus. I knew the day would come when we might need every bit of help to eliminate Primus."

"What's stopping Primus from destroying humanity? Why hasn't he done it already?" I asked.

"Without Kadax, I'm sure he's having trouble convincing the others to help him. He won't be able to do it on his own, he's too weak without his dagger. Which brings us back to the weapon you stole on Cosanus. During their invasion of Tuscan, the fae stole several daggers. Each of them belonged to a god, each imbued with a piece of the gods' magic. It amplifies a god's abilities. And in my hand alone, each dagger is capable of killing the god it's linked to. I thought the one on Cosanus might belong to Primus. I was wrong, though. On closer inspection, it appears to belong to Mahleia, Goddess of Pleasure. We still don't know where Primus' dagger is."

I ran a hand across my face, rubbing at my eyes. "What does any of this have to do with me? With the Mortal Trials and the Rite?"

Kilian released a tense breath. "Centuries ago, after my exile, a god went missing. Aerie, the Goddess of War. It is rumored that she chose death rather than a betrothal to Primus. But I didn't kill Aerie, and it was thought that her soul spent many years wandering Tarlor, looking for a new host to occupy. So long that she forgot who she was. *What* she was. The real purpose of the Mortal Trials is to find her, so she can break the curse placed on me by Primus. It's a curse that only another god can break. Believe me, I tried to find a way around it. We approached every single elven and still regularly conduct checks on the children being born each year on the off-chance one of them can help. I have had to explain everything to the elven. It took ages to convince them of Primus' plans for the mortals – plans which I am not certain will stop *only* with the eradication of humanity. The elven's distaste for the gods is no secret, and I believe Primus intends on weeding them out once he's done with the mortals. But even after all that, none of the elven had the ability to break the curse. Septimus, Syrina and I spent decades searching for an alternative solution, only to land at the conclusion that it must be another god who can break it. The Mortal Trials were born out of necessity to find Aerie, not entertainment. None of the elven approve of it, but they understand why it needs to exist, the repercussions if Primus is not stopped."

"Why didn't you just ask one of the other gods to break the curse?" My voice fractured, disbelief coursing through me at the conversation we were having. The flippant discourse about the gods, as if they were not omnipresent, all-powerful beings.

"Aside from me killing one of our own, which fractured most of my relationships, I don't trust any of the others to help. They are the ones who voted for the exile, after all. But not Aerie..." He gave me a soft, sad look like there was a secret shared only between the two of us. One I couldn't remember. "I trust Aerie. I have spent decades looking for her. The only way to unbind her, though, if she had chosen a mortal host, was to subject her to the Rite."

His words struck something deep and familiar inside of me. That name... A barrage of images ran across my mind's eye, just as they had on the summit, after the lightning had subsided from my body.

Kilian said slowly, "It's why you were able to process the current."

I shook my head. It didn't make sense. None of it did. "I don't understand what you're saying."

"Lirah..."

"I'm mortal!"

"You *were* mortal. Because that is the body you chose to occupy. Your soul has spent so long stuck between the spiritual and physical realms that you have forgotten who you are. You are not mortal, and you are not elven. You may occupy an elven body, but make no mistake, you are no more elven than I am. The Rite has transformed you into your true form."

"I'm not Aerie," I said. "You're delusional. I don't believe any of this!"

Kilian gave an exasperated sigh. "The fae in Cosanus... he didn't speak to you in Grilish. Calendula told me. That's why Caleb didn't understand it. It was the old language of the gods – a language you understand because it is ingrained into the very fiber of your being. Your power manifests as darkness, an unusual manifestation of mine, which usually presents as lightning. Darkness was always Aerie's specialty. It's why you're drawn to my energy. I've had my theories about you since that day in the park; I just didn't dare to hope it might be true."

"If you had these theories, why didn't you want me to participate in the Rite?" I retorted.

"I didn't want to risk you if my theories weren't correct. Loving you has clouded my judgment somewhat."

I clutched at the sides of my head as the images stirred again. No, not images, I realized. *Memories.* Faces I no longer recognized, a crumbling house, a forgotten land. A male whose face was so twisted and cruel that I shuddered at the fleeting image.

"What if I had *died* during the earlier Trials? Before you *'loved me'*?" I flung my words at him, hoping they would cut. There were so many times I had come close to death. It seemed like an awfully risky gamble to take on finding someone *so* important.

Kilian shook his head. "Aerie would know how to survive."

"Right. Of course. I suppose this is why you seduced me, then?" I spat. "On the off-chance I might be this missing goddess you're looking for? All to break your curse?"

Kilian winced. "Of course not. I had my theories, and still, I told you not to participate in the Rite, with all that is at stake, despite this being *centuries* in the making. There was a chance you were Aerie and would pass the Rite, but I did not want to take it. Because if you weren't – if I was wrong – I would lose you. And I cannot lose you. I *love* you. You know that."

"I don't know anything about you!" Bitterness colored my words, anger licking at my flesh.

Hurt flashed through Kilian's eyes, but it vanished in a second. "I have never lied to you about my feelings, Lirah. But you don't have to be in love with me to break the curse. If you won't do it for me, do it for everyone Primus will decimate if he ever finds his dagger."

"How can you even be so sure I am Aerie? What if it's Lana?" It made more sense for it to be Lana, who was so brave and strong-willed. I was just Lirahna Aldhur, scullery cook in the governor's house. I couldn't be a missing goddess. The thought was preposterous.

"I can feel your energy. It's a distinct impression that belongs only to you," Kilian said softly. "I scented it on you after the Rite. It's similar to what I feel from Septimus and Syrina."

My eyes snapped to his and he nodded. "Primus cursed them too, when they aided me in the rebellion against him and Kadax."

My brain was going to explode. "Septimus and Syrina... are *both* gods?"

"Like me. Cursed with only a kernel of power," Kilian confirmed. "Septimus controls luck and favor. Syrina, the arts. We're still gods, but just... weakened, unable to break each other's curses. We're shadows of who we once were in this form and bound to most of its limitations – like the inability to cross rock salt. Even if I had Primus' dagger, I'm far too weakened as is to even get close enough to him to use it."

I sank to the ground, my thoughts a jumbled mess. Nothing made sense. Not the foreign memories roiling through my mind, nor the idea that Kilian was the God of Death. Even more ludicrous was the fallacy that I was the Goddess of War.

"I know it's a lot to take in," Kilian said, and I let out a harsh scoff. "But the future of everyone really is at stake. If I am not released from this curse in time to stop Primus, if we do not find his dagger before he does, he will exterminate the entire mortal race to make way for Winipyr to create a more malleable species. And when he's done with that, there's no telling what he'll do. I'd rather we didn't find out."

His eyes searched my face, like he was hoping for some sort of understanding.

I gave him nothing.

"Take some time to let it soak in. And when you're ready, come find me."

I stiffened as he walked past me to the door. His hand curled around the frame, and he paused, looking back at me. "I may have omitted the truth, Lirah, but I didn't lie to you. What I feel for you has nothing to do with the curse or the gods. I love you for who you are. And I really hope you make the right decision."

And then he was gone, leaving me alone in the bedroom with only my reeling thoughts and a sour taste in my mouth.

CHAPTER 26

I closed the blackout curtains the minute Kilian left and crawled into the bed, hoping blissful sleep would take me. But my mind was restless and kept turning over every piece of information he had lobbied my way. Even worse, disjointed memories kept flooding through my brain with no context attached.

I saw the harsh, thin-lipped smile of a male who looked elven, but instinctively I knew was not. A beautiful, dark-skinned female with thick hair and rose-tinted lips stood in a room filled with books. She handed me something, but when I tried to look at the object it vanished in a swirl of color. A crumbling house came next, on a burning island, the shingles on its roof faded blue and charred. A burnished helmet fell to my feet, rippling sand in its wake. Sizzling hot pain seared my leg as a hand inched up my thigh, and when I looked to my left there were only depthless teal eyes.

I shoved the covers off me. They smelled too much like Kilian. Like *Azrael*. I was going insane in this bedroom, with nothing but questions burning inside of me. I rose from the bed and began pacing, replaying my entire conversation with Kilian over and over again, turning each word and sentence in my head. A knock issued through the room, and I paused mid-step.

Lana was outside, with a bottle of what looked like wine, two glasses and a cheese board held in her hands.

"I thought we could drink and commiserate the fact that you're supposedly a goddess?" she said.

I snorted. Only Lana could make the ridiculous news seem casual. I held the door wide. "Come on in."

She trooped inside, setting the cheese board on the middle of the bed, before plopping onto the covers. I nestled on the opposite side of the board and stuffed a pillow behind my head.

Lana reached for a glass, unscrewed the cap off the wine and poured a generous serving into each cup. She handed me one before clinking her own against mine.

I took a sip of the wine. It was fizzy and tasted slightly of apple. "Septimus told you everything, then?"

She popped a piece of cheese in her mouth. "Oh, yeah. We had a really long talk about all of it. In fact, he thinks I'm related to Augustine."

My brows rose, and I looked at her with renewed perspective. She did resemble Augustine quite a bit, especially in elven form. With her pale hair and light blue eyes, she could have been his twin. I didn't know how I hadn't seen it before.

"How crazy?" she continued. "But not as crazy as finding out that Septimus is a literal *god*. I mean, I always thought he looked like a god, but more in a *he's so hot, I want to fuck him* kind of way."

I pinched her and she batted my arm away, saying, "I did not see the Azrael-slash-Aerie curveball coming my way, though."

"How do you think I feel? I'm completely baffled by the entire thing. Part of me doesn't even believe it," I said.

"But then that means... part of you *does* believe it?" she prodded.

I hesitated for a second. "Ever since the transformation, I keep seeing these things. Images of faces and places. They feel so vivid and real. Almost like..."

"Memories?"

I took another sip of my wine, nodding. "It sounds so farfetched. I grew up in Serila. We prayed to the gods. And now, I'm being told *I'm* one of them. Some missing goddess. And that I've fallen in love with a death god!"

Lana gasped. "You love him?"

I realized how woefully behind she was on my love life. "That's a story for another time."

"Right," she agreed. "More pressing issues at hand."

"I just don't understand why all this is happening. If these... memories are real, and what Kilian told me is true, then why did Aerie – why did *I* – choose death over betrothal to a god? Why did I wander Tarlor for so long that I forgot who I was? Why did I choose a mortal body to occupy and not an elven one? It all makes me wonder whether there was a purpose behind forgetting. Perhaps, life as a mortal was more appealing than being a god? Or maybe I wanted to run so far from that life that I could never be found." The words tumbled out as the thoughts formed, jumbled and messy. Nothing made sense.

"Except you have been found."

"Yeah. And if that was a life I didn't want, then what do I do now?"

Lana sighed deeply. "Nothing you don't want to do. No one knows about this except for Kilian and Septimus. And Syrina, probably. You're free to leave Lortan now. If you want to go back home, you should be able to do that. If you are this goddess that they say you are, then nobody will be able to make you do anything you don't want to."

I chewed on my bottom lip. "But if I don't do what Kilian wants... if I don't release him from his curse, then the entire mortal race is at risk of being destroyed. Primus will eliminate everyone if he's not stopped."

Lana placed a hand on top of mine. "This is your choice, Lirah. And no one can tell you what to decide."

I clenched the stem of the glass in my hand, frustration tensing my muscles as I remembered telling Kilian, moments before the Rite had begun, that not even Azrael could keep me from him. He had smiled in response. "I just feel so angry at the lies."

"But can you blame him?" Lana asked softly. "Maybe he didn't want to put that kind of pressure on you during the Trials. Or maybe he wasn't even fully sure who you were. It would have raised too many questions if it hadn't worked out how it had."

Her words made sense, but that didn't make them chafe any less.

I leaned my head against the pillows, considering everything. "I know what I have to do, but there's something I need first."

* * *

I found Kilian in the sparring room, taking out his anger on a punching bag. Every inch of his exposed torso was taut, sweat dripping between the curves of his abdomen as it flexed with each powerful jab at the bag. He hadn't used gloves or tape. With my newfound crystal-clear vision, I could see his knuckles had split. Blood pooled between his fingers and speckled the floor below.

He held the bag still as I approached, eyes wary.

I stopped a few feet away from him and folded my arms across my chest. "I need proof."

His eyes narrowed. "Proof of what?"

"Of whatever you've claimed to be. Of what you think I am."

Kilian rolled his eyes. He rolled his *fucking* eyes, and I nearly punched him. "I already told you, Lirah, I've been cursed. I only have a literal drop of my power. I cannot decimate entire cities as evidence right now. As for you, the blood of the Goddess of War courses through your veins. Go incite a rebellion if you need proof."

My jaw dropped. "Wow. Where did all that sass just come from?"

"I've been learning from the best." He tipped his head toward me. "But seriously, I can't give you the proof you're looking for. If you believe it, you'll feel it."

"That's a load of crap," I hissed. "And you're a lying asshole."

Kilian strode purposefully toward me. I swallowed nervously but stood my ground. He stopped mere inches away. "Close your eyes."

"What? Why?"

"Just do it."

I could practically feel the annoyance radiating from him.

"So fucking bossy," I muttered, but I closed my eyes.

He ran a hand across my bare arm, along my collarbone. My body hadn't seemed to get the message that I was pissed at him, because it leaned into his touch.

"What do you feel?" he asked, his fingers still trailing delicately across my skin.

"You," I answered truthfully.

"And do I feel any different to you?"

I licked my lips. "No."

"Do I smell different to you?"

I inhaled deeply. Sweat, blood, leather, peppermint, *him*. All of it heightened now, but still very much familiar. "No."

I felt the air stir softly around me, and then his mouth was on mine, his hands gripping my waist gently. My lips parted as his tongue licked at the seam, desire flooding through me.

"Do I taste any different?" His voice was husky and raw.

"No." I pressed my lips back against his.

His fingers gripped my hip bone, digging into my flesh. One hand lightly traced the seam of my leathers, his mouth absorbing my moan, before tearing away to whisper, "Do I make you feel any different?"

He was doing something with his hands that made speaking very difficult. And all I wanted was for him to unzip my pants and take me right on the floor of the sparring room.

But his tongue was on my throat now and the sensation was overwhelming. "Answer me, Lirah."

"No." The word tore from my chest.

"I am not claiming to be anything other than what I have always been. I am Kilian. And I am Azrael. I am the same person you have fallen in love with. Can't you see that?"

He set each and every one of my nerves alight. When he bit down on my earlobe, I whimpered softly. At this point, with the way he was teasing me, I was not above begging for more.

"I fucking love you," Kilian said in my ear. "Does knowing everything make you love me any less?"

I finally opened my eyes and stared at him. His eyes were a silver beacon in a sea of chaos. And I knew then, I would never be able to stop loving him. "No."

A sense of calm washed over me and the thing prowling beneath my skin yawned awake. Darkness unfurled inside my chest, and whispered, *Hello, wicked lovely. Have you finally come to wield me?*

I tensed but did not pull away from it. For so long, I'd thought the darkness was a manifestation of Kilian's power. A piece of him bestowed upon me through the link, but the link was gone, and it was still there. It still called out to me exactly as it had as a mortal. I wasn't hearing voices. I was hearing the magic. And the only reason was the simplest one. It had always been mine.

The shadows rippled through me, soft and familiar. *Welcome back, Aerie.*

I shivered, and Kilian ran warm hands up and down my arms. I blinked, my tether to the darkness disconnecting.

"What's wrong?" Kilian's brows were knitted in concern.

"Nothing." I rose on my toes to kiss his clavicle before stepping back, the decision finally settling in my core. "Tell me what I have to do to break your curse."

CHAPTER 27

"I'm coming with you," Lana said, plopping down beside me.

I eyed her innocently over the toast I was nibbling on. The mess hall was quiet at this time of day, in between the breakfast and lunch rush. Kilian, Syrina and Septimus had run over the plan with me three times before heading to an armory I had never heard of before, but I should have known Septimus would spill his lovestruck guts to Lana. "Coming where?"

Lana smacked the toast from my hand, and it fell to the plate with a clatter. "You are not going to Dorisport without me. That is *my* home."

"You aren't coming, Lana."

"Like hell I'm not. I will be waiting at the scry whether you like it or not. I'm not letting my best friend enter the land of the gods alone."

"I won't be alone. And besides, it's too dangerous."

"Too dangerous?" Her voice rose in pitch, and I winced. "I've just competed in the most dangerous challenges in Tarlor. Fuck that. I'm coming."

I sighed. I should have known by now that trying to stop Lana from doing anything was impossible. It was easier to give in. "Fine. We're leaving this evening."

She pressed a kiss to my cheek, then stood. "I have to get weapons. Speaking of, isn't it kind of pointless heading to Tuscan without the dagger imbued with Primus' magic? Don't you need that to kill him?"

"We'll have to look for it after the curse is broken. I think Septimus has a new lead. It's not ideal, but at least if Kilian's unbound that's one issue resolved."

"And explain to me, why does this unbinding have to take place in Tuscan?" Lana asked. "Why can't you do it here?"

"The powers of the gods are amplified in their homeland. And it's where the curse was performed. It can only be broken there," I recited what Kilian had said when I'd asked him the exact same question.

"Right." Lana sucked on her teeth. "So, we'll be needing weapons, then."

"Lots of them." I pushed away from the table, my toast no longer appetizing. If the gods caught us in Tuscan before I managed to unbind Kilian, Septimus and Syrina, it would be over for all of us. I doubted the gods would take kindly to a renegade pitching up after centuries only to unbind the one who could kill them all.

We could only hope that we managed to slip into Tuscan undetected. I supposed we could try to fight our way out, if it came to that. But truthfully, I didn't think four elven and an amnesiac goddess stood a chance against eight wrathful deities at full strength.

It was best to be as prepared as possible. Steeling myself for the day ahead, I followed Lana as she led the way to the armory.

The sun had just begun its descent, turning the sky a beautiful shade of peach, when Lana and I stepped into the courtyard. We were both armed to the teeth, an extra bandolier of weapons slung across my hip.

Syrina paced across the courtyard. She looked up when she saw us, her face breaking into a grin.

"You're cheery," Lana said to her.

Syrina's smile grew wider. "I'm going home! I haven't felt the Tuscan breeze on my face in centuries. And there are so many things I want to paint. So much music I want to create and share with the world. How can I not be excited about that?"

She seemed to not be remembering the threat of egregious bodily harm that the land of the gods posed were we to be discovered.

The door opened behind us and Septimus and Kilian strode out, dressed in full battle armor. Metal dripped from every inch of their bodies and Kilian's mouth was set in a grim line. He looked like the elven who had taken me from Serila on Augustine. Except this time, I was going into war at his side.

"Are you sure you want to come?" I turned to Lana.

"Yes, Lirah."

"I tried convincing her not to," Septimus muttered, but the look he gave Lana was so soft, so loving, it felt like I was intruding on a private moment. "But arguing with Lana is like trying to take on a hurricane."

The same conclusion I had come to myself earlier that day.

Kilian's gaze slid to Syrina, who was tinkering with the scry. "Are we all ready?"

I took a quick gulp of the cold air and marched forward. "Ready."

My fingers linked through Kilian's and, together, we stepped through the murky smog.

My feet touched smooth, even stone. A loud blare blasted through the air, grating against my eardrums. It sounded like a horn. My eyes roamed around my surroundings, drinking it all in. I had only ever lived on Serila, and now, Lortan. Aside from my brief trip to Greyhaven, I had never been anywhere else in Tarlor.

Dorisport was a coastal town. The scry had spat us out on the edge of a pier, around a large harbor. Rust-covered ships lined the dock, towering above us. Shipping containers were stacked across the length of a massive vessel, and I marveled at their size.

Septimus and Lana appeared behind us, and then Syrina. The scry hummed quietly and went silent.

The pier wasn't empty at this time of day. The mortals who milled about, walking along the wooden planks, eating food and slurping at drinks, took one look at us and turned in the opposite direction. I knew they were used to seeing elven on the mainland – Lana had told me as much. The governor of Dorisport often had meetings with the elven to broker trade agreements, and they were free to come and go as they pleased, so long as they kept to the terms of the peace treaty by blessing the land and only ever taking the mortals needed for the Trials.

Kilian paid them no mind as he tugged on my hand, pulling me away from the dock. I could hear the others' footsteps behind me as we hurried across the quay, toward a set of steps. The scry had brought us to the closest beacon near the Amber Temple, and I could see the pointed peak of its centermost turret. It was a solid block with a sharp spire made entirely of amber. The gemstone glistened in the setting sun, the orange glow of the sky seeming to set it ablaze.

Even at this time, mortals gathered outside, pointing out the architecture and history. The slabs of amber which made up the temple had been stacked and arranged so that several smaller chambers formed a semicircle around the larger chamber in the center, the one the tallest turret rose from. A large archway was nestled right in the middle, against the centermost chamber. The door was left open, and mortals spilled out as a bell chimed.

"It's the last prayers of the day," Lana said, gesturing to those who were slipping their shoes back on at the base of the temple.

If only they knew their gods were closer than they thought.

When the last of the mortals had filtered out, we strode for the temple. The steps echoed beneath my feet, and I felt an odd sense of familiarity wash over me as I entered the chamber. Stained glass and mosaic murals decorated the windows and walls. There were several washbasins lined against the wall and an altar at the epicenter. Thirteen statues made of amber circled the dais. I peered up into the faces of the gods.

It was clear that the statues had been hewn by hand, and I did not recognize any of the faces set in stone.

"Over time, many of the gods have chosen new bodies to occupy," Kilian murmured beside me as I peered up at a stunning female. Her eyes were closed, lips curled into a gentle smile. "That was once Winipyr. And this is how I remember Aerie." He pointed to a statue on the opposite end.

The female's face was perfectly symmetrical, so beautiful my chest constricted. Whoever had carved the statue had managed to capture the wrath and fury that burned in her eyes. She held a sharp, angular helmet. With a pang, I realized I had seen it before, falling to my feet on a sandy beach.

"We should keep moving." I tore my gaze from the statue. Whoever I had once been, it was patently clear that I was not her anymore.

Septimus, Lana and Syrina had moved past the statues and were now heading through a second, smaller chamber. I followed them, Kilian trailing behind me. The second chamber was not as decorated as the first. It only housed a set of wooden pews before a wide altar.

"Over here," Septimus called from behind the altar. It seemed as though a hidden door had been fixed into its back. It was dark inside, but I could see the top of a set of steps leading further down.

"This leads to Tuscan?" Lana asked dubiously.

"It's a portal, yes. Only a god can open the doorway," Septimus explained. "It's not too late to chicken out, sunshine."

"I'll show you 'chicken'," Lana huffed and stepped across the threshold. She turned to look back at us. "Well, are you coming?"

Septimus grinned and followed suit. Syrina went next.

Kilian gripped my wrist, spinning me toward him before I could cross into the stairwell. He pressed a soft kiss to my lips, and my hand rose automatically to cup his cheek.

"What was that for?" I breathed.

He ran his nose along my neck, and I shivered. "In case I don't get the chance to do it in Tuscan. I don't want to regret not kissing you at every chance I get."

"There'll be plenty more chances," I murmured, my eyes shuttering as I breathed him in.

"I know." His hand skimmed my side, reaching for my own. I let him pull me through the altar and into the depths below.

The steps were steep and the darkness endless. It consumed me the second I entered the stairwell. But Kilian's hand clasped mine, his grip steady as he guided me through the descent. Eventually the stairs plateaued, the ground evening out, and, in the distance, a pinprick of light appeared.

The light grew steadily larger the further we walked. My eyes strained as crushing darkness gave way to milky twilight. I stepped onto soft sand, my boots sinking into the ground. The sound of roaring waves crashing over rocks greeted me, along with the scent of salty air. My eyes flickered shut as an ocean breeze stirred the loose strands of hair at my neck. We were on a beach. Waves lapped at the shore, leaving frothy white foam in its wake. Up ahead, I could make out the silhouette of mountain peaks, covered by a layer of fog.

Lush vegetation sprouted beyond the beach, rolling hills of green as far as my eyes could see. A heady sense of ease filled me, the kind of feeling you only got from being back home. It was both familiar and foreign, the sense of déjà vu. My brain felt like it was hurtling through misty space and time, searching for the right pieces to slot into place.

Syrina's head was tilted to the sky, and I followed her gaze. I knew we were no longer in Tarlor because there wasn't a single star in the sky. Pale moonlight cast our surroundings aglow, but aside from that, the sky was cloudless and barren.

Apprehension coursed through me.

I looked at Kilian and whispered, "Where are all the stars?"

Kilian swiveled slowly on the spot, his eyes raking across the beach, the land, and finally, the sky. Agitation lined the corners of his mouth. Septimus faced us, a similar look on his face.

"I haven't been back here in centuries," Septimus murmured. "But something doesn't feel right about this place."

"It's too quiet. We should go back," Kilian said, reaching for me.

"No." I pulled away. "We came here to unbind the three of you. I'm not going anywhere until it's done." I understood the process. I knew what to do. I looked between the three of them. "Now, who's going first?"

Kilian stared at me for a beat. He must have noted the grim determination in my eyes because he said, "Septimus. Then Syrina."

Septimus shook his head. "No. Kilian first."

Syrina nodded in agreement. "You're our best shot against Primus. We'll go afterward."

Kilian scowled. "We've been through this. Septimus first, then Syrina. We don't have time to argue. Lirah, go ahead."

I stepped toward Septimus, reaching out for him. Reluctantly, he curled his fingers around my forearm. I did the same to him. And then I reached deep inside of me for the shadows.

Hello, again, wicked lovely, the darkness cooed. *How would you like to wield me?*

The magic coiled and unfurled inside of me, like a serpent's tail or the feathered wings of a raven. *What shall we do first? Shall we lay waste to Tarlor? Or shall we stop the hearts of our enemies and eat them for supper?*

Neither. I gritted my teeth. *We will unbind Septimus. We will release him from the bonds inflicted by Primus. And we will forge him anew in his rightful place as Adonitis, God of Luck and Fortune.*

How dreadfully boring, the darkness clucked. *But as you wish.*

Cold magic seeped through my veins, black and dripping. Sparks erupted at the point of contact between Septimus and I, charcoal embers of starlight, crackling and fizzing, heating my skin from the inside out. Energy thrummed in my veins, pooling in a vibrant cascade that morphed and twisted into a thread of midnight. It flowed through me, and I sent it onward from my fingertips, into Septimus. I felt it balk as it touched his skin, touched the curse, retreating along the edges and curves, looking for a way in.

I pushed it further, willing it as Kilian had instructed me. The magic rippled through me and against the intangible walls of the curse. It pulsed once, then twice, and I felt the curse crack, splintering like fine china. The thread of power seeped out of me and into Septimus, in a rush that left me dizzy and breathless. I knew the second the curse broke, because golden light poured from Septimus in an arc so brilliant, it burned through my closed eyelids, eating away at the lingering shadows wreathing my hands.

My hold broke on his arm as a gust of warm wind wrenched through the air. I skidded back, sand skittering beneath my feet. And then, as quickly as it had come, the wind vanished. Light dimmed into a pale twilight once more. When I blinked, Septimus stood before me, a devilish grin on his face.

He didn't look any different, but it had definitely worked: seconds later I was swept into a tight embrace. My feet lifted off the ground as he spun me. I couldn't help the laugh that bubbled from my throat.

There was relief on Kilian's face, but beyond that, so much hope. Septimus set me back on the ground and strode over to Lana to kiss her.

Syrina bounded toward me, her hand outstretched and a wide smile on her face. "I'm next."

I reached for her hand as Kilian said, "We should hurry. Someone might have seen the flash of light."

Syrina grasped my hand, and I reached for the darkness once more.

It happened so quickly.

Scarlet light split through the sky and the entire ground trembled. My knees hit the beach as a thick coil of cold metal snaked around my thighs. I gasped, blinking against the fading light. A male stood a few feet away, shrouded in red mist. When I turned to the others, I saw they had each been similarly bound. Kilian's arms were clamped firmly at his sides, knees sinking into sand, but his gaze was on the male. A look of such hatred and fury blazed in his eyes that I knew exactly who had appeared on the shore before us.

"Well, well, well. Look what the tide dragged in," Primus crooned.

CHAPTER 28

Primus gave the air of someone who was used to getting what he wanted. He had a shrewd look about him, accented by a pointed chin and clever, sly eyes. Brown curls framed his face, and he carried a thin wooden staff in his hand.

He surveyed the five of us like we were roaches that had trespassed on his beach. A cruel smile touched his lips as his gaze flitted to Kilian. "I am curious – how has life amongst the commoners been, Azrael?"

"Fuck off, Primus," Septimus said. The binds around him tightened, his skin straining against it. Septimus had been given his full power. Surely, he should be able to break out of the binds?

Unless… even as a god, he was no match for Primus.

Primus looked to Septimus and tutted softly. "After all these centuries, I still cannot fathom that this is the rabble you've chosen to associate yourself with, baby brother."

Brother? My jaw hung slack. Lana's eyes widened significantly, but she didn't say a word. I didn't think I could handle any more surprises, honestly. My heart couldn't take it anymore.

"You are no brother of mine," Septimus hissed as the binds turned his skin red.

"Stop," Kilian commanded, angry thunder rumbling across the cloudless sky. "This is between you and me, Primus. Let the others go."

"Always the hero. I assume you've come to break the curse I placed on you? I gather this one was going to do it for you?" Primus' head jerked to me, and bile rose to my throat.

I saw him then, hazy and distant, teal eyes locked on mine as his hand slid up my thigh. Inching, inching... scarlet hot pain flashed through me, and I pulled myself away from the memory.

"I must thank you," Primus continued, his eyes back on Kilian. "For finding my Aerie. I have been searching for her for many years. Now that she's back, we can resume our courtship."

"Courtship?" Syrina scoffed. "Do not act for a second like we do not remember the curse you placed on her. When Aerie finally realized that what she felt was of your own doing, that you manipulated her, she chose death! She chose to wander the elven and mortal realm rather than warm your bed."

It was strange, hearing them talk about a life I could not remember, but I knew Syrina's words were true. I felt it in my bones and through the brief flashes of memory of that past life. I had left Tuscan for a reason. I had chosen a mortal life to escape Primus. And here I was again, on my knees before him.

"If you so much as look at her," Kilian spat, "I will peel the flesh off your bones and feed it to you before I grant you the mercy of death."

Primus gave him a bored look. "Those are pretty words from a bound male. From where I'm standing, there's not much of anything you can do."

Golden sparks fell from Septimus and his eyes flashed dangerously, yellow and gleaming. The chains around him were melting. His face was a contortion of pain as the restraints burned through his skin, but still he pushed against them. The metal was red hot when he gave one final shove. The manacles cracked and tumbled to the floor, leaving behind red welts and bleeding indentations in his wrists.

Septimus ignored his wounds as he rose to his feet, menace in his eyes. So swift it was a blur, he shot an arc of dazzling light at Primus, but the other male dodged easily. Drawing his staff outward, Primus hurled gusts of wind toward Septimus. He stumbled backward, hands clutching at his neck as he wheezed for breath. He fell onto one knee, eyes wide as he choked and gasped against the pressure.

Lana cried out, reaching for him. Primus looked from her to Septimus and smiled.

The wind ceased and Septimus gulped, his fingers clenched in the sand beneath him. He stared up at his brother, sparks dancing on the ground, but Primus' smile did not slip.

He wagged a finger at Septimus before turning it onto Lana. Her chains tightened, reddening with heat, and she screamed. It wrenched through my heart, ripping it to shreds. Septimus crawled to her, pulling at the chains, but they only tightened.

"Stop!" I shouted.

But Primus did not stop. In fact, his grin only widened.

Lana shouted in agony, blood welling from the points where the chains sliced into her. Septimus' eyes were frantic. He turned to his brother, voice pleading and pained as he said, "Primus, stop! I'll do what you want!"

The chains halted their progression through Lana's skin, and she whimpered softly, tears streaking her cheeks.

"Get back," Primus commanded.

Septimus inched away from Lana, allowing fresh chains to snake across his body.

I looked to Kilian, wild panic slamming in my chest. Lightning pulsed directly above us. It fractured and sizzled along the beach, each strike leaving imprints on the ground.

Primus stared at the purple streaks with mild fascination. "What a lovely lightshow, Azrael. It's a real pity that's all you can do."

"Unbind me and you'll see exactly what I can do." Kilian's deathly calm unnerved me.

"Now, why would I do that?" Primus tutted. "It's so much more fun seeing you on your knees, weak as ever." He turned to me then, raising his staff to my chin. He slid the hard wood along my jaw, tipping it up to face him.

Kilian hissed, thunder clapping overhead.

"I much preferred your old body," Primus said. "But I suppose I can make this one work."

Oily hatred slithered through me, and I spat at his feet. "I will never be yours."

He raised his brows, cool amusement quirking his lips. "You've still got that fire in you, Aerie. I can't wait to break you."

"I am not Aerie. My name is Lirahna. Whatever life I lived here is over. I want nothing to do with you," I snarled.

"And you think I care what you want?" Primus murmured. "Once this is all done, I'm going to put my curse right back on you. And you will love me, whether you like it or not."

Icy fear stole my breath. The shadows inside of me growled in response, reaching out to wash over the terror with cold, dark fury. I was not some plaything for Primus to use. And I was no longer a weak mortal. I had the power of a goddess running through my veins. I just needed to reach for it.

So, I reached.

I delved deep inside of me, feeling for the darkness.

What shall we do? it asked.

We shall feast on the bones of our enemies, I responded. Ancient spite swirled along every atom and molecule inside of me, pure instinct kicking in.

Delightful, it purred.

Shadows slammed out of me in a torrential wave. The chains binding me snapped in half, falling to the sand, and Aerie, the Goddess of War, rose.

Primus shoved his staff in the sand to keep from falling to his knees, his eyes burning with wrath and what looked like... desire. It disgusted me. I reached my hand out, my fingers clenching as the darkness pressed against Primus, digging its talons inside his mind. I bent and twisted at the walls of his conscience, relishing at the anguish that carved his face.

There was such cold malevolence and hatred there, enough to make me want to double over and wretch at the images drawn from him. Burning flesh and screams of torture. Women and children fleeing, their lives dim and inconsequential to him. At the helm of it all, slimy, slithering curses that drained the lives and souls of everything they touched.

I pulled back slightly, the death and destruction so overwhelming, and it was enough for Primus to regain control. He shoved his staff toward me, and I buckled beneath the weight of an invisible hand pressing me down.

And then he did the one thing that broke me.

He turned his staff onto the others and a dark cloud appeared above them. It gave a threatening rumble and drops of liquid began spilling from it, each one the size of a fat berry. They fizzled where they landed. At Lana's screams, I knew it was not water. The fluid left red welts in its wake, seeping into and dissolving the flesh it touched. When Kilian's gaze met mine, I knew it was over.

Dread pooled in my stomach at the sight of my friends – of Kilian – bound and chained, acid rain dripping onto them.

The darkness reached forward again for Primus. To stop him. But the God of Curses had layered his mind with titanium now, and it was an impenetrable fortress. Kilian's neck bowed as the rain washed over him, blood streaking across his face. Lana was no longer crying in pain, and I realized she had passed out from the agony. Septimus' body covered hers as much as it could. Angry red blisters marked both his and Syrina's skin.

My heart splintered wide open. I dropped before Primus, my voice raw and broken. "Stop." But the rain did not cease. A sob wracked through me. "Please! Stop! I will stay in Tuscan. I will stay as yours. I will never leave you again."

Kilian's head jerked up. His silver eyes snapped to mine. "Lirah. No!"

But I had to do this. It was the only way.

"Let my friends go," I told Primus. "Let them return unharmed to Tarlor, and I will remain here, with you."

Primus' gaze slid to me; finally, I had caught his attention. The rain paused but the thundercloud still drifted above, poised to resume its assault at any second. "You expect me to believe you will not run at the first chance you get? That your friends won't simply return to collect you?"

"Curse me, then," I whispered. "Curse me to forget them. And when they leave, place rock salt around the entrance. They will not be able to re-enter."

Primus looked like he was considering my words. "What of Septimus? He is unbound."

"Leave him be. He won't come back. He has too much at stake."

Primus' eyes fell on his brother, still covering Lana in case the rain started once more. "I suppose," he murmured.

Lightning scattered across the sky. Primus raised an idle hand as a bolt struck. It glanced off what seemed to be an invisible shield around him. The energy dissipated and crackled into nothing.

"Your efforts are valiant, Azrael. But I'm afraid in this half-form, you don't stand a chance," Primus said.

I knew how helpless Kilian must've felt. I could see the anger and pain in his eyes, but beyond that, desperate, hopeless terror.

"Please," I begged, before Kilian could do something else to bring Primus' retaliation tenfold. I couldn't bear his pain, the suffering of all of them, when I could prevent it.

"As you wish. Think of it as a homecoming gift." Primus gave me a nasty smile. "Rise."

I stood on shaky legs, the darkness inside of me quieting into dull submission. Primus stepped toward me. It took everything in me not to recoil as his hands touched my face. He smelled like old wine and cellars, of damp dungeons and rot. It was a bitter, musty scent that made me nauseous.

He pressed two fingers to my temple. Kilian's face contorted into a mask of rage and fury. One of the chains snaking around his arms groaned with the exertion of his struggle, but it did not give way.

"Primus!" he yelled. "She is not who you want. I am the one who brought her here, the one who intends to kill you. I am the one you want! Let her go!"

My gaze slid to Kilian and a tear slipped free, sliding down my cheek. I wished the link still existed between us so I could show him exactly how I felt. So I could tell him to stop talking. To leave me here and get the others out.

The darkness stirred itself inside of me, and I realized with shocking clarity that I did not need the link. I had invaded Primus' mind as easily as stepping from one room to the other. It had happened through pure, instinctual muscle memory.

I reached for Kilian now, allowing the shadows to fill me once more, commanding it to my new will. And when I caressed the bounds of his mind with gentle, scraping fingers, he let me in. His eyes widened a fraction before he schooled his expression into perfect neutrality, so Primus would not know what was happening.

I need you to leave. Get the others out, I told him.

Not without you. Even mentally, I could hear the insolence, the rebellion, in his voice.

I gave him a supplicating look. *I know what I'm doing. Trust me.*

Lirah...

You asked for my trust before. Now it's your turn.

There was a moment of hesitation, and then his gaze dipped to the ground. I took it as silent agreement.

When it's over, take the others and go. I love you.

His eyes gleamed fiercely. *I will come back for you. I will always find you. Even when you no longer remember me. My heart has always belonged to you, and I will spend the rest of eternity reminding you of that. If I have to burn the world to save you, I will.*

The tears were flowing freely now. I held onto the connection for as long as I could, but as the first tendril of Primus' oily power grazed the walls of my mind, I let it go.

EPILOGUE

KILIAN

The agony of the acid rain eating at my flesh was nothing compared to the moment Lirah's expression turned blank, her eyes glassing over as Primus dug his fingers into her temple.

She asked me to trust her, but how could I, when I knew what the monster before me was capable of? The things Primus had done… the lives he had ruined… It was enough to have me ripping at my bonds once more, terror my driving force.

The chains tightened, digging into my skin, and my power lay just out of reach. A fragmented, pathetic pit of nothing. What use was I if I let this happen, if I could not protect her? If I remained on my knees and watched history repeat itself? But it was already too late. I had already failed. Just as I had centuries ago. It always fucking ended like this.

Primus trailed his hand down Lirah's cheek, and I wanted to burn the skin off each finger that touched her. He took on a satisfied look, lips curling into smug arrogance.

"Aerie, my dearest." He held his hand out to her, and… she took it.

My stomach dropped, sinking as my worst nightmares unfolded.

Lirah turned her gaze on us. There was no recognition in her eyes, no affection when they cast over me. Only cold emptiness. Lirah had been angry and snarky, vicious and cutting, soft and sorrowful, and, on the rare occasion, happy. But never had I seen her so... reserved. The shift was unrecognizable.

Her voice was lofty when she asked, "Who are they, my love?"

"No one of concern." Primus flicked his fingers and the chains binding us fell to the ground. "You're free to go. Don't even think about doing anything stupid. You will end up in the exact same position, and I guarantee you I will not display any form of mercy a second time around."

I flexed my fingers, rising swiftly, thunder rumbling somewhere in the distance. Or maybe that was the blood pounding in my ears. I barely felt the chafing of my skin, my focus solely on Lirah. She wasn't even looking my way. She was staring at Primus, the way she'd once looked at me.

Syrina sobbed quietly beside me, struggling to stand, and I reached for her, helping her up. My friends... I should never have brought them here. I needed to get Syrina out. I needed to stay here and fight for Lirah. I was too fucking weak to do any of it.

"Can you walk?" I asked Syrina.

She shook her head and my chest caved.

Primus grinned like he had won a prize. "You had best return home, Azrael. There is nothing left for you here." He was goading me, and it was working.

Anger raged through me, worse than a forest fire. This was the type of fury that destroyed entire worlds. I took a step toward him, but Lirah, standing just behind Primus, caught my eye. Her charm – the one imbued with protective upper magic – dangled from her fingers and she slipped it quickly into her pocket, out of sight.

Her gaze flicked up, met mine. And she gave me the smallest shake of her head. A movement so brief, I blinked, questioning if I'd actually seen it.

She was back to looking down on us, a haughty tilt to her chin that suggested we were as insignificant as the sand beneath her feet.

We were out of our depth, caught like fish in a trap. Lana was unconscious, Septimus carrying her in his arms. He gave me a wild look, an anguished one, pleading to put this to an end. Syrina was so covered in blood, only the brown of her eyes shone through.

There was nothing I could do. No tricks up my sleeve.

Syrina wheezed beside me, clutching her stomach as she coughed. Blood spilled from her lips, dribbling down her chin.

"I grow weary of this," Lirah said to Primus, boredom in her voice. "Make them go."

"You heard my Aerie," Primus drawled. "If I have to make you leave, I'm afraid some of you won't survive."

I cast another look at Lirah, scanning her face for any sign of reluctance, any indication of unwillingness, but she remained impassive, her outward demeanor stony. Every fiber of my being ordered me to reach for her, to take her with me. She was so close, yet so far away.

Septimus shook his head at me imploringly. There was once a time he would not have accepted defeat, but the stakes were different now. He knew I could not do this alone, but he had Lana to consider. He was asking me to stand down.

There was no right decision in this impossible situation, but I knew what I had to do.

I spat at Primus' feet, my rage just barely leashed as I drew Syrina to my side, letting her lean on me.

Septimus released a relieved breath, gave his brother and Lirah one last look, and strode back toward the portal with Lana in his arms.

Syrina coughed again and I tightened my grip on her.

The distasteful curl on Lirah's lips did not slide.

I gave her a final desperate look, hoping it conveyed how much I loved her. How much the thought of leaving her here, with *him*, broke my heart.

She gave me nothing in return.

Syrina clutched at me, using me as support as I helped her back to the portal, my insides splintering with each step I took away from Lirah.

Hidden in the shadows, I paused. Panic clutched me. I did not know when I would see her again and it terrified me. I turned back to look at Lirah, at war with myself, unable to simply carry on down the portal and let her go for now.

Primus stared at her, his eyes running predatorily down the length of her body. I'd take his eyeballs first.

"Apologies for that," Primus told Lirah. "Business matters are so tedious."

Lirah gave him a rare smile. One that lit her entire face and made life worth living. I committed it to memory, for the days of complete darkness that would follow her absence.

"Then let us not dwell on such dull affairs," she answered.

"I share the exact same sentiment." Primus tugged her along the beach, toward the grassy bank and out of sight. "We're going to have so much fun."

Utter fucking helplessness clawed at me, scratching its way from the inside out.

"What shall we do first?" Lirah asked, her voice distant now.

"What you are best at, my dearest." Cold malice from Primus. "War."

Dread stabbed through me, and I made a promise then. To myself. To Lirah.

I would not rest. I would not eat. I would not sleep. Not until I got her back. My world reduced to a single focal point, rage razing everything else.

Primus had a head start and he better begin running. Because I was coming for him.

ACKNOWLEDGMENTS

To Stephanie, my best friend and the very first person to read this story – you are quite literally the other half of my brain. From reading every chapter as soon as it was completed, to your invaluable critique, guidance and uncanny ability to somehow make every single situation funny, you have shaped both me and this book in innumerable ways. Thank you for sixteen years of friendship and your endless, unwavering support. I am so grateful for you.

To Gemma, thank you for every comment, line edit and note on how to improve this story, for getting my characters, and being unfailingly kind and supportive.

To Desola, editor extraordinaire. Thank you for polishing this story into the very best version it could be. Working with you has been a dream.

To the team at Angry Robot, you have made this entire process so easy and wonderful. I could not be luckier to have such an amazing team at my side. Thank you for all your hard work and tireless efforts in pushing this story out into the world.

To Alice and Rachel, for championing this story. Thank you for all your hard work.

To my lovely agent, Bethany. I am so lucky to have you in my corner.

To Rebecca, who I met in the query trenches many years ago and has remained a steady constant in my life ever since. With each text and voice note, continents apart, we have been on this rollercoaster from the very beginning. Thank you for your support, advice and kindness throughout this journey.

To Grace and Norees, navigating the publishing world would be overwhelming without your support and friendship. I am so lucky to have you both in my life.

To everyone who blurbed, thank you so much for taking the time to read *The Mortal Trials* prior to publication and provide such wonderful words. I am endlessly grateful.

To Jenny, who introduced me to some of my closest friends, thank you.

To Megan, Mariana, Taylor, Kalie, Sophie and Rachael, for your constant support.

To the Discord – we've finally made it off the group chat! You are all the most talented, supportive rays of sunshine, and I am so fortunate to have been part of such a brilliant group of writers.

To my mom, Samantha, who took me to libraries and introduced me to books from a very early age. Everything that came after belongs to you. Thank you for your support in the good times and the bad, and for encouraging me, even when this dream felt impossible to achieve.

To my dad, Clive, who always taught me that I can do whatever I set my mind to. You're the hardest worker I know. You inspire me every day.

To my brother, Rayden, who is wise beyond his years and always makes me laugh.

Last, but certainly not least, to the readers. Thank you so much for picking up this book and following Lirah and Kilian to the end. I am so grateful for each and every one of you.